The Orange Blossom Special

The Orange Blossom Special

Betsy Carter

W F HOWES LTD

This large print edition published in 2006 by
W F Howes Ltd
Unit 4, Rearsby Business Park, Gaddesby Lane,
Rearsby, Leicester LE7 4YH

1 3 5 7 9 10 8 6 4 2

First published in the United Kingdom in 2006
by Piatkus Books

A CIP catalogue record for this book is available
from the British Library

ISBN 1 84632 602 8

Typeset by Palimpsest Book Production Limited,
Grangemouth, Stirlingshire
Printed and bound in Great Britain
by Antony Rowe Ltd, Chippenham, Wilts.

For Gary Hoenig

PART ONE

1958

CHAPTER 1

The morning after the letter arrived, Tessie Lockhart dressed with care in a navy blue skirt, red cinch belt, and blue-and-white-striped cotton blouse. Instead of letting her hair lie limp around her shoulders, as she had since Jerry died, she pinned it up in a French twist. And for the first time in God knows how long, she stood in front of the mirror and put on the bright red lipstick that had sat unused in her drawer for nearly three years. She pencilled on some eyeliner and even dabbed on Jean Naté.

Jerry died two-and-a-half years earlier and Tessie hadn't given her appearance a second thought since. When he was alive, he would stroke her hair and tell her that she looked pretty, like the actress Joanne Woodward. He even nicknamed her Jo. She'd never fallen under a man's gaze quite that way, and though she'd studied pictures of Joanne Woodward in the movie magazines and even started wearing her hair in a pony tail the way Joanne Woodward did, Tessie never really saw the resemblance. Not that it mattered. Just the look in Jerry's eyes when he would say, 'God, Jo, you are so beautiful,' that and the way he'd pull her toward him was all the impetus she needed to turn up the collars of her shirtwaist dresses, and wear her bangs short just like Joanne Woodward had worn hers in *Sweet Bird of Youth*.

She told her boss that she had to go see Dinah's teacher at school and would be away for a couple of hours. Instead, she got on the bus and went to Morris Library at Southern Illinois University. She'd gone by it hundreds of times in the past thirty-six years, but had never set foot inside. Never had any need to. Now she ran up the stairs as if she were coming home.

Going to Morris Library filled her with a purpose that seemed worth primping for. Besides, she knew there'd be mostly young people there, and she still had enough vanity in her not to want to be seen as old.

'I've forgotten, but where is the travel section?' Tessie asked the young woman behind the front desk. 'One flight up,' she answered, without looking up from her filing.

Approximately 449,280 minutes after her father died, Dinah Lockhart brought home a letter that her teacher had written to her mother. The word *PERSONAL* was written on it in small block print.

'What's this?' Tessie asked.

'Who knows?' Dinah shrugged, as her mother took a kitchen knife and slit open the envelope.

Dinah knew. It was a letter from her seventh-grade teacher, Mr Silver.

Tessie read each word carefully, her lips moving imperceptibly. Dinah watched her mother struggle with the words, holding the note, written on lined loose-leaf paper, at arm's length. She could see the vein over her mother's left eye start to pulse, the way it did when she felt anxious.

' "... crying in class ... distracted and disinterested ... the seriousness of the situation ... our recommendation that you seek counselling for her ..." '

Tessie had noticed how Dinah talked in a monotone voice and how she never seemed to be completely there. But she hadn't connected it to the truth: that Dinah was lost. No friends, no language to put to her feelings, no way to help herself. 'Distracted and disinterested,' Mr Silver had said.

'You cry in class?' she asked her daughter.

'Yeah, sometimes.'

'How come?'

'Can't help it.'

Tessie stared at her daughter, her beautiful thirteen-year-old daughter with the red ringlets and shiny face, and saw the pleading eyes of a child about to be hit. She was not a woman likely to make hasty decisions, but as she read the teacher's words, she was struck by one unequivocal thought: We have got to get out of here.

Tessie knew without knowing how that leaving

Carbondale was the right thing. She couldn't spend another day selling dresses at Angel's. The smell of cheap synthetics filled her breathing in and out, even when she wasn't in the store. Only the taste of Almaden Chianti could wipe it out. The sweet grapey Almaden, which she had taken to buying by the case, was her gift to herself for getting through another day of assuring customers that 'no, you don't look like a gosh darn barn in that pleated skirt.' Just four sips. She'd have four sips as soon as she came home from work. Right before dinner, there'd be another four sips and a couple more during dinner, and so the Chianti got doled out through the evening in small, not particularly worrisome portions. It got so that she was finishing a bottle every other night. When she'd go to buy another case at the liquor store, Mr Grayson always greeted her the same way. 'Howdy do Tessie. You wouldn't be here for another case of Almaden Chianti, would you?'

Embarrassed that he noticed, Tessie would bow her head and pretend to be making a decision. 'Hmm, sounds like a good idea. Might as well have some extra on hand for company.' Of course the last time Tessie had had company was back when Jerry was alive.

We have got to get out of here. The words moved into Tessie's head, each letter taking on a life of its own – arches, rolling valleys, looping and diving until they sat solid like gritted teeth. She thought about their desolate dinners – macaroni and

6

cheese or one of those new frozen meals. She'd ask Dinah how school was. 'Fine' was always what she got back. Then she'd claim to have a lot of homework. Tessie would light her after-dinner cigarette, and the two of them would retreat to their rooms. Tessie's only solace was talking to her dead husband. 'What she needs is a fresh start,' she would whisper to Jerry. 'What we both need is a fresh start.'

We have got to get out of here. The sentence buzzed inside her like a neon light.

Tessie and Jerry Lockhart had spent their honeymoon in St Augustine, Florida, seventeen years earlier, in 1941. It was the only time in her life that Tessie had ever left Carbondale. The memory of that had all but faded except for the sight of Spanish moss draped over live oak trees like a wedding veil. She had never seen anything so beautiful.

Although the ads for Florida always claimed that it was so, she never really believed that it would be warm enough to swim in the ocean at Christmastime – until she was there, and then it was. So different from Carbondale, with its gray winters and ornate Victorian houses always reminding her what was out of reach.

She checked out every book about Florida that was available in Morris Library. She balanced the giant atlas on her knees and, using St Augustine as the starting point, made a circle with her fingers north to Jacksonville, west to Tallahassee, and south to Sarasota. As she leafed through the reference books and read about the cities on the map, she found herself staring at pictures of Alachua County, swampy Alachua County, where the sun shining through the moss- covered oaks cast a filigree shadow on the boggy earth. Alachua County, whose name came from the Seminole-Creek word meaning 'jug,' which referred to a large sinkhole that eventually formed a prairie.

'What a beautiful place,' she thought to herself, pushing aside any doubts about an area that was essentially named after a sinkhole. Then she read that Gainesville, in the heart of that county, was home to one of the largest universities in the United States. Pictures of the redbrick Century Tower at the University of Florida reminded her how much she liked being part of a college town. It gave her status, she thought. People in Carbondale assumed other people in Carbondale had been schooled there, or were in some way a part of the university. She liked the exposure that Dinah got to higher education, and it thrilled her that Dinah might be the first in their family to go to college.

Could Gainesville be the place? she wondered.

Just by asking the question, she knew she'd already answered it.

That night she would tell Dinah how they would leave by Christmas and that she would begin 1959 in a new school.

★　　★　　★

Dinah Lockhart never made a precise effort to tally up the number of cigarettes her mother smoked each day, or how many minutes it had been since her father's death. She knew these things instinctively, the way she knew to avoid stepping on cracks and knew to lift her feet and make a wish whenever her mother drove over railroad tracks. She wasn't superstitious exactly, but why risk it?

Things had been taken away from Dinah, so the things that were there counted. Things like the fourteen honey-locust trees and sixty-two squares of sidewalk on her block.

Two-and-a-half years earlier, when Dinah was eleven, her father had dropped dead of a heart attack. 'It came out of nowhere,' her mother told her when she picked her up from school that day. There was a foggy look in her mother's eyes. She hugged Dinah close to her and said, 'Ashes to ashes, dust to dust. Gone, just like that.' Dinah pictured the heart attack racing around the corner, hoisting her father under his arms and hurrying him off. In the days after, teachers and parents of friends would tell her that her daddy had gone to heaven. Dinah would close her eyes and try to imagine her father up there in pillowy clouds with the doting angels, but nothing came. Besides, her mother refused to buy into paradise. 'He's gone, honey,' she would say. 'Now it's just you and me. We're all we've got.'

When she was little, Dinah's father used to wrap her red curly hair around his finger and call her his little Boing Boing Girl. He was always making up names like that. This nickname stuck, and Dinah turned into the personification of it. Skinny and agile, with her dad's thin shoulders, she had a laugh that kept going like marbles spilled across the floor. Her mother, whose bloodline was swamped with melancholia, would watch her daughter with wonderment. 'Thank God you inherited your father's good nature,' she would say. Dinah knew what she was expected to answer. 'Yes, but I've got my mom's good looks.' They would both raise their eyebrows in that what-can-you-do face and Dinah would giggle, secure in knowing that she was her father's daughter.

Now, her mouth had become fixed in a tight line. Since her father died, everything changed and yet nothing was different. Dinah woke up in her narrow bed every morning and went to the same school with her same old classmates. 'You're still my Boing Boing Girl,' her mother said one day, her stiff voice trying to sound jaunty.

'Sure am,' Dinah answered, trying to sound as if the bounce was still in it.

Inside her, things were mounting that she couldn't control: the way her socks needed to be arranged by color in her dresser drawer; the sixteen times she would run her brush through her hair at night, the eleven times in the morning. These were the things she could depend on when everything else seemed to be coming untethered.

★ ★ ★

Tessie spent the entire bus ride back to work practicing how she'd tell Dinah of her decision. 'Guess what? We're moving to Florida!' Too abrupt. 'Can you imagine moving far away from here to a new house, and a new school?' Too scary. 'Given all that's happened here, a change of pace would do us both some good.' Too vague. She floated through the rest of the afternoon at Angel's, her head filled with what she'd read in those books: the Spanish architecture, the Seminole Indians, the fact that the average temperature was seventy degrees.

'Well somebody's in a good mood today,' said Irene the cashier, her brown eyes buggy with expectation. Irene, Irene the talking machine, was what Jerry used to call her. The noisiest person in Southern Illinois. Tessie stared back, knowing how it would irritate Irene if she didn't give her an answer. Then she picked up a sweater that had been thrown back on the display table and studied the price tag. 'Seven dollars for a cashmere, now that's not bad at all.' Irene smiled and waited for more, but Tessie had given her all she was going to give.

Tessie got through her days at Angel's by taking cigarette breaks and remembering the rhymes that Jerry used to make up about her co-workers:

> Edna McGee in the tight red sweater,
> Loves herself, loves her boobs better.
> Smelly mean old Warren Nash
> Keeps the books but hides the cash.

11

That night she repeated the doggerel to Dinah. 'They still make me laugh,' she said. 'I can hear his voice and see the little laugh lines around his eyes when he said them.' Then she told Dinah how she talked to Jerry every day. 'I tell him about you, I ask him questions. I know he can hear me.'

'You're lucky that way,' said Dinah. 'I can't find him.'

Tessie paused and took a drag on her cigarette. 'I've been thinking about us moving to Florida. There's this place called Gainesville. It has those grand oak trees I've told you about and it's a university town, like this one. The difference is it's warm year-round.'

The way it had been with Dinah lately, Tessie had no idea what she would say. Dinah stared at her and Tessie looked back, expecting to see that scorched look in her eyes.

'You mean leave Carbondale and never come back?' she asked.

Tessie shook her head yes. The ash that dangled from her cigarette fell to the floor.

Dinah thought about how her days had become about walking home alone from school every day, then climbing into bed. She recognized that it could be different somewhere else where people didn't know about her father, and the teacher wasn't writing notes home about her odd behavior. She felt her face soften into a smile.

'That could be okay,' she answered. 'I might like that very much.'

Her smile made Tessie remember how the warming sound of her daughter's laugh nourished her in ways that nothing else did. 'I'll give notice at Angel's tomorrow,' she said.

CHAPTER 2

Three years after his death, Jerry Lockhart took up residence with Tessie and Dinah in a cedar-shingled Gainesville house with its upside-down V roof. Here, Tessie became bolder about talking to him, not bothering to whisper anymore. She welcomed him in the morning and blew a kiss to him at night. She would ask for his opinion in arranging the furniture – 'What do you think, the couch under the window or facing outside?' She accepted his compliments on her initiative. 'What choice did I have? She couldn't keep on the way she was. I think she'll be better off here.' And she made him some promises. 'I'm going to be the best mother I can. And the drinking. I'm worried about the drinking.' During the last couple of months in Carbondale, the four sips of Almaden had become eight, and so on, and she had begun stashing empty wine bottles in the laundry hamper, waiting until she'd accumulated six or seven. Then she'd wrap them in double-lined grocery bags and drive them to the large trash container outside the Bee Wise supermarket. She told herself she did that because she didn't want to be a bad influence on Dinah, but in truth, she was ashamed that the garbage men might see the bottles day after day. 'I'm going to cut down on that,' she said meekly, looking skyward. 'Maybe you can help me.'

In this new place, the sun bore down, softening the cold edges of her memory and making hope a dim possibility. Tessie could feel it in her step and see it in the way her eyes took on definition, separate from the rest of her face.

The night before Dinah started school, the two of them had schemed like schoolgirls about what she would wear. Tessie held up a piece of clothing, then pretended she was doing a television commercial. 'This fine white blouse, with its perfect Peter Pan collar, is guaranteed to make whoever wears it the prettiest *and* the most popular girl at Auberndale Junior High School. Tired of snow pants and woolen sweaters? Try our Florida delight, a pumpkin-colored chemise with white piping.' Finally, all that time spent at Angel's had paid off. Tessie couldn't remember when the two of them had laughed so much together, certainly not since Jerry had gone. They finally decided that the sleeveless dress with the red cherry print and brand-new white bucks with white socks would be perfect.

Before school the next morning, Dinah Lockhart brushed her hair in front of the bathroom mirror and hummed the Davey Crockett song to distract her from counting the number of strokes. She practiced smiling in the mirror and studied her lips as she said 'Nice to meet you.' She could be a whole different person in this place. She could walk barefoot in the backyard, and there was a tree house in the vacant lot across the way. Her father had never been to Gainesville, Florida, so this town wasn't his the way Carbondale had been. Here it was easier to make herself believe that he was somewhere watching over her, maybe even helping her out on the first day of junior high. She would no longer expect to walk out of school one day and find him waiting for her in the car.

Tessie came into the bathroom and studied Dinah's face in the mirror. She saw her daughter's eyes brimming with eagerness and stroked her hair. 'Knock 'em dead, baby,' Tessie said as Dinah walked out the front door, noting the soft clopping sounds her daughter's new white bucks made against the bare wood floors.

Dinah walked the three blocks to school alone; at thirteen, she was too old to have her mother come with her. Stolidly, she walked into the principal's office. 'I'm Dinah Lockhart, the new girl in seventh grade,' she said. Mrs Widby, with her gray hair in a bun, and a large bosom that sank down to her waist, grasped Dinah's shoulders with her spiky fingers. 'Ah, yes, Mrs Morris's homeroom. I'll escort you.'

'Class, this is Dinah Lockhart,' said Mrs Widby in her drowsy, formal manner. 'She has come to us from Carbondale, Illinois. I want you to be

16

gracious and extend her a welcome.' All the while she spoke, her fingers dug into Dinah's arm.

Dinah scanned her new homeroom. She noticed the girls with their Veronica Lake pageboys and pointy Capezio flats, and the boys with their perfectly angled flattops and button-down shirts. There was a girl in the front row staring at her. She was pretty and well dressed and Dinah could swear she saw a smile play on her lips. Then Dinah's eyes fell on the boy who sat in the front row closest to the door. She didn't mean to fix on him, only to block out the principal's voice and avert the curious stares from others. Was it the shoes? The shoes and the dress? Dinah's white bucks were sturdy enough to get her through a snowstorm if they had to. These kids languished in the sweltering unmoving air as if at any moment their clothes might slip to the floor: straps fell off their shoulders, hair hung in their eyes, their shoes were cut low enough so you could actually see where the cracks of their toes began.

After a while the boy became more than a distraction. She noticed his bluish fingernails and the spidery lines on his forehead. He had both hands on the desk and was clenching and unclenching them in an agitated manner. He'd make a fist then flash three fingers on his left hand, two on his right. The fist would ball up again and then there'd be two fingers on his left and four on his right. Over and over he would make this motion, the fingers flashing in different

17

configurations and pointing straight at her as though he were trying to tell her something in code.

Mrs Widby left and Mrs Morris put Dinah at a desk fourth from the front, on the opposite side of the room from the boy with the flashing fingers. Now as Mrs Morris took attendance, no one paid her any attention at all, except for the boy who kept shooting his mysterious hand signals at her: four fingers on the left hand, five on the right. Dinah, no stranger to secret logic, tried to make sense of the sequences. So intent was she in figuring out the meaning of his numbers that the most obvious fact of what she had seen that morning only occurred to her during her algebra class. The boy had five fingers on his left hand, plus a thumb.

Six fingers.

The pretty girl from homeroom was also in Dinah's algebra class. Her name was Crystal Landy and she had crafty brown eyes and a crooked smile. Crystal studied the new girl from Carbondale. The girl had shoulder-length curly hair and the whitest skin Crystal had ever seen. This morning, as she'd stood in Mrs Widby's grip, she looked stricken, as if she'd just been captured. She wondered if the new girl had noticed how the rest of the class regarded her white bucks. And that sleeveless dress with its cherry print pattern: Good Lord! It seemed downright contrary, like something you'd wear to church.

At lunchtime, Dinah sat with a couple of girls from her classes. As Crystal Landy passed their table, each girl looked up and said, 'Hey, Crystal,' in a way that Dinah knew it was important that they get noticed by her. They told her that Crystal was one of the richest and most popular girls in the school. She wore madras shirts, they said, the kind that bled when you washed them, and Harpur skirts with real leather on the belts, not the fake ones with plastic. The girls talked fast and their words blurred together. 'You are from up north in Illinois. Well, I don't think I ever met anyone from that far away,' said a girl named Caroline. Ruby, a blonde with foxlike eyes and a mouth full of braces said she'd been as far north as Tennessee to visit her cousin but they'd never gotten out of the car because her sister developed scarlet fever, and they had to turn around and come home, so she guessed it didn't really count. Dinah struggled to come up with something clever to say back, but the best she could do was, 'Tennessee. Gee that is so interesting.' By the end of lunch, word traveled through the cafeteria that Crystal Landy had dubbed the new girl the Redhead in the White Bucks.

Dinah got through the rest of that day by noting the time and then counting the minutes until she could go home and get under her green quilt with its white periwinkles. By the time she'd left Carbondale, in the middle of seventh grade, her calculations of MTH (Minutes to Home) filled pages of her notebook, like fragments of a theorem. The moment she walked into the house – the daily miracle of her life, as she saw it – she would stop counting. From there, she knew it was only two minutes and forty-six seconds until she was on her bed.

In Carbondale, she'd enter her bedroom at 3:35. Then, as if in a trance, she'd take off her shoes and dress, rub her hand back and forth over her pillow, making sure to catch a whiff of her own hair, then pull back the covers ever so slowly. She'd run her hand over the bottom sheet, erasing any lumps or creases that might have materialized during the day, then slowly mount the bed and lie on her back. The luxury of letting her body relax, of not having to remind herself to breathe, of no one watching her, gave her such an intense feeling of relief, she had to give in to it slowly. She'd pull the quilt around her shoulders and watch out the window as the sun got duller in the winter sky. Dinah would close her eyes and let the pleasure of it wash over her. Involuntarily, her arms would flap up and down the way they did when she and her father used to make snow angels in the backyard.

Ecstasy, that's what you'd have to call it.

After some time, when the sheets warmed and her body settled into just the right spots, she'd imagine herself into scenes where she was a little baby in a crib and her mother and father were sitting next to her waiting for her to fall asleep. Or she'd put herself in a pram, her father at the handle. It was cold outside, but she was warm because he'd tucked in the blankets around her. Sometimes she'd allow herself the ocean fantasy. It was a warm ocean with waves that rocked her. Each time the water washed over her, it cleaned out the poison in her body. Other days, she'd lie frozen in position for what seemed like hours and make believe that she was dead.

Now that she was in Gainesville, Dinah was determined not to fall into that awful pattern again. When she walked home, she worked hard *not* to count the number of steps between home and school and purposely *didn't* avoid stepping on the cracks.

Tessie was waiting for her at the front door. She threw her arms around Dinah. 'So honey, tell me everything,' she said. 'How did it go?' Dinah told her about how everyone wore a white sleeveless gym suit in Phys. Ed. with their last name sewn in purple thread above the breast pocket. She talked about the girls and their funny accents and the way everyone called Mrs Morris 'Ma'am.' Then she said, 'My dress, and those shoes, what a mistake. No one wears clothes like that down here. I looked like such a clod.' But she never mentioned the boy with six fingers.

'Seventh grade in the wrong clothes! No one should have to go through that,' said Tessie. Dinah looked at her as if to ask if she was kidding. 'I'm on your side, honey,' said Tessie. 'C'mon, let's find something for you to wear tomorrow.' Dinah forgot about her longing to dive under the quilt. Choosing the right outfit for tomorrow, that's what really mattered.

The closet in her room had a sliding door. Few houses in Carbondale had sliding doors. To Dinah it seemed very modern, especially the sound it made when it rolled back and forth – like electric trains on a track. 'Madame, open the door please,' said Tessie as they stood in front of the closet. Dinah slid the door open slowly, as if what lay on the other side was precious and mysterious.

By the time she showed up for school the next morning, the white bucks were in the back of the closet. This time, she wore a simple white blouse with a navy skirt and flats that had rounded toes instead of pointy ones. They would have to do until her mother said they could afford new ones. She took her seat in homeroom and caught the boy's eye. Before he could move a finger, she flashed him three fingers. She didn't know why, except that she was drawn to his intensity. Besides, he was the only person in the class who had made an effort to connect with her. Excitedly, he shot back four. She returned with five and he came back with seven.

Dinah started writing down the numbers in her notebook. She'd find herself daydreaming about the significance of *five*. At night she'd lie in bed and run the numbers through her head. She'd add them up and look for meaning in the sum. She'd play them backward and try to make sense of them that way. One afternoon, while she was straining to hear what Mr Nanny, her algebra teacher with the shoe-shaped face was saying about like terms and common factors, her father's voice suddenly filled her head.

The boy with fingers has nails that are blue,
but his heart's as pure as you know who.

That was when the thought struck her. Her father was speaking to her through this boy. Of course that was true. For three years, she'd been trying in vain to hear her father's voice, catch a glimpse of him in her dreams, pick up a signal from somewhere that he was watching. But nothing came. Now there was this mysterious boy with his spastic gestures. Her dad was talking to her through this boy. She'd never tell anyone, they'd think she was insane. But in her heart she knew this was so.

On a Saturday afternoon, Dinah was downtown with her mother when they passed by the movie theater on Main Street. There was the boy with six fingers waiting in line with his parents. 'I see someone from my homeroom,' whispered Dinah. 'I'm going to say hi.' Delighted that her daughter had made a friend, Tessie watched as Dinah ran up to the boy.

'Hey,' she said, not looking him in the eye.

'Hey,' he answered in a low drawl.

'What movie are you seeing?'

'*Rock-a-bye Baby*, you know the one with Jerry Lewis,' he smiled.

'Well, enjoy the movie,' she said, running back to where her mom was waiting.

Tessie noticed both parents beaming at their boy who was so popular that a pretty redheaded girl came over to say hello to him.

Dinah could barely catch her breath as she said to her mother, 'They're going to a Jerry Lewis movie, can you imagine? A Jerry Lewis movie.' She must have repeated that four times that day. That boy, those words, they stirred something inside of her.

That night, she took out her notebook and went through the numbers from the first day. Three: 'Are you there?' (three words). Four: 'I am here always' (four words). Five: 'Are you talking to me?' Nine: 'This is the only way that I can now.' For the first time since he died, Dinah felt her father's presence.

From then on, she would come to school each day filled with questions for her father. 'Are you happy?' she'd send Eddie a three finger sign. 'I miss you and Mom,' he'd answer with five. She and Eddie became like silent lovers, so contained in themselves they never noticed that anyone else was watching. But Crystal Landy was watching. On a day in early March she caught up with Dinah as they were walking to algebra class.

'Hey,' she said, nudging Dinah's arm.

'Hey,' she said back, wondering why such a popular girl would even bother with her.

'So what's going on between you and Eddie Fingers?'

'Eddie who?'

'You know, the freaky guy in homeroom with the . . .' Crystal made her eyes go crossed and wagged her pinky in Dinah's face.

Dinah giggled. She'd never thought of him that way.

'What do you mean what's going on with us? I don't really know him.'

'Well I see all that crazy stuff you do with your hands. Everyone does. You in a secret club or something?' Crystal used her forefinger to move a piece of her sprayed hair off her face.

Dinah heard a tinge of want in her voice, and at that moment she realized that she had something that Crystal Landy couldn't have. Mostly she was aware of what Crystal had that she couldn't.

Crystal's father, Maynard Landy, owned a group of liquor stores, Landy's Liquors. It was where people went to shoot the breeze, plan the tailgate party, reclaim lost dogs and parrots. You can bet that Landy's Liquors figured one way or another into Saturday night for anyone who grew up in Gainesville. Maynard liked to boast that he was responsible for at least three weddings, and uncountable births. When his customers went on vacation, they would send Maynard picture post-cards. He kept every one of them, from the Trevi Fountain to a milk truck in Wisconsin, taped over his cash register. Among them was a framed letter from a University of Florida alumna.

'I won't go into the gorey details,' it read, 'but let's just say that if it wasn't for your store I don't think that little Landy Williams would have entered this good earth on July 29, 1954.' Maynard would watch people read that letter, then laugh his nicotine laugh and start counting back-ward on his fingers to September. 'It doesn't take a genius to figure out what this girl was doing during homecoming weekend, now does it?' He was a hard man to read, always friendly and laughing, but decidedly opaque when it came to his own feelings. When people like Anita Bryant or Rocky Graziano passed through town, Maynard and his wife, Victoria ('If you call me Vicky, I swear I'll scream'), would get their hooks into them and have them to a dinner party at their grand house in the Cypress Woods section of town. That's the kind of people they were.

Maynard Landy came by his money honestly. 'The House That Landy's Built,' as he liked to call it, was one of the biggest in Gainesville. There was a kidney-shaped pool in the backyard and the only cabana in the neighborhood. By any-one's standards the place was deluxe. There was a sunken living room decorated in all white – 'The Graziano Room,' they called it because they

26

used it only when a famous person passed through. There was a soda fountain in the real living room, and a built-in television set that swiveled into the adjacent den. The bath in Victoria and Maynard's bedroom had a glass wall that looked onto a palm tree and a hibiscus bush growing outside their window. 'It's like bathing in Bali Hai,' Victoria Landy would say, repeating the decorator's intention.

The older of the two Landy children, Charlie, lived in an all-blue bedroom with a painted blue wooden desk, a blue toy box, and three pennants on the wall – one from the newly minted Los Angeles Dodgers, another from the University of Michigan, and a third from the New York Giants football team. This wasn't because Charlie rooted for teams that were from three completely different parts of the country, but because all the pennants were blue, another of the decorator's inspired details. Crystal's room was painted in what the decorator called 'Crystal Pink.' There was a pink telephone, a pink shag rug, a pink stereo. Even the hangers in her closet were pink. Maynard would tease Crystal: 'If you ever get a sunburn, we'll never find you in there.' Victoria saw the pink and blue motifs as strokes of genius. 'He had all his creative juices flowing,' she would say of the decorator when showing off her children's rooms to guests.

Maynard never forgot that he was short and thickset with droopy turtle-like eyes, and that the redhead on his arm was as statuesque as Gina Lollabrigida. Even after two children, Victoria was still the most beautiful woman he had ever met. 'Maynard is the brains of our family,' she would say with a half smile. 'All I have to do is keep up my appearance.' She said it because it seemed to explain everything, and because Maynard liked hearing it. Maybe she even believed it herself.

Every Saturday morning, Victoria had her hair done at the fanciest beauty parlor in town, J. Baldy's. And once a week, she had a massage therapist come to the house. 'Suppleness is the most important thing,' she would instruct Crystal, with the assumption that her daughter had the same grooming ambitions as she did.

Maynard came from a poor family. The men on his father's side helped to build the Seaboard Airline, the railroad line that connected the southeast to the north-east along the Atlantic coast. His father, Matthew Landy, would tell stories about how they had to dig up the trenches and use landfill to hold back the ocean water. The first passenger train that came down those tracks from New York to Miami was called the Orange Blossom Special, and Maynard and Charlie shared a fascination with it. They saved matchbooks and key rings from it, and built a model of the orange, green, and gold locomotive that sat like a trophy on a special table in the living room.

Like most American towns in the early part of the century, Gainesville was built around its court-house and transportation hubs. The downtown was a grid of commercial and government buildings, most of them redbrick with tin roofs, and everywhere the lanky Laurel oak trees. Gainesville had long been serviced by railroads that carried away lumber and phosphate and replaced the citrus and cotton crops that still hadn't recovered from the record-setting freezes of the 1890s. When word came that the town would be a stop along the route, the dream was that some of the rich folk traveling south would stop off and leave some of their money behind. Matthew shared that dream. When he rode the heaving work trains up and down the budding mainline, he would imagine the office buildings and hotels and banks and saloons that would inevitably grow up around the new station. He squirreled away a piece of his wages, and in 1927 he bought a little corner lot some five blocks from where the new station was to be built. Then came Black Friday and the Depression, and while work on the tracks went on, building in the rest of Gainesville, as in the rest of the country, screeched to a halt.

But the Orange Blossom Special turned out to be its own little works project. Matthew took out a loan from one of Roosevelt's new programs and built a liquor store on that corner lot. He called it the Rest Stop, figuring travelers stopping over would need a little something to wash away the fatigue from a twenty-hour train ride. That's not what happened. Instead, the store became the crossroads for those working at the budding businesses that sprang up around the station.

When Matthew died of a heart ailment at age fifty-two, he left the store to Maynard who changed the name to Landy's Liquors. Later, when he acquired three other liquor stores in nearby towns, he gave them his name as well. 'Hell,' he said, 'it's like getting married, I might as well.'

Crystal learned early in life about expensive jewelry. Her mother would stare tenderly at the five-carat diamond Maynard had given her and say, 'Now that's class.' About moisturizer, she cautioned, 'Hands tell more than half the story.' And she was forever telling Crystal horror stories about sudden weight gain and pot-bellied 'tummies.'

Slightly overweight, with a snaggle-tooth and crooked smile, Crystal would never be the beauty her mother was; she knew that. It left a space in who she was that she filled by being the class cut-up, the one who always sassed the teacher and made people laugh with her smart mouth.

Wednesday night dinner at the Landy's was always fried chicken, canned green beans, and potatoes. It was Crystal's favorite meal. The housekeeper, Ella, spooned a mound of the thick and buttery mashed potatoes onto her plate. Victoria narrowed her eyes and watched as Crystal reached for a warm Pillsbury dinner roll.

Charlie caught the edge of his mother's glance and tried to divert the conversation. 'Auburn's playing Alabama this weekend,' he started. Ella stood behind Victoria's chair, waiting to serve her. 'Just a ti-eensy bit please,' she said to Ella. 'I'm watching my figure.' She pronounced 'figure' like 'vigor.' Nobody spoke. Victoria stepped into the silence and reported what the landscaper had suggested that day. 'Eric says Saw Palmetto and Bear Grass over by the cabana would look lovely, because they're – you know – indigenous, they give it a very natural look.' As she waved her hand to show where in the backyard the new plantings would go, she observed with pleasure her Strawberry Crème nails, sharp as stilettos. 'Crystal honey, it's not too soon for you to start thinking about weekly manicures,' she said. 'You can't go around with peasant hands for the rest of your life. And sweet thing, don't you think one roll is plenty?'

Charlie raised his eyebrows. It always struck him funny how his mother's conversation traveled like a switchback. He also wondered if she would ever get over the fact that Crystal was thick-boned and hadn't inherited her tiny waist. Charlie worried about things like that, even though Crystal couldn't care less.

At seventeen, he was short and thickset and weighed down with an unyielding sense of what

31

was just and what wasn't. He thought that because he was a boy, or because of his likeness to his father, that his mother rarely directed her critical comments toward him. In truth, Victoria always felt Charlie saw through her. He would look at her funny when she talked about the landscaper or used fancy words like *indigenous*, as if he knew she was pretending to be somebody she wasn't. Unlike her, he was not comfortable with the visible wealth of his family. Even as a child, he rarely invited other kids over. He was the one who demanded that Ella join them at the dinner table and that she share their Easter and Christmas. When he was seven, the family went on a picnic to the Ichetucknee River. As they sat eating their egg and cheese sandwiches, two black children circled their blanket, screaming and laughing as the big one chased the little one. Victoria became uneasy and whispered to Maynard, 'You'd think they'd have their own place to go.' Charlie had looked at her as though she had just given him a scolding. 'Mama,' he said, 'God just wants them to have a good time. He doesn't care where they do it.'

The remark became part of family lore, and left Victoria feeling that Charlie was special in a way that the rest of them weren't. Normally she didn't give things like that much thought, but just in case this was so, she treated him with consideration. Crystal was different: life rolled off her like sweat. Victoria didn't have to watch herself around her.

'Mmm, love these rolls,' said Crystal in a taunting voice, reaching for another. 'So listen to this. There's this sort of new girl in my class. And, well, there's this guy we call Eddie Fingers. They've got some secret code going on between them. They do this signaling thing with their hands, shooting numbers back and forth, like they know what they're talking about. It drives me crazy.'

For the first time since they sat down, Maynard seemed interested. 'Who's Eddie Fingers?' he asked.

'Oh, you know.' Crystal sounded impatient. 'This kid in my class who has an extra finger on his left hand.'

'Is that why you call him Eddie Fingers?'

'No, Dad. We call him Eddie Fingers because his hair's so short. Of course that's why we call him Eddie Fingers!'

'What does the extra finger look like?' Maynard asked.

'It kind of looks like a baby's pinky, real skinny, with an eensy weensy fingernail.'

'Crystal, that is disgusting.' Victoria put her fork down. 'Why on earth would you concern yourself with a boy and his deformity, and some pathetic new girl starved for friendship? Could we please talk about something a little less gruesome? When do the cheer-leading tryouts begin?'

Maynard ignored her. 'What do you think they're talking about?'

Crystal shook her head. 'It started a couple of months ago, the first day she walked into class, like they'd known each other forever.'

'Do you know anything about her?' Charlie asked.

'Only that she wears the worst clothes,' said Crystal. 'I think her father's dead or something. She lives alone with her mother in The Glades subdivision.'

'What about him?' said Charlie. 'Eddie what's his name?'

'Eddie Fingers!' said Crystal, sounding annoyed. 'Is that so hard to remember? He walks with a slight limp. He doesn't have a whole lot of friends and he always seems to be out of breath.'

Maynard and Charlie exchanged glances, like they were both puzzling over the same thing.

'So this new girl and Eddie have things about them that are apparent to everyone, yet they probably wished they could keep secret?' said Maynard.

'That is not an enviable position to be in,' said Victoria, sounding genuinely sympathetic.

'Outsiders,' said Charlie. 'They're both outsiders, and they must have recognized it in each other right away.'

Ella, whose brother Reggie had one leg that was eight inches shorter than the other, collected stories about people with physical abnormalities. 'You ought to invite that boy to dinner someday,' she said.

'Eddie Fingers? Here?' said Victoria. 'That'll never happen.'

'Well, the girl then,' said Ella. 'Sounds like she could use a nice home-cooked meal.'

CHAPTER 3

O nly a fool assumes that everything will be okay tomorrow,' Tessie said to Dinah one night. 'But tonight, I am willing to be a fool.'

That day, she had gone for an interview at a printing plant where there was an opening for a receptionist. She drove for a half hour out of Gainesville, and was sure she had the address wrong because when she got there, all she saw was a windowless stucco building the color of apricots, with a flat tar-paper roof. But no, there was the sign, the black letters outlined in red: 44 Butler Highway, LITHOGRAPHICS.

Tessie put one hand to her chest as she told Dinah the details. 'It has this wonderful smell, like new wood and fresh paint. And the presses sound like that song, you know . . .' Tessie stretched out both arms, as if yawning, and began to sing: '*Shoo doo bee shoo bee doo, shoo doo bee shoo bee doo* . . . It had that rhythm,' she said, still swaying her head to the beat of 'In the Still of the Night.' 'I tell you, Dinah, it was amazing. And the bosses – a father and son – they seem real nice. It pays eighty-six dollars a week. Can you imagine?'

The early evening light slipped through the jalousie windows, painting stripes on the living-room wall. They'd lived in the house for three months and the furniture that felt so heavy in Carbondale – the dining-room table with its lion's paw feet and the couch with arms that twisted like snails – took on a fairy tale lightness in this place. Tessie's cheeks flushed with excitement.

'That sounds great, Mom,' said Dinah. 'I really hope it works out.'

'Well, you know what your father used to say about counting chickens before they're hatched. Still . . .' Tessie smiled a dreamy smile. 'And what about my teenage girl? How was your day?'

'Well I kind of have some news too,' said Dinah. 'Remember that girl in my class, you know, Crystal, the popular one I told you about? She invited me over after school on Friday.'

'The one whose father owns the liquor store?' Tessie had met him several times. 'He seems like a nice man.'

'Yeah, that's her. We've become sort of friendly. She's very funny.'

It had become a regular thing, Crystal and Dinah, waiting for each other after homeroom. They began to have their private jokes, making up nick-names for the other kids. Jessie Rudd, the fat girl with the tiny mink-colored eyes that were too close together became Diesel Weasel. Henry Tobin, the pale boy with the pudding face, became the Slab. They'd sit together in the cafeteria during lunch and invent pretend menus. 'The nausea soup of the day is coconut beef,' Crystal would say. 'And the nausea meat of the day is antelope brain,' Dinah would add. 'And for our grand nausea dessert, we have cockroach cookies.' By this time, their heads would be touching their trays, they'd be so bent over with laughter.

They could barely make it through Mr Reilly's Civics class without having a giggling fit over how he would ask questions, then answer them himself.

'You know why America is the greatest country in the world?' he would shout. 'I'll tell you why. Americans have "can do" values. How else could we have built this vast country? With blood and sweat, that's how.' Crystal and Dinah would look at each other and roll their eyes. They spent hours trying to devise ways to touch his flattop. Dinah guessed that he could stand on his head and not a hair would bend. 'That's because his hair is made of wood,' said Crystal.

After Dinah went to bed that night, Tessie lay on her own bed playing back the day's events to Jerry – the possible new job, her concern about Dinah visiting that rich girl. What if she invites her here? Will she be ashamed about how little we have? Whenever Tessie posed a question to Jerry, the answer would come back to her in some way. Two weeks ago, when she'd seen the ad in the *Gainesville Sun* about Lithographics, she wrote on a scrap of paper: *Will I be in over my head if I get the job at the printing plant?*

She folded it up and put it in a little cedar box she took to calling her Jerry Box. Three days later, the answer appeared to her clear as the rising sun, when a teacher at Dinah's school told her, 'Your daughter is so young to have to bear the burden of sorrow that she does. But she has a gift for words. She should read everything she can get her hands on.' And now here was Tessie, hoping to get a job in a place that printed words. If that wasn't a sign, what was?

Her thoughts ran to the new rattan chair, with its palm-leaf-print fabric, and the matching ottoman, and how perfect they looked in the Florida Room. 'We are building a life without you,' she said, staring at the little box. The truth of it made her sad, and a little exhilarated.

Dinah lay in the adjoining room and listened to her mother talking. 'He's dead,' she wanted to scream. 'You are talking to yourself.' She worried that her mother was crazy. If she's crazy, what does that make me? she wondered, having just decoded that day's exchange with Eddie Fingers. She imagined how Crystal would laugh if she told her that she and her mother were a two-nervous-breakdown family. But then again, maybe it wasn't that funny. I don't want to come off as a drag, she thought.

When Dinah came home from school on Thursday, the house felt too quiet. She noticed her blocks, the alphabet ones that she'd kept from childhood, spilled across the dining-room table. At first she thought they were randomly and inexplicably tossed there, but when she looked again she realized that they spelled out four words: WE ARE HOME NOW. Her mom got the job. Just then, Tessie ran out of the kitchen. She threw her arms around Dinah, thinking to herself that this was the moment that their new life was starting. 'I'm so happy for you, Mom,' said Dinah, her head filled with Pappagallos, transistor radios, and other things that they could now afford. That night, Dinah dreamed that she and Crystal Landy were walking through the corridor at school holding hands. Crystal's grip was firm and reassuring.

Friday morning, Dinah woke up an hour early. Her first thought was, If I start now, can I make this day move faster? She wore her new blouse, cotton with a madras print, and wondered if Crystal would notice that it wasn't the real thing. Her new black flats with the clip-on bows had already rubbed blisters on her heels. But this was not the day to go back to the white bucks, that was for sure. She pulled her reckless hair back into a ponytail and put on some blush lipstick that tasted like wax but made her lips pink and shiny.

With her hair off her face like that, Tessie noticed Dinah's jaw-line – Jerry's jawline – jutting like a plane taking off, full of determination. Dinah had her father's childlike brown eyes; they were round with curiosity and possibilities. Her face, like his, was long and thin like a knife sheath, but unlike Dinah's, his hair was thick and black and straight and hung like a satin cap around his head. Tessie used to run her fingers across his full pink lips and say, 'Whoever created you, used too much paint.' Today, Tessie thought, Dinah's face looked that rich and filled with life. She'll be a beautiful woman, she thought, though she was sure Jerry already knew that.

In homeroom, Dinah exchanged her usual numerical greeting with Eddie. She flashed nine fingers: 'Do you think it will work out this afternoon?' He came back at her with eleven. She knew right away it was one of her dad's silly rhymes:

> Crystal Landy seems quite dandy,
> In the end, your best friend.

Dinah nearly laughed out loud.

Crystal waited for her by the back door after the bell rang. 'So you still want to come over?' she asked, as though it might have slipped Dinah's mind.

'Well, yeah,' said Dinah trying hard not to sound like it was the only thing she'd thought about all week.

A giant replica of a sea wall, pitted and rough with barnacles, surrounded Cypress Woods. It was only

41

three miles across town from where Dinah lived, but in those three miles, the houses became larger, the backyards more spacious, and the addresses changed from numbers to storybook names like Cedarcrest Heights and Seaward Road.

'Here we are,' said Crystal, pointing to a modern L-shaped house that snaked around the corner and took up half a block. A black woman with eyes the color of antique wood opened the door. She gave off a faint whiff of Borax.

'Hey Ella, this is my friend Dinah from school.'

'Nice to meet you,' she said. 'Y'all come in the kitchen now. I've fixed you a snack.'

A nest of french fries, each with perfect brown edges, and two glasses of cherry Coca-Cola were waiting on the kitchen counter. Crystal hoisted herself up onto the stool, Dinah next to her. The two ate in silence, never looking up from their plates. When they finished, they went to Crystal's room, where they listened to the new Johnny Mathis album.

'This is the best make-out music,' said Crystal.

'Don't you think "Chances Are" is the most romantic song ever?'

'Not better than "Unchained Melody." So how many boys have you made out with?'

'Really . . . not any,' said Dinah. 'You?'

'Maybe one,' said Crystal.

'Maybe? You mean you don't know?'

'Well, we kissed and stuff and he stuck his tongue in my mouth, but it didn't go on very long.'

'That counts,' said Dinah. She took off her shoes and sank her feet into a pink carpet as lush as overgrown grass. Nothing in this house was like anything she had ever seen – the speckled gold-and-black Terrazo tiles on the porch floor, the maid, the french fries. Even Johnny Mathis sounded bolder on Crystal's pink hi-fi.

'How come your family moved to Gainesville?' asked Crystal.

'My mom picked it out of a book one day,' said Dinah. 'So we didn't have to stay in Carbondale.'

'What was wrong with Carbondale?'

'Everything. After my dad died, it got bad.' It had been so long since Dinah confided in a friend, she forgot to be careful. 'I never left my room. My mom started having out-loud conversations with my dad; still does. She started drinking. We moved here to start over, you know, to try and get away from all that.'

'Did it work?'

'Well, I seem to have left my room,' she laughed. 'And my mom just got a job at Lithographics. She's going to make eighty-six dollars a week. She's trying real hard.'

Why was she telling Crystal all this? It was like the french fries. After one, she couldn't stop.

Crystal reached behind her head with both hands and pulled her black hair on top of her head. 'God, you're lucky your mother works. Mine's around all day. She makes schedules about the stupidest things. In the morning, she wakes

43

me and my brother up and says, "Okay, kids, what's on the schedule today?" She's been asking us that since before we even knew what the word "schedule" meant. Her idea of a schedule is to shop all day, and then spend the next day exchanging everything she bought.'

They started with mom stories, and somehow the conversation wended its way to world affairs.

'Do you think there are a lot of Communists in Gainesville?' Dinah asked earnestly.

Crystal let her hair fall around her face. 'Charlie says that if he and Khrushchev could have a conversation, he knows that he could fix the situation and make the two countries friends.'

'Neat,' said Dinah, thinking he must be one strange kid to want to talk to Khrushchev.

'So here's the sixty-four-thousand-dollar question,' said Crystal. 'What's the deal with you and Eddie and the fingers?'

Dinah had wondered when this would come up and had debated with herself whether or not she would tell the truth. She took a deep breath and let out a sigh. 'When I walked into class that first day and Eddie started doing all that stuff with his fingers, I couldn't figure out what was going on. Later I thought that maybe it was my dad, and that maybe he was sending me messages through him.' Dinah suddenly felt embarrassed. 'God, you must think I'm such a moron.'

Crystal stared at her for a few seconds without answering. 'No, I don't. You could be right. I mean, don't you think Eddie could be from another planet?'

Ella interrupted the girls. 'Mrs Landy wants to know if your friend would like to stay for dinner.'

'Can you?' asked Crystal.

'I'll call my mother.'

Rich people inviting her kid over for dinner aroused uneasiness in Tessie. Yet the exuberance in her daughter's voice made her put it aside. 'You have a good time, sweetheart,' she said. 'I'll be waiting in the car outside at eight.'

'Manners. That's the thing that distinguishes people with class from people who are coarse.' Tessie had a couple of maxims that she lived by, and that was one of them. She had the annoying habit of swiping Dinah's elbows off the table and tapping her on the small of the back when she slouched. This night, at the Landy's house, Dinah sat with her forearms resting on the kitchen table just so, and her back straight as a ramrod. She thanked Ella each time she served her some shrimp or rice, and was careful to address the Landys as Mr and Mrs

She was seated next to the brother whom, she noticed, would cast swift glances at her then look down at his plate. The father called her by name several times, and once spoke to her directly. 'Dinah, it sure must be something for a snowbird like you to find yourself on the sunny streets of Gainesville.' The mother never so much as looked

45

her way. It seemed to Dinah that she just talked to fill the air. 'Maynard, darling, don't you think it's time we took Crystal jewelry shopping?' she said out of nowhere. 'She is fourteen, old enough for some starter pearls.' Crystal raised her eyebrows and mouthed the words 'nausea pearls' across the table to Dinah. Dinah put her hand over her mouth trying not to smile. She could see why Mrs Landy got on Crystal's nerves.

At exactly eight o'clock, Dinah thanked the Landys for 'a really terrific dinner,' then ran outside to the green Plymouth parked outside their house. She was breathless with news about the day: the inside of Crystal's closet, where all the clothes were arranged by color (her mother's idea), the shrimp dinner, Mr Landy. 'He was really nice,' she said, without adding that, before she left, he put his arm around her and said, 'You must come and visit us again real soon,' and said it as if he meant it.

Tessie seemed distracted. 'You'd think they'd have more streetlights in the rich part of town,' she said. Dinah could tell driving in the dark in this new neighborhood made her nervous. With Tessie's unsteady foot on the gas, the car lurched forward like a drunk in the dark. Dinah wasn't paying attention to the unfamiliar streets; Tessie wasn't listening to Dinah describe the Landy's pool table.

Then came a sudden thump, an unearthly yowl, the shriek of brakes. Tessie and Dinah sat frozen.

Fear, sour as sulfur, filled the car. The screams of a little girl got louder as she ran toward them. Before she reached them, Tessie stepped on the gas and sped away as fast as she could.

'Mom, you hit a cat,' cried Dinah.

'No, no I didn't,' said Tessie, her voice trembling. 'I hit nothing of the kind.'

CHAPTER 4

Above the receptionist's desk at J. Baldy's, where the women who could afford it dropped twenty-five dollars to have their hair washed and teased, was a framed document from the Gainesville Chamber of Commerce. 'J. Baldy's,' it said in block letters. 'Business of Distinction. 1956.' The paper had an official offwhite color. On the bottom right-hand corner was a shiny gold seal.

Jésus Baldisarri took a foreigner's pride in that certificate of recognition. After he received it, he wrote his mother in Spanish: 'The American government has given me an award for excellence. It is signed by the mayor and there is a big gold star on it. You must come here soon. Everything is possible in this America. Your loving son, Jésus.'

J. Baldy was the name Jésus took after a teacher at beautician school told him that Jésus Baldisarri was too foreign for the people in this town. He earned his success by exploiting the otherness that his teacher had warned him against.

His Cuban accent and rum-colored skin were a novelty among the slow drawls and white faces of Gainesville. That, plus his thick black curly hair and slight six-foot frame: How could the women resist a man like Jésus? 'My friend,' he would say when one of his ladies came into the beauty parlor. 'I am honored to have you in my shop.' Sometimes he would kiss her hand. 'You look so rested, you have been on a vacation?'

When one of his ladies sat in his chair, he would snap a white gown closed behind her neck like a giant bib, rest his large hands on her shoulders, and stare at the reflection of the two of them in his mirror. His mahogany eyes would widen with interest as they explored the possibility of bangs or the latest bubble cut. Then he'd brush his fingers through her hair, pulling it away from her face or sweeping it above her head. Sometimes he'd lightly stroke her face for emphasis. 'These bones are so – ah, expressive. I will make it that everyone can see the sparkle in your eyes.'

If Jésus knew that there was something sensual in his touch, a seductive promise in his voice, he kept it to himself. It was something the women looked forward to. They would never admit it, of course, but they kept coming back for more. They told him things, stories, indiscretions, nearly forgotten dreams. He never repeated what he heard or made judgments about what he intuited. Behind his back they gossiped about whether or not he'd left a wife in Havana or dated one of the customers. No one could remember ever seeing him outside of his shop.

Victoria Landy had a standing appointment,

Saturdays at eleven. Jésus had a high regard for the natural beauty of this woman and chose his words carefully around her. 'How your skin glows today,' he would say, or 'You are a happy woman. This is true, no?' Accustomed to being flattered, Victoria would answer with a flicker of a smile, then fall into easy conversation with him. He'd been teasing her hair for the past three years. When she and Maynard had their twentieth wedding anniversary party, it was Jésus who suggested floating flowers in the pool. And the time she had to go into the hospital overnight to have a cervical cyst removed, Jésus was the only one she told, and the only one who sent flowers to her room.

The morning after Dinah came to dinner, there was an unusually ferocious rainstorm. Victoria ran into the beauty parlor, her auburn hair tightly packed under a clear plastic bonnet. 'Honestly,' she said to Delilah, the receptionist, 'sometimes I think all of Gainesville will just float away.'

'We should be so lucky,' answered Delilah.

Victoria changed her clothes and went, like a schoolgirl, to her usual chair. '*El beso del sol*,' said Jésus. 'You look like you've been kissed by the sun.' They both stared at her damp matted hair in the mirror. 'I don't either,' she said. 'I look like some toad come out of the rain.' They laughed, she at his transparent attempt at a compliment, he because he thought she was right.

'We have a new girl today,' said Jésus, leading

her over to the magenta sink. 'Sonia, a friend of the family from Havana. She will shampoo you.'

Victoria usually ignored the women who washed her hair. She'd lie back in the chair, arch her neck into the crook of the basin, and close her eyes as the warm water and the smell of ripe apple shampoo washed over her.

But Victoria noticed that the girl had a pouty lower lip and a gap the size of an almond sliver between her two front teeth. Sweet face, she thought, as she rested her neck in the crux of the cold sink. Gently, as if she were lifting a baby, Sonia picked up Victoria's head and placed a rolled towel beneath it. She washed Victoria's hair, massaging her scalp at the same time. Her fingers danced deftly beneath the storm of lather and the sweet smell.

'Cream in my coffee.' The song came unbidden to Victoria. 'Her skin is the color of cream in my coffee.' The words took on a tempo of their own, in time to the tango that was playing in her body. Only when Sonia wrapped a towel around her head and pointed to Jésus's chair – 'Mr Baldissari, please' – did Victoria remember where she was. 'Well, Sonia,' she said, 'you do that awfully well.' Later she slipped a five-dollar bill into her hand, more than Sonia earned for the day. She looked at the money and then at Victoria. 'Is too much,' she said, holding it in her open palm like an offering. 'No. Is too much.' 'Don't be foolish,' said Victoria in a hushed voice. 'Just keep it.' Sonia tucked the bill down the front of her pink blouse. 'Thank you, miss,' she said, then began sweeping the floor before Victoria could change her mind.

'Who's the new girl?' she asked Jésus.

When Jésus smiled, feathery laugh lines played around his eyes. 'Sonia. She is the daughter of a friend. She is one good looker, eh?'

Next to them, Sonia began sweeping up the damp pieces of Victoria's hair that had fallen from Jésus's scissors. She wore tight white capri pants and leather sandals with straps that tied around her bony ankles. Victoria noticed her narrow waist and imagined that if she held it with both hands, her fingers would practically touch. She had no hips, which only accentuated the surprising slope of her rear end.

'Yes sir, she is one good looker,' said Victoria. 'Have I told you about the landscaping we're doing around the pool?' They both embraced the new conversation.

'Saw Palmetto grasses are perfect,' he agreed. 'Nature as it was meant to be. You have a rare appreciation for beauty.'

She did, and fortunately she had the money to surround herself with it. Indulging in her desires? Now, that was something separate and perhaps the one thing that she couldn't afford to risk.

Two weeks earlier, Crystal's friend, whatever her name was, had stayed overnight. She and Crystal had become inseparable, going to the drug store for Cherry Cokes after school, calling each other the minute they got home. Victoria worried that there was something unnatural about their close-ness, and their secret language, and the way they'd both laugh so hard at the same dumb things that tears would stream down their cheeks. Victoria encouraged Crystal to bring home other friends, but it was always Dinah who ended up visiting. Victoria remembered how, the night she stayed over, they went straight to Crystal's room after dinner. 'We have a project to work on,' Crystal had said, with an irritating emphasis on the word *project*. The two girls could barely hide their smirks when Victoria answered, 'Sarcasm is not a very feminine trait, young lady.' Later, she heard them laughing and realized that the drumming sound behind them was water running. They were taking a bath. Together!

Steam blotted the mirrors and made everything in the pink bathroom foggy. The first thing Victoria noticed when she stormed in was Crystal and Dinah sitting in the tub. Their faces were red from the heat, and they had both fashioned hats and moustaches out of bubbles. Victoria reached down and yanked Crystal by the arm, pulling her out of the tub. 'Oh no you don't, not in this house,' she hollered. Dinah sat alone in the sudsy water with her arms wrapped around her knees. She suddenly felt humiliated.

'You girls get dressed now and act decent,' she said, before throwing a robe at Crystal and slamming the door. When she walked out of Crystal's room, Charlie was standing in the hall waiting for her.

'Gee, Mom, don't you think you were a little hard on them in there?'

Victoria, her face scarlet, dried her hands on her blue cut-off shorts. 'How the hell do you know I was hard on them?' she asked.

'Well anyone who lives within a mile from here could hear,' he answered.

'Listen, Charlie Landy. You are a smart young man, smart enough to get yourself into Auburn University. And Lord knows you have knowledge of things other people your age do not. But – and correct me if I'm wrong – it just might be possible that you do not understand every goddamned thing that goes on in the universe!'

For all of his intuitiveness and sensitivity, Charlie drew a blank when it came to his mother. Try as he might, he failed to detect a glimpse of what was going on inside of her. Like his father, he had learned to back off whenever she started swearing. But this time felt different, as if there was something he needed to defend.

'I may not understand every goddamned thing in the universe,' he shouted back, 'but I do know one thing. Everyone in this house, including you, would be a whole lot happier if you cared less about how things looked and more about how they felt.'

He waited for her to lob back that he was a self-righteous little pug, like she sometimes did. She'd scrunch up her face when she said 'pug,' to remind him that he was thick and jowly, just like his father. But she didn't say any of that. Instead, she placed her hands together, as if she were trying to cup raindrops, and buried her head in them. When she spoke again, the anger was gone. 'Well, darlin',' she said with surprise in her voice. 'I can't remember the last time you and I went at each other like this. That was really something, wasn't it?'

That was an awful night, thought Victoria as she left J. Baldy's. By that time the storm had passed and the steamy streets smelled like early morning. Her heart and head were running at different speeds, as if the two were disconnected.

CHAPTER 5

She had to know she'd hit the cat.

Dinah lay in her bed, puzzled over why her mother hadn't even stopped the car. God, she was weird. No friends, all the drinking and smoking, talking to her dead husband. And now this! Her mother was a liar; worse even, she was a coward. Dinah stared at the moon, so round and pale it looked like Khrushchev's head out her window. She thought about whether she'd tell Crystal what had happened. Adults weren't to be trusted, that was for sure. They'd disappear on you, just like that, or try to make you believe something that happened really hadn't. Would Crystal think that was interesting, she wondered, as she concentrated on not listening to her mother talking to her father in the next room.

The next morning, Tessie woke up with a fiery rash. Prickly little blisters ran down her arms, behind her neck, and across her stomach. It felt as if there were pine needles inside her trying to get out. Her bed sheets were soaked.

The heat, that's what this must be about, she thought, rubbing her fingers over the nubby terrain of her arms. The books never mentioned the humidity. Tessie constantly felt as if she were wrapped up in a coat that was too heavy. It made her steps cumbersome and her thoughts sluggish. The air in Carbondale was brisk; it didn't try to sink you. Here the heat took root and strangled everything in its path. Staying cool was the biggest accomplishment. They had fans in every room, but fans just moved the hot air around. Sometimes Tessie took three cold baths in one day.

She stood in front of the bathroom mirror dabbing Calamine lotion on her skin. 'Look at this,' she said to Dinah, who had just woken up. 'All over me, just like the measles.' Dinah considered the little eruptions and saw the tension in her mother's face as she tried to keep from scratching. 'Don't I look attractive today? How ever will I go to work like this?' Dinah wondered if it wasn't as obvious to her mother as it was to her: it was the cat, scratching back. What Dinah didn't know was that the night before, Tessie had placed a piece of paper in the Jerry Box. 'Should I tell Dinah the truth?' she had written in a shaky hand. Now the answer was written all over her.

'Dinah, honey,' she said, rubbing the Calamine into the crook of her arm. 'We should talk about what happened last night.'

'Forget it, Mom. I've got to get ready for school.'

Suddenly Dinah couldn't wait to get to homeroom. She knew Eddie Fingers would be in his seat when she got there. Without realizing it,

Dinah had come to rely on him. She felt safe in his presence and took comfort in their silent dialogue.

When she got to her seat, Eddie was waiting. She flashed him a quick four. *What about the cat?* He considered her message before responding. For the first time, he used all six fingers on his left hand to signal back. Maybe he smiled, Dinah couldn't tell. She carried the number six with her through Phys. Ed, through Civics, English, and to the cafeteria. As she was looking out the window of Mr Nanny's Geometry class, the six words revealed themselves to her: *The answer is clear as glass.*

It made her smile to hear her dad's voice as she played the words over in her mind. That afternoon, she and Crystal walked home together. 'My mom ran over a cat last night,' she said.

'Did it die?' asked Crystal.

'I'm sure it did. The weird thing was, she drove off real fast and pretended like it didn't happen.'

Crystal bit the inside of her lip. 'My mom's like that too, you know, doing one thing and saying it was something else.'

Dinah felt the warmth of relief flood her belly. She had told Crystal a forbidden secret. Crystal understood, even made it sound as if Mrs Landy and her mom had something in common.

The answer is clear as glass.

Crystal. That's what was clear as glass.

★   ★   ★

'The Baron's coming today,' said Glenn Bech Jr, handing Tessie a bunch of carnations for her desk.

'So that explains the suit,' she said.

'And the haircut,' he answered, wiggling his ears.

Ever since she started her job, the Bech family, owners of Lithographics, would tease her about her flat *a*'s, and ask her to pronounce words like *pajamas*. 'Pajaahmahs,' she'd say, purposely stretching out the second syllable. Then she'd poke back: 'Well, at least I don't have that Florida y'all drawl.'

Only one month into the job, Old Man Bech had said to her, 'Just call me Glenn, and my son here Glenn Junior. Don't you think that will be easier all around, Tess?' The Bechs were part of the business elite in Gainesville, yet they made her feel as if she could match up. No one had ever called her Tess before. It sounded efficient yet familiar. She liked the sound of her own voice on the phone, 'Lithographics. How may I help you?' But her favorite thing was having her own desk. At Angel's, she was on her feet all day. Some nights, she would hobble home and collapse on the sofa. Jerry would pull out his mother's old white enamel basin and fill it with warm water and Epsom salts. 'We've got to find you a sit-down job,' he'd say, taking one foot at a time in his hands and kneading her toes. She hoped, somehow, he could see her seated at her gray metal desk with the words *Mrs Lockhart* engraved on the plastic nameplate in front of her.

* * *

Twice a year, the Baron would come from Fort Lauderdale to get programs printed for his Jai Alai games in Dania. Dania Jai Alai was Lithographics' fastest-growing account, with all the snowbirds eager to throw money at one of the few legal gambling joints in the South. The Baron, whose real name was Barone Antonucci, was an older man with tight gray curly hair, slightly thinning on the top, dark pitted skin, and black narrow eyes that seemed to take everything in but let little out. On this day, the second day of Tessie's rash, he walked through the door wearing a gray shark-skin suit, a royal-blue shirt, and a thick ID bracelet with the initials B.V.A. engraved on it. Everything about him defied you not to notice him.

'Well hello, you must be . . .' the Baron squinted at the nameplate before him. '. . . Mrs Lockhart. Barone Antonucci. Nice to meet you.' He paused for a moment, taking in the sight of the funereal white carnations and this slight woman who resembled Joanne Woodward with mosquito bites. 'Looks like you had a roll in a patch of poison ivy.' He winked as if he were part of the joke.

'No I didn't really,' she answered. 'It's the heat. This heat . . . how do you people stand it?'

'Our people are hot-blooded. We can stand anything,' he answered. 'How long have you been here?'

'We moved here three months ago.'

'It gets easier,' he said. 'You'll see. Do you know where I can find Junior and Senior?'

'Oh, you mean Mr Bech and Mr Bech?' she asked.

'Yes and yes.' His laugh was deep and sharp.

She picked up the intercom to call them. The Baron stood over her with his hands at his sides. She noticed how his dark fingers curled as though he were carrying heavy valises. While they waited for the Bechs, Tessie tried conversation. 'You've come all the way from Fort Lauderdale?'

'Did indeed,' he said. 'Your joint makes all the printing plants in South Florida look like crap.'

'That's so nice,' she said, wishing the Bechs would hurry.

'Especially now.'

'I suppose so.' Oh God, where were they?

Finally, the Bechs appeared.

'Well, if it isn't the Glenns! How you guys hanging?'

'Long time, no see,' said Glenn Jr. 'How the hell are you?' As the two men pumped each other's hands, the Baron's ID bracelet made a chunky noise.

'All the better for having met your new gal here. Now you take care of that heat problem,' he said, with another wink.

'Thank you, I sure will.'

The three men disappeared into the office. Tessie went to the ladies room to put some Calamine on her stomach. She pulled a cigarette from her bag. Where do men like that get their confidence? she wondered, taking a long drag on her Marlboro.

When she returned to her desk a few minutes later, she found a piece of paper neatly folded on her chair. Vellum. Expensive. She knew that. There was a silhouette of a man in the right-hand corner. Feet together, he was jumping into the air about to hit a ball. She recognized the *cesta*, the carved basketlike racket strapped to his forearm, from pictures she'd seen of Jai Alai. 'Dania Jai Alai,' read the embossed letters next to the figure, and under that, in the inverted handwriting of someone in a hurry: 'Have lunch with me today, Mrs Polka Dottie. I promise it won't be too hot. BVA.'

As she studied the note, her heart started pounding, her face flushed, and all hell broke loose inside of her. She raked her nails over her screaming skin until the angry pinpricks swelled into hives and her body turned crimson.

Who does he think he is? she thought, tucking the note into her purse.

Ten minutes later, after the Glenns had walked the Baron to his green and white Impala, Tessie's phone rang.

'Lithographics, how may I help you?'

'For one thing, you can meet me for lunch at Sundowner's in fifteen minutes.'

Tessie was silent as she collected her thoughts. 'Oh, thank you, but I already have an engagement.'

'With whom? The crocodiles in Alley Pond?'

Tessie was so startled at having used the word

62

engagement, she didn't even hear the Baron's answer.

'Well, it's not an engagement, really. It's just that I said I would meet a friend.'

'Okay, Dottie,' he said. 'I'll call you soon and we'll make our own engagement.'

'Yes, well, thank you.'

'You're welcome.'

The phone went dead.

Three days later, a letter landed on her desk. It was addressed to her and had the word *personal* scribbled in the bottom left-hand corner. Tessie recognized the heavy paper and the busy backward handwriting. Inside, there was one sheet of paper with no greeting, just the following words. Tessie made sure no one was watching when she read them to herself in a faint whisper.

Last night I took a walk along the beach. The setting sun cast a golden glow across the water. From out of nowhere a little girl in a purple pinafore and a flowered scarf on her head came to me.

'Mister,' she said. 'Won't you buy some of my magic shells?' I said to her, 'What do your magic shells do?'

She said to me, 'They make sad people happy and sick people well.' I thought about my new friend Dottie with the mean rash all over her body and said, 'I know somebody who needs to feel better so I'll buy your shells.' I threw in an extra five to make sure the happy part was covered. Here they are. I hope they do the trick.

When Tessie turned over the envelope, fragments of shell fell onto her desk. She wondered how a man who looked like Caeser Romero and wore a gold pinky ring with an opal came up with such a sweet story. That night, she slipped a note into the Jerry Box. 'There's a man,' was all it said. The answer came back in the next day's mail. Again, the heavy envelope, the zigzag handwriting.

I went back to the beach last night. Our little shell friend was there again. 'What've you got for a guy with a big fat crush on a woman who doesn't even know he's alive?' I asked her. She pulled out a cigar box and opened its lid. Inside were little creatures in the shape of an S.

I ended up shelling out (no pun, ha ha) ten bucks for a handful of seahorses.

'Whatever you ask for will come true,' she promised.

That you'll have lunch with me was what I wished for. Just lunch. How bad could it be? June 4. Noon at Sundowner's.

'Just lunch. How bad could it be?' She could hear Jerry's voice. It was funny to think that he and Barone Antonucci might be in cahoots. I can't do this, she thought. What would we talk about? He's a dangerous man. It's more than a month away. He'll forget by then. Besides, what would I wear?

Barone Antonucci was raised in a household of boys who were never expected to be any more than a lot of trouble. Their father, Christian, had worked his way up through the restaurant supply business. For thirty-two years he got up every morning at 5:30 and took a trolley half an hour from Bay Ridge to Red Hook, where he reigned over Peerless Restaurant Supplies, an old warehouse full of cast-iron fryers, ceramic plates, and stemware with names like the Salud Grande martini glass. Christian always told his boys that he could walk into any restaurant in New York City and spot his butter dishes or table settings right away. 'I've laid the groundwork,' he would tell his sons. 'All you guys have to do is not screw it up.'

Barone was seven the first time his father came across the book he used to sketch close-ups of things like his own hand or his sleeping brother's face. Christian noticed the thick black pad that was stuck in the middle of a pile of comic books when he came in to say good night to the boys. 'What have we here?' he demanded, pulling the book from the stack. Christian didn't like surprises; he knew what was best for his boys and what course their lives should take. He sat on Barone's bed studying the drawings. He licked the tip of his index finger to turn the pages, making sure none of them stuck. The last picture in the pad was a still life of Mrs Antonucci's apron hanging from a hook behind the kitchen door. Barone had sketched it while he kept his mother company one night as she cooked.

'Why'd you draw this one?' Christian asked, his thick finger jabbing at the image of the apron. 'You think that's pretty?' Barone answered tentatively. 'I liked the colors. I liked how the apron looks like a shell.

'What are you, a little faggot or something?' Christian slapped Barone on the side of the head. 'Drawing is for sissies. Aprons are for sissies. There are no sissies in the Antonucci family. You get that?' Christian smacked him on the other side of the head for emphasis.

Barone absorbed his father's blows. 'That didn't hurt,' he said, as if asking for more. But Christian just stood up, dropped the sketch book to the floor, and walked out of the room. After that, no one in the Antonucci family ever mentioned the word *drawing* again, and Christian fell back to his assumption that his boys would follow him into the restaurant supply business.

Every now and again Barone's mother, Dora, would obliquely ask him how his work was going. 'Good,' he'd say, not bothering to mention that by eighth grade he was doing oil on canvas and by his freshman year he'd decided that he was going to become a painter and live in Paris. All through high school, he worked for his father and stashed every penny he earned in the brass safe box that his grand-father had given him on his confirmation. By the time he was seventeen, Barone was five feet nine inches, four inches taller than Christian. On the night that he announced to his parents that he was going to Paris after graduation, he watched his father's face turn the color of a rainy day. 'Is that what you call work?' he shouted. 'Over my dead body, no son of mine is going to be some high-falutin artist.' He balled his fist, getting ready to strike. But Barone grabbed him by the wrists and pinned his arms to his sides. 'There'll be no more of that,' he said, leaving red handprints on each wrist. One week later, he sailed for Paris.

He found a small walk-up studio with just enough room for a bed and his easel. He'd paint all morning and in the afternoons take his sketch pad and a box of colored pencils to the café down-stairs where he'd sit with a sign that said LES BEAUX PORTRAITS DIX CENTIMES. Barone attracted people with his dark exotic looks and easy manner. Turned out, he'd inherited his father's talent for sweet-talking.

He was in Paris for three months before he met another American. That afternoon, he was sitting at the café when he heard a woman ask the waiter for '*un demitasse sil vous plais.*' The waiter scrunched his nose as though he had just smelled rancid butter, then shrugged. Once again she said, '*Un demitasse sil vous plais,*' and once again the waiter pulled away and knitted his eyebrows as if the mangled French were a physical assault. Barone knew the waiter and knew that he understood English perfectly. The woman seemed to be getting angry and Barone sensed there could be a scene. 'Henri, give this lovely woman a demitasse and put it on my bill,' he said.

'*Okay dokey, Monsieur*,' said Henri, and hurried off to make the coffee. The woman turned around. She had large horseshoe-shaped lips the color of holly berries and tawny-colored hair. She wore a tight purple sweater and had, as Christian would have so eloquently said, 'tits that could knock you from here to Yonkers.'

'How do you do, Miss . . .'

'Fran. Fran Faberge,' she said, in a fractured accent part-English part-American.

'Fran Faberge. What a refined name,' said Barone.

'You can tell so much from a name, don't you think? And speaking of names, may I ask, what is yours?'

'You're going to find this hard to believe,' he said. 'It's Barone Antonucci.'

She laughed, an unguarded husky laugh that was purely American. And then she said the thing that he would always remember. 'Get outta here. You're as much of a Baron as I am a Faberge.'

'Ah, but,' he said in an exaggerated French accent, 'My father is Christian Antonucci, the king of the restaurant supply business in Bay Ridge, Brooklyn. And I have come to Paris to be an artist.'

'Yeah, well, my father is king of the royal pains in the asses in Teaneck, New Jersey,' she said in her native accent. 'Joey Moresco. Maybe you heard of him?'

Fran, it turned out, had also come to Paris to pursue her art. She'd been a ballet dancer since she was eight years old. Her teacher at Swan Studios, where she'd studied for twelve years, had urged her to follow her dreams. 'Fran,' she'd told her, 'It's in your blood. A natural like you comes along once in a lifetime.' She told her she must go to Paris, France, where the ballet was thriving, unlike in Teaneck. So Fran went to Paris where her gifts were just what they were looking for at the new strip club, Café Crazy. 'What the hell?' she told Barone. 'Art is art.'

About the time that Fran packed up her leather valise and moved into Barone's flat, he got a letter from his mother.

Your father has a horrible cough. Sometimes he spits up blood. He tries to hide it from me by covering his mouth with his handkerchief, but I see the awful stains later. He gets tired very easily. I want him to go see Dr Phipps, but he tells me that nothing is wrong and that I carry on too much. You know how he is. He is so stubborn and proud. I worry about him all the time.

He showed the letter to Fran. 'You gotta go home and help her,' she said. That was the thing about Fran – Barone never had to spell things out. She was canny without being a know-it-all. One month later, Fran and Barone landed in the United States.

The first time Barone saw his father, he thought it was the old neighbor from down the street. Christian had lost so much weight that it seemed as if his face was falling away. The sheer effort of taking in air exhausted him. He knew better than to let on about what he saw or how it shocked him. So he said the only thing he knew would be okay. 'Papa, how's the business?'

'Never better,' his father whispered. Later that night, after everyone had gone to bed, Christian asked Barone to join him in the living room. Barone rarely had a conversation alone with his father. He didn't even know where to begin. Finally Christian broke the silence. 'I won't beat around the bush,' he said. 'I'm sick. I need someone to help me with the business. God should forgive me for what I'm about to say about my sons. They're my children and I love them but they are as dumb as rocks. You're the only one of them who has a brain in his head. I am asking you as your father to do me a favor. I promise you if you do, you will be a rich man some day.'

Six months later Christian was dead and Barone was president of Peerless Restaurant Supply. Fran and Barone were married in a small wood-framed church in Teaneck, New Jersey, on an early fall day in 1927. Their first dance was to the song 'Someone to Watch Over Me,' the popular George Gershwin hit from the year before. When the singer sang, 'I'm a little lamb who's lost in the wood . . .' Fran and Barone each thought of themselves as the lost little lamb, and each felt blessed.

After that, no one ever asked Fran what kind of a dancer she'd been in Paris. She'd put behind her the brief but colorful career of Fran Faberge. From now on, she would simply be known as the Baroness.

CHAPTER 6

Victoria hated Memorial Day weekend. It was a different kind of being alone, as if everyone was at a party and she was left behind. When she would say something to Maynard about wanting to go away, he'd flat-out refuse. 'It just isn't right for me to leave the kids alone at the store,' he would answer, shaking his head. 'This is one of the busiest weekends of the year.' On the Saturday of this long weekend, she showed up for her usual appointment at Baldy's.

'Where the hell is everyone?'

'They've all gone to the fish,' said Jésus.

Victoria squinted. 'You don't mean that.'

'Yes,' he said. 'To Key West. To the fish.'

'Oh, they've gone fishing. Well, the hell with them. It's just you and me and that new girl.'

'Sonia?'

'Yes, Sonia. Where is she?' Victoria scanned the room.

'She's off today.'

'Gone to the fish,' she said, her voice flattening. She told Jésus how she hated these long week-ends, and how Maynard always felt as though he had to be at the store. 'What's the point of having buckets of money if you don't get to do what you want to do?' she asked.

'Maybe Mr Landy is doing what he wants to do,' said Jésus.

'Well, what about me? When do I get to do what I want to do? Charlie's off to college in the fall. That leaves Crystal, who right now can't stand the sight of me. Maynard's never home. I'm not getting any younger.'

'Mrs Landy, you don't look . . .'

'Cut the crap, Jésus. You know what I mean. It's lonely, just me and Ella rattling around that monster of a house.'

Jésus rubbed her shoulders. 'Sonia will be back next week,' he said. Victoria patted his hand. 'You're so good to me, even when I mouth off like a witch.'

'I've been thinking about your hair.'

Victoria perked up.

'Maybe it's time for a change. Something young and fresh like a bouffant.'

Right after they were married, Maynard made her promise to keep her hair long. 'How it flows on the pillow,' he'd said, staring down at her. 'Like ripples in the ocean.' It was an uncharacteristically romantic sentiment from Maynard and Victoria never forgot it. She wore the same flip for the next twenty-two years. Now, Jésus piled her hair on top of her head and pulled a few tendrils around her face. 'It would be very Ann-Margret,' he said.

'Ann-Margret? My goodness.' Victoria giggled. 'Shucks. Why the hell not?'

As Jésus trimmed the hair around her face – graduating the hair, he called it – she could see her younger self emerge: she began telling him about Victoria, the president of Kappa Delta. Victoria, with the loud mouth and beautiful smile. 'Miss Pearly Whites,' of the University of Georgia, 1935. Got put on suspension when she was found kissing Nora White, a freshman pledge, on the lips one night behind the sorority house. Got turned in by Sandra Beasely, some ugly small-minded girl from Asheville, who said that Victoria had unhealthy tendencies and was a threat to the other girls of Kappa Delta. Just like that, Victoria turned around and found herself a steady boyfriend. The first girl in her year to get pinned, the first to go all the way. Married before graduation. Donald Pierson. Football player, president of his fraternity, great dancer. Took her back to the family farm in Hawthorne, Florida, where his daddy raised cattle. Away from the razzmatazz of college and frat parties, Donald's drinking took on an ugly desperation. One night she found a handful of hairpins in his night-table drawer.

'Where'd these come from?' she asked him.

'What the hell you doin' going through my things?' he shouted. His face turned gray.

She told him she was looking for the nail clippers.

'Don't you ever, ever go through my stuff again,' he said. 'Do you get that?'

'What've you got to hide, anyway?' she asked
'Nothin',' he said.

'Sure doesn't sound like it.' Her voice was playful, taunting if you wanted to hear it that way.

'Just stay the fuck out of my things,' he said.

Out of nowhere, a fist slammed into her right jaw. It was as sudden as a bad dream. Before the pain, she felt a gap where her bottom incisor used to be. The tooth was floating in a pool of blood. The blood tasted bitter, metallic. The two of them put their hands to their mouths in disbelief.

'Oh my God, honey, I am so sorry.' He reached for her, but she slapped his hand away.

'You touch me and I'll kill you,' she said, then ran inside the bathroom, slamming the door behind her. She rinsed her mouth, ran water over the tooth, wrapped it in a piece of toilet paper and tucked it inside her pants pocket, just in case.

Donald was mewling at the other side of the door. 'Sweetie, I didn't mean anything. You know what a hothead I am. I swear, this will never happen again.'

She opened the door, moved him out of the way without looking at him. Went to the closet and pulled her valise from the top shelf. He watched cow-eyed as she threw her clothes into the bag.

'C'mon Victoria, you gotta gimme another chance.'

'Not on your life,' she answered and walked out of Donald Pierson's life forever. She hitchhiked to Gainesville, where she stayed with a sorority sister.

'The weird thing is, I never found out if the hair-pins were his or someone else's,' she said.

'Where is he now?' asked Jésus.

'Dead. He volunteered when the war broke out and was killed in Italy. That's the last I heard, anyway.' She gave a little laugh.

It pained Jésus to think of someone wounding his beautiful friend. He stroked her right jaw.

'It ended all right,' she said. 'I met Maynard Landy three weeks later. The kindest man I've ever known. He was generous, you know what I mean? Dressed well, didn't ask too many questions about my past. We went out for a while, and then he asked me to marry him. I didn't hesitate for a minute. There was a man I could depend on. He'd make a good living. He'd always respect me. These are the important things when you're thinking of building a life with somebody. Physically, it was okay, but between you and me, that's never been the big thing between us.'

Peace of mind, that was worth more to Victoria than all of it. Maynard was a strong man. His thick arms and barrel chest were a barrier between her and the rest of the world. No one in his right mind would pick a fight with a guy built like Rocky Marciano. If someone takes a punch at you from out of the blue once, there is never a time when you don't think it could happen again.

Whenever Victoria felt restless or like Maynard

wasn't paying enough attention, she'd pull out the little music box he had given her one Christmas. It had a skater figurine on top, which twirled in circles, while the box played its frothy version of 'As Time Goes By.' Lying like a jewel on the green velvet lining inside was Victoria's old incisor. The center of the tooth had long since rotted, but the carcass remained. Her only link to Donald Pierson, a reminder of how far she'd come.

'Can I ask you a personal question?' she asked Jésus.

'Of course,' he said.

'Do you ever feel safe?'

'I always feel safe. I am an American citizen.'

It never dawned on Victoria that for many people, that was enough.

'And you? Do you feel safe?' he asked.

'Not for one iota of a second,' she answered. 'My daddy left when I was eleven. Seven years later I got married. Life is a matter of avoiding one hazard after another as far as I'm concerned. Lord knows, without shopping I would be a psychological wreck, always worrying about what it will be next.'

She laughed as pieces of freshly cut hair trickled down her neck.

'If I may say, Mrs Landy, sometimes it is just matter of allowing yourself to be okay. Because you are waiting for the next bad thing doesn't mean you can keep it away. It is unfortunate to waste the times in between.'

'Jesus H. Christ!' shrieked Victoria.

'What is it?'

'You're right, I do look like Ann-Margret!'

Charlie swamped his mother with attention when she came home with the short curly hairdo.

'That's very modern,' he said.

'Oh sweetheart, I am so glad you like it. You know how a little thing like a new look can shape a person's attitude. Jésus is an artist. What that man knows about hair, I swear, he could write a book.'

Charlie never said he liked it, but his mother seemed less edgy, almost giddy, and so silently he thanked God for the brilliant and gifted Jésus Baldisarri. That night, when Maynard came home from work, he pulled her into a hug.

'You look beautiful,' he said.

'Thank you, honey,' said Victoria, nuzzling into his chest.

'How about we open up a bottle of nice Rosé and get an early start on the party?'

Every Memorial Day, the Landys had a family barbecue. The tradition was that they'd each do some sort of performance. This year, they invited Dinah and Tessie because, as Ella put it, 'Poor souls, to be alone on Memorial Day is a crying shame.' Victoria had little interest in meeting the girl's mother. She could barely stand having the girl around.

Still, on issues of what was right and wrong, Victoria was always on shaky ground. She had the self-awareness to recognize that about herself, and to yield to Charlie, Maynard – even Ella – all of whom she felt had a greater sensitivity toward other people than she did. So begrudgingly, she invited Tessie Lockhart to the barbecue.

'If the merry widow is half the jackass that her daughter is, this will be one zippydeedoodah Memorial Day,' she said to Maynard.

'You are so graceful with the English language,' he answered.

Victoria never knew whether or not he was kidding.

Dinah tried to prepare her mother for her meeting with the Landys. 'She's a snob,' Dinah said. 'For all the times I've been there, I don't even think she knows my name.'

Dinah didn't say that Mrs Landy made her embarrassed about being poor and not having a father. 'The only thing she's ever said to me was that she had this fancy beautician who knew everything about hair straightening.' And she surely didn't mention that time in the bathtub.

'Well that's pretty awful,' said Tessie, who'd been agonizing about the invitation for the past week. She'd already figured out that, since the barbecue was called for seven, she could have a glass of wine at six in the privacy of her own home.

'You're dreading this, aren't you?' Dinah asked her on that afternoon.

'I'll be honest, I am a little. I mean these people don't exactly sound like my cup of tea.'

Dinah thought about how her mother hadn't visited anybody since her father died, nor had anyone visited her.

'Mom, you haven't had a cup of tea in four years,' said Dinah.

'That's so, isn't it?' said Tessie. 'Well, I've had cups of other things.'

The house was even grander and fancier than Tessie had imagined. 'What am I supposed to say to all this?' she wondered as Ella took them through it to the backyard: 'Nice place you have here?' She decided against saying anything and joined Maynard and Victoria in a semicircle of lounge chairs by the pool.

Conversation got off to a desolate start. 'So, how are you snowbirds enjoying Gainesville?' Maynard asked as Tessie sipped her Rosé and Victoria picked at her cuticles.

'I have a wonderful new job,' she said. 'Lithographics, the printing plant on old Butler Road.'

'Of course,' said Maynard. 'It's the biggest one in central Florida.'

'I'm the office manager,' said Tessie embellishing her position.

'I know Senior and Junior,' said Maynard. 'We're in the Rotarians together. Devout Baptists, both of them. Can't drink, can't cuss, can't gamble. Junior comes into the store every once in a while looking as guilty as an underage kid. "I just need

80

one of those little bottles of Scotch," he'll say. And each time, he reminds me, "Flora doesn't have to know about this now, does she?" Nice guy, but scared to death of his wife.'

Tessie was buoyed by the knowledge of Glenn Jr. being a little henpecked. The thought emboldened her to remark on some of Lithographics' clients, as though they'd all been friends for years. 'There's this fella who comes up from Fort Lauderdale, he runs the Jai Alai fronton down there. We print all of his programs.'

'The Baron!' said Maynard.

'You know him?'

'Everyone in the state of Florida knows the Baron,' said Maynard. 'He used to be a starving painter in Paris. Now he's a businessman worth more than a million. Fascinating story.'

'Quite a character,' said Tessie, trying to sound neutral.

'A horny one at that,' laughed Maynard. 'Though he's a monk compared to the Baroness.'

'The Baroness, who's that?' Tessie cocked her head.

'Fran Antonucci. Barone's wife. The former – quote, dancer from Teaneck, New Jersey, unquote.' Maynard raised his eyebrows. 'Whoo, that woman can drink any man under the table. And she's built like a brick you-know-what house.'

Tessie took another sip of the wine. 'I've heard that,' she lied.

Just then, Victoria jumped up and clapped her

81

hands together. 'All right now, it's showtime. Crystal and her friend have prepared a song for us.'

Dinah's right, thought Tessie. That woman really doesn't know her name.

The girls had made up their own dance to the popular song 'Lollipop.' They snapped their fingers, bent their knees, and wiggled their hips in time to the simple rhythm. 'Lollipop, lollipop, oh lolli lolli lolli . . .' Charlie sat behind the girls, playing the bongos as they acted out the song. He watched his sister with a smile. Crystal could put a bag over her head or jump up and down in place, and she'd still be cute. She danced with the ease and confidence of someone who didn't worry how she looked. But the other girl, Dinah, there was an awkwardness in her step, something hesitant about the way she kept looking to Crystal for confirmation that she was doing it right. If Crystal abandoned herself to joy, Dinah seemed intent on keeping it at bay.

He watched Mrs Lockhart take deep drags on her cigarette, her eyes darting as if to take in the ceramic birdbath, the pool, the brass sundial, the fountain that cascaded into the pool, the cutting garden, the grasses, the enormous house that went as far as the eye could see. Nervous, he thought. She wonders what she's doing here. She can't figure out how a nice man like my father ended up with a spoiled woman like my mother. She's not bad looking. If she did something with that limp hair and wore less dowdy clothes, she would be quite attractive. God help me, I am starting to sound like my mother.

Victoria lit a Salem and lay cross-legged on her chaise. The nighttime air was smoky and sweet with frangipani. There was a soft breeze. 'For all the misery in the world, there is this night,' Victoria said to Maynard and Tessie. The girls were winding it up, thrusting their arms forward, and rolling their *l*'s from the back of their palettes. '. . . oh lolli lolli lolli. Lollipop!'

'Whoever wrote that song had the IQ of a water bug,' Maynard whispered. Victoria laughed and swatted him on the thigh. Tessie wondered what Victoria could possibly know about misery. Everyone clapped for the girls. Then Victoria stood up again and announced, 'Charlie has a special song he would like to sing. And he will accompany himself on the guitar.'

Charlie stood next to the grill, his wide face backlit by a citronella candle. He strummed the guitar and bobbed his head up and down before he began to sing. The song started out innocently enough – something about an old man and his cat. But then came the chorus:

The cat came back, the very next day
The cat came back, we thought she was a goner
But the cat came back, she just couldn't stay away.

He never took his eyes off Tessie. When he finished, Tessie clapped harder than anyone. Dinah tried not to stare at her. 'What could he know?' she wondered. Crystal nudged her on the arm and whispered, 'I swear, I never told him a thing. He's just weird that way.'

Victoria followed with some song she'd learned in her sorority: 'It's a great big wonderful world we live in, when you're in love you're a master of all you survey, you're a gay Santa Claus . . .'

Her voice was sweet and warbled and slightly off tune. It was one of the few times she seemed nakedly vulnerable, and when Maynard got up to do his imitation of Nat King Cole's 'Mona Lisa,' he dedicated it to her. They all tried to get Tessie to sing, but the most she would do was chime in on the 'Mona Lisa' chorus. Afterward, they ate barbecued ribs and killed three bottles of Rosé. At the end of the evening, Victoria actually used Dinah's name when she said, 'Thank you for coming, Tessie and Dinah. This is one of those nights we'll never forget.'

'So was it as bad as you thought?' asked Dinah later as she and her mother drove through Cypress Woods.

'If a woman is built like a you-know-what brick-house, does that mean she's attractive?' answered Tessie.

'It's a compliment, Mom, like *va va va voom*.'

Tessie got lost in her thoughts. How did Dinah know about all this? How could a married man send the kind of notes that the Baron had written to her? What else did Dinah know that she didn't?

'I had a very nice time,' she finally said.

'Yeah, it was pretty neat,' said Dinah. 'The brother's nice.'

Neither of them mentioned the cat.

CHAPTER 7

On the second day that Eddie Fingers didn't show up for class, Mr Reilly stood in front of the class, his hands clasped and his head bowed like an altar boy's. 'I have an announcement. You know our friend Eddie Howell? He will not be back for the rest of the school year. Why? Because he is sick and will have to be in the hospital for a while.' Mr Reilly continued, as though he were a ventriloquist using two different voices. 'What's wrong with him? The doctors think it might have something to do with his heart, but they're going to do their darndest to find out.'

Normally, Dinah and Crystal would be biting the insides of their cheeks to keep from laughing. But they didn't even exchange glances. Dinah knew how people could disappear forever, and Crystal knew that her friend had a strange attachment to Eddie. That's why she never revealed what Charlie had told her months earlier. Eddie had caught his eye at the end of a school assembly. 'How ya doing?' Charlie had asked. 'Can you help me?' Eddie had answered. 'I've wet my pants and need to get to the men's room.' Charlie told

Crystal that Eddie seemed to have a wheeze in his voice. He also said that the way Eddie had spoken to him, so straight forwardly and without embarrassment, made him think that Eddie was used to asking for help.

All day, Dinah thought about Eddie. About his bluish fingernails, the way he slumped in his desk, how he looked thin and used, like a much older person. While she hated listening to her mother talk to her father each night, she was certain that this boy was the direct connection to her father. Should she write him a card? What would she say? Maybe she should send a present. She couldn't imagine someone her own age being in the hospital. With him not at school, how would she talk to her father?

If Jerry Lockhart was in heaven, he wasn't having much fun. Between doling out advice and devising cryptic numerical codes to transmit through a six-fingered fourteen-year-old boy, when would the poor man have time to indulge in the glories of his new location? For the past week Tessie had besieged him. What about the Baron? June 4th was only two days away. Should she have lunch with him? And now there was a wife. Her notes were becoming more desperate.

One night she wrote: 'It seems like a betrayal to think of any other man but you. Of course you are the only one.' And on another night, after she'd had a couple of glasses of wine, she'd slipped this note into his box: 'You know, Jerry,' it began with a tone of belligerence. 'I am a woman and have desires sometimes. It is so strange to me that you are not here and that I have to think about these things by myself.'

On the morning of June 4th, Tessie woke with a start. She'd dreamed that she was driving Victoria Landy around Cypress Woods, looking for Crystal and Dinah. The women were lost, and the longer they drove, the further away their daughters seemed to get. 'We might never see them again,' Victoria said. It was as if her words took shape and ran in front of the car. Tessie slammed on the brakes and heard the awful noise of shells breaking beneath her wheels. 'Don't even say that,' she shouted, then woke up. She jumped out of bed to get as far away from her dream as possible. She threw on her vermilion robe with beige flowers, the same robe she'd worn for fifteen years. 'Rise and shine,' she said, trying to sound chipper as she opened Dinah's door.

But Dinah had long since risen. She lay in bed, her head propped up against the pillow, her eyes narrow and swollen. 'Didn't sleep much,' she said. 'Can't go to school today.'

Tessie hadn't heard that dullness in her daughter's voice since Carbondale. She felt her own anxiety, the clutch in her stomach, the lure of getting back into her still-warm bed. It tugged at her like an old habit, and it took every form of will she could muster to resist it. Instead, she climbed into bed next to Dinah. 'We can't, you and me, go back to the way we were,' she said gently. 'I know how you feel. There are some days I can't imagine going on. It's just a step at a time. You get up, you brush your hair, eat breakfast. And before you know it, you've gotten through an hour, and then another hour, and soon you're not thinking about the time you put behind you. You just have to keep moving forward.'

Dinah started to cry. 'Sometimes it's just too hard.' She wasn't about to tell her mother about Eddie. 'I miss Daddy so much.'

Then Tessie told Dinah about her Jerry Box and how, whenever she had a question, he always seemed to answer. 'I believe there's a part of him that watches us,' she said. 'I know him well enough to be sure he'd hate it if either of us was hiding in our rooms. Tell you what. Why don't you have Crystal come over after school today. I'll come home early and make you girls some french fries. I'll buy some Coca-Cola with cherry syrup, too.'

They lived on a strict budget; Dinah knew never to ask for any of the extravagances. Trips to the supermarket became lessons on indulgence. 'Too rich for my blood,' her mother would say, returning an item to its shelf after examining its price. 'Some people can afford to kiss their money goodbye, I guess. Hooray for them.' Consequently, Dinah had never had Coca-Cola with cherry syrup until that first time at Crystal's house. She turned on her side and rested her head on the inside of her mother's arm. The familiar smell of stale cigarette smoke and last night's Noxzema made her feel safe, as if she was a little girl again bundled in her mother's lap. 'Coca-Cola? Really?' she asked.

Tessie could hear the life come back into Dinah's voice. She thought about the teacher's words a couple of months back. It broke her heart to realize how hard every day must be for her. 'Yes ma'am,' she said to Dinah, mocking the Southern accents that surrounded them. 'Don't y'all think it's time I get to try some of those potatoes you're always carryin' on about?'

'You sure are *unpredickable*,' said Dinah, laying on the accent, thinking about her mother and that box, and how much worse off her mother was than she even imagined.

They lay there for a while until Dinah rolled on her back. She thought that maybe she would write a poem for Eddie, the way her dad used to do for her. That way it could be a little funny, not all so serious.

Tessie's thoughts had also wandered to what she would wear today. The two of them came apart guided by their distractions. Tessie went back to her room and picked out a shirtwaist dress with orange lines that crisscrossed against a gray background. The dress was tight in the bust and accentuated her narrow waist and thin legs. She studied herself in the mirror, pleased with what she saw, then turned the collar up and wrapped her fingers around the back of her neck the way she'd seen the fashion models do it in magazines. 'What am I doing?' she worried, as she dabbed Jean Naté on her wrists. In her head, she had not yet decided whether or not she would meet Barone Antonucci for lunch today. As far as what she would wear was concerned, the matter was already settled.

Meanwhile, Dinah had pulled out her notebook and was sitting on the metal folding chair in front of her small wooden desk. She opened her notebook and began writing:

Dear Eddie Howell,
   The first day I saw you, you held up four fingers.
   I knew what you meant, and the memory lingers.
   Every day there you are, in Civics and Home Room.
   Now your chair is empty, I hope you'll come back soon.
   Mr Reilly said you were sick, then asked us why?
   For once, he didn't have an answer. What a strange guy.

She wanted to end with something like:

You are the best friend that I've ever had.
In so many ways you're just like my dad.

No, she could never say that. She crossed out the last two lines and tried:

Get better soon, I hope your sickness is mi-nah
Best wishes to you, from your friend Dinah.

That sounded dumb.

Just then her mother came back into her room. 'So, what are you going to wear to school today?' Dinah looked up from her notebook. She saw that her mother's face was flushed. Or was it dots of rouge? She'd put a barrette in her hair and there were slashes of blue eye shadow on each lid.

'You look really nice,' said Dinah.

'Thank you. And you, my little Boing Boing Girl? When are you going to get dressed?'

'Mom, I'm too old to be anyone's boing boing girl. Could we please move past 1956?'

Tessie fought back tears. She'd been so pleased by Dinah's compliment that she'd momentarily forgotten her daughter was fourteen. If I cry every time her tone is harsh or she pulls away, where will that leave me? she wondered. 'Well young lady,' she said in a stiff voice, 'you have a half hour to shower, eat breakfast, and get dressed. So I'd suggest you get moving.' She used her hurt feelings to push out the guilt she felt at rushing Dinah to school. After all, it wouldn't be proper for a mother with a sick child at home to go off and have lunch with a married man. Besides, she didn't want Dinah moping around the house all day. Even if her motivations weren't pure, Tessie was sure she was acting in her daughter's best interest.

God, she really was *unpredickable*. Dinah stared after her mother as she headed toward the kitchen. She remembered how her father used to tease her mother. 'Jo,' he'd say. 'You have the temperament of a tropical weather pattern. It's sunny. It's stormy. You never know.' The other night, the Ritchie Valens ballad 'Donna' was playing on the radio. From her bedroom, Dinah could see her mother dance by herself, one arm wrapped around her stomach, the other held in the air as though she was clasping the hand of an invisible partner. Her eyes were half-closed and her head was swaying to the music. There was something about the way she let her hair graze her bare back, from one side to the other – Dinah couldn't put words to it but she knew she was watching something she shouldn't.

Now Dinah could hear her mother slam the cupboard doors and set the cereal bowls down so hard on the dinette table that they might have cracked. The emphatic noise usually meant, 'I am the only one who does anything around here.' But this morning, the banging was more urgent than usual. Dinah shut her notebook and shoved it under her pillow. There was no use trying to finish her poem. School would be a relief after this place.

Mother and daughter ate in silence. As she left, Dinah let the screen door slam. 'See ya,' she said behind it, not 'I love you,' the way she did every other morning. Tessie grabbed her unused napkin and the ballpoint pen by the telephone. 'Damn you Jerry Lockhart,' she wrote. 'What kind of a man dies leaving his wife alone with a teenage girl?' She pressed so hard that the napkin shredded. For the first time she allowed herself the notion that just because people are dead, doesn't mean they come back to you wiser or better than they were in life. She balled up the napkin in her hand until it was no larger than a nub, then stuffed it into the box.

'Tess Lockhart, don't you look nice today?' said Glenn Jr passing her desk. 'Whatever you're wearing, it smells real pretty.' Tessie pressed her lips together, trying to hide her satisfied smile. Her new Coral Ice lipstick felt waxy on her mouth, and she worried that she'd gotten some on her teeth. 'Oh you,' she said, discreetly trying to remove it with her tongue, 'it's just toilette water, you can buy it in any drugstore.' What if the Glenns guessed she had an engagement? Worse, what if they figured out with whom?

When Tessie told them, 'I may need a little longer for lunch today. Doctor's appointment,' she lowered her eyes as if to say, 'enough said.' At precisely 11:45 she left the office. The lemony scent of Jean Naté trailed behind her. The two men watched out the window as she drove off in the Plymouth. 'Doctor's appointment, my ass,' said Glenn Sr.

'Yeah, really,' answered Glenn Jr 'What a crock of shit.' The two men flushed at their use of profanities. It was the one indulgence they shared when they were alone.

The word *Sundowner's* was carved into a plank of driftwood that was affixed to a royal palm; the letters were painted turquoise. A fisherman's net was draped around the sign and a giant conch shell sat at its feet. Two weathered oars framed the front door of the restaurant, and inside, mounted sharks, marlins, and tarpons loomed over the rickety wooden tables and straight-back chairs. The cocktails had names like Planter's Punch with a Porpoise and the Martini That Got Away. The Baron seemed more tentative than he had the first time they met. He ordered a gin and tonic and twirled the wooden end of the paper umbrella that came with it. His notes had been so intimate, yet sitting here inside the badly lit Sundowners, he couldn't even meet her eye. They were virtual strangers with no history to turn into light conversation. Tessie pulled apart a roll, then set it on her plate. She lit a cigarette, then ordered a glass of Chablis. Finally, the Baron broke the silence. 'So, the last time I saw you, you were covered with spots. Did you ever find the culprit?'

Without thinking, Tessie blurted out the first thing that came into her mind. 'Fish,' she said. 'I'm allergic to fish.'

They stared at each other like two people who'd been underwater and surfaced at the same time.

'You're kidding me?' His eyes bulged.

'No I'm not,' she answered, not wanting to break the tension.

'Fish? I can't believe it.' His face got red and a sound rumbled up from inside of him and exploded into laughter. Tessie laughed at the sight of him laughing. Tears rolled down his cheeks. She covered her mouth with her hand and fell back against the chair, helpless with her own laughter.

'Fish,' he said, barely able to sputter out the word. Now they were heaving, gasping for breath.

'Fish,' she screamed, wiping her nose. People from the other tables stared at them, unsure whether there was a fight ensuing or someone had gotten a bone lodged in their throat. He wiped his cheeks with the back of his hand and with the other opened the folded menu. 'Well, I guess you won't be having' – he raised his voice as though he were a television announcer – 'A FINE KETTLE OF SHRIMP.' His careful enunciation caused the two of them to collapse into more gales of laughter. Tessie, barely able to catch her breath, answered, 'And NO to the FISH GOTTA SWIM CLAMS GOTTA FRY.' The Baron waved his arms as if offering surrender. 'Please,' he gasped. 'Please, stop, I can't. I'm gonna faint.' Tessie could feel deposits of mascara settle into the lines around her eyes. 'Oh God, I haven't laughed this hard since who knows when,' she said. They slumped forward, elbows on the table. The inside of their arms brushed. Still caught in the hysteria of their laughter, the Baron reached across the table, pulled Tessie toward him, and kissed her hard on the mouth. Tessie lost her place. Her left hand grappled with the air, as if she was looking for something to hold on to. Her right hand traveled the span of Barone's cheekbone, behind his ear to the back of his neck where his thick black curls met his baby soft skin.

When they finally broke apart, he looked at her face as if for the first time. Her lipstick was smeared around her mouth; her eyes were streaked with makeup.

'You look like a far-sighted clown,' he said using his thumb to wipe the lipstick off her chin. His cheeks were still covered with tear tracks; a thicket of hair stood up on the top of his head. She smoothed his hair and dabbed his cheeks with her napkin. 'The two of us, what a sight,' she said.

She ordered filet of sole; he had the stone crabs. He ordered a second gin and tonic and she another Chablis. Conversation came easy. Tessie told him about Dinah and Carbondale and how after six months, she still couldn't figure out how to set up her hi-fi system. Barone explained the game of Jai Alai, and talked about his childhood in Bay Ridge, Brooklyn. 'There were five of us, all boys,' he said. 'Every morning before he went to work, my father would smack each of us. "Why'd you do that?" we'd ask. "Because I know you're going to do something to screw up," he'd say. "Respect your mother today, or there's more where that came from."'

He told her about Fort Lauderdale. 'It's a small redneck town now,' he said, 'but the way the tourist business is going down there, things will soon be booming. I can't wait to show it to you.' He never mentioned anything about his family. When it was time to leave, he said to her, 'When will I see you again, Dottie?'

She had been Tessie all of her life, except for those years when she was Jo. Dottie was someone new, someone she didn't know very well and wasn't even sure she liked. 'I don't know,' she said. 'You know with Dinah and the job, I don't have a lot of free time.'

'Guess we'll have to work around that,' said Barone.

'Thank you for lunch,' she said, as he walked her to her car.

'Next time we'll have dinner at The Cattleman,' he said. 'Unless, of course, you're allergic to beef.'

By the time Tessie got back to Lithographics, she'd put on fresh lipstick and fixed her eye makeup. Glenn Sr came by her desk later that afternoon. 'Everything okay at the doctor's?' he asked.

'Oh sure, you know, just routine women stuff,' she answered. Glenn Sr stiffened, afraid she'd give him more details. 'Okay then, that's good,' he said. But when Tessie tried to work, she thought of Barone. She leaned her chin into her right collarbone, pretending to be stretching her neck. In truth, some of his Old Spice had rubbed off onto the shoulder of her blouse. The smell of it made her lonesome and incredibly nervous.

At around four o'clock, she remembered that she'd promised Dinah she'd be home early. The french fries and Coca-Cola; the fight, the slamming screen door. Was that just this morning? She knocked on Glenn Jr's door. 'I know it seems as if I'm asking for a lot of time off today,' she said, 'but I promised Dinah I'd be home early. It's kind of important.' Glenn Jr nodded. 'Sure Tess, whatever you need.' Later, he and Senior would exchange conjectures about the nature of Tess's 'women stuff.' Glenn Jr, who had a bloodhound's nose when it came to alcohol, said he could swear he smelled it on her breath when she came back from lunch. Senior laughed. 'Do you think our Tess was having herself a nooner?' Junior's voice deepened. 'She's a nice piece of ass. Probably hasn't gotten laid since her husband died.' The two men shook their heads and made snorting sounds.

By the time Tessie got home with the Coca-Cola, potatoes, and cherry syrup, the girls were already there. She could hear their voices behind the closed bedroom door. Tessie had never made fries. She cut up the potatoes into stick shapes that she thought approximated french fries, poured a cup of oil into a pan, waited until it bubbled then threw in the potatoes. It sounded right. She stirred up the drinks in two large jelly glasses. She put all of it on a blue metal tray along with a salt shaker, two plates, and two napkins, and carried the offering to Dinah's room. 'Okay, girls,' she sang out. 'I have a little something for you.' Crystal opened the door. 'Ta dum,' said Tessie placing the tray on Dinah's desk. That's when she noticed Dinah lying on her bed, tears running down her cheeks. 'Thanks Mom, I'm not hungry,' she said, turning her face to the wall.

'What's wrong?' asked Tessie. Crystal sat next to Dinah on the bed. 'It's our friend from school, Eddie Howell,' she said in a hushed voice. 'Mr Reilly told us he died last night.' Dinah had never mentioned the boy, but clearly she was saddened by his death. Tessie sat down next to Crystal and rubbed her daughter's shoulder. 'Sweetheart, I am so sorry,' she said, but Dinah stayed facing the wall. Instinctively she knew that it would be Crystal, not she, who could comfort her daughter. She walked out of the room and beckoned Crystal to follow her. 'She knows too much about death,' said Tessie. 'Promise me you'll help her get past this.'

'Yes ma'am, of course I will,' she answered.

For so many years, Tessie was her daughter's everything. Now it was becoming painfully clear that there would be others who would take her place. She closed the door and left the two girls alone. Back in the kitchen she poured some wine into a ceramic coffee cup. It mattered to her that

Crystal might tell Victoria Landy she'd seen Tessie drinking from a wineglass at five in the afternoon. Tessie took the drink and went into her bedroom. She closed the shades, angled the fan just right, and lay on her bed, placing the cup on her night table. She thought of Dinah, of Barone, of the Glenns and how none of this would be happening if she hadn't gone to the Morris Library that day and been captivated by the black-and-white pictures of the old colonials and Spanish moss. 'Oh my Jerry,' she cried, turning toward the wall. She envisioned Dinah on the other side of that wall, toppled by her own misery; the two of them like ends of a wishbone, snapped apart.

She drifted off to sleep and awoke a half hour later determined to make things right for her child and herself. As was her habit when she made vows of renewal, she wrote a note to Jerry.

It is all so hard without you. Today I kissed a man. You know who I mean. Dinah's friend at school died. My darling, it might seem as though we are moving away from you. We will never do that in our hearts. It's just everyday life that pushes us forward. I feel ashamed about the man. Can you forgive me?

Sometimes Jerry's answers seemed obscure, but she always recognized them when they came. Two days later, an ad in the *Gainesville Sun* caught her eye: 'Don't Get Caught Up Short – Or Long – By Summer,' it read. 'We know just what to do with all your hair problems. J. Baldy's. Bring this ad and get a 20% discount on a wash, cut, tease or perm.'

As Tessie dialed the beauty parlor, she remembered how people used to say, 'That Jerry Lockhart. What a wicked sense of humor.'

Crystal and Dinah might as well have been on the other side of the moon.

'What if I've lost my dad forever?' said Dinah.

'I'll bet you haven't,' said Crystal.' 'You just need to find another way to talk to him.'

'You're the best friend I've ever had,' said Dinah.

'Me, too,' said Crystal.

'Let's be best friends forever.'

'I promise.'

CHAPTER 8

The world was a sorrowful place; whatever Ella knew of it was proof that it was so. By the time she was eight years old, her mother had died from smallpox, and her father had been shot dead in a robbery over eleven dollars. She and her younger brother, Reggie, were all that was left. Them and their grandma Olie. Olie had three children of her own and one husband, dead for the past seven years. Two of the children lived up north and the other was a caretaker for some fancy man on Lake Okeechobee.

From the time she was a young girl, Olie worked at the First Baptist Church of Alachua. She swept the floors and washed down the pews. When Arthur Finn, the white minister of the church, got too old to walk unaided, Olie held his arm and made sure he ate three meals a day. At night, she would lay out his pajamas and pray with him before he went to sleep. Olie was self-schooled and learned to read by following the text of songs she had long since memorized. Reverend Finn had always read aloud to her the letters he got from his relatives in North Carolina. After he was

103

finished, Olie would read them back to him. Sometimes they would spend a whole evening working on the words she couldn't pronounce.

Olie was well into her fifties when she took in Ella and Reggie. It was no problem, she said. She was glad for the company. The three of them lived in a cramped two-room house right outside of Gainesville. There was no running water, and Reggie and Ella slept separated by a sheet tacked across the middle of their bedroom. Later Ella would say that Olie gave her gifts worth more than all the money in the world. She taught her to read. She taught her the words of Jesus and to put her life in His hands. That trust, unbroken and truer than anything she had known, was what defined her world and made living in it bearable. Her faith remained unshakable in the face of formidable odds: Olie's descent into dementia, Reggie's instability, Victoria Landy.

Ella came to work for the Landys right after Reverend Finn passed and Charlie was born. Olie's husband had worked for Matthew Landy laying ties on the Seaboard Airline. 'He worked until the very last,' Olie had told her. 'And when he was gone, Mr Landy said to me, "Olie, as long as I and my family are still drawing a breath, you and yours will never want for bread on your table."' Olie had a way of making everyone sound as if they spoke right out of the Old Testament. No matter, Matthew Landy proved to be good to his word.

She was fourteen when Maynard Landy gave her a job delivering liquor to people's homes. 'Now Ella, make sure you go to the back door,' he'd instructed. 'People in this town aren't used to coloreds calling.' When he married Victoria, he had her come to their house once a week to wash the laundry and straighten the house. 'Victoria has many talents,' he'd said then, 'but housekeeping isn't one of them.'

After Charlie was born, Ella moved in with the Landys. She slept in a small room off the pool-room, with her own bathtub and toilet. From her window she could look into the neighbor's yard, where there was a mango tree and a hibiscus bush. There was a Venetian blind, which she could pull up or down depending on the time of day. She slept in a narrow single bed, and the roundness of her body left its imprint on the mattress. At night, she fit into all the right places like an old pair of shoes. There was a little closet to the right of her night table, and over her bed she hung a cross made of birch wood and twine that Olie had made for her sixteenth birthday. She called the room her sanctuary.

When Charlie was a baby, Ella would rock him in her arms and sing the songs she had learned in church. Victoria knew better than to complain too much about Ella. She was as much a part of her life as Maynard was. In truth, the woman's constant singing drove her to distraction. 'Either the baby or me – one of us is going to start talking in tongues any day,' she told Maynard one night. 'I mean, religion is one thing. Obsessive behavior is quite another.' What Victoria did not know was that Ella was as compulsive about reading as she was about singing. She read everything she could get her hands on, though her taste ran to mysteries by Agatha Christie and novels by Harold Robbins. From those books, she learned about men's needs and women's compliance, and the practicalities that attended these impulses.

Having given herself over to Jesus, there were certain facts of life that she knew would never be relevant to her, though she figured that He would want her to be fully informed. Just in case she was wrong, she hid the books under her mattress and in an old plaid suitcase in the back of the closet. Every now and then, some salacious reference would creep into her conversation. Once, when Maynard and Victoria went away for a three-day weekend, Ella stopped them as they headed out the door. She wrapped her long dark fingers around Victoria's wrist and whispered to her, 'Don't get pregnant.' Victoria turned and said, 'Ella, what goes on in that head of yours? Where do you come up with this stuff?'

Ella smiled, taking this as a compliment. 'You know what happens on those sultry moonlit nights, Miss Landy. A woman can let go her senses and the next thing she knows . . .' Ella patted her stomach, then went back inside the house and continued singing her hymns. Alone with baby

Charlie, she would read to him from the Bible and talk to him about the stories they read. She'd even baptized him in the pool once. Mindful that he was an infant, she only held him under the water for a few moments, long enough to get the job done.

Ella lived by the principle that if you don't set yourself up to be judged, no one can judge you, and she in turn never judged those around her. Judging was the Lord's work, hers was just to watch. Many mornings when she'd make up the Landys' bed, she'd notice that no one had slept on Mrs Landy's side. She'd gone and spent the night on the couch in the television room. One day she found Crystal Landy's diary open to a passage that read, 'I wish Mom and Daddy would get a divorce, and he would marry someone with a head on her shoulders.' She heard Victoria cuss at the landscaper: 'I'm not interested in your goddamned excuses, just get those grasses in the ground before Memorial Day!' Whenever Victoria bought a new dress or blouse, which was almost always, she'd model it for Ella. She'd twirl around and arch her back, and her voice would get all girlish. 'How do I look, Ella? Isn't it beautiful?'

Ella always said the right thing. 'Mrs Landy, that might just be the prettiest thing I have ever seen.'

But it was Charlie Landy's secrets that Ella nurtured as her own. From before he could talk, she could see the child was blessed with a soul like no one else in that family. 'You have the gift of God in you,' she would tell him.

When he was four, he said to his parents, 'Where's my sister?' That was a year and a half before Crystal was born. Charlie told Ella that he had these strange feelings. They rose from a knot in his stomach and made his head throb the way eating ice cream too fast did. Sometimes the images came before the words. They filled his dreams and ripped through his thoughts.

He would tell Ella about dreams that were so specific and vivid, it was often hard for him make the distinction between what had happened during sleep and real life. One night in his dreams he saw a bowl of cooked peas, a platter of roast beef, and roasted new potatoes on the kitchen table. He watched Crystal's hand grab the gravy boat and accidentally knock it over, spilling the hot brown liquid onto their mother's lap. 'Christ almighty,' Victoria cried, plucking a gravy-sodden mushroom from her white slacks. 'Crystal you are as uncivilized as a hobo.' When the scene played out the following night, just as he had dreamed it, he couldn't stop Crystal from reaching across her mother's chest for the gravy, nor could he reconfigure the claw-shaped stain fanning quickly over his mother's white pants.

Sometimes the dreams were frightening enough to pull him out of sleep. He'd wake up drenched in sweat, with horrible sounds from some far-off place ringing in his ears. One night he dreamed of lights flashing; crunching metal, moans, and cries in the distance. In the middle of it, all he could make out was the number 65. The next night, he heard on the news that there'd been a plane crash sixty-five miles south of Mexico City.

Crystal called him the Mad Mutterer because he was always singing to himself. That was because he thought by filling his head with Buddy Holly lyrics and the batting average of the Dodgers' starting lineup, there wouldn't be room for anything else. He tried exorcising the visions by playing football, tennis, by waterskiing – anything to keep his body in motion until exhaustion set in. That girl Dinah, the one with the red hair who his sister had been palling around with the past few months, kept showing up in his thoughts. Nothing specific, just her looking at herself in the mirror, her on a bike, her with Crystal rolling their eyes behind his mother's back.

'Don't you go telling people this stuff,' Ella would say to Charlie when he'd tell her these things. 'You and me know it's God's way, but not everyone will understand that.'

Since the poolroom was in a wing of the house that was seldom used, Ella felt as though she was living in a house of her own. 'This is where I'll stay until it's my time to go,' she would tell Reggie when she saw him at Christmas. 'No place gonna be finer than this.'

On the Thursday morning before the last day of

school, Charlie yelled upstairs to Ella. 'Are you there?'

'Sure honey, come on up.'

When he was a boy, Charlie would lie on Ella's bed and they'd talk. Sometimes, she'd sit next to him and he'd place his head in her lap. Now he was too big for all of that. On this morning, he sat on the foot of her bed, his legs crossed Indian style.

'I had one of those dreams last night,' he said. 'This one was so real. There was fire and burning trees and twisted metal. Do you think you can smell in dreams? I swear, I could smell the smoke, feel the heat on my skin.'

Ella settled herself down on the bed next to him. She didn't look straight at him, but let her eyes wander back and forth among the titles on her bookshelf. It was awhile before she spoke, and when she did there was a heaviness to her words.

'God gave Noah the rainbow sign. No more water, the fire next time.'

'What does that mean?' asked Charlie.

'God's telling you there's changes coming. Big changes. Charlie, pray with me.'

The two knelt by the small bed. Ella bowed her head and closed her eyes. Charlie kept his open. 'From now on I will watch closely,' he said to himself. 'When the changes come, I want to be ready. Please God, help me be strong.'

That night, the Landy family sat together at dinner. Ella had baked a Virginia ham with glazed

110

apricots. It was the color of terra-cotta and smelled like the Fourth of July. Along with it, she served peas topped with butter and fresh hot cornbread. 'Ella, you have outdone yourself,' said Victoria, cutting a sliver of ham and forgoing the cornbread. Charlie could see her tense as Ella carried the platter of ham around to Crystal. 'No thanks,' said Crystal. 'I'm not hungry.'

Charlie held his breath, hoping his mother would have the sense not to say anything. But of course, she didn't. 'Great day in the morning,' Victoria exclaimed, as if a rabbit had leaped out of the ham. 'I never thought I'd live to see the day when this little girl of mine said no to something edible.'

'Congratulations, Mom,' said Crystal sullenly. 'I guess today is your big day.'

Victoria narrowed her eyes as if trying to discern whether or not she had just been insulted. The little smile on Maynard's face told her all she needed to know. 'Crystal Landy,' she said, putting down her fork for emphasis, 'I am sick and tired of whatever adolescent crap you're going through. It is boring and impudent, and I don't want to hear any more of it.'

'That makes us even,' said Crystal, pushing her chair away from the table. 'Because I am just as sick of whatever hysterical thing you're going through.'

Ella continued to serve the ham, as though she hadn't heard a word. Crystal ran from the room. 'I'll talk to her,' said Charlie, leaving Maynard and Victoria alone at the table.

'She seems upset,' said Maynard.

'Oh, pooh! It's just one of her attention-getting tantrums,' said Victoria.

Maynard stabbed some peas with his fork. 'I see you've been reading your Spock again.'

When Charlie caught up with Crystal, she was sitting on a hammock in the backyard, pushing herself back and forth with her bare feet. Charlie grabbed the hammock long enough to sit down beside her. Together they rocked back and forth. 'That woman is a moron,' said Crystal.

'That woman is our mother,' he answered.

'Our tough luck then.'

Charlie leaned into his sister. 'I heard that boy died last night,' he said. 'That's why you're so upset, isn't it?'

'I was over at Dinah's this afternoon,' she began. 'You know she had this weird thing with him. She was real sad, of course. Her mother came home from work early and made us fries and cherry Cokes. It was this big deal, I think. Dinah wouldn't touch any of it. Her mother got all teary and said that Dinah knew far too many dead people. 'She has to think about the living,' she said. Then she made me promise her that I'd help Dinah get over this. I said I would. But I also told Dinah we'd go to Eddie's funeral, you know, to say goodbye. I mean I promised, so now, what am I supposed to do?'

Charlie knew exactly what she should do. 'You need to go to that funeral,' he said. 'I'll help you get there. Let's keep it between us.'

'You're the best,' said Crystal, poking at his naked toes with hers. Had Charlie been anybody else's brother, she'd have dismissed him as a goody-goody. But to her he was unique and heroic – the one sane thing standing between her and a cuckoo mother and preoccupied father.

'We'd better get back to the ham,' said Charlie. 'Ella worked on it all afternoon.'

After dinner, Maynard and Victoria went to watch Walter Cronkite, Crystal went to call Dinah, and Charlie helped Ella with the dishes. He told her about Eddie and Dinah, and Crystal's promise to Mrs Lockhart. The more she concentrated, the more Ella creased her brow. Charlie used to kid her that she listened with her forehead.

'There ain't no question about it,' she said. 'That boy needs a proper send-off. We're going to that burial.'

'Who's 'we'?' asked Charlie.

'You, me, and them two girls,' she said. 'Who'd you think I meant?'

As much as anything, Ella loved a good funeral. Any right of passage that showed the Lord's hand was worth celebrating. Besides, hadn't she long ago taken responsibility for Charlie Landy's deliverance? It gave her pause to think that, in all the seventeen years she had known him, this would be the first time they would ever stand together in a house of worship. 'I know this is a sign, Lord,' she prayed silently, raising her eyes to the skylight above the sink. 'Thank you for this moment of opportunity, and may you accept into your glory the poor young soul of Eddie Fingers.'

On Saturday morning, Ella told Victoria she was taking Charlie, Dinah, and Crystal to a school function. 'Well, isn't that sweet,' Victoria answered, thinking she'd call Baldy's and see if she could squeeze in a manicure. She'd gotten used to filling in the time alone on weekends with what she liked to call visits to her helpers. When else do I have the time to get all this maintenance work done, she asked herself while dialing Jésus's number.

Weekends were the hardest for Tessie Lockhart. When Jerry was alive, she luxuriated in Saturday mornings. Jerry would wake up around eight. She'd hear him prepare the coffee and talk to Dinah and the sound of him underfoot would lull her back to sleep for another hour. When she awoke, she'd call out his name and he'd come to her with a cup of hot tea. If Dinah was watching television, he'd get back into bed. 'God invented Tom and Jerry,' he'd always say, 'so man could procreate.' And then they would make love. The rest of the weekend, they would run errands, take long car rides, go out for an early Sunday dinner of meatloaf and hash browns – the things that families do together. Those days would float by. There'd be no accounting for how they'd fill the time.

Without Jerry, every hour of the weekend took on great moment. On Saturdays, before Dinah went off with Crystal, Tessie would lie and tell her daughter, 'Oh gosh, I have so many errands and things that need fixing around the house, I don't know where to begin.' In truth, after straightening the house and shopping for groceries, she would find herself with hours to fill. Sometimes, she'd park the car and walk around the campus at the university. She'd fall in step with a group of girls, and imagine herself a co-ed talking about tonight's fraternity party and worrying about the biology test on Mondays. She liked daydreaming about these girls because their stories were just starting, their lives so full of possibility. It was easier on her than her other pastime, wandering through Grumman's department store pretending to look at glassware and washing machines. That's where the families were, touching or leaning into each other as naturally as puppies in a crate.

On this Saturday, Dinah left earlier than usual. She told her mother that Gainesville Junior High was having an all-day party in honor of the last day of school. 'You are dressed to the nines!' Tessie said, when she saw Dinah in a black shirtwaist dress with her black patent-leather pumps and her hair up in a twist.

'What kind of party did you say this was?'

'Oh, you know, kind of formal. There'll be speeches and songs and stuff like that. Crystal and me, you know, we're going together from her house.'

Lately Tessie was feeling bogged down by all of

her daughter's 'you knows' and 'stuff like that.' For a girl who gets As in writing, she can barely speak English, thought Tessie. But she wasn't in the mood to correct her grammar or tell her to quit squeezing the pimple on her chin. Horrified by the relief she felt that Dinah was leaving, she kissed her on the cheek and told her to have a good time. Then, she looked at the time sprawled out ahead of her. It was nine o'clock; the temperature was already eighty-six degrees. 'The hell with it,' she said out loud. 'This is my morning, and I'll do exactly what I want.' She poured herself a cup of coffee, then got back into bed with the latest copy of *Life* magazine. On the cover was a picture of Mr and Mrs Sherman Adams in fly-fishing gear with the words 'The Adamses Relax' underneath it. Adams, who had resigned his position as Chief of Staff to President Eisenhower several months earlier because he'd accepted a vicuna coat from a businessman, was wearing a tam-o'-shanter and squinting into the sun. Mrs Adams had on a fishing vest and a toothy smile and looked like Jerry Lewis in drag. Both were wearing waders. 'Sturdy people,' was the last thing Tessie remembered thinking before dozing off. 'I wonder if they really have sex.'

The sound of a ringing phone called her back from sleep. The voice on the other end was husky and familiar.

'This is your lucky day, Dottie Lockhart,' it said. 'Mr Fixit has come to town.'

'Who is this?' she said, still groggy from her nap.

'I fix cars, sinks, screen doors, and hi-fi's. You name it, I fix it.'

'Is this who I think it is?'

'I don't know. Who do you think it is?'

'Oh golly. Hi. What are you doing here?'

'I told you. I've come to town to fix your hi-fi and anything else that needs repairing.'

Tessie didn't know how to answer that.

'Can I come over?' he asked, slightly hoarse.

'Here? Now?'

'That's what I had in mind.'

All Tessie could think of saying was 'You're married.' But she didn't.

'I suppose so.'

'It'll take me fifteen minutes to get to your house,' he said.

'How do you know where my house is?'

'What's the matter? You don't think I can read? It's in the phone book, page 218 under Lockhart. See ya soon.'

Tessie put the phone in the cradle and stared at her hand putting the phone in the cradle. 'Jerry, what have I done? What am I going to do?' she cried.

Tessie showered, washed her hair, combed it straight back the way she'd seen Grace Kelly wear hers in some magazine. She put on a pair of black slacks and a plain white jersey blouse. Shoes. It was important to wear shoes. Barefoot was too informal, too intimate. Flats, not sandals. Brush teeth. Lipstick, no Jean Naté, the strand of little pearls, perfect as baby's teeth. Music? Shouldn't there be music? Nothing too mushy. Hank Williams. Perfect. Oh nuts. Hi-fi's not working. Answer the bell.

The Baron stood at the other side of the screen door. A look of uncertainty crossed his face as they stared at each other through the gray mesh. 'You will let me in, won't you?' he asked.

'Oh sure.' Tessie laughed.

She undid the latch and opened the door. They stepped as close to each other as they could without touching.

'Hello,' he said.

Tessie in her flat shoes was a few inches shorter than he was. She watched the perspiration zigzag across his rutted skin. In this morning light, his eyes shone amber and green. The smell of Old Spice caught in her throat.

'Hello to you,' she said.

'So, let's get to work,' he said. 'Where is it?'

'Where's what?'

'The hi-fi. I'm here to fix your hi-fi. Why'd you think I came?'

Tessie jumped, as though his words had snapped her out of something. 'Sure,' she said, pointing to a mahogany consul with Magnavox scripted in chrome across one of the cloth speakers. She lifted the lid and showed him the inside, where the turntable and spindle were taped up like mummies.

'Just another job for Mr Fixit,' he said, rubbing his left bicep. 'Ya got a screwdriver?'

For the next twenty minutes, he spliced wires and screwed the turntable back together. He worked in silence. The snaky veins around his temples became prominent the more he concentrated. When he was finished, he wiped his hands together, stood up, and straightened his trousers. 'That's done,' he said. 'I guess we should test it.' He looked through the small pile of records stacked on her bookshelf and pulled out a 45 rpm.

'They asked me how I knew, all who loved were true . . .' The luscious chords of the Platters filled the room like a church choir.

Suddenly Tessie felt like a sixteen-year-old waiting for a boy to ask her to dance. She played with her pearls and stared at the floor. Barone stood with his hands at his side, his arms bowed as if he were about to start running.

'Will you dance with me?' he said.

'Gladly,' she said, and stepped forward. He put his arms around her waist, she wrapped hers around his neck. They rocked back and forth, not really dancing at all. The Old Spice mixed with sweat. She could feel his heart beating. Slowly, he let his hands drop from her waist to the bottom of her spine and then again, until one was under each side of her buttocks. He held her with such force that if Tessie had picked up her feet and wrapped them around him, they wouldn't have tipped forward. She slipped her hand into his open shirt and felt the hair on his chest and the swell of muscle underneath it. With the little sense that was left in her, she forced herself not to nuzzle her face into the reassuring nest of black hair. She just kept running her hand back and forth in the same spot, taking in his smell, letting the sweetness of the music carry her to a place beyond reason.

Barone circled her cheeks with his hands, each motion getting harder and more urgent until it felt like he was already inside her. Either her legs gave out, or he pulled her to the floor, or both happened at the same time. They tugged at each other, discarding their clothes as fast as they could. When they were naked, he stopped and held her away from him. 'My God, Dot,' he said, catching his breath. 'You are so ripe.' He placed his hands between her legs and she heard herself moaning. 'Take me. Please, take me.' Tessie had never said those words out loud. They came out like a growl, the voice of an animal, not anyone she knew. Barone slid inside her. He lay on top of her, and held her by the wrists as they rushed forward. '*Ay, Ay*,' he yelled. '*Ay, Ay*.' She heard herself scream and felt the tears on her cheeks. He held her tight: her tears, their sweat, what came from their bodies. She buried her head under his arm, afraid that he would see the naked want on her face. 'I never thought I would love again,' she cried into his armpit. He stroked her wet hair. 'Child,' he said. 'My poor child.'

Tessie finally came back to the world: the floor, the clothes strewn around her. She heard the sound of the needle skipping at the end of the record, the ringing of the phone. She needed to say something that would get them from this moment into another, the one where they could be Tess from Lithographics and Barone Antonucci from Fort Lauderdale. But it was too late for that.

'Is that what you yell at Jai Alai?' she asked. '*Ay, ay*. Is that where it comes from?'

'You're a real smartass, aren't you?' he said, kissing her on the forehead. 'The phone's ringing.'

'No one calls me on a Saturday morning.' The ringing was persistent.

'Someone is calling you now.'

Tessie pulled away from Barone and ran into the kitchen. The voice at the other end had a forced evenness to it.

'Mrs Lockhart?'

'Yes.'

'This is Arnold Kamfer, I run the Kamfer funeral parlor?' His inflection rose to a question. 'Everything is fine, but your daughter, Dinah Lockhart, is here. She's a little under the weather.'

'Under the what? Who is this? Where is she?'

Tessie heard her voice rising and tried not to scream.

When Ella, Charlie, and Dinah walked into the Kamfer funeral parlor that Saturday morning, Eddie Howell's body was on view in the back room. The Howell family – Earl Howell was a plumber who had fixed nearly every sink and toilet in town – had been talked into the open casket by Arnold Kamfer, the owner and mortician at the home. 'Eddie was a beloved student at Gainesville Junior High,' he had told them in a monotone. 'And you are pillars of the community. You owe it to your friends in Gainesville to let them say their last goodbyes to Eddie. And don't you worry,' he added, his voice filling with pride. 'I will make him look as good as ever.'

Early that morning, before any of the mourners arrived, Arnold Kamfer pushed open the lid on the coffin and showed the Howells what he had done to their son. Eddie's face lay peacefully against purple satin as though he were propped up in a jewel case. He looked handsome enough, just as Arnold had promised. His hair was slicked back into a suave pompadour. His cheeks had been plumped up and rouged and the blueness was gone from his lips. He wore his only suit, a striped gray one, and his arms were folded atop the black cotton blanket that covered the bottom half of his body. His mother, Betty, noted that his fingernails had been buffed and that in death, he looked healthier and less strained than he had during the last two of his fourteen years.

She sat on a folding chair by the head of her son as visitors walked past and paid their respects: Earl's partners from the plumbing business. Eddie's teachers, including Mr Reilly, who said to

Mrs Howell, 'We'll miss him. Why? He was a wonderful student and would have been a great American. I'm so sorry for your loss.' Their former neighbors, the Dickersons, who'd moved to Ocala, had driven seventy-three miles to be here today. They'd brought their son Bruce who was a little younger than Eddie. Betty only heard the last part of the scuffle between Bruce and Wilma Dickerson. 'Because I said you can't touch him, that's why,' she whispered.

As the funeral home filled with people, the cloying smell from all the flowers made Betty light-headed. Wilma could see Betty fanning her fingers in front of her face, and wiping her brow. She ran across the room and put her arm around Betty.

'Honey, you feeling faint?' she asked.

Betty nodded yes.

'Here I brought this just in case.'

Wilma pulled a bottle of smelling salts from her handbag and moved them under Betty's nose. 'I never go to one of these without them,' she said. 'There now, that's better, isn't it?' Betty sat upright and took a deep breath. That's when the two women noticed a curious group gathered around the casket. There was a black woman, all dolled up in coral beads, a blue dress with white polka dots, and a navy blue cloche with a plume that streaked up the side of her head. A stocky white boy whose neck spilled over his dress shirt held her arm, and across from them were two young girls about Eddie's age, hand in hand.

Wilma turned from Betty and let the salts drop to her side. 'That's the Landy boy, isn't it?' she whispered. Betty nodded, 'Yes indeed it is.'

'But who's the nigrah?' asked Wilma, turning to Eddie as if he held the answer.

Ella, an old hand at studying the dead, was scrutinizing Eddie. 'So pretty and virginal, laid out like this,' she smiled. Charlie stood next to her, trying to take in the sight of the first dead person he had ever seen. 'He sure didn't look this way when he was alive,' he mumbled.

'I reckon he's found his peace now,' said Ella. Charlie looked across the casket at Crystal and Dinah. They were peering inside and pulling away at the same time.

Wilma placed a gloved hand on Betty's shoulder. 'I'll handle this, don't you worry,' she said.

She stood up and stared directly into Ella's eyes. 'Y'all are so kind to come here today. I suppose you are friends of the deceased?'

'Yes, ma'am,' said Ella. 'Dinah and Miss Landy were his schoolmates. This is Mr Charlie Landy.'

'And you are?' asked Wilma?

'My name is Ella Sykes.'

Ella didn't seem to sense trouble, but Charlie did.

'Ella's been with our family for seventeen years,' he said.

'That must be very comforting at a time like this,' said Wilma, her voice dropping. 'But I am sure you know that the Kamfer Home does not allow any coloreds.'

124

Ella continued speaking. 'Dinah came new to the school this year, and Mr Fingers was the first person to befriend her.'

Wilma looked at the coffin, then back at Ella. 'He was a kind boy,' she said, lowering her eyes. 'But I don't think you heard what I said. The Kamfer Home doesn't allow any coloreds.'

Charlie squeezed Ella's arm, took a step forward, and opened his mouth to speak his mind. But before he could say anything, a sound like a train switching tracks tore through the room. It was Dinah. She had leaned forward and stuck her head into the casket where Eddie was resting his left hand on his right side. Gone were the blue spidery veins in his long fingers. Three of his six fingers were curled up like dying petals of a flower. The other three, the middle ones, lay rigid and pointing right at her.

'Three fingers. He's flashing three fingers!' she cried. Her face turned the color of skim milk and her body went loose and floppy, like one of those collapsible wooden dolls held together by rubber bands. Charlie watched her go down slowly. For a moment he worried that she would fall on top of Eddie. But instead she wound up knocking over little Bruce Dickerson, who was standing on tiptoes trying to pry open one of Eddie's eyes. The two of them ended up sprawled on the floor at the feet of Wilma Dickerson.

Charlie and Ella ran to Dinah. Ella got down on her knees and started wiping her face. 'Salts,

I need salts,' she ordered. With one hand Wilma dug into her bag and retrieved them; with the other, she pulled Bruce to his feet. 'I told you to stay away from him,' she said through clenched teeth. Bruce pointed to the prostrate Dinah and wailed, 'I didn't do nothin'. She pushed me.'

Crystal and Charlie knelt on the floor with Ella. The color was starting to come back into Dinah's face. 'Honey, you're gonna be fine,' said Ella, wiping the sweaty red curls off her forehead. Dinah looked up at the sea of concerned faces staring down at her: Mr Reilly, kids from school, Charlie Landy, Crystal. 'Oh God,' she muttered. 'I am so embarrassed.' Charlie got on all fours and crawled to her side. He leaned down, gripped her arm, and whispered something in her ear. She said something back to him. It took a while for him to answer, but after he did, the world stopped spinning and she felt well enough to sit up. 'You may be right,' she said. He put an arm around her shoulder. 'I know I'm right,' he answered.

By now it seemed as if half of the funeral party was on the floor. It was Arnold Kamfer who broke the silence. 'Ladies and gentlemen,' he said, wringing his bony hands. 'May I remind you that we are here to honor the dead, not gawk at the living.'

If a funeral was a production, Arnold Kamfer was the impresario; he was not about to be upstaged by some hysterical teenage girl. Arnold crouched down next to Dinah and, in a stage whisper loud enough for everyone to hear how kindly he was, said to her, 'Darlin', give me your phone number, and I'll make sure your parents come and pick you up.'

'It's just her mom,' said Crystal. 'Highland 30874.'

Arnold Kamfer was experienced at dealing with the overwrought. He knew to modulate his voice evenly and speak slowly, in order to emphasize his concern and empathy.

'Mrs Lockhart, everything is fine, really it is. It's just that your daughter, Dinah Lockhart . . .'

'I know her name,' shouted Tessie on the other end.

'. . . has had a little fainting spell,' he continued. 'But she's okay, really she is.'

'What is she doing in a funeral parlor? Doesn't sound okay to me.'

'Please, just take down the address and come pick her up. I assure you, everything will be just fine.'

Tessie grabbed a pad of paper, wrote down the address, and hung up the phone.

'Who was that?' asked Barone, his eyes half closed.

'That was the Kamfer Funeral Parlor,' said Tessie. 'The Kamfer Funeral Parlor. My daughter's under the weather at the Kamfer Funeral Parlor!'

'What's she doing there?'

127

'That is the question, isn't it?' said Tessie, grabbing his shirt from the floor. Suddenly, being naked in front of this man seemed the most inappropriate thing in the world. 'She's supposed to be at this school thing. How should I know what she's doing there?'

'Let's go.' said Barone, putting on his pants. 'I'll take you.'

Mechanically, she put on her clothes and combed her hair. 'It's just that a girl her age shouldn't have so much death around her,' said Tessie as if they'd been in this conversation the whole time.

'Tell me, is there a good age to have death around?' he asked.

She stared at him. The morning sun created a shaft of white light that split the room in two. Then her eyes bulged as if she'd just remembered something. She ran to the hi-fi and switched it off. Carefully, she lifted the record from the turntable, slipped it back into its sleeve, and returned it to the bookshelf. 'Ok, let's get out of here,' she said.

When Barone and Tessie drove up to the Kamfer Home, Dinah and Ella were sitting at the edge of a stone planter. Ella was wiping Dinah's brow with a cold cloth. Charlie and Crystal stood like sentries on either side of them. Dinah saw her mother before her mother saw her. She saw the older man behind the wheel and noted that he wore a pinky ring. Dinah stared at her mother as if she'd never seen her before.

Barone stopped in front of Kamfer's, and Tessie jumped out of the car. 'Sweetheart, what happened?' she asked, her hands crisscrossed on her chest.

Dinah's words froze in her throat. 'I'm all right,' she said flatly.

'She took one look at that boy inside his coffin and gave out quite a holler,' said Ella. 'Then she fainted.'

Tessie turned so white, for a moment it seemed as if she might faint as well. 'Tell me what happened,' she whispered to her daughter, taking her by the hand and pulling her to her feet. 'You wouldn't understand,' said Dinah, pulling away from her and grabbing her friend's arm. Tessie stood there alone, surrounded by strangers and by Barone, who might as well have been a stranger. She felt as if they knew her secret: that she'd just made love to this man she'd had lunch with once. That's why Dinah was punishing her now. The Landy children and Ella. She'd met them only at the picnic after she'd had way too much to drink. *They* knew why Dinah was here, and she didn't. She was the outsider: a northerner, a widow. Even her own daughter didn't want anything to do with her. She watched as Dinah and Crystal walked together, their heads bent in toward one another as though they were sharing secrets she would never know.

'What went on in there?' asked Crystal.

'When I looked at Eddie, all dead and stonelike,

I noticed he was pointing three fingers at me, just like he did in school. That's when I screamed and fell down. I could tell it was my dad trying to tell me something. Charlie knew what was happening. He came over and whispered that I was right, it was my dad. He was talking through Eddie, and Charlie said he knew what my dad was saying.'

Crystal ran her hand up and down her neck as if she were trying to swallow Dinah's words. 'What did Charlie say he was saying?'

'"Let me be," that's what my dad was trying to tell me. I know Charlie's right about that.'

Crystal thought about what she'd told her, about her mom talking to her dad, leaving him notes, asking his advice. She thought about Dinah and Eddie going on and on with their numbers every day. 'Charlie knows about stuff like that,' she said. 'Maybe he's right. Maybe your dad just needs a break.'

'I can see why,' said Dinah with a little laugh. Both girls walked toward the car and looked at Barone.

'Oh, honey, this is my friend from work,' said Tessie, trying to sound casual. 'His name is Barone Antonucci.'

'That's quite a name,' said Dinah.

'Yeah, well, he's just a friend. You all right?'

'About what?'

'You know, all that's just happened?'

'I'm fine. Let's get out of here.'

★   ★   ★

130

Victoria arrived at J. Baldy's earlier than usual that morning. On a whim ('Whim, that's the story of my life,' she liked to say) she'd picked up a couple of mangoes, some fresh strawberries, and a bunch of bananas. Jésus ran to help her with her bags as she walked through the door.

'What is all this?'

'I've been shopping!' she said.

'Food?'

'Why sure. What else would I buy?'

Jésus was genuinely confused. In all the years she had talked about what she had bought, not once did it ever involve food.

'It's a beautiful Saturday morning,' she said, bursting with enthusiasm. 'Perfect time for a party, don't you think?'

Victoria dumped the contents of her bags onto the receptionist's desk.

'I need a bowl, a knife, some water,' she announced. Delilah put down the crossword puzzle she was doing. Sonia stopped sweeping and the two of them opened drawers and rummaged through closets until they found exactly what she needed. Victoria peeled, sliced, and arranged the fruit in two stainless steel bowls that were usually used for hair dye.

'Now then, *muchachas* and *muchachos*,' she said to the other customers, 'let's celebrate *el sol, la vida,* and the best damn hairdresser in the entire state of Florida.' Victoria's eyes swept past Jésus and Delilah and landed on Sonia. Shyly, the girl

131

picked the pieces of mango from the bowl and plopped them whole into her mouth.

'I knew it!' Victoria's voice rang out. 'Mangoes! Everyone loves mangoes, don't they?' She smiled her best Miss Pearly Whites as the others devoured the treats and licked the sticky nectar from their fingers. When they finished, Jésus clapped his hands. 'We are so grateful to Mrs Landy for her wonderful party. But we are a house of beauty, not a house of fruit,' he lifted his lips and gave a little smile. 'So now we must get back to work.'

Victoria and Sonia picked up the dirty bowls and walked together into the little back room where there was a sink and a cabinet full of dishes, tea, and instant coffee. Victoria took a handkerchief from her purse and dabbed at a little bubble of mango juice on Sonia's chin.

'I'll bet you like to swim, don't you?' Victoria whispered. 'A girl like you, from Cuba, you're probably part mermaid.'

'I like to swim,' said Sonia, obviously pleased that she had formed a full sentence in English.

'I have a pool. Is *muy grande*,' said Victoria, holding her arms out in the HOW BIG? THIS BIG position. 'Maybe when I'm done here, you'd like to come home with me during your lunch break and swim in my pool. I'm sure Jésus wouldn't mind.'

Her eyes widened. 'Yes, Miss I would like it to swim in your pool,' she said quietly.

'Good then,' Victoria winked. 'It's a date.'

Victoria tucked her handkerchief in her bag and sat down in Jésus's chair. He cut her hair without his usual pleasant banter.

'I see the way you're looking at me,' said Victoria.

'There is nothing,' he said. 'I am just concentrating.'

They knew each other better than that.

'Look, Jésus, Maynard's working, Ella's got the day off, and the kids are at some school function. I just want some company. All I did was invite Sonia home for a swim. And besides, it's hot as Hades out there.'

'Every day is hot as Hades,' he said as he swished his comb up and down, creating great frothy wings in Victoria's Ann-Margret do.

'My God, you're mad at me, aren't you?' she laughed.

'You come here. I do my very best work. You pay me a lot of money. And then you want to go home and get into a swimming pool? If you paid Picasso to paint your portrait, would you throw it in the water a half an hour later?' Jésus stopped teasing and shifted his weight from one foot to another, wearing his wounded pride like a too tight pair of shoes.

'Well I'll be a monkey's uncle. It's about the hair, isn't it?' said Victoria, who had never seen this side of Jésus. 'I've really offended you, haven't I?'

Embarrassed by his raw emotion, he went back to work and to his old demeanor. 'Mrs Landy, you could never offend me. It is very generous of you to bring the fruit.'

Just before Victoria left the beauty parlor, she went over to Sonia and said softly, 'I'll meet you at my car.' Then she walked up to Jésus, who was already running his fingers through another customer's hair. 'I'll only go in up to my chest. I swear it,' she whispered in his ear.

Victoria's turquoise Chrysler Imperial swooped down on Pine Hills like a hawk on its prey. 'This is it,' she sang when they arrived home. Sonia stared at the Landy house in disbelief. 'Many families live here?' she asked.

'Oh no,' laughed Victoria, 'just mine.'

Sonia's almond-shaped eyes narrowed as if to take in what she was seeing.

'C'mon, silly,' said Victoria. 'Let's get into the pool before we die from the heat.' She ran into the house, with Sonia following close behind. Sonia walked on her toes, afraid to leave tracks or soil the perfect white shags and the polished marble floors, and followed Victoria into her bedroom.

'We need to find you a bathing suit,' said Victoria. It made her shudder when she thought how anything of Crystal's would hang loosely, maybe even fall off of Sonia's fine-boned body. She went through her drawers and pulled out an old blue-and-gold-striped T-shirt that belonged to Maynard and a pair of her old shorts.

'This should do it,' she said. 'There's nobody here but us girls.'

Sonia went into Crystal's bathroom to change. Victoria slipped into her pale yellow Jantzen suit with the pleated bodice. She put on a pair of Wedgies and threw two beach towels over her arm.

'Last one into the pool is a rotten egg,' she shouted at the closed pink bathroom door.

Victoria caught a glimpse of Sonia behind her, the shorts, baggy above her knees, as they ran through the Florida room, past the cabana, and to the pool. True to her word, Victoria stepped down the ladder and waded in the water until it was slightly above her waist.

Sonia did a perfect swan dive into the deep end, emerging with her black hair behind her ears, falling to just below her shoulders. She swam from one end to the other and back and forth a few more times. Her hands sliced through the water, her legs moved quickly just below the surface. She was as sleek and fast as a dolphin, and it was clear from the joy on her face that water was where she felt most at home. Everywhere else she was just passing through.

All the while, Victoria watched from the shallow end. She had her hands in the air like someone who was being held up, wary of what the chlorine might do to her manicured nails. At some point, Victoria became aware that Sonia was encircling her like a lasso underwater. When she finally surfaced, she was inches from Victoria's face.

'Miss, you keep your hair dry?' she said. 'You keep your hair dry for Mr Baldissari, right?' She hopped up and down, a small smile playing across her face.

'Well, yes, Sonia, Mr Baldissari worked very hard on my hair. I'd prefer to keep it dry.'

Sonia kept bouncing up and down.

'And if it gets wet?'

'If it gets wet because a certain water nymph makes it get wet, I will have to . . .' Victoria sprang forward and dunked Sonia's head under the water. '. . . kill her!' she shouted.

When Sonia surfaced, she wiped the water from her eyes. Then she clenched both fists and splashed Victoria, aiming right for her hair, soaking every other part of her as well.

'Goddamn,' shouted Victoria, putting her hands on top of her head. The water mixed with hairspray fell like glue around her face; her hair flattened like a raw egg. 'I'm gonna get you for this,' she shrieked, but Sonia was gone before she could. The two women yelled and splashed and chased each other around the pool. The sounds of their screaming were loud enough to be heard on the street when Barone's Impala pulled up in front of the house.

The six of them had ridden in silence. Dinah was wedged between Barone and Tessie in the front seat. In the back sat Charlie, Ella, and Crystal. What had taken them an hour and a half by bus that morning, turned out to be a thirty-minute car ride back to the Landys'. Tessie thought they would pull up in front of the house, drop off Crystal, Charlie, and Ella, and drive off before any chance encounters with Victoria or Maynard. But when they pulled up, the teal door with the giant brass doorknob was askew.

Charlie was the first to notice. 'That's odd. No one ever leaves the front door open.' As they stared at the door, they heard the shrieks coming from the pool. Barone got out of the car. 'Stay here, I'm sure it's nothing.'

No one stayed anywhere. They piled out of the car and followed Barone to the front door. They went through the house until they came to the sliding door that led into the backyard. That was open too. In single file, behind Barone, they marched to the pool. There was Victoria, her hands on Sonia's shoulders, screaming, 'Now you drown.' And there was Sonia, her hands on Victoria's shoulders, her T-shirt riding up around her breasts shouting, 'Now Miss, *you* drown.' The two of them went under and when they came back up stared into six pairs of stunned eyes.

'Mrs Landy!' cried Ella.

'Mom!' shouted Crystal.

'Mrs Landy?' asked Tessie.

Victoria stood up and pulled her hair away from her face. 'Well now that we've established who I am, who the hell are you?' she said, staring at Barone. 'And what are you doing here?'

'I am Barone Antonucci. I am a friend of Mrs Lockhart's from work,' he said.

'Well, this is Sonia. She is also a friend from work.'

Charlie looked at Dinah, and so did Crystal. Victoria stared at Barone, who was watching Sonia hop up and down in the water. The Lord works in mysterious ways, thought Ella.

'My my,' said Victoria. 'Aren't we a cozy bunch?'

CHAPTER 9

Dinah, Tessie, and the Baron drove home in silence. Tessie kept telling herself that it wasn't her fault, the way Dinah pushed her away just then. She was a teenage girl. Teenage girls kept secrets from their mothers and confided in their best friends. She thought back to herself at fourteen and could still see her mother wipe her hands on her apron. 'Honestly, Tessie,' she'd say harshly, 'I hope some day you have a girl of your own and she's just like you. That would be some punishment, let me tell you.' It made Tessie wince to think that she ever caused her mother this kind of pain. And besides, how could she blame Dinah for having secrets when, God knows, she had secrets of her own. She didn't dare look at Barone, but worried that, having left the house in such haste, there would be signs everywhere of what they had done. And what was going on with Victoria Landy and that young woman? Why was her housekeeper all dressed up? She wondered how she and Barone would say goodbye and what she would tell Dinah about him when he left.

Barone caught Dinah's eye in the rearview

mirror. Her head was bowed, as if she were praying, but her eyes were looking up, studying the back of his head. She's a clever girl, he thought. There was something wistful about her, like her mother, though she seemed more willful and less pliable. Barone's bravado worked with adults. They admired his shrewdness and were taken with his stylish clothes and ease with money. But he had little experience with children. He had none of his own, and the ones he did know belonged to relatives or friends who had taught them to act respectfully toward him. This one, he thought, his eyes meeting Dinah's in the mirror, had no reason to think anything but the worst about him.

'A fine pickle.' His father always said that when one of the boys messed up. 'A fine pickle you've gotten yourself into this time. Now what're you gonna do?' Funny phrase, that one. What made a pickle fine? And if a pickle wasn't fine, what was it? Pickle. Where did that word come from anyway? Picklepicklepicklepickle. He couldn't help himself; he broke out into a smile. Dinah was still watching him. She noticed how purplish his gums were, and how wide and flat his teeth were, not small and delicate like her dad's. Barone saw her staring and winked at her, the smile still on his face.

Dinah tried not to smile back. She'd rather die than give him the satisfaction of knowing how pleased she was that he included her in the joke, whatever the joke was. He'd winked at her, as if she were an adult, not some clueless fourteen-year-old. She turned her attention to the back of her mother's head. Different hairdo, combed behind her ears like that. Her mother hadn't moved since she got in the car. Didn't look at her or the man. Like a horse with blinders, she kept facing forward.

Dinah thought about all the things that had happened today: Eddie, Mr Kamfer, Ella. Did Charlie really know what her father was saying? Mrs Landy? Why did her voice get so piercing and shaky when she said that thing about them all being a cozy bunch? Who was this Barone fellow, and how come no one was talking in the car? Dinah realized that there was a lot she didn't know, but she also understood that by asking these questions, she knew a lot more than she thought she did.

When they pulled into the carport, she swung her legs out of the car as fast as she could and slammed the door behind her. 'Got stuff to do,' she said, running into the house before anyone could talk. Barone and Tessie sat in the front seat; Tessie still faced forward. Barone moved his hand across the front seat and squeezed hers. 'She likes me, don't you think?' he said. For the first time since they got in the car, Tessie faced him and stared at him sternly.

'That was a joke,' he said.

'That was a disaster,' she said. 'Everything about today was a disaster.' Barone moved his hand to the inside of her thigh.

'Not everything about today was a disaster, Dottie.'

Tessie had to will herself to get out of the car. She stood, one hand on the hood the other on the door and gave one of those laughs that dovetails into a sigh.

'Thanks for coming with me to . . .' she fluttered her hand in front of her face, '. . . you know, all this.'

'Wouldn't have missed it for the world,' he said. 'I'll call you.'

Tessie walked quickly into the house and called Dinah's name. But she was already on the phone whispering to Crystal. 'He winked at me in the rearview mirror. She never turned her head the whole time in the car. So weird. Uh oh, here she comes. I'll call you later.'

Somebody was going to have to talk to somebody about what had happened that afternoon. Later that night, Crystal told Dinah that her mother spent the rest of the day acting put upon. After she drove the young woman back to the beauty parlor, she came home to everyone's eyes fixed on her like floodlights. 'She pretended that nothing was going on,' Crystal said. 'Just got all spiteful and mean. "Surely you have better things to do on a beautiful Saturday afternoon than hang around staring all cow-eyed at your mama. I know *I* do," she said all hoity-toity. And then she says to poor Ella, "Ella, you gonna walk around this house all day in those fancy church shoes of yours? Do that and you'll be spending all of tomorrow following your footsteps cleaning up those scuff marks." Jeez, she drives me crazy. Did your mother say anything?'

'She came in and walked around the house like a zombie, picking stuff up from here and there, straightening the books on the book-shelf, staring out into space every couple of minutes. When I asked her if she was okay, she kind of blinked, like she'd forgotten I was there. "Sure I'm fine. Why do you ask?" She's been in her room most of tonight. I'm worried that she hasn't eaten all day. Wait a minute. We're the children. Aren't they supposed to worry about us?'

'Fat chance,' said Crystal.

'Do you suppose both our mothers are crazy nymphomaniacs?' That got them both to laughing so hard, it pushed aside the events of the day.

'Crazy nymphomaniacs!' They kept saying it until it was unclear whether the thought of it or just saying it was what made them helpless with laughter. From that moment on, all one of them would have to do was raise her eyebrows in a knowing way, glance toward the other, and say 'CN,' and they would laugh as if it were the first time.

On the following Saturday, Tessie opened her Jerry Box, took out the ad from J. Baldy's, and stuffed it in her handbag. She had never been to a fancy beauty parlor. In Carbondale, she'd gotten her hair cut at the same barber's where Jerry had his cut. In Gainesville, she went to Regina's, a place a few blocks from her house. For six dollars, Regina, whose copper-colored hair was piled atop her head and flowed down her face like lava, would wash and cut Tessie's hair. 'Ain't no point in teasing this,' she'd say, holding Tessie's limp hair in her hands as if it was some spit-up from a baby. 'It'd be like trying to make a bee hive out of a spider web.' Then Tessie would tip Regina fifty cents and leave the one-room windowless shop feeling more worn and haggard than when she'd first come in.

J Baldy's was like no place she'd ever been. The walls were a soothing peach color, not white peeling paint, and light streamed in from the large bay window in the front. There was a receptionist, and classical music played softly from a hi-fi. Tessie pulled out her clipping with the 20 percent discount coupon. 'I have a noon appointment with Mr Baldy.' She kept her voice steady and made it a point to look Delilah in the eye.

Delilah looked her up and down. Another scholarship case, she thought to herself, and said he'd be with her in a moment. Tessie sat down on a blue brocade armchair. She reached into her purse for the envelope she received Thursday morning. Again she read the note written in the hasty hand of Barone:

Dottie, We only danced one dance and yet the music keeps playing in my head. I took you in my arms and the world melted away. Then life intruded, with a bang (and a splash) and our magic bubble burst too soon. Have the next dance with me. Your place, a week from this Saturday night. I'll bring the food and music.

A familiar voice sliced through her daydream. 'Why of course I don't plan to go into the water today,' it said, rather shrilly, 'not with this master-piece I am carrying on my head.' It was Victoria Landy, unmistakably. Tessie looked up, straight into Victoria Landy's ice-blue eyes.

'Well, of all people,' said Victoria. 'I didn't expect to see you here.' Tessie covered the Baron's note, as if someone might cheat off of it. She hoped that Victoria hadn't seen her hand Delilah the coupon. 'Yes,' she answered, running her hand through her hair. 'I thought I'd try something new.'

'You've come to the right place. This man,' said Victoria, turning to Jésus, 'is the Albert Einstein of hair. Aren't you, Jésus? Jésus, this is my friend, Tessie Lockhart.'

Victoria never took her eyes off Tessie when she called her 'my friend.'

'How do you do, Jésus,' she said, aware that by accepting Victoria's gesture of friendship, the two women had sealed a pact.

'What are you doing after your appointment?' asked Victoria.

'Nothing much,' shrugged Tessie, who planned on spending most of the day waiting for the night.

'Tell you what. I have a lunch date, but I'll meet you back here at one. We can have a cup of coffee.'

'Sure,' Tessie said, surprised by Victoria's offer. She had too much on her mind already to worry what the women would talk about. She watched Jésus, his dark long fingers floating over Victoria's hair, pulling a strand here, patting another one in place there.

He'll find me so plain after her, thought Tessie. But her anxiety dissolved once she sat in his chair.

Jésus rubbed Tessie's shoulders in a way that no one, not even Jerry, had. 'Mrs Lockhart,' said Jésus. 'I'm sure that everyone has told you of your resemblance to the actress Joanne Woodward.'

'Not everyone.' Tessie blushed. Jésus ran his hands through her hair with respect. 'You have fine silky hair. We should open up your face, let the world see your radiant eyes. Have you ever worn bangs before?'

Tessie shook her head yes. 'But that was years ago.'

'There is so much to work with here,' he squeezed her shoulders. 'Sonia will wash you first.'

The young girl from the pool: Tessie recognized her immediately. Sonia watched her silently as she washed her hair and gently massaged her head with a towel. As she led her back to Jésus's chair, she said to Jésus, 'Sir, I go to lunch now.'

Of course, thought Tessie. She has a lunch date too.

'Your friend Mrs Landy is an extraordinary woman,' said Jésus. 'She has, like you, very fine hair yet she has managed to do so much with it.'

'Yes,' Tessie agreed, 'Mrs Landy is a very versatile woman.'

By the time Jésus had finished with her, Tessie had a short bob with bangs. 'You look like the daughter of the woman who walked in here an hour ago,' said Jésus, pleased with his own creation.

Tessie stared in the mirror. It was as if she were looking at a face she hadn't seen in nearly four years.

'Thank you, Mr Baldy,' she said, unable to take her eyes off herself. 'This is amazing. Thank you so much.'

Jésus noticed how Tessie's hands were red and dry, and how her nails were jagged as if hastily clipped. Normally, he would have suggested a manicure, but something about her unabated gratitude made him hold back.

'I hope I will see you again,' he said.

'The next time you have one of those coupons in the paper, I'll be first in line,' said Tessie, trying to make light of it.

Jésus was moved by her honesty. He knew what it was like to be poor and proud.

'It gives me such pleasure to cut your hair, Mrs Lockhart, I'll tell you what. Anytime you come here, I will give you twenty percent off. It would be my honor.'

'Oh I couldn't do that,' said Tessie. 'Besides, you do such a good business, why do you need me?'

'It's the women like you that make my work such a satisfaction,' he said graciously. 'We will keep it just between us.'

Maybe Jerry brought her here to remind her that there was kindness in the world if you knew how to see it.

CHAPTER 10

'Well if that isn't the sweetest little hairdo,' said Victoria, rubbing her hands together with satisfaction. She was seated across from Tessie in a yellow vinyl booth with red trim at Harmon's Luncheonette. Harmon's was right across the street from Baldy's and the ladies of town would meet there for a BLT or tuna melt before their appointments or for one of Harmon's famous sticky buns after. 'I swear, you look twenty years younger,' Victoria went on.

It might be construed that by using the words 'sweet little hairdo' or implying how old Tessie had looked before, Victoria was talking down to her. But seeing as Tessie had never conversed with any of the women in town, much less sat face-to-face with one here at Harmon's, she chose to think that Victoria was being kindly in a Southern sort of way.

'Have you ever tried one of the sticky buns?' Victoria continued. 'It's just the best thing I've ever had. You're such a petite little thing, you could eat a room full of sticky buns and never gain an ounce. Me? I take one look at those things and my thighs turn to mud. Go ahead, try one.'

The twenty dollars she'd spent at Baldy's that morning, plus the two-dollar tip she'd left, had already put Tessie in the hole for next week's spending. Another thirty-five cents for coffee and fifty cents for the bun would leave her with not enough money for groceries that week. But she didn't want Victoria Landy to know how carefully she had to count her money.

'I can't pass that up, can I?' said Tessie, trying to sound casual.

When the bun came, warm and smelling like something baked on a snowy winter afternoon, Tessie slowly pulled it apart. The white icing oozed into the swirl of cinnamon. Had Tessie been alone, she would have licked the sugary stuff off the plate. But with Victoria's eyes on her, she simply swallowed and took a gulp of coffee.

'Bet they don't bake like that in Ohio,' said Victoria.

'Illinois,' said Tessie. 'Carbondale, Illinois.'

'Jiminy! Idaho, Ohio, Illinois. I never can keep those vowel states separate,' said Victoria.

Tessie smiled broadly, revealing a brown fleck of cinnamon stuck in a back tooth. 'I know what you mean. Like Okefenokee Swamp or Lake Okeechobee.'

Victoria's eyes narrowed with the knowledge that in some way, she'd just been put in her place.

'Seeing as our daughters have become inseparable, I thought it best we get to know each other,' said Victoria, her voice lowered by an octave.

'How nice,' said Tessie sincerely. 'Dinah's father died four years ago. Since then, she's been so awfully sad and lonely. Her friendship with Crystal has brought her back to life. I am so grateful for that.'

'And what about you? Are you lonely too?'

Tessie placed both hands over her heart. 'You have no idea.' Her voice choked. 'Sometimes I can't believe I'm still alive. If it weren't for Dinah, I don't know . . .'

Victoria had planned to spin the conversation right along and ask about Barone. She thought she'd make it clear that she knew about him, and she'd enjoy Tessie's discomfort with the knowledge that she also knew he was married. Maybe it was the way Tessie's voice went all tight when she talked about her dead husband, or how she was so naked in her gratitude toward Crystal, or maybe it was how pathetic she looked with the brown crumb stuck in her tooth. Victoria wasn't sure what it was, but she had lost her taste for cornering her.

Tessie's eyes filled with tears. 'We moved to Gainesville to get away from the memories. We were in such terrible terrible shape, me and Dinah. Jerry – that was my husband's name – and I had honeymooned in St Augustine. We thought it was the most beautiful place in the world, so I decided . . .'

It occurred to Victoria that this feeling of tenderness, curbing her impulse to lash out, was what

Charlie meant when he talked about having compassion for other people. She could do this. She could have compassion for another person. What was so hard about that?

Tessie stopped herself midsentence, as if she hadn't been aware that she was talking. 'I'm so sorry. You have better things to do than listen to me go on like this.'

Awash in righteousness and gripped by the desire that Tessie Lockhart view her as a kind person, a *compassionate* person, Victoria reached across the table and took Tessie's hand in hers. 'Don't you go worrying about me, honey, I have all the time in the world. My heart goes out to you, for all you've suffered,' she said, biting back the urge to tell her that Nivea Creme would do wonders for her dry hands. 'You and that poor little girl of yours.'

Tessie finished her sticky bun in silence, under the mournful gaze of her new friend. After a moment, Victoria's eyes brightened. 'Oh my word, I have just been struck with the most brilliant idea. Crystal is going off to Camp Osceola in two weeks. There's another of those vowel places, isn't that a scream? Dinah should go with her.'

'Oh, no,' said Tessie, 'I could never afford that. It must cost hundreds of dollars.'

'Doesn't either,' said Victoria. 'Crystal is going to be a counselor in training; Charlie's going to be a counselor. They both go for free. Maynard and I have known the people who run the camp for years: the Frankels, Audrey and Ralph. They're Jewish, but very nice. I'm sure we could get Dinah a position. It would do her a world of good.'

'It's worried me, about the summer and what Dinah would do,' said Tessie. 'With me working and Crystal being away and all . . .'

'Then it's decided! I'll call Audrey as soon as I get home,' said Victoria triumphantly. 'Oh, and this is on me. Now that you've had a sticky bun at Harmon's, you're an official citizen of Gainesville, Florida.' Virtue coursed through her veins.

'Do you think they put strange things in the water down here?' Tessie asked Dinah as she told her about lunch with Victoria. 'Honestly, she was like night and day.'

'Crystal says when God gave out brains, her mother was off shopping' said Dinah, slightly distracted. 'Can I really go to Camp Osceola?' Dinah hadn't even noticed Tessie's haircut. Tessie might have been annoyed about her daughter's self-absorption if she hadn't been lost in her own daydreams about seeing Barone alone in the summer.

That night, Dinah had a sleepover at Crystal's. She sat with Crystal on her pink chenille bedspread, poring over the Camp Osceola brochure. 'That's the lake,' said Crystal, pointing to a picture of a lake with a raft in the center. Dinah kept staring at the photo as if in her staring, something more would reveal itself to her. On shore, upside-down canoes were stored like wine bottles on a rack. There was another rack with row boats. The setting sun illuminated the water the way it does when lightning strikes in the night. Crystal moved on. 'This is the tennis court. Oh, and there's the main dining hall.'

The two girls looked at the pictures slowly, turning the thick glossy pages of the brochure as if they were Dead Sea scrolls. 'Could we go back to the picture of the lake?' asked Dinah. She stared at the photo, trying to put herself in that scene, in that water. 'The bottom is rocky, so you'll have to bring a pair of water shoes,' said Crystal.

Water shoes, sneakers, nametags, tennis racquet, duffel bag, soap dish, poncho: there were so many things she'd need for camp, and Dinah didn't have any of them. When she asked her mother how they were going to afford everything, she shrugged her shoulders and held out her hands. 'Beats me,' she said. 'We'll figure out something.' It sounded to Dinah like no big deal. Little did she know that later in the afternoon, Tessie wrote an agonized note to her Jerry:

God help me, but I'm going to ask the Glenns to borrow some money. It's not how I choose to live, but it seems worth it for this camp business. You would be surprised at some of the things I'm doing these days.

I had coffee and a sticky bun with Victoria Landy today. I've changed my hairdo. Who would have ever dreamed I could go on like this without you?

It wasn't rational, being so coy, but Tessie preferred not to talk to Jerry about Barone. Of course, if he could understand her notes and entreaties, how could he not be aware of what else was going on? She chose not to ask herself this question. That night, before Barone came over, she found a five-dollar bill in the back pocket of a pair of dungarees she hadn't worn in years. Five dollars was a heck of a lot of money: a message from Jerry loud and clear.

Crystal and Dinah were still looking at the Camp Osceola brochure when Charlie came home that night. Dinah hadn't seen him since the Eddie Fingers episode, and she worried what would happen when she did. She liked him. He probably thought she was a real loser. He better get used to her, she thought, as they were about to see each other every day for the next two months.

'Charlie, guess what? Dinah's coming to Camp Osceola with us!' said Crystal when he came into her room.

'Have you taught her the songs?' asked Charlie.

As if on cue, Crystal leaped from the bed and stood next to Charlie. They both narrowed their eyes and pursed their lips together in mock seriousness. Then they began to sing in thundering voices:

The blue and gold we'll êer remember
Though we are far apart
And friendships made during camping days,
We will cherish in our hearts.
To thee we raise our banners, pledging our allegiance.
And we, your loyal sons and daughters all be true.
We'll keep the memories of each golden day of summer,
Till someday we return Osceola, back to you.

They finished their song and took a bow. Dinah stared at them.

'Was that English?' she asked.

Charlie and Crystal laughed.

'No, I'm not kidding,' said Dinah, 'was that really English?'

Crystal looked at Charlie. 'That was color war English,' she said.

'Yeah,' he said. 'Color war English. You'll get the hang of it when you're there.'

'Color war, what's that?' asked Dinah.

'That's the highlight of camp,' said Crystal. 'Toward the end of the summer the whole camp gets divided into two teams: the blue and the gold. Everything is a competition. How you make your bed, baseball games, the songs you write. At the end of color war, the team with the most points wins. It's so neat.'

'It sounds really stupid,' said Dinah.

'Not when you're in it,' said Charlie.

'Wait, somewhere I have last year's songs. I can show you,' said Crystal. As she stepped into her closet to look for the old song sheets, Charlie nudged Dinah with his elbow. 'You doing okay?' he mouthed.

'Okay,' she nodded.

'I'm glad.'

The way he smiled and looked right at her when he said 'I'm glad' made Dinah feel safe, as if they'd known each other always. It wasn't unlike the feeling she got from Eddie Fingers. Ever since the funeral, when Eddie Fingers sent her that last signal, the numbers and the need to count didn't matter so much anymore. The dread that used to add up, the desperation to be in her bed, they were gone now. Lately, she'd stopped counting and measuring her life. It made her wonder if, after Eddie Fingers, her father had been in touch with Charlie Landy as well.

On Thursday, Tessie got another note from Barone.

I look forward to resting in peace with you on Saturday. That was a bad joke, maybe, but you know what I mean. I am assuming that you have pots and pans, and that your

157

stove works. I'll bring the music and the food. Wait until you taste my cooking. I hope it will knock you right off your feet and into my arms.

Underneath that sentence he had drawn a sketch of a woman biting down on what looked like a lamb shank, and swooning into the arms of a man wearing an apron who was a cartoon version of Barone. As she fell into his embrace, lamb shank and all, the following words were coming out of her mouth: 'I knew you were tall, dark, and handsome. But this, too?'

In the bubble above the man's head, it said, 'Oh Dottie, this is nothing. Wait until you taste my veal cacciatore.' The sketches were drawn in the same clean and tight style as the Jai Alai symbol of the man jumping in the air with the *cesta* strapped to his arm.

When Barone came to the door on Saturday night, his arms filled with grocery bags, Tessie was dressed more casually than the last time. She wore her dungarees and a red-and-white-checked blouse with a Peter Pan collar. No pearls. Red slippers on her feet.

The screen door slammed behind him as he stepped inside the house. 'Nice to see you,' said Tessie, her arms folded in front of her. Barone put the bags on the floor and thrust his head forward like a turtle coming out of its shell. 'Polka Dottie in squares!' he said. He kept staring at her.

'And wait a minute, those bangs – Christ almighty you are a sight to behold.' As Barone pulled her toward him, he was overpowered by the odor of Spray Net. 'You look so beautiful, I don't even mind that you smell like ether,' he said, his lips sticking to lacquered pieces of her hair.

Tessie had promised herself that she wouldn't get 'physically involved' with Barone until after they had a conversation. And maybe, after that particular conversation, they would never get 'physically involved' again. He kissed her collar-bone and ran his fingers down the sides of her breast. Her resolve weakened.

'So what's for dinner?' she asked, trying to sound as if it mattered.

'Mmm, dinner,' he murmured. 'Let's have dessert first.'

'No, really,' she said, more adamantly. 'I'm hungry. What's for dinner?'

'Okay, dinner.' Barone slid his hands down Tessie's sides until he was holding her around the waist. 'Iceberg lettuce with blue cheese dressing; Beef Stroganoff with a side of noodles and butter, Apple Brown Betty for dessert, and a wonderful bottle of French Beaujolais.'

Tessie had never tasted Beef Stroganoff. Or French Beaujolais. She tried to think of something to say that wouldn't betray her lack of sophistication. 'Noodles, I love noodles. What kind?'

'I know a hungry gal when I see one,' said Barone. 'Let's cook.'

For the next thirty minutes, Tessie watched Barone chop onions, whisk flour, mix up a salad dressing. She noticed the curly little veins in his wrist and natural grace with which he wielded a knife. The only mushrooms Tessie ever had came from a can. They had a slippery texture and no taste at all. Barone had brought a small bag filled with real mushrooms. Carefully, he wiped the grit off of each one and sliced them in thin slivers that looked like the columns outside the Victorians in Carbondale. Then he sautéed them in butter. These things, they smelled sweet and earthy unlike anything she had ever smelled. Barone moved around the kitchen as if he'd been there a thousand times before. Sometimes he hummed, but mostly he let the sounds of the crackling butter and the odor of onions frying and meat roasting do the talking for him.

Tessie set the table with her white dishes, so worn and plain for this meal. She stepped into the front yard and snipped some hibiscus from the bush, hoping that their gaudiness would make her utilitarian Formica table a little more festive. Damn, she didn't even have proper wine glasses. That was a laugh. For all the wine she drank, all she had were dumb old jelly glasses. She'd put out the ones without bears on them hoping Barone wouldn't notice. Oh wait, the silver candlesticks she and Jerry had gotten for the wedding. God knows, she hadn't had any use for them in years. There were still some white stubs of candle left and in the dim light, maybe he wouldn't notice how tarnished they were.

'You sit now,' he said.

He served her the beef with the thick sour cream, butter and mushrooms and noodles; and against her will, she wondered what Jerry would think if he could see her sitting here, her face flushed in candlelight with this food, this wine, this man.

Barone poured generous helpings of the wine into each jelly glass. 'To Polka Dottie in circles, squares, and whatever other shapes you come in,' he toasted.

Tessie clinked her glass against his. She remembered his last note. 'I knew you were tall, dark, and handsome. But this too?' It was confusing having both men in her mind at the same time. The notion that somehow their notes might cross made her smile, but she didn't dare speak her thoughts out loud.

Instead, they talked about the week, about Dinah going to camp, about Victoria Landy. 'If her brains were as big as her ass, she'd be the better for it,' he said. They drank more Beaujolais.

Tessie waited for the wine to take her to that warm and sure place. Then it was just a matter of finding the right moment, which finally came when Barone did his imitation of a velvet-voiced disc jockey on a local radio station. 'It's Saturday night, date night in Miami, and I send this next song, Paul Anka's "Put Your Head on My Shoulder," out to all the lovebirds on the beach, in a car, robbing a 7-Eleven, or simply getting drunk at home.' He watched her face, waiting for her to laugh.

'So what are you doing here on a date night?' She heard her voice get starchy. 'I mean, what about Mrs Antonucci? Where does she think you are?'

Barone's face went dark, accentuating the deep furrows that, in the light of the candles, made him look every one of his fifty-four years. He ran his hand over his mouth as if trying to hold back the words.

'Tessie, don't use that high and mighty tone with me.' His words quavered with anger. 'You have a thing or two to learn about judging people. Because I dress well and know about fancy wine doesn't mean I'm some vulgar Don Juan. What if I judged you by what I saw on the surface? Do you think I'd be here tonight?'

It was the first time he had ever called her Tessie. It crossed her mind that in his fury he might hit her.

'No, no, I wasn't judging, it's just that . . .'

He didn't wait for her to finish her sentence.

'My wife doesn't know I'm here,' he said slowly, the anger leveling his sentences. 'When I'm home, she doesn't know I'm there. Fran Antonucci has been sick for twelve years. It's a horrible disease of the nervous system. She lies in our home, in a special bed. I have round-the-clock nurses. I promised that I'd never put her in a hospital. Now she can't move, she can't speak. When I talk to her, she stares blankly. If I squeeze her hand, nothing.' He shook his head. 'God, that woman had such life in her.'

The room became chilly and the candlelight suddenly seemed like a foolish artifice. Tessie got up from her chair and walked to where Barone was sitting. She cradled his large head in her arms. The dead weight of it made it feel as though she was holding a Thanksgiving turkey. 'I had no idea,' she said. 'I'm sorry.'

Barone got up from the table and walked to the kitchen where he pulled the Sarah Vaughan album *Swingin' Easy* from one of his bags. He put it on the hi-fi and set the needle down on the fourth cut. He'd imagined how they would dance and how she would soften in his arms when she heard the words. Now they were sitting inches apart, many worlds between them.

Looking at the woman seated across from him, he saw his own ache and longing reflected in her face. They sat in their chairs, silently dancing with their private memories as Sarah Vaughan sang.

Back before they knew that the tingling in her fingers and the weakness in her legs were a sentence from which there was no reprieve, Barone would make Fran dinner while she lay in bed. This was after he'd sold Peerless and made enough money to move to Miami and make a killing in the real estate boom. A friend had just visited Havana, where he'd seen the game of Jai Alai. It was like super-speed handball, he said. He told Barone how the *cestas* made the players look like vultures with huge claws, and how they moved with such grace and cunning, leaping in the air and hitting the hard little ball as fast as 180 miles per hour. He wanted Barone to help him open a Jai Alai fronton in Fort Lauderdale. Barone was rich enough to retire, but Fran had discouraged him, saying she'd kill both of them if he spent more time at home. So he went to Havana and saw the Jai Alai and understood the thrill and simplicity of the game as well as how much money there was to be made when overly excited people bet on it. Their first fronton was built on what later became the parking lot of the Hilaeah race-track. Just six years earlier, in 1953, Barone and his friend opened the big fronton in Dania.

Most nights he'd come home around eleven and fall into bed, but on the nights he was home early, he'd put on the radio, lower the lights, and bring Fran a tray covered with a linen cloth and their best silver. There'd always be a glass of wine and a cut flower – a rose, a carnation. He'd carry in the beautifully arranged setting and she'd say something like, 'If your father could see you now, he'd beat the shit out of you.' Anything to undercut the tenderness of the gesture. Years later, when she couldn't walk and her speech was badly slurred, it was an ordeal for her to leave the bed. On one of those nights, Barone brought her a plate full of roast beef and mashed potatoes, her favorite. When he walked into the room, he saw that her eyes were closed as if she were straining to hear something. The radio had gone static but in between the hissing sounds he could make out the melody: 'Someone to Watch Over Me.' When he passed a certain spot in front of the floor lamp, between her bed and the radio, the static dried up and the music became clear. He put down the tray and stood in that spot, a human antenna, until the song played out. Neither of them mentioned the tears that slid down her cheeks.

'Mother of God, that is a sentimental piece of crap,' she said, when she opened her eyes again. Her words were woozy and unconvincing, and he knew then that the fire had gone out of her.

The music brought Tessie to the time when Dinah was sixteen months and just starting to walk. They were in downtown Carbondale and Tessie had her by the hand when somehow Dinah slipped away and started to toddle into the street toward an oncoming car. Tessie swooped down to pick her up and fell on her knees. As she went down, she held Dinah up, like a trophy, and, miraculously, she was unhurt. But both of Tessie's knees were raw and bloody. That night, when Jerry came home, he looked at the Mercurochrome and Band-Aids and said, 'Holy cow, Jo, what did you do, crawl all the way to the supermarket?' She'd considered making up a story about tripping down the basement stairs, but thought if she told this lie, there would be nothing to prevent it from becoming the tail of a kite of lies to follow. So she told him the truth. She remembered the way he tilted his head when he listened hard, and how, when she cried and said, 'What kind of a mother am I, to let my child wander into the street like that?' he'd taken her into his arms and said, 'You're the kind of a mother who has a willful child and does the best she can.'

Lost in their thoughts, Tessie and Barone sat at the table long after Sarah Vaughan finished singing, and the Beef Stroganoff gravy had congealed into a viscous puddle around the edges of their plates. How sad he looked when his face was in repose. She had never seen his energy depleted.

'I ran over a cat and killed it,' she said, breaking their silence.

'You what?'

'A few months ago, after we first moved here, I was picking up Dinah from the Landys' and on the way home, I hit a cat. Dinah told me I'd killed it, but I told her no I didn't, that she was being ridiculous. But I did. I killed it.'

Barone could have said, 'Why are you telling me this?' or 'That's a terrible thing, to run over a cat and kill it,' and though neither of them might ever know why, that would have been the end of that.

Instead, he put his elbow on the table and

cupped his chin in his hand. 'I'm sorry. You must have been terrified.' He could picture it, the wild scared look in her eyes. Dinah's voice high and whiny. Tessie's impulse not to admit to herself, much less to her daughter, what had actually happened.

'You bet I was,' she said. 'You know, you're new to town, and everything is strange and you want to do things right. And then you do the most wrong thing you can possibly do, in front of your own daughter no less, and it leaves you feeling . . . I don't know . . . hopeless I guess.' She twisted her mouth and looked off to the side.

'There's no percentage in hopelessness,' he said. 'You lose hope and what've you got? I mean as human beings, Dottie, it's the only thing we have that makes us different from animals. Well, we have thumbs, I suppose, but think about it: you moved from Carbondale with a young girl because some-where inside you thought things could be better. And you came here and you got a job and your daughter is happier and you've met me and tonight we ate Beef Stroganoff. Could you ever have imag-ined any of this would happen? If you only accept life's bad surprises, and don't believe that there are good ones of equal weight waiting to happen, well, then I don't really see what the point of going on is. Do you?'

'Some people have no choice but to go on,' she said. 'If they go on and get the rest of what you said, then that's gravy.'

As the words came out of her mouth, they both looked down at the table.

'No, *that's* gravy,' laughed Barone, pointing at the gelatinous mess on his plate.

'Could I hear that song again, the one about polka dots and pug noses?' asked Tessie.

Back came Sarah Vaughan, her rich throaty voice singing all about the country dance in a garden. They got up to dance and just as he had planned it, Tessie leaned into him when she heard the words, *polka dots and moonbeams*. When they walked, their arms around each other, into her bedroom they did not act like two grasping teenagers in the backseat of a Chevy. This time they were tender and slow, two grateful grownups turning to each other for comfort and a respite from pain.

CHAPTER 11

Ella and Charlie hadn't talked since the day of Eddie Fingers's funeral. They weren't avoiding each other exactly, it's just that they knew when they finally did get together it would be to bring up things neither was ready to discuss.

For her part, Ella unburdened herself to God. 'Please help me understand what I seen with my own eyes,' she prayed. She went to church every morning and tried to make sense of her troubled thoughts. Her oldest friend, Pauline Brown, had been going to the Old Stone Baptist Church with her for nearly twenty years. Since they worked for families only six blocks apart, often they walked back and forth together. On one of those cloudless mornings, when the sun breathed fire and they huddled under the shade of Pauline's faded red umbrella, Pauline said to her old friend, 'What's wrong with you? You're not yourself lately.'

Ella, whose voice always soared like a creaky old bird when they sang the hymns, had lately been singing flat, with none of her usual exuberance. Pauline had noticed that, and how she didn't stick around after services and chat with the other parishioners. So Ella told her old friend about what had happened that Saturday at the funeral, and then later, at the pool with Mrs Landy and that young girl in the T-shirt.

'Do you think Mrs Landy is one of those women who likes other women?' Ella said.

'What of it?' asked Pauline. 'They said the same thing about Mrs Eleanor Roosevelt, and she was the best friend colored folks ever had. They said she looked like a man, and dressed like one too.'

Ella was not one to judge other people by their looks, she with a nose so flat that it looked as if it were always pressed against a windowpane, and the double chin that wrapped around her other one like a crinoline. The two women fell into thought as they moved closer together under the umbrella.

'What if it's true that Mrs Landy turns out to be like that? What will become of Mr Landy, the Landy children, the house, my room?'

'Ella,' said Pauline, 'your imagination will drive you to distraction. You keep your nose out of what's not yours to know. Whatever is meant to be, will be.'

She knew Pauline was right, but she couldn't stop herself from thinking about all that had happened on that day: Mrs Lockhart and that man – that nice-looking older man. She saw how Mrs Lockhart's nostrils would flair every time he looked at her. Sure as sugar, there was something between them. And what about the girl, Dinah Lockhart, seeing her dead friend laid out in his coffin. She nearly up and died with him. Poor child, her father being dead and all.

Like a swarm of bees, the thoughts kept coming, until Ella felt they would bury her alive. She might have stayed locked inside herself had she not received a letter from her brother Reggie two days later. In the last few years, she and Reggie had lost touch. She knew he was a porter on the Orange Blossom Special, and that he had a wife, Portia, in Hendersonville up in North Carolina. She held the letter in her hand, staring at his jagged handwriting. 'He writes like a pecking chicken,' Olie used to say. Reggie only wrote when the news was bad or he wanted something. The last time she heard from him was when he needed money for a new orthopedic shoe. 'Now what?' she wondered, slowly pulling the flap from where it was glued to the envelope. She noticed that his handwriting looked shakier than usual. The letter was dated May 28, 1959.

My dear sister Ella,
    The past years have not been good to me. For reasons that I cannot explain here I lost my position at the railroad. Portia and I scraped by on barely nothing and now she don't want me in the house no more. You are all I can turn to and I don't want to be a burden but I would like to come

and stay with you in Florida. I will be arriving in Tallahassee on Saturday June 19.

Your loving brother Reggie.

As if she didn't have enough on her mind.

The Landys knew about Reggie and spoke kindly about him, the way you would about any infirm person. But frankly, Ella couldn't imagine how Reggie, with his missing teeth and dragging his too-short leg behind him as though he were tethered to a ball and chain, and Mrs Landy, who was repulsed by anything that wasn't physically attractive, could exist under one roof.

Later that afternoon, she caught sight of Charlie as he was pumping soda from the fountain off the living room. 'How you been?' she asked, squinting at one of the glasses on the shelf to see if it needed washing.

'If it seems like I've been avoiding you, I'm sorry,' said Charlie. 'Between everything that's going on . . .' Charlie didn't finish his sentence. For the past week, he'd been having visions of Ella trying to hide some kind of trouble. It was something she wouldn't be able to conceal much longer. She wasn't pregnant, it wasn't that kind of trouble, but it was something that disturbed her deeply. And there was the fire. Always the fire. 'Can we talk up in your room?' he asked.

'You say when,' she answered.

'After dinner,' he said. 'While my mom and dad are watching the news and Crystal's on the phone.'

Later that night, as planned, Charlie found himself sitting on Ella's bed as always. He took off his shoes and pulled his knees underneath his chin. He stared across at her bookshelves filled with *Kids Say the Darndest Things, Peyton Place,* weathered romance novels, and small religious paperbacks.

'This is a good woman. Why would anyone throw stones at her?' The thought came and went like a draft.

Ella noticed Charlie scanning her books and pointed to them with the back of her hand. 'Who needs all of them when we got more drama going on here than we know what to do with?'

'You can say that again,' laughed Charlie.

'I've been at church every day since then,' said Ella. 'This is what I know. God gives us as much as we can handle and not one bit more. It may not seem so when it happens, but I've seen it time and again with my own eyes.'

Charlie said what had been on his mind for the last week. 'Ella, I'm sorry that woman spoke to you that way at the funeral. She had no right to say you couldn't be there.'

For a moment Ella looked as if she didn't know what he was talking about. Then she remembered. 'Oh that,' she said. 'That's the way things are. That woman was a silly old fool. Don't go letting her upset you.'

All her life Ella had sat where she was supposed to, drunk from the drinking fountains assigned to her. It never crossed her mind not to. She had her place at the Landys' and that was that.

'It doesn't have to be like that,' said Charlie. He didn't know how it would change, only that it would.

Charlie and Ella let the silence that followed sit between them like a prayer. After some moments, Ella was the first to speak. 'For all that's happening I got even more news today.' She told him about Reggie and the letter. 'I think Mr Landy will be okay with it, but Mrs Landy? Well, you know.'

Deep inside, Charlie knew Ella was right, but there was no point adding to her worries. 'My mother isn't always the most hospitable person to strangers, but my daddy will do the right thing.'

Charlie wasn't used to saying half-truths to Ella or keeping secrets from her. But he'd also never had the kinds of thoughts that had been filling his head ever since what happened with Dinah at that funeral last week. How could he describe to Ella how heavy the girl's body felt when he first gripped her arm, how he knew that her dead father needed some peace and quiet, and how, when he told her that, he could feel her body fill with life. It made him feel a kind of tenderness that he had never felt before. How could he tell anyone these thoughts – even Ella?

What he felt about the girl was what he felt about what was happening around him in general. Her world was as fragile as a hawk's egg just before it cracks open. When that happens, the bird becomes so big and rapacious so quickly, it is hard to imagine that it was ever contained within anything at all.

When Ella asked Charlie to pray with her, he fell on his knees next to her as he had since he was a little boy. Now he was seventeen, a young man filled with new thoughts and looming premonitions. He needed all the help he could get.

CHAPTER 12

'I wonder if she's gotten herself knocked up?' Glenn Sr lit his pipe and sucked in the thought.

'Oh shit. Maybe she needs the money for one of those abortion doctors.'

'Goddam,' said Junior.

'Goddam is right,' said Senior.

Earlier that day Tessie had asked to speak to them in Glenn Sr's office. The men stood while Tessie sat in a gray metal chair, staring up at them suppliantly.

'I wouldn't ask this if it weren't absolutely necessary, and I promise I will never ask again. But I wonder if I could borrow two hundred and fifty dollars.' She didn't wait for an answer, just continued with her planned speech.

'I know it's a lot of money, but if you agreed, we could take five dollars out of my pay every week for the next year. I'd be so grateful.'

Glenn Sr nodded at Glenn Jr, and then Glenn Sr shook her hand and said, 'Of course we can do that, Tess.'

'We're glad to help you out, Tess,' said Junior,

giving her a warm smile that lifted her above her humiliation.

'Hot damn,' said Senior.

After Dinah left for Osceola, it got so quiet at night sometimes, Tessie imagined that she was hearing the distant roar of the ocean, or maybe it was the rhythm and flow of her own body. Her letters to Jerry became more urgent and less questioning.

> Dinah's gone off to camp. I borrowed $250 from the Bechs. I know they wanted to know why I needed the money but they were too decent to ask. I used to think that for all the bad things that happened good things would happen to make up for them. I don't think that anymore.

In death, Jerry was as generous as he had been in life, and even though she didn't ask for it, he sent Tessie an answer, which came in the form of a note from Barone the next day.

> Dottie,
> Have you ever had champagne from room service in a hotel? It'll make you feel like a princess. I have to go be in Tallahassee next Monday morning. Come with me and let's make it a bang up July 4th weekend. If you say yes you'll be my Tallahassee Lassie, I'll pick you up Friday after work

and we'll go to Wakulla Springs Lodge, where all the bigwig senators and politicians stay. Vote yes for Tallahassee and be my first lady. I promise you we'll have a Good Time with a Capitol G (ha). Wear something sexy but stern, like one of those women from Washington. I'll call you on Wednesday.

Tessie wondered how long it took him to write these notes. She thought about spending the night in a new place with Barone; how she hadn't stayed in a hotel since St Augustine, and never in a fancy one. Glenn and Glenn had been so kind to her, lending her the money. They'd be closed that Monday for July 4th anyway. She'd been at Lithographics for nearly six months and hadn't taken a full day off, so really, what was the big deal? Dinah had been at camp for a week and still no word, not even one of those addressed and stamped postcards she'd packed away for her. Everyone would be out of town. No one would even know she was gone.

Even Maynard Landy closed up for the July 4th weekend. He had promised to help Victoria prepare for their big party. Anita Bryant was coming to town, the same Anita Bryant who was last year's Miss Oklahoma and this year's second runner-up in the Miss America contest. Her song, 'Till There Was You,' was a big top forty hit on the radio. 'Let me tell you,' Victoria said to Jésus on the morning of the party, 'having Anita Bryant come to your house is no small honor.' She was Victoria's idea of the perfect woman: beautiful, talented, and well respected. 'Aside from all the Baptist bullshit, who wouldn't want to be Anita Bryant?'

As Victoria stared at her image in the mirror, it crossed her mind that other women probably felt that way about her. Who wouldn't want to be Victoria Landy? Of course she inspired envy; her life was close to perfect. Perfect except for one thing: that awful brother Ella had visited upon them, Reggie Sykes. She told Jésus about his short leg and missing teeth, and how it offended her to hear him thumping around her house. He had taken the small room next to the garage, just big enough for a cot and a shelf for his things. 'He's clean, and Lord knows he's polite, always "Yes, ma'am" this and "No, ma'am" that. It gives me the willies. But hell, why am I talking about that wretched fellow when I've got a party to tend to? I am fortunate to have such a sunny nature, aren't I?'

'Spit curls,' said Jésus, tugging and twirling the ends of her hair. 'They are very Anita Bryant.' She examined the curlicues that sat like scimitars on her cheeks and smiled at Jésus. 'You sweet man. You do bring out the best in me. Thank you for letting Sonia come and help out tonight.'

Victoria rushed out of Baldy's with purpose in her step. There was so much to do before the party: food, flowers, the Maraschino cherries. Maynard was bringing home a case of Verve Cliquot champagne. He suggested that she also make her special strawberry punch. 'Baptist booze,' he called it. Knowing how Anita would hold her in esteem for her sensitivity, Victoria kissed her husband on the lips and said, 'Maynard Landy, you never fail to surprise me.'

Maynard and Victoria weren't the kind of people who told each other 'I love you' very often. She would squeeze his arm, or he would tell her how beautiful she looked, and they would know what they needed to know. That night, as they waited for their guests to come, they stood looking at the white living room bathed in candlelight. The bouquet of Talisman red roses filled the air with the smell of wealth and promise, and all over there were sterling silver platters with exotic cheeses and crystal bowls filled with the finest Greek olives and fresh shrimp. 'We are happy together, aren't we?' said Victoria, placing her hand on the back of his neck. 'Yes we are, darling,' he smiled. 'We're very happy together.'

In the kitchen, Reggie helped Ella baste the nine cornish hens. Sonia, in her white apron and her hair pinned up in a bun, was putting hors d'oeuvres onto trays. 'You're doing a wonderful job,' Victoria whispered in her ear. 'Muy bueno.'

Reggie was dressed up in his porter's outfit and had promised he'd help serve dinner. 'Carrying things. If there's one thing I know how to do is carry things.' Ella was concerned that with his uneven gait, all nine hens would end up slipping onto the dining-room floor, but she didn't have the heart to tell him so. Oh my, wouldn't that be the final icing on the cake. In the days since he'd arrived, Reggie had done his best to be helpful and unobtrusive. But Victoria would never address him directly. She'd always say, 'Ella, could your brother mow the lawn today,' or 'Ella, shouldn't your brother try wearing shoes with rubber soles.' There was always an edge in her voice.

That night, after the guests left and Ella and Reggie had cleared the dishes, Maynard and Victoria were getting ready for bed. In between brushing his teeth and gargling, he shouted to Victoria, 'You know, this may have been our best party ever.'

Victoria lay in bed, rerunning the night through her head. Of course the Grists – Marilyn and Bill – had been the first to arrive. God, what would she ever do without Marilyn? Marilyn had grown up in Barnsdale, Oklahoma, and knew the Bryant family from there. Whenever Anita came to town, she'd stay with the Grists, which was how Victoria had gotten to know her. Marilyn and Victoria had been in the same sorority Marilyn was tall and rangy with a face the shape of Flicka's: the girl most likely to succeed. Victoria liked her because she was accepting and funny and said whatever came to her mind. When Victoria's marriage to Donald Pierson came to an end, she went to stay with Marilyn, who had just married Bill and was living in Gainesville. She remembered how Marilyn had taken one look at her bruised face and broken tooth and given her a hug. 'You need a warm bath and a long sleep,' she had said. 'Then we'll think about tracking down that little creep who did this to you.' But they never did track him down. Instead, Marilyn introduced Victoria to a friend of Bill's. They were on some civic board together. 'He's a gentle man,' Marilyn said. 'Cute in a bearlike way – and real smart. Bill says he's going to own this town one day. His name is Maynard Landy.'

Victoria smiled at the memory and shouted back, 'I think you're right. It really was our best yet.' Maynard got into bed and they talked about how strange Glenn Bech Sr and his wife, Lillian, were. Before the party, Maynard had joked that the Bechs ought to sit with Anita so they could share their pure thoughts and alcohol-free punch. 'Just be sure to put me at the other end of the table,' he'd said. She'd swatted him on the arm and said, 'You are so bad.'

'He is kind of weird,' said Victoria, who happened to be standing next to Glenn when Anita Bryant came in. 'I swear I heard him say, "nice tits" under his breath. But Glenn Bech Senior? How could that be?'

'Maybe he was just telling Lillian where to put the olive pits,' said Maynard.

'*Pssh*,' said Victoria. 'Did you notice his wife drag

182

poor Doctor Simons into the corner to look at one of her molars. She stood there with her mouth wide open and her tongue hanging out. What a silly woman! Has she never been to a civilized party before?'

'It was your brainstorm to invite the Simons,' said Maynard.

Doris Simons ran the drama department at the University of Florida, and always dressed as if she were in a barroom scene. Tonight she'd showed up in a bright-red full skirt with a low-cut peasant blouse and gold hoop earrings. Victoria figured she dressed that way to make up for her husband, Peter Simons, the family dentist and the dullest man in town.

'Well, there was some logic to it,' she said. 'I thought Anita and she could talk show business together, and they did. Wasn't Anita radiant tonight?'

Victoria could still envision her. Her hair was in a bouffant, as round and airy as the Goodyear Blimp. She'd worn a blue taffeta sheath with a scooped neck and wide belt. Her blue taffeta pumps matched the dress exactly. When she walked in, the room had fallen silent.

'I was worried that everyone would just gawk at her for the rest of the evening,' said Victoria. 'Thank God for Marilyn.' Wonderful Marilyn had just loped across the white mohair carpet and taken Anita's arm. 'Honey, you must meet Doris Simons, she's our local thespian.' Doris had directed a production of *The Music Man* the year before. The two of them immediately fell into conversation about the song from that musical, 'Till There Was You.' At some point in their conversation, Anita even sang a few bars to Doris. 'It was amazing how everyone just froze in place when that happened,' said Maynard.

'That'll give that dimwit Lillian something to talk about at her next Bible study,' she said.

'You've got quite a mouth on you, don't you?' He leaned over and kissed her on that mouth – so vulgar and vicious and beautiful. They made love, and Maynard fell asleep on Victoria's shoulder. She stroked his hair and noticed how bald he was becoming. This is how it will always be, she thought, and that isn't half-bad. She imagined Sonia's elflike ears and the tiny bumps she had on each earlobe. Later, whenever she tried to put the pieces of that night back together, what she would remember most clearly was the sweet unadorned voice of a young Anita Bryant singing 'Till There Was You.'

Three hours later Maynard woke up abruptly. He sat up in bed listening for what it was that might have disturbed him. There were no sounds, but there was a strong smell. He felt as if something were being crammed down his throat: something thick and lacerating. He was having trouble taking in air. When he turned on the night lamp next to him, he saw ghost-like puffs of smoke slipping under the door. Fire. That's what it was. There was a fire in the house. He shook Victoria. 'Get up. We've got to get out of here.' Victoria sat up in bed, her heart pounding. She saw something in Maynard's face she'd never seen before, then smelled the smoke. Inexplicably, she grabbed a hair brush and ran it through her hair, then searched through her closet for her cream-colored silk robe. 'Goddamnit, Victoria,' he shouted. 'There's no time. Just get the hell out of here.' He grabbed her by the arm and pushed her toward the window. He stood on the dresser and punched out the screen. Then he helped her up and told her to jump. He jumped out after her. They landed in the saw grass that grew under their window. For a moment, they lay in the grass staring up at the perfectly clear night. 'You okay?' he said. 'Yes, you?' she said. He stood up and pulled her to her feet. The fresh air washed over them. Maynard noticed that the lights had gone on in the houses down the streets. He hoped someone had called the fire department. 'My God, Maynard,' screamed Victoria, watching black smoke pour from their beautiful house. 'Do something. We have to do something.'

'What we can't do is panic,' he said. 'We've got to find Ella. And Reggie.'

They heard Ella before they saw her. 'Oh, Lord. Oh, help me, Lord,' she was crying. She was crouched in the bushes by the garage, barefoot and dressed only in her cotton nightgown. Reggie was crouched next to her. The hairnet that she wore to sleep every night had fallen over her eyes, and her face was wet with tears. She was hugging the birch-wood and pine cross that Olie had given her for her sixteenth birthday and Reggie had his arm around her shoulder.

'Ella, it's okay. We're here. Ella, please stop crying. Victoria and I are here. It's okay.' Maynard reached for Victoria's hand, but couldn't find it.

'Victoria,' he shouted. 'Victoria!'

Victoria was running back toward the house. Maynard ran behind her in the smoky shadow. 'Victoria, where are you going?'

'The ring,' she shouted. 'I left it on the bathroom sink.'

'Screw the ring,' he shouted, 'You can't go in there.'

'I gotta get the ring,' she yelled, before disappearing into the blackness.

Maynard had given Victoria the five-carat-diamond ring for her thirtieth birthday. He remembered that she'd cried when she'd opened the box and how she shook her head and said, 'This means everything to me.'

'Victoria,' he shouted into the air. 'Don't be an idiot. I'll buy you a new one.'

There was no answer.

Maynard ran into the garage. It was dark and beginning to fill with smoke. His eyes burned and he had trouble keeping them open. He had to concentrate on breathing. 'Victoria,' he yelled, in what came out as a whisper. He listened for Victoria's footsteps. 'Victoria!' His voice was hoarse. 'Victoria,' he tried to shout again. He told himself: concentrate, breathe in, breathe out. Somewhere from the center of the house, he heard an explosion. He felt the ground shake beneath him as he stumbled forward, not knowing anymore if he was walking closer or further from the fire. He tripped over a pipe or a fallen bicycle – who knew – and fell face down on the floor. Breathe in, breathe out, goddamnit. The breaths were coming heavier now, sharp pains as he breathed in, bubbly cough as he breathed out. The cement floor was cool, like the ocean floor. The pain in his arms, his chest, it was as if he were cracking apart under the weight of the wave, a ship broken by the storm. Part of him stayed in the same place watching over the other part of him that was spinning off getting smaller and further away, until he finally disappeared beneath the sea.

Victoria had run into the bathroom and jumped out the bedroom window just before the explosion. She found Ella and Reggie and waited with them for Maynard. The two of them had to restrain her from running back in after Maynard. 'Get your cotton-pickin' hands off me,' she shouted. 'Maynard, Maynard honey, I'll be right there.' But they wouldn't loosen their grip on her. When the Fire Department finally went in and got Maynard out, they said it probably was a heart attack that killed him. Other than the black smudges from the smoke, he didn't have a mark on him – not even a scrape.

It took until early morning to get the fire under control. Only part of the house remained intact: the part that contained Ella's room and Reggie's beneath it. The Skullys down the road took Victoria, Ella, and Reggie in for the night, though no one slept. At eight a.m., Victoria and Mr Skully went back to the house. Victoria roamed the street in front of the house in her long silk robe and her shiny diamond ring. Stooped by shock, she looked wraithlike in front of the scorched landscape. The sky was still overcast with smoke, and the smell clung to everything.

The metal circular staircase that connected Ella's room with the kitchen was charred, melted into the shape of a seahorse. Plastic glasses from the soda fountain were curled like fingernails grown too long. There were black stubbles of things that once were other things. The springs from a bed looked rusted, as if they'd been left out in the rain for months. Victoria picked up a piece of paper from a magazine preserved in a nearly a perfect circle, its edges browned but still readable. Something – a pot, a plate – must have sat on top of it and kept it from burning. There was a photograph of a Mr and Mrs McCall, with a caption identifying them as 'visiting snowbirds from Toronto.' The McCalls were leaning toward the camera smiling. His brown hounds-tooth jacket and her gray checked blazer looked as if they'd been hand painted. Mr Skully came over to Victoria. 'The wind was blowing to the north last night. If it had gone the other way, all the houses around here would be goners. Someone was watching over us.' He glanced up toward the smoky heavens before realizing that Victoria probably didn't feel she'd been watched over terribly well. 'It's horrible,' he said, placing his hands on her shoulder. They were a builder's hands, and she could feel his calluses through her thin robe. She stared at Mr Skully, her blue eyes swollen. 'Oh, Maynard,' she sobbed on his shoulder. 'My poor Maynard.'

Later that morning, Marilyn Grist came to get Victoria. As Marilyn got out of her car, Victoria embraced her old friend. 'Everything's gone,' she cried. 'This is more than I can stand.'

'You'll stay with us,' said Marilyn. 'C'mon, let's go to my place. As they drove into the carport of Marilyn's small redbrick house, Victoria leaned her head on Marilyn's shoulder. It surprised her how irritated she felt by the two little dwarfs in Marilyn's front yard holding, between them, the words 'The Grists.' Inside, Marilyn brought Victoria into the pale blue study with Bill's framed diplomas from the University of Florida on the wall. She opened the beige-and-brown- plaid pullout couch beside his desk and made the bed. It smelled old and musty, but Victoria climbed under the covers, grateful for the clean sheets.

Marilyn tucked Victoria into the bed and sat beside her. She held her friend's hand. When Victoria cried, 'It hurts, it hurts so much,' Marilyn wrapped her arms around her and rocked back and forth. 'I know, baby, it hurts real bad.'

On Monday morning, July 5th, Tessie Lockhart was lying in a queen-size bed next to Barone. They ordered up breakfast from room service and drank coffee and ate from a basket of sweet rolls. There was a silver vase with a single tea rose in the middle of the tray. Tessie was rubbing her nails lightly up and down Barone's back as he read the newspaper. Barone was thicker, more muscular than Jerry. She liked how her thin white fingers looked so small against his dark hairy skin, and wondered how much it would cost to get a manicure at Baldy's. Suddenly Barone straightened his spine. 'Holy Christ!' he said, breaking the lazy rhythm of the morning. 'Look at this.' He thrust the *Tallahassee Democrat* in Tessie's face. There, on page two, was the headline: 'Maynard Landy, 49, Prominent Gainesville Businessman, Killed in Early Morning Fire.' They stared at the photo of the blackened remnants of the house. In the right-hand corner, they could see the pool and the cabana, which appeared to be unharmed. The article said that the cause of the fire was unknown. Neighbors claimed they'd heard an explosion, leading police to surmise that the fire might have been caused by faulty electrical wiring, but they hadn't located the source. Mr Landy was found lying facedown dead in the garage. The cause of death was a heart attack. The other three residents of the house, Mrs Maynard Landy, Ella Sykes, and Reginald Sykes, were unharmed. Mr and Mrs Landy's two children, Crystal and Charlie, were away at camp.

Tessie reached for the phone to call Dinah.

A woman with a chipper voice answered, 'Good morning, this is Camp Osceola, how may I help you?'

'This is Tessie Lockhart, I'd like to speak to my daughter, Dinah.'

'Oh yes,' her voice got terse. 'They've been trying to reach you. I'll get her.'

While Tessie held on, she exchanged looks with Barone. She reached for his hand.

Dinah finally got on the phone without even saying 'hello.' 'Where've you been?' she shouted. 'Everyone's been looking for you. We even tried calling the Bechs. How can you just disappear like that? This is so awful. I just want to come home.'

'Don't worry, honey,' said Tessie, 'No one's disappearing. We'll come and get you right away.'

'Everyone is disappearing!' cried Dinah. 'And who's "we"?'

'You know, me and my friend from work. You've met him.'

'Oh, him.'

PART TWO

1962

CHAPTER 13

'It's not just because you're Cuban, but you remind me so much of that fellow Fidel Castro.'

For weeks, Victoria had been watching the Cuban dictator on the news, and each time she'd say to Charlie and Ella, 'Damn, that face is familiar.' Finally, she got it. 'My God, he looks like Jésus, that's who it is.'

Charlie said, 'Do you think every Cuban person thinks that every American man looks like John Kennedy?'

'Don't be silly,' she answered. 'Not nearly half of them are that handsome.'

Jésus did look like Fidel. He had the same petulant bottom lip and those spooked brown eyes that often gazed into nowhere.

'Charlie says I think all Cubans look alike,' Victoria continued, 'but he's a silly. You don't look anything like Desi Arnaz.'

'How is the young Mr Landy?' asked Jésus, eager to change the subject.

'Work, work, work. He's in that store fourteen hours a day. That's not normal for a boy his age.'

'There is nothing wrong with the son taking care of his mother,' said Jésus. 'It is an honor.'

'It's an ordeal, that's what it is.' said Victoria. 'Me and him living under one roof with Ella and Reggie. And he's a boy who should be getting drunk at fraternity parties rather than standing behind a counter and selling liquor. That is not normal. No sir, that is not normal.'

Victoria's voice was harsh now, the sound of metal against metal. Since the fire, her face had become fuller. It seemed as if her eyes were setting into her cheeks. She was still beautiful; she'd always be beautiful. But with the veneer of loss that set over her, it was a more ordinary beauty, like a washed-ashore fragment of coral that was once part of a magnificent reef.

'I think this bob makes my cheekbones more prominent, don't you?' asked Victoria, running her fingers across her face.

'Like Raquel Welch,' answered Jésus, grateful that she could never stay away from the subject of herself very long.

Jésus sprayed her hair, shielding her face with his hands. Victoria squinted through the mist as Tessie walked in for her twelve o'clock appointment.

'There she is now, Miss Hot Type of Gainesville, Florida,' shouted Victoria.

Tessie gave her a friendly punch on the shoulder. 'You're too much.'

They now had the easy friendship of two women who had seen the worst of each other and had nothing left to hide. After Maynard died, Tessie offered to have Crystal come and stay at her house. 'The girls could share a bedroom. Dinah would love the company,' she said. It was all Victoria could do to hold herself together, and after thinking about it for less than a minute, Victoria said, 'Yes. That is a very kind offer. Of course I will pay her expenses.'

Three years later, Crystal still hadn't come home.

The new Landy home was U-shaped with white lap siding and an orange shingled roof. There was no sunken living room, no garden in the bathroom that conjured up Bali. There was little room for Eric, Victoria's landscaper, to work his magic, not that she cared anymore. Still, Charlie had made good on the promise he made to Victoria the day after the fire. 'I'll take care of you,' he'd said. 'I promise, I won't leave you alone.' On the Monday before the funeral, he called the Auburn admissions board and said he wouldn't be coming in the fall, and on Tuesday, he put the whole chain of liquor stores up for sale except for the one right in Gainesville. The joke around town was even people who never touched the bottle bought from him just to keep his business up. He was a saint, that Charlie Landy. That's what everyone said.

Charlie insisted that Ella and Reggie move in with him and Victoria. Had Victoria been less depleted, she would have never let things get that far; never would have let Reggie live under the same roof; Reggie with his watery eyes that she would never meet, for fear she would see reproach within them. Reggie and Ella knew that Maynard Landy would be alive today had Victoria not run back to find her ring, and the knowledge haunted all of them in different ways. Reggie dwelled on the fact that for once, the horrible consequences were not a result of his drinking, womanizing, or lying when it would get him somewhere. If a man can be redeemed by being faultless for once, then Reggie was that man. Each day the conviction that it was his destiny to serve Victoria Landy for the rest of his life became more powerful, and despite her irritability and severe aversion to him, he made a vow to himself that he would do just that.

The way the house was arranged, Reggie and Ella had the rooms at the upper arms of the U, and Charlie and Victoria had the rooms at each end of the curve overlooking the backyard. Reggie called his tiny room off the garage My Palace. Ella lived in the little bedroom off the kitchen. The Nun's Room, Victoria called it, because it was white and sparse with just a small hospital-style bed, her birchwood and pine cross hanging over it, and a small oak night table standing next to it. Ella had a small book collection. There was the Bible, of course, the latest Harold Robbins novel (*The Carpetbaggers*), and a book about puppies by Charles Schulz. But she was slow to add things to her room, just as she was slow to rebuild her life since the fire.

The fire tested Ella's faith. You could see it in the way her shoulders had rounded and her pace had slackened, as though she was yoked and dragging a heavy load behind her. You could hear it in the sadness of the songs she sang: '. . . When nothing else could help, love lifted me.' Shame had gnawed a hole in Mrs Landy, and Ella prayed for her salvation with the same fervor that she prayed for Mr Landy's soul. If she ever spoke of the loss, she would only say, 'God has his reasons. I am in His hands now.'

As they did nearly every Saturday, Tessie and Victoria went to Harmon's after their hair appointments. Each time, they'd pick up the pink menu with its line drawings of pillow-size burgers and creamy malted milkshakes and pretend to study it for a while. 'I guess I'll have a BLT with mayonnaise on white toast and a Cherry Coke,' Victoria would say. Then Tessie would say, 'Sounds good. That's exactly what I want,' as if they hadn't been ordering the exact same thing every Saturday for the past three years.

Even their conversation took on a routine. First they'd discuss each other's hair, then they'd share some gossip. Inevitably Victoria would talk about the latest thing Reggie did to try her patience.

'The other day he was hanging around me. "Miss Landy, can I drive you to church? Can I pick up the groceries? Do you think the garage could use a fresh coat of paint?"' She mimicked his slurry speech. 'I finally said to him, "Listen, Reggie, if I am going to be seen in a car with you, or let you go into town and do errands in my name, you cannot wear those scuzzy overalls and the same brown polo shirt. And those curls out of control. My God, you look like Methuselah on a humid day."' Victoria threw her head back and laughed. Tessie noticed a thickening around her neck. 'So I said, "Here is twenty-five dollars. Get yourself a haircut and buy some decent clothing." When he came back, his hair was short and he was wearing a pair of chinos and a blue blazer, and I said to him, "Now Reggie, that's what a respectable man ought to look like."'

When Victoria looked at Reggie, what she saw were gaping black holes where his teeth should be and a short impaired leg that threw his body into a disarray of awkward shapes and sloppy movements. It was an ugly and painful sight to see, and one that sometimes caused Victoria to wonder if the way he looked on the outside was what she was on the inside. If she could fix Reggie, maybe it was possible that she could fix herself. What happened to Maynard taught her humility, she believed. Widowhood had made her more compassionate. Her voice rose, filled with magnanimity. 'And now to our favorite subject, the girls.'

They talked about how, between her boyfriend and cheerleading practice, Crystal didn't have much time for schoolwork. 'She doesn't come home until after seven,' said Tessie. 'And by then, she's so tired, it's all she can do to make it through dinner and a little homework.'

'Let's face it,' said Victoria. 'She'll never be an honor-roll student like Dinah. Maybe cheer-leading is her true talent. Did it ever occur to you that these might be the best years of her life, and we should let her be? I'll tell you this: It's a good thing that girl will inherit some money, because she sure isn't going to make any with those brains of hers.'

Later that night, Tessie dropped a note in her stuffed Jerry Box: Had lunch with V. Cruel as ever but kinda funny.

Even though she wrote to him in shorthand sometimes, Jerry's capacity for sending her signs had not diminished. Last year, the night after she wrote 'C & D fight all the time. Isn't it time for C to go back home?' Crystal and Dinah had surprised her with a home-cooked dinner: chicken potpie, salad, ice cream, the works. Before they ate, Dinah held up her glass of Cherry Coke and said, 'To the best mom in the world.' Crystal raised her glass, looked Tessie in the eye, and said, 'To the best mom in the world.' Later, in her note to Jerry she wrote, 'Tonight C & D made me feel like a million dollars. Crystal may never go home.'

Begrudgingly, Crystal went to see her mother once a week. 'At least call her sometimes,' Tessie would urge.

'Why, so she can ask me if I've lost any weight yet? Think of it this way. I have broken up with my mother. If my daddy was alive, I'd go home all the time. Of course if my daddy was alive, I wouldn't be here in the first place, would I?'

When Crystal left Tessie speechless – which she often did – Dinah would step in. 'Get off it, Mom. She thinks her mother's a real yo-yo, and she's not going home.' It was more like three girls in a dormitory than two girls and a mother. Secretly Tessie felt that the arrangement gave her an edge over Victoria. Her daughter had chosen to live with her instead of her own mother. But more importantly, the arrangement was worth it to Tessie for how the two of them could help each other.

Dinah and Crystal spoke the same language of loss. Often that meant not speaking at all, or letting one or the other of them cry without making a big deal of it. As they lay in bed at night, they would tell 'daddy' stories. 'My daddy once took me to the botanical gardens near Carbondale. He knew every flower by name.' Or, 'Daddy never screamed or cussed, his voice just dropped and got real cold. Charlie used to call it Daddy's ice voice.' The stories never had punch lines, and no matter how many times they'd repeat them, they'd laugh as if they were hearing them for the first time. Often they'd drop their fathers into conversation as a gift to each other. When Crystal got picked to be a cheerleader, Dinah said, 'Your daddy would be so proud of you.' And when Dinah wrote a funny poem for Crystal's birthday, she said, 'That's the kind of thing your dad would write.' They'd pretend that their fathers were friends in heaven, and would fantasize about what they were doing. 'Tonight they had spaghetti and meatballs, don't you think?' one would tell the other. Sometimes Dinah would pull an old Barton's candy box out of her top drawer. Inside were her 'treasures' – her father's old harmonica, his pocketknife with its pearl handle, his address book, an old pair of pliers. She'd spill her treasures on the bed, and the two of them would pour through the address book and try to analyze her father's loopy Y's and wispy T's. She'd imitate how he'd cup his hands around the harmonica when he'd play, like he was telling it a secret. They never spoke of their fathers to anyone else.

Crystal had no treasures from her father; the fire took everything. Occasionally people would send her photographs of him, but her hurt was too fresh; she couldn't look at them. All she had was the locket she wore around her neck: a little gold heart on a chain that he gave her when she turned thirteen. At every football game, right before she'd run onto the field with the other cheerleaders, she'd press the locket to her lips and look up at the sky. She'd rather no one noticed.

As intimate as the girls were at home at night, during the day it was as if they had never met.

Crystal was more popular than ever. Suffering a formidable and public tragedy had elevated her status with the kids at school. 'You are so brave' or 'You are so strong,' they'd tell her. They assumed she knew things that they didn't. She had become the person that everyone thanked their lucky stars they weren't, though if she knew, she didn't let on. Rather than pity her outright, they made her a cheerleader and president of the Pep Club and anointed her a member of the Homecoming Queen's Court. She'd walk down the hall and people would say 'Hey' and she would say 'Hey' in an animated voice, as if their greeting had taken her by surprise. At lunch, she'd sit at the table with the football players and the other popular boys who were members of The Key Club, and Wheel Club. (When Dinah said, 'They should merge and become 'The Bicycle Club,' Crystal pursed her lips and said, 'Ha ha. So funny, I forgot to laugh.') Crystal thrived in her heroism, and accepted her popularity as her due.

If anything, Crystal's popularity made Dinah more headstrong than ever. She cared less about curbing her tongue and being polite, and more about saying what she felt to be the truth. 'You should hear her with the boys,' she'd tell her mother. 'She has this loud shrieky laugh. She never laughs that way when I say something funny, and trust me, I'm a lot funnier than they are.' Crystal swore she hadn't gone all the way with her boyfriend, Huddie Harwood, a thick, squarely built boy with small gray eyes so close together that he looked perpetually confused, but Dinah was convinced it was just a matter of time. On Saturday nights Huddie would come to the house reeking of Canoe, his flattop perfectly waxed. His cheeks were angled like the bow of a boat, and his moist red lips gave him a sated look, as if he had just polished off a baby. 'How do you do, Ma'am,' he'd say to Tessie, as though they'd never met, and to Dinah, 'Hello there,' which she did not consider a substitute for conversation.

Crystal was tall now, and stacked. The few pounds of baby fat that drove her mother crazy now gave her hips a sexy curve and filled out her breasts, which only added to her popularity. She'd always wait until Tessie, Dinah, and Huddie were seated in the living room before making her entrance. That way, everyone would have to notice her hair done up in a tight French twist, the extra load of frosted-blue eye shadow and black mascara, the low-cut chemise she'd bought on her mother's credit at Mina Lee's. 'Hi Huddie,' she'd say in a singsong way, as if she knew his secrets. She had this way of lowering her head and raising her eyes toward him like a little girl. Dinah hated that eye-rolling thing. Couldn't anyone else see what an act it was? Then Huddie would smile, only one side of his mouth turning up, and look at Crystal through his slothlike eyes. 'Ready-O?' he'd ask, and each time Crystal would laugh as if this was the most original thing she'd ever heard.

'Ready-O,' she'd say, her eyes sweeping past Tessie and Dinah and landing right back on Huddie.

Huddie was president of one of those bicycle clubs. He played varsity football and was running for class president. He had a deep round laugh and laughed often so that everyone around him thought they were having a good time. Crystal was helping him with his campaign. At least that's what she'd say when she'd come home from his house at seven o'clock on week-nights, her lipstick smushed around her mouth. 'Huddie and I were working on strategies for his campaign.'

Dinah would laugh, 'I'll bet you and Huddie were working on strategies.' Crystal would give her one of those 'Oh you,' looks and claim she had to finish her homework.

'The great thing about Crystal Landy, when you get her away from her crowd, is what you see is what you get,' Dinah would tell Charlie. The same could not be said about Dinah Lockhart.

No one knew that during lunchtime Dinah left school, ran south down University Avenue, turned right after the bright orange Gulf sign and just before Fremac's luncheonette, and ducked into the store with the purple and blue neon sign outside that buzzed like a fly zapper. She'd kiss Charlie on the cheek and tell him what kind of sandwiches she'd brought for lunch. 'It's Bologna Day!' she'd exclaim, or 'Peanut butter or peanut butter? Your choice.' They'd sit on the two folding bridge chairs behind the counter. 'So, BB Girl, how's your day going so far?' he'd ask. She'd tell him about her math teacher who'd showed up with a brown shoe on his left foot and a black one on his right, or how she got the highest grade on her English test. He called her BB Girl after she'd told him how her dad used to call her his Boing Boing Girl. She felt dopey telling him, but then, a few days later he'd said, 'How's BB Girl today?' and the nickname stuck. If her dad had lived to see her at sixteen, tall, lean, and graceful with her short curly red hair and quick brown eyes, she imagined he'd know that she'd grown too old and elegant to be anyone's Boing Boing Girl. He'd probably have come up with BB Girl himself. Charlie was amazing that way.

He liked to talk about things that were not necessarily of that time or place, questions you could talk about infinitely and still not come up with answers. He talked about faith, war, the cure for cancer, loss. 'Nothing is really gone,' he said one day. 'What's gone or taken comes back in different ways. You just have to recognize what they are. My house burned to the ground, but I feel certain I will live in my house somewhere sometime again. It just won't look the same.' Dinah could listen to Charlie talk forever. Sometimes he spoke of the things he saw that later came true. When he told her how he'd had dreams about the fire before it happened, it didn't scare her. She told him about Eddie Fingers, and how after her dad died, she would sometimes lie in bed as still as she could and pretend she was dead, too. 'If it hadn't been for Crystal, I might just have died.'

'That girl is a source of life,' said Charlie. 'Even though she may be the death of my mother.'

'It would take more than Crystal to kill your mother,' said Dinah.

'My mother. That's a whole other story.' He moved his lips as if he were about to say something else, but then covered his mouth with his hand as if to stop the words from coming.

'What?' asked Dinah, knowing that Charlie rarely spoke unkindly about anyone, even his mother. 'You can tell me.'

'What I was thinking is my mother is a life force who feeds her soul by depleting others. Crystal knows that and she refuses to let hers be eaten up. That's why she won't come home.'

As they ate their peanut butter sandwiches – the corners of their chairs bumped up against each other – they stared into the streets of downtown Gainesville. The two-story stucco office buildings looked like sugar cubes under the blaze of the noonday sun. The low-slung phone wires draped across the landscape like sheet music. It was a cloudless afternoon in October, just before homecoming weekend at the university. There were blue-and-orange signs everywhere that said 'Go Gators.' Blue-and-orange strips of crepe paper hung from the lampposts and were wrapped around the young live oaks. The festive streamers looked dejected on this humid windless day. The streets were empty, and the whole place had the feeling of a party waiting for its guests. 'Take a good look,' said Charlie. 'This is the last of it.'

Even though she didn't understand what he meant by his remark, it was the kind of thing he would say that made her feel special. He knew things she would never know and in his wisdom she felt as reassured and comforted as a child enfolded in her father's arms.

It was 12:45, time for Dinah to get back to school. With her pinky, she daintily wiped a piece of peanut butter from the crease of his mouth. 'See you tomorrow,' she said. 'Tomorrow,' he said, planting a virginal kiss on her forehead. For a long while after she left, he could feel a slight throbbing on the crease of his mouth from where her finger had been. Always this physical discomfort, the afterlife of her touch, the smell of her clean shampooed hair. For a young man who lived mostly in his head, the rest of his body was making quite a hullabaloo, and he hadn't the slightest idea of what to do about it.

That night, when he came home from work, he could hear his mother and Reggie in the living room, working at the same jigsaw puzzle they'd been putting together for the past three days. It was one of those puzzles with thousands of pieces that came in a large deep box. The picture on the cover was of a cable car running up a street in San Francisco. There were painstaking details of people on the cable car, the tracks in the streets, the bay in the background. Charlie couldn't understand why anyone would spend days re-creating what was already so clearly depicted. Where was the surprise or the mystery? He could tell by the sound of his mother's voice that Reggie must have just tried to force a piece with curves into a space defined by edges. 'Think, Reggie,' she demanded. 'Use your head. God didn't give you brains just to hold up your ears.'

Victoria rarely just spoke to Reggie. She shouted at him in loud imperative sentences, as though she had just grabbed him by the lapels and was shaking him to make a point.

'Hey, I'm home,' said Charlie, rubbing his mother's shoulder as she deliberately fitted what appeared to be the brim of the conductor's navy cap into the tableau on the dining-room table.

'Hello, my precious boy,' said Victoria, her voice suddenly sweet and fluffy, her eyes never leaving the puzzle. 'Reggie and I are doing our puzzle.'

Charlie suspected that Reggie felt like a man in jail. 'You've done your time,' he wanted to say, but something told him that Reggie was still doing penance. So he winked at him instead.

'Your mama sure does give my brain a work-through,' said Reggie, using the back of his hand to wipe beads of sweat from behind his neck.

'Reggie, if you're going to mop yourself up, be civil and use a handkerchief,' said Victoria, glaring at Reggie's neck. Then, in her softer voice, she said to Charlie, 'Darling, Ella's in the kitchen, and I know she's cooked up a nice roast beef. I'll be along shortly.'

'They're quite a pair,' Charlie said to Ella, pointing with his eyes toward the living room.

'This goes on all day long. The cussing and the yelling. I'm telling you, I've known Reggie Sykes since the day he was born and I never saw him listen to nobody the way he listens to Mrs Landy. That boy's got such a bad temper on him, I wonder that he hasn't raised his hand. But he's as meek as a lamb. Lord, forgive me for saying this, but he's a man who has seen the other side – and it wasn't heaven either. I pray for his soul.'

Normally, Charlie would have relished discussing Reggie Sykes and his up-for-grabs soul, but not tonight. He had other things on his mind and he couldn't wait to talk to Ella about them. His sit-downs with Ella had become routine, every night after dinner. Though he was less gregarious than his father, Charlie was a good listener. People at the store told him things that were personal or revealing, and never felt in danger of being judged or talked about behind their backs. They were comforted by his broad smile and solid demeanor, and noticed how, when they would talk, he would cock his head and stare straight on at them with his soft blue eyes, so as not to miss a word. Because he said so little, people felt free to interpret his silence in ways that would suit them, and as a result, they revealed even more.

All day he listened, keeping the stories in his head so that when he and Ella had their time together, they could discuss the characters she had come to know through his telling.

'Betty Foley was in today.' She was the registered nurse with the crooked nose and the veined hands who usually showed up around four, just off her early morning shift.

'How's old Mr Thayer doing?' asked Ella.

Ben Thayer was the pharmacist, muted now by a stroke.

'Betty says she can see something going on in his eyes. She says that when she sings to him, particularly the Irish songs, his eyes seem to get moist.' Betty told Charlie that she sang to Mr Thayer while she bathed him. Charlie could imagine her voice, husky and intimate, as if she were talking to someone she couldn't see. 'Just so's you don't think there's anything lewd in my manner,' she said, her voice tilting to a question. 'I think it makes him feel less shamed about his nakedness.'

'Mr Thayer's a real proud man,' said Ella. 'I'm sure Betty Foley is a fine comfort to him.'

Then she asked about Isaac Solomon, the gardener. 'Did he have anything to say today?'

Isaac came in for a pint of scotch every couple of days and always paid with exact change. Each time he'd say, 'Howdy doo, Mr Landy, it certainly is a fine day, isn't it?' Isaac had a terrible stutter. A good day for him was when he didn't have to speak. He let his gardens – magical designs with bursts of color, secret pathways, and exotic sweeps of grass – talk for him. Charlie knew how hard it was for him to utter that cheerful greeting. He'd always tried to say something in return to make Isaac aware that people noticed him, but without obligating him to give an answer. 'Nice job with the Roscoes' rock garden, it's the pride of the neighborhood,' he'd say. Isaac would nod and purse his lips, as if he were mulling it over.

Last winter, after Isaac didn't show up for over a week, Charlie learned that he was sick with pneumonia. Isaac didn't have a phone, but since he went to Ella's church, she knew where he lived. On a Sunday afternoon, she and Charlie walked through the colored section of town to Isaac's one-room wooden house. They found him lying in bed, his eyes glassy and his face flushed with fever. The windows in the room were closed, and judging by the stale and sour smell inside, they hadn't been opened for days. 'All of God's creatures need light,' said Ella, throwing open the two windows in the room. 'As if you, Isaac, of all people, were ignorant of that fact.' Ella fed him some chicken soup she'd cooked, and left him a potful of boiled beef on the stove. Charlie brought him a pint of his favorite scotch in a brown bag and placed it on the kitchen table. 'This is for later, when you're better,' he said.

Ella got a kick out of hearing about the Glenns –
how they'd dart in, their eyes searching the corners
of the store like bank robbers, and say something
like, 'One man's poison is another man's guilty
pleasure,' before exploding into sharp bursts of
laughter and rushing out again.

If it was close to the weekend, the university kids
would come in – the frat boys with their cocky
smiles and fake IDs, the grad students with their
airs of indifference. Charlie had come to know
many of them by name and sometimes they'd invite
him to their parties. 'C'mon, Charlie, take a
busman's holiday,' they'd say. 'Thanks, but I've
got to finish up here,' he'd answer. He knew they
thought he was a queer one. Still, they confided in
him their fears about flunking out or problems with
girlfriends. Charlie Landy could keep a secret – that
was for sure. Who was he going to tell anyway? He
told Ella, of course, but she was only interested in
the ones who got pregnant.

The Grists, Marilyn and Bill, dropped in from
time to time when they needed a case of wine for
a party. Nice people. She would always have a
kind word about his father: 'Every time I walk
through this door I can hear your dad's infectious
laughter.' She continued to see his mother, even
though by now, Charlie told Ella, he was certain
it was more a chore than a pleasure. Bill would
find a moment to come real close and whisper so
Marilyn wouldn't hear: 'You know if you ever find
yourself short of cash, or in any kind of trouble,

I'm always here.' He knew the Grists were strapped for money and that it made Bill feel proud to hold out the offer. 'Thanks Bill,' he'd say, grasping him by the shoulder. 'It's a comfort to know that.' He told Ella how he thought Bill felt responsible for him, since he was his dad's friend from long ago.

Charlie told Ella everything but this: each time Tessie Lockhart came in he felt embarrassed, as if being near her stirred up the disorientation he felt being around her daughter. He also felt a little greedy, knowing that Tessie might talk about Dinah and in that way, bring another piece of her to him. Aside from that, or because of it, she was the customer he liked the best. She always seemed nervous and disorganized. 'Just stocking up,' she'd say, pulling four bottles of Almaden off the shelf. Charlie could tell when her married boyfriend, the Jai Alai mogul, was coming for dinner. She'd suddenly get particular about her choices, citing specific regions of France. 'I need a champagne from the Loire Valley,' she'd say, her voice a little louder. (Tessie still nursed the belief that no one knew about her affair with the Baron.) But his favorite moments were when they would have one of their chats.

He would start by saying, 'How's my sister, your new daughter?' Tessie would pause, as if the question caught her off guard, then reach into her pocketbook for a pack of cigarettes and lighter. She'd hand Charlie the lighter and bend into the flame as she sucked in the burning nicotine. A ring of smoke would form a halo around her head after she exhaled. Then the conversation would begin.

'Did you ever have a best friend?'

'Not really. Well, Ella, but she kind of came with my life. Did you?'

'None except my husband. But the two of them, they know each other's secrets and read each other's minds like they come from the same womb.' She pushed the bangs off her forehead as if to clear the way for her next thought. 'They carry in their heads the expectations their fathers had for them. And when they fight, it's because one of them knows that the other isn't meeting up to those expectations.' Until she said those words, Tessie had no idea she knew this.

'We keep people alive however we can, I guess,' he said.

'How do you keep your dad alive?'

'By taking care of my mother and Ella and Reggie under one roof. By doing the best I can. The truth is, it doesn't seem enough. Does Crystal seem happy?'

'You know her adorable boyfriend, Huddie Harwood,' she said, making it sound like a question.

'I remember the Harwood kid,' said Charlie. 'A little runt when I knew him, but not a mean bone in him.'

'That's good to hear. Dinah doesn't seem to do as well in the social department as Crystal does.'

'I wouldn't worry about her.'

'She's brainy, that one. Takes after her father.' Tessie got a faraway look in her eyes. Charlie knew she was too tactful to add that she was concerned that Crystal was headed down the wrong path, but with everything else on her mind she didn't have time to worry about that too.

These were the people that populated Charlie's world. He recognized his good fortune, but it was not enough to quell the restlessness. The river that ran beneath him was how he pictured it. He knew that in order to become who he was meant to be, he would soon have to leave this place. He'd been running the store for nearly three years now. This is what he needed to discuss with Ella tonight. After dinner, Reggie and Victoria returned to the cable car in the dining room ('I swear they must've built San Francisco in less time than it's taking us to do this friggin' puzzle'). Charlie and Ella went to her room.

Charlie sat beside her on her narrow bed. From that close, he could see how white her hair had become. Her hands, which were normally busy, rested wearily on her lap.

'You're tired,' he said, putting his head on her shoulder.

'I'm old,' she said. 'Old and tired, yes I am.'

'Not too old to give this old man some advice, I hope.'

'You've only seen twenty years. What you mean, "old"?'

'Sometimes I feel I'm living the life of a fifty-year-old man. I get up, I go to work. I come home. Instead of children, I have my mother and Reggie going at each other like magpies. I go to sleep. I get up, and it starts all over again. This can't be what I was meant to do with my life.'

'Oh honey,' she said, scratching his head the way she had when he was a little boy. 'This is just the beginning. God dealt you a mighty blow. He's testing you and you doing just fine. Whatever it is he has in mind for you, you're getting ready to handle it. God's funny that way. It don't always seem like he has a plan but you've got to have faith that He knows what's best.'

'We used to talk about the changes coming. You think my dad's death was the change?'

'No I don't,' she answered. 'I think your dad's death was just the beginning.'

They sat in silence, breathing in the truth. After a while, Charlie said the thing he planned on not saying.

'Did you ever find yourself thinking about one person all the time, and getting this kind of nauseous feeling in your stomach when you did?'

Ella looked at Charlie as if meeting him for the first time. Then she let out a whoop of laughter and rocked back and forth with it until her cheeks were wet with tears. Finally, when she caught her breath she said, 'Well, thank the Lord, Charlie Landy has fallen in love. From the first day that girl walked into the house, I saw something in your eyes and I knew what it was. WAHOO.' She let out another yelp. 'You got it bad.'

'I'm glad you're enjoying this,' said Charlie.

'I've seen how she looks at you, the way she wets her lips when you walk in the room. I see how you get a bullfrog in your throat . . .'

'Ella,' he interrupted. 'Could we please not talk about this anymore?'

'Don't be embarrassed, it's the most normal thing in the world, even for you.'

'Yeah, well it doesn't feel normal.'

Charlie had kissed girls before, even made out with them. He thought he understood what there was to understand about desire. But Dinah was different. Her smell, her habit of lifting her skirt and pulling it across her knees before she sat down, the way her eyes, in a certain light, sparkled with saffron flecks – these things filled him and never left him, even when she wasn't present.

After his talk with Ella, he agonized over Dinah. Did everyone see what Ella saw? Did Dinah know this too? Dinah was practically his sister. Wasn't this incestuous and not very normal? He wondered how he would act the act next time he saw her.

The next afternoon, she came to the store. It was Bologna Day. They sat next to each other and watched out the door. Words, which always came naturally to him, froze in his throat.

'Would you like to go to the movies on Friday night?' He knew how mundane that sounded.

Dinah leaned her face so close to his you could have barely passed a blade of grass between them.

'I'd love to,' she smiled mischievously, then looked at him out of the corner of her eye. 'Charlie Landy, did you just ask me out for a date?'

CHAPTER 14

Barone knew that what he had in mind sounded crazy even though it made perfect sense to him. He was sure that Tessie would understand too, this need to introduce her to Fran. He had real feelings for Tessie and didn't want to keep half of his life hidden from her. He never gave up on the thought that Fran knew what was going on around her, she was just too locked in to show any signs. If that was so, then she already knew about Tessie. If it wasn't, then he was honoring their marriage by making this gesture of truth. Tessie had told him of her conversations with Jerry, and how she felt his hand in the unfolding of her life. He didn't know how he would find the words to say this to her in person, so late one night he composed one of his notes.

Dear Dottie,
　　I know my letters are usually filled with suggestions of where we should go, what wine we will drink, which clothes I would like you to wear on that little body of yours. This time is different. I have a favor to ask

of you. It's a request really, and something I have thought about for a long time. You don't have to give me your answer right away, but it's something I'd like you to think about.

For the past five years I have been living my life in shadows. I say shadows because Fran, while she is not here in the usual ways, looms large over my life. You tell me how Jerry always knows what is going on. Sometimes he even guides you. I feel that way about Fran. If it was possible for me to meet Jerry, would you want me to do it? It is still possible for you to meet Fran. It is something I would like very much. Will you come to Miami Beach for the weekend? We could stay at the Fontainebleau Hotel (very ritzy). Sammy Davis Jr and Frank Sinatra perform there. We can go to the nightclub and dance the night away. If you decide to come, wear bright colors. Fran likes bright colors. I hope my request doesn't trouble you. I thought you would understand.

Instead of signing his name, Barone made a drawing of Tessie. Her mouth was the shape of an O and her eyes were popping out of her head like two jack-in-the-boxes. Underneath he wrote, 'What will he think of next?'

Tessie received the letter one morning while she

was at work. She was no longer the receptionist at Lithographics; after taking a night course in accounting, she was now the head bookkeeper. She had an office, not a very big one, but large enough for a typewriter on a table with wheels and a two-drawer filing cabinet with a lock. That's where she kept the company's bills and records. And behind all that, in a tin Christmas-cookie box, she kept Barone's letters. By now there were so many of them, she kept the older ones behind them in a taped-up manila envelope that said, *mail*. She kept the letters here because keeping them home, near her Jerry Box, seemed a violation of something she couldn't put a name on.

Tessie put the letter back in its envelope, and sat at her desk with it in her hand. As she thought about meeting Fran and what Barone had said about how she'd want him to meet Jerry if he could, she absent-mindedly began tapping the tip of her nose with the envelope.

'Well, someone's in a thoughtful mood today.' It was Glenn Jr, hovering at the door of her office. 'It's too nice a day to wear such a dark frown. It can't be that bad now, can it?'

Tessie considered saying, 'My boyfriend wants me to meet his semidead wife and I am sitting here waiting for a sign from my completely dead husband about whether or not this would be a good idea. It is ninety-three degrees outside and the humidity is ninety percent. Just getting from here to my car, I'll be drenched in sweat and will feel as if I'm trying to breathe in gum. Yes, things really are that bad.'

Of course she said nothing of the kind.

'Have you ever been to the Fontainebleau Hotel?' she asked.

'I had a drink in the bar once,' he said. 'You know, a Shirley Temple. It's quite the place. Why, you planning to go?'

'No,' said Tessie, pressing the envelope to her lips. 'I've just heard a lot about it, you know, how Frank Sinatra and Sammy Davis Jr perform there, that's all.'

Of course Junior was quick to report this exchange to Senior. 'Our lady friend is moving up in the world.' He lowered his voice. 'The Fontainebleau.'

It was an unspoken secret that Tessie was seeing the Baron. She never mentioned it, and the Glenns never let on that they felt a begrudging respect for her because of it.

'The big guy is playing a little close to home, don't you think?' said Senior.

'What does he care?' asked Junior. 'His wife certainly won't catch him.'

Now they'd crossed a line. Neither of them had ever alluded to Fran or her illness before. They shook their heads and laughed uneasily.

That night, Tessie wrote Jerry the following note:

The man wants me to meet his wife. She can't speak or hear and is almost dead. Yet he says she is alive to him. She's kind of like you that way (no offense). It seems strange and not right, but I don't want to hurt his feelings and it matters a lot to him. I can't imagine how I got into this.

Tessie waited days for a response from Jerry, but none came. She took this as an answer itself: 'Too weird. You're on your own.' Thursday morning, when Barone phoned, she cupped her hand over the receiver and said softly, 'Yes, I'll do what you asked, but you have to promise me one thing. Promise me that you'll never tell anyone I did this.'

'It's our secret,' he said. 'Just mine and my sweet little Dottie's.'

Crystal and Dinah had come to like Barone. He called them each Sweetheart, which they assumed he did because he couldn't remember who was who. They nicknamed him Señor Swanky. They liked how he teased Tessie and called her Dottie, though they never knew where that nickname originated. Mostly they liked that in his presence she laughed more and seemed lighter. He never asked them what they were doing in school, or any of the other usual grown-up-to-kid questions. Instead, he talked to them about painting and music and Jai Alai, and about what it was like to live in Paris in the early 1920s. When they giggled or rolled their eyes at one another, he just ignored them and kept the conversation going. One night, the four of them went out to a fancy Italian restaurant. He ordered a bottle of wine and poured a glass for each of the girls. Tessie looked at him as if to say, 'Are you sure about this?' 'They're going to drink wine anyway,' he said. 'They might as well learn about the good stuff from someone who knows.' The girls nodded, despite their surprise. 'And who better to teach us than Señor Swanky,' said Dinah.

'Exactly,' said Crystal, lifting her glass to everyone at the table.

At Christmastime, he gave each girl a charm bracelet with a gold *pelotari* (Jai Alai player) dangling from it. They gave him a beautiful book with thick paper and many colored plates called *The Italian Painters of the Renaissance*. On the frontice page they wrote, 'To Señor Swanky, Thank you for bringing some really neat things into our lives. Your friends, The Sweethearts.'

Barone smiled when he read the inscription. His face flushed as he ran his fingers over the vivid color reproduction of Leonardo da Vinci's *Mona Lisa* on the book's cover. Then he reached out and cupped Crystal's and Dinah's chin in each hand: 'If I'd ever had children of my own, I would wish they'd be exactly like you.'

'Except for one thing,' said Tessie. 'You'd both be boys.'

When Tessie told the girls she was going to Miami Beach for the weekend – 'Well, actually,

I'll be staying at the Fontainebleau' – they nudged each other.

'The Fontainebleau, only the most famous hotel in the world,' said Crystal.

Dinah picked it up. 'The Fontainebleau, home to the richest and most glamorous people in the universe.'

'The Fontainebleau,' shouted Crystal, 'the most expensive and the fanciest place on earth.'

'The Fontainebleau, the biggest and . . .'

'Stop already!' Tessie interrupted. 'I know about the Fontainebleau. What I don't know is what to wear.' The three of them headed for Tessie's closet.

On Saturday morning, when Tessie got on the Trailways bus in Gainesville, she had on orange toreador pants, red shoes, and a red sleeveless blouse. She wore two Bakelite bracelets that the girls had picked out for her: one red, the other orange. When she stepped off the bus in Miami, she was so blinded by the noonday sun that she didn't notice Barone standing there in khaki shorts and a Hawaiian print shirt. 'You came,' he shouted, and threw his arms around her. She could feel the hairs on his chest scratch against her cheek. 'You look perfect.'

Barone carried Tessie's suitcase to his waiting Impala. 'What have you got in here, a whole set of china?'

'No, just a lot of stuff.'

They were quiet in the car. Tessie had never been to Barone's house. He lived on Palm Island, one of the most exclusive addresses in Miami Beach. She knew the house would be big and that it would face the bay. She knew there would be paintings by famous artists on the wall and that the furniture would be in impeccable rococo style with lots of scrollwork and silk upholstery.

The house turned out to be bigger than she imagined. There was a fountain in the front surrounded by life-size statues of angels and cherubs. Barone took her hand as he opened the antique oak door, one that he'd purchased in Italy many years before. 'Let's sit by the pool and have a glass of wine first.'

'A glass of wine sounds good right now. Where's my suitcase?'

'In the trunk of the car.'

'I'll need it.'

Barone hauled the luggage into the house and left it in the front hall. They went to the kitchen where he poured two glasses of wine. Outside they sat at a wrought-iron table under a striped umbrella. The bay was on one side, the pool on the other. There were two statues of lions sitting on their haunches and staring at the water. Were there too many statues, wondered Tessie, or was this just a Miami Beach thing?

'Are you okay about this?' he asked.

'Umm, I guess,' she said, twisting the bangles on her arm.

'You're sweet to be here. It sounds stranger than it will be, really.'

'No, I think it sounds exactly as strange as it will be.'

They drank their wine in silence, staring at the boats that went by. When they'd emptied their glasses, Barone asked Tessie if she was ready.

'Ready-O,' she said. 'Oh, and my suitcase, please.'

They walked down a lemon-colored hallway, Barone dragging Tessie's suitcase behind him.

'This is Fran's wing,' he said. Off to the side were rooms with floral spreads on the beds, and some of Barone's old paintings on the walls. She couldn't tell whether anyone lived in those rooms or if they stood empty. At the end of the hallway they came to a white bedroom filled with sunlight. It was an oval-shaped room with large windows that faced the water. The room was filled with the sound of the waves and the fresh salty smell of the sea. There were photographs on the walls and on the bureaus, hundreds of them, snapshots and portraits of Barone as a much younger man, with a woman with smoky-green eyes and the smile of a seductress.

Not until Barone said, 'Tessie, this is Verona. She takes care of Fran,' did Tessie realize they weren't alone in the room. Verona stood and came forward to shake Tessie's hand. 'How do you do,' she said. Her handshake was as firm as her voice and her thick rubber-soled shoes were soundless against the white marble floor. 'Pleased to make your acquaintance.'

'Me too,' said Tessie.

'How is she this afternoon?' asked Barone.

'We've had a good day,' said Verona. 'We had a bath, a shampoo. Got all dressed up for the company, didn't we, Fran?'

Barone stroked the form that lay under the colorful blanket. 'Fran, honey, Tessie is here. Fran, this is Tessie. Tessie, this is Fran.'

Tessie didn't know where to look or what to make of Verona's firm tone and Barone's relaxed voice, as though all of them were about to sit down for tea. She stared at the pale and wasted face on the pillow, trying to match its scant features with the voluptuous ones in the photos. She listened to Fran's breathing, labored but steady, and tried to imagine her lifeless form in full. After a long pause, she said, 'Hello Fran. It's so nice to meet you.'

Verona smiled and Barone seemed pleased. The two of them sat in chairs on either side of Fran's bed. Tessie sat in a love seat across the room. There was an awkward silence, until Verona said, 'I'll leave the three of you alone.' When she was gone, Tessie walked over to the suitcase that Barone had placed in the center of the room. She knelt down beside it, and as she snapped open the metal latches, she began to talk in a slow monotone. 'Fran, I've brought some things I want to show you.' Carefully, she took out an object that was wrapped in a towel. 'I was married once too. His name was Jerry Lockhart and we were very happy together.'

Barone gripped both sides of his chair and hunched forward so he could see what Tessie was doing.

As she pulled back the layers of terry cloth, he could see the graying cover of what was once a white photo album.

'I've brought my wedding pictures.'

Tessie got up and carried the album to the chair where Verona had been sitting. She sat down and started going through the pictures, tilting the book so that it was within Fran's view. She went through the album page by page. 'That's my Uncle Dick,' she said, pointing to a short stubby man with a swatch of a mustache. 'He got so drunk that when he tried to dip my Aunt Shirley, he dropped her on the dance floor.' She pointed to a shapely woman in a neat pageboy. 'This is my Aunt Shirley, the one in the low-cut – *very* low-cut – dress. She was so angry that she called him a 'stupid ass' loud enough for everyone to hear.' Tessie never looked at Barone, never noticed how he sat with his mouth leaning into his clenched fist. She described all the people in the pictures, the food on the table. 'We couldn't decide between chicken supreme or roasted lamb, but we ended up with the lamb because we decided lamb was more elegant. Don't you think?' She searched Fran's face for a sign of recognition. When she showed her a picture of the wedding cake – 'a little too lemony for my taste' – Barone took Fran's hand. Later he told Tessie that he was sure she squeezed it. When Tessie finished the wedding album, she went back to the suitcase and pulled out some scrapbooks.

'We had a little girl. Her name is Dinah and she's seventeen now.' She showed Fran baby pictures of Dinah, and locks of her hair that she'd pressed between pieces of waxed paper.

'Here's Dinah and her dad at the botanical gardens. Look at those curls. He used to call her his little "Boing Boing Girl," and I guess you can see why.' Her voice was animated. Barone slipped the picture out of its cellophane sleeve and outlined little Dinah's face with his thumb. 'It's amazing how much she looks like her father,' he said, looking first at Tessie and then at Fran.

'She's got his IQ and my melancholy nature,' said Tessie.

'She also has your big heart.' He smiled.

For the first time since she received Barone's letter, she understood why she was there.

'Do you want to see our wedding album?' he asked.

'Why not?'

Through the pictures, she met his stern father, his martyred mother, and his four brothers. The just-married young Barone – his smile so sure – had his hand resting on the curve of Fran's lovely bottom as they walked down the aisle. 'She's beautiful,' said Tessie.

'A pistol, she was.'

The sun was on the horizon by the time they

finally got up to leave. Tessie patted Fran's bony hand, 'I'm so glad I finally met you.' Barone kissed his wife's cheek.

That night, he and Tessie drank champagne and ate roasted lamb with mint jelly and just as he promised, they also danced. After they made love in their suite at the Fountainebleau, Tessie rested her head in the crook of his arm. 'Doesn't it feel weird to be here with me knowing that your wife is at home?' she asked.

'To tell you the truth,' he answered, 'it feels exactly as I hoped it would.'

When she wrote to Jerry about that afternoon, Tessie said that Fran seemed like a nice person and she was glad the four of them could finally get together. His message came to her a week later, after she realized that she had left the picture of Dinah and Jerry at the botanical gardens on the nightstand next to Fran's bed.

CHAPTER 15

'The mind is one of the most important body parts,' Victoria told Tessie, during one of their Saturday lunches. 'It's as vital as your hair. You wash your hair, you trim it, you keep it stylish. If you don't, it gets dull, shapeless, pathetically out of date. The same is true of your mind, you see what I mean?'

Tessie shook her head and tried to keep a straight face, imagining what Barone – who was losing his hair rapidly – would think of this analogy.

'My best inspirations come to me when I am able to put all thoughts out of my head,' Victoria went on. 'Sometimes when I am shopping, I swear I go into a trance. I am there, but part of me is far away.' Victoria closed her eyes and pictured herself in a dressing room, slacks, and blouses draped over chairs; dresses still waiting at attention on their hangers, each garment promising new possibilities. She'd place her hands on her hips and study her figure in the mirror. The years would slip away: she was nobody's mother, there had been no fire. She was Miss Pearly Whites, the young Mrs Landy, the hostess of parties where

Anita Bryant ate shrimp and oysters leaning back on satin pillows in her all-white living room. That's when the ideas – wild ideas – would come to her.

'So last week, I was trying on bathing suits – Catalina does the most slimming styles, by the way – and I started to think about Reggie and what it was about him that repelled me the most. There's a lot to choose from in that area, believe me, but I realized it was his teeth. Seeing his gums and the way the spit comes through the open spaces where the teeth should be – well, that is disgusting – never mind about that. And then it dawned on me. I could get Doctor Simons to build Reggie a set of teeth. I could buy Reggie some teeth.'

Again, Tessie had to control herself. She thought about the poem that Jerry would write to go with the teeth:

> This special present is made for you,
> Think of me when you bite or chew.

Victoria stared at Tessie, her eyebrows raised with expectation. She wanted Tessie to tell her what a fine idea this was, what a humanitarian gesture she was making.

'Do you think Reggie wants teeth?' Tessie asked.

'What kind of a question is that?' asked Victoria. 'Why wouldn't he want teeth. Do you think he likes the way he looks?'

'Maybe he does,' said Tessie, knowing how her answer would get Victoria riled up.

'Do you mean to tell me that if he has the choice of looking like a decrepit old fool or a man of some substance, that he would choose the former? Tessie Lockhart, you have a lot to learn about human nature.'

Tessie didn't know how much longer she could keep up her end of the conversation. She thought about poor Reggie and how his life had become inextricably bound with Victoria's, so much so that if Victoria decided he was going to have teeth, he was going to have teeth whether he wanted them or not. She wondered if Victoria worried about Crystal half as much as she did about Reggie, and was about to steer the conversation in that direction when she felt a silence drop over the room like a sheet.

A group of four young black people – three boys, one girl – had walked into Harmon's. Their movements were sharp and determined, as if they had all been given the same commands. Deliberately, they took their seats on the red vinyl stools and placed their elbows on the yellow countertop. They didn't speak to each other, and their mouths were fixed in small tight expressions, as if they knew that they had put themselves in harm's way, and now they were sitting stiffly waiting for it to arrive.

Victoria turned to look where everyone else was looking. Then she looked at Tessie. 'See that young colored fellow, the one with the white Oxford shirt,' she said. 'He looks neat and well groomed. And look at those teeth! There's no reason that with some teeth Reggie couldn't look like that. You can see my point, that teeth . . .'

The young man at the counter asked the waitress for toast, jam, and a cup of coffee. The waitress's name, according to the yellow nametag she wore, was Patsy. 'I'm sorry,' she said with strained politeness. 'We don't serve colored people here.' The young man was unmoved. 'Please, I'd like some toast with jam and a cup of coffee.' Patsy stared steadily at the hem of her apron as she picked at it with her fingernail. 'Damn,' she said. She had snagged her nail. Almost as an afterthought, she looked up at him. 'Mr Harmon has a policy about serving to coloreds. Would you like me to get him?'

'That would be a fine idea,' said the young man.

It didn't take long for word to spread around the neighborhood about what was happening at the lunch counter. Arnold Kamfer, whose funeral parlor was just a block down the street, came into the restaurant to see for himself. Some of the fraternity boys who were buying liquor a block away at Landy's, also stopped in. Mr Harmon, who had earned the nickname Big Red because of the color of his hair and the permanent flush on his face, walked over to where the young people were sitting. As he wiped his hands on a dirty dish towel, he stared down at the young man who had asked for toast and coffee. 'I thank you to leave here, son, before there's any trouble.'

'I would like some toast with jam and a cup of coffee,' said the young man again.

'You leave me no choice but to call the police,' said Mr Harmon.

As he turned to go back into the kitchen and use the phone, Arnold Kamfer stood up, walked slowly to the lunch counter. He stood there, studying the crowd in the restaurant to make sure that all eyes were upon him. Then he picked up the red plastic ketchup container from the counter and squeezed it into the hair of the young black woman. She lowered her head and kept her elbows on the table as the ketchup dribbled down her face and onto her blouse. She barely moved except to bring her hand to her face and, with a simple flicking gesture, wipe the ketchup from above her eye.

'That poor girl,' said Tessie. 'Should we do something?'

The noise of the crowd grew louder.

'Yes,' said Victoria. 'We should get the hell out of here.' She reached in her bag, pulled four dollar bills from her wallet, and left them on the table. With Tessie following behind her, Victoria pushed aside one of the fraternity boys who blocked the door. 'What are you staring at?' she said to him, then turned to Tessie. 'My God, have you ever seen a worse complexion?'

At about that time, Charlie had left the liquor store and was running up University Avenue to find out what was happening. He got there just in time to see two police cars pull up in front of Harmon's. Four policemen, their hands resting on the nightsticks that hung from their belts, marched into the restaurant. When they came out, each was holding a protester by the scruff of the neck. Outside, a crowd was starting to assemble. Someone threw a rock; someone else threw a shoe.

Four blocks to the north of the liquor store was the black section of town. At the Old Stone Church, Ella and Pauline were attending a prayer meeting when word came that some Freedom Riders had staged a sit-in at Harmon's. It was Pauline who urged Ella that they sneak over to see what was happening. Charlie was standing on the sidewalk across from Harmon's when he noticed the two women walking down University Avenue. He rushed toward them. 'What are you doing here?' He was incredulous. 'This is no place for you to be.'

'We wanted to see,' said Pauline. Ella kept her eyes fixed on her friend. She looked scared and small. Charlie grabbed each woman by the arm and started off down the street away from Harmon's and back toward his store.

Suddenly, a face that Charlie recognized as one of the fraternity boys who came into the store once in a while, pushed himself up close to

Charlie's face and shouted 'Nigger lover!' Charlie moved in front of Ella and a rock caught him on the side of the head. One of the guys who worked across the street at the Gulf station sunk his fist into Charlie's ribs. For a moment, it was the bulk of the old women that kept Charlie standing. Then, a bunch of young boys came out of nowhere, just like the rock and the first, and formed a circle around Charlie, Ella, and Pauline. Charlie prepared himself for another blow. One of the boys shouted to the gathering crowd, 'Get the hell away from these people, or we'll beat the crap out of you.' Charlie recognized the boy as Huddie Harwood, Crystal's friend. The small posse moved clumplike down the street. It was a startling sight: the young man with the plump baby-fat cheeks arm-in-arm with two old black women, bent over as if they were struggling against the wind; and the boys that surrounded them in a 'Ring around the Rosy' circle. People turned and stared. Even the policemen towering over the crowd on their quarter horses stopped to take in the curious sight. Ella, Charlie, and Pauline, their arms entwined, their eyes fixed straight ahead, just kept walking.

Then Charlie saw the beauty parlor up the street from Harmon's. He'd grown up hearing about the genius, J. Baldy. This seemed a good time to meet him. 'Let's go in there,' he said, nodding toward the bright red door with its brass handle. The boys guarded Charlie, Ella, and Pauline as they ducked into Baldy's doorway. 'I'll tell my sister I saw you,' Charlie said to Huddie. Huddie winked and took off with his pals.

Charlie pushed against the door. It was locked. The curtains were drawn and there were no lights coming from inside. Then he saw the curtain move and a face pushed against the window staring at him, a face he recognized as Mr Baldy's. 'I'm Charlie Landy, Victoria's son,' he mouthed slowly. And again, 'Victoria Landy's son.' Charlie watched the taut face at the glass soften with recognition. He saw the man reach his hand up to unlatch the lock. Charlie and Ella and Pauline pushed through the door. 'Come quickly,' said the man with his hand still on the lock. Once they got inside, he locked the door again, and leaned up against it.

It was quiet inside the shop. The smell of apples and the soothing sight of the peach-colored walls were a sharp contrast to the shouting and the press of bodies outside. Charlie, Ella, and Pauline still clung to each other. Jésus had recognized Charlie from Maynard Landy's funeral.

'This is Ella and her friend Pauline,' Charlie said.

'Of course, Ella,' said Jésus. 'You must be the sister of Reggie.'

Ella stared at Jésus, unable to find words. Being in this place with its leather chairs and fancy pictures on the walls was as scary to Ella and Pauline as being outside with a mob of angry people. Was it proper for them to sit down? They stood before Jésus like two schoolgirls.

'Yes, sir,' said Ella meekly. 'Reggie Sykes is my brother.'

Jésus heard the tightness in her voice echoing his own fear. That's when he noticed the blood trickling down the side of Charlie's face. 'You are hurt,' he said. 'Come, Sonia will fix it.'

Sonia beckoned Charlie to follow her to the magenta sink where she washed the ladies' hair. 'Please, sit,' she said.

To hear a soft voice and have a place to lie back seemed like a miracle to Charlie. The tightness in his stomach was finally relenting. He lay back on the chair, rested his head on the curve of the porcelain, and fell soundly asleep. He didn't even feel it when Sonia dabbed his cut with hydrogen peroxide, then pressed a cloth with cold water against it to stanch the bleeding.

Jésus invited Ella and Pauline to sit. 'Please, it would be my pleasure,' he said, offering Ella his hand to help her into the seat. 'Is a horrible thing, what's happening,' he said. 'I never thought I'd see something like this in America.'

'Mr Baldy,' said Ella. 'Often times me and Mr Landy talked about the times ahead. We have to put our faith in God and pray. He gives us the strength for whatever comes.' As if summoned by Ella's words, there was a pounding at the door. Nobody moved as the pounding got more insistent. Tentatively, Jésus stepped closer to the window and tugged the curtain aside to see who it might be. 'Oh my goodness,' he cried and unlocked the door. In flew Victoria, with Tessie holding on to the back of her blouse as if they were playing tag.

'Good God, what's going on out there?' said Victoria, her voice rising. 'We were stuck in that crowd for nearly half an hour.' Victoria's hands were trembling. 'I swear, we nearly got trampled to death.'

It was Tessie who saw Ella first. 'Ella?' she uttered in disbelief. It was one more thing in an afternoon of too many things.

Terrified that Victoria would be angry with her for being where she shouldn't, Ella got up and offered Victoria her chair. 'I'm so sorry, Mrs Landy,' she said, stumbling over her own words. 'Pauline and me, when we heard about the incident at the coffee shop, we came downtown to see what was going on. We saw Charlie and the three of us were walking down the street when someone hit Charlie in the head with a rock.' She was talking faster now. 'And then these boys, they came and made a circle around us and told the crowd that if anyone touched us, they would be mighty sorry. And then Charlie said he thought nobody would follow us in here, so the boys took us here and Mr Baldy let us come inside.'

'Charlie's here, too?' said Victoria. 'Oh, boy.' She puffed out her cheeks, snorting as if she'd just had a close call.

'Yes ma'am, he's in the back with Sonia. She's washing up his wound.'

Victoria took in the sight of Charlie lying in Sonia's chair, of Ella and Pauline in this place, this expensive place – her sanctuary – of Jésus, his usually impassive face, rigid with anxiety, of Tessie, frightened witless.

'Well this is . . . for God's sake, Charlie Landy.' She crammed a piece of Juicy Fruit in her mouth. 'Can't you just be with people your own age and act normal for a change? Why do you always have to go butting your nose into other people's business?'

By now, Charlie was sitting up, holding the cold compress to his head. 'It wasn't other people, it was Ella,' he said softly.

'You care more about everyone else than you care about me. I tell you . . .' Victoria didn't finish her sentence. She was diverted by Ella's face in the mirror. For all the years she had known her, Ella wore her hair in a bun, hard and neat as a golf ball. Now, for the first time, Victoria noticed her high cheekbones, her broad forehead, her strong masculine hands – maybe there was even some Cherokee blood in her. How could she have never seen this, that with a more flattering hairdo and some weight loss, Ella might be an attractive woman?

Victoria cracked her gum. Charlie could never understand how she could create a little gum-bubble, then pop it open using only her back teeth. The cracking was steady as Victoria stared off into space. Charlie knew that when she cracked and stared she was thinking about something, and whatever it was, it was something he would never have predicted. Victoria turned her attention to Jésus. 'I know this sounds crazy at a time like this, but you know me, always Miss Practical. While we're all stuck here with this zoo going on, I wonder what could you do with Ella's hair, you know, to give it a little pizzaz.'

'Oh Mrs Landy,' Ella protested. 'I couldn't. That wouldn't be right.'

'Go on,' urged Pauline. 'A little prettying up won't hurt you.'

Jésus gestured outside. 'We could be here for hours. It would take our minds off of the unpleasantness. Besides, I would like nothing more than to trim your hair. May I?'

Charlie came and stood behind Ella next to Jésus. He winked at Ella in the mirror. 'It's time for a change, don't you think?'

'All right then,' said Ella, turning to Jésus. 'But don't you go making me look like Audrey Hepburn.'

Sonia led Ella to her station and placed a smock around her neck. 'You relax now, I do the work,' she said, as she adjusted the water until it was just so. Victoria watched Sonia's little face become studious as her hands moved like a conductor's through the froth and tangle of Ella's hair. Sonia was particularly beautiful when she was serious and engrossed.

Ella sat rigid, as if she were about to get a cavity filled without a painkiller. This was all too different, someone serving her – a man, a white man no less, all the attention she was getting over what, over a haircut? Ella was always amazed by the vanity of some people. In God's eyes, everyone was humble, so why did they bother to spend so much money going to beauty parlors and buying too many clothes? Maynard Landy was one of the few who knew the value of a dollar. She'd seen how hard he'd worked for every penny he earned. Just the thought of him, may he rest in peace, filled her with sadness and longing for a time that had passed. How embarrassed she'd be to have him see her like this. And Charlie Landy. What must he think of her done up in this fancy smock with Mr Baldy running his fingers through her hair like she was some kind of a fashion model. She hoped Pauline would have the good sense not to talk about this to the other parishioners.

Tessie asked Jésus if she could use the phone. She hadn't stopped fidgeting, lighting one cigarette after another, since she got here. 'I ought to call the girls and tell them what's going on.'

'Yes, and find out if they're okay,' said Charlie.

Victoria sat down next to Ella. 'I have to talk to you about something.' Ella heard the lilt in her voice and her heart sank, knowing she was

246

trapped. 'It's about Reggie.' She chewed her gum thoughtfully. 'I can see that underneath it all, Reggie has some potential.' Victoria was oblivious to Ella's discomfort. 'Of course, when you have certain physical defects, it's hard to have any self-regard. I mean, how could you? So I was thinking that maybe I could get Dr Simons to fix him up some teeth. You know how important first impressions are. People look at your eyes, your hair, your teeth, and right or wrong, they sum you up before you've even said a word.'

'Reggie could sure use some teeth. That's very kind of you to offer,' said Ella in a monotone.

'Well, you know how I like to help in any way I can,' she said, glancing up at Jésus.

Jésus nodded, as he always did when Victoria wandered beyond his comprehension.

'There's not much left,' Pauline said to Ella. 'You see what's going on here?'

Ella's hair had gathered around Jésus's feet like a nest. With all the excitement, no one seemed to notice that he had cut off most of it, leaving a nimbus of soft white curls framing her face.

'My God, you look like Ella Sykes's daughter, if she had one,' said Charlie. 'That is amazing.'

'It's very nice,' said Tessie, who kept staring at her watch. She had finally reached Dinah. 'You won't believe what's going on here,' she told her.

'What?' Dinah sounded distracted.

'Victoria, Ella, Pauline, Charlie, and I have been

locked inside J. Baldy's. There's some kind of demonstration . . .'

'Charlie's there too?'

'Yes, there's some kind of demonstration . . .' She tried to describe what had been going on but Dinah was only interested in one thing.

'Yeah, but what's Charlie doing there?'

She looked at her watch again. 'Jeez, we've been here for over an hour.' She could tell Dinah wanted to get off the phone as fast as she could.

'I'll call back at Baldy's in an hour. If you're still there, we'll figure something out,' Dinah said.

Tessie tapped a cigarette against her knuckle. 'Oh, and please call Barone and tell him where I am,' she said, trying not to sound too frantic. 'I mean, he may want to know.'

'Yeah, sure,' Dinah said, and hung up.

Dinah could be so irritating at times. It was no picnic raising one teenage girl, never mind Crystal, who, let's face it, was more than she had bargained for. Everyone wanted something from her. And Barone, everything had to be done on his schedule. She always had to wait until he called her. It was hard having to take care of herself. Jerry protected her. Now who was watching? Son of a gun, Victoria was still talking! She hadn't shut her mouth once in the hour and a half they'd been there.

'Everybody!' Victoria clapped her hands. 'Look how beautiful Ella is.' They all looked up except

Sonia, who was sitting in the back of the shop reading a romance magazine in Spanish.

Victoria walked to where she was sitting. 'Hi, Sonia,' she said tentatively.

'Hello, Mrs Landy.'

Since the fire, Victoria had barely spoken to Sonia, though she still gave her generous tips each week. Whenever she thought about that night, how she had visualized Sonia while she and Maynard made love, she would flinch and turn away as if what she saw before her was too overwhelming. She rationalized it by thinking how she desired all things beautiful. And Sonia was certainly beautiful. All she wanted was to see what she was like up close, away from the salon. Victoria was sure that was all there was to it. But each time she looked at Sonia, she was forced to stare at her own guilt over Maynard's death. Victoria waved her hand in front of her face, trying to shush away these thoughts. 'Charlie, honey,' she said, distracting herself with her own chatter. 'How is that wound? You feeling better, sweet boy? Tessie, are the girls okay?'

If Sonia wondered why Mrs Landy didn't bring bags of mangos to the shop or invite her back to her house anymore, she never asked. Now she waited for Victoria to stop talking so she could go back to reading her romance magazine.

When the phone rang, they all started, as though they'd never heard the sound of a bell before. 'I'll get it,' shouted Tessie, nearly knocking over

Charlie on her way to pick it up. From the way she lowered her voice and turned toward the wall, they knew it was Barone at the other end.

Jésus kept his eyes fixed on the front window, trying to catch a glimpse of what was going on. 'Don't worry,' said Charlie, placing a hand on Jésus's arm. 'It's just a bunch of crazy boys. It's already quieted down, we'll be fine.' Jésus kept staring at the window. 'Where I come from, police would take these poor people away, torture them, sometimes even kill them. This, what is going on outside, is what I've feared the most.'

'No one will be killed or tortured,' said Charlie. 'It's just what happens when things change. People don't take to new things easily.'

'I am very happy with the old things,' said Jésus, who cherished the predictability of life in Gainesville. 'I see no need for changes.'

'I know what you mean,' said Charlie. 'New things are scary.' He thought of his own changes – his feelings for Dinah, the growing awareness that he would have to leave this place soon and make a bigger life for himself – and how they darted his nights with unease and sleeplessness. 'I worry about my mother,' said Jésus. 'I write her every day and pray that someday she will come here to Gainesville. She misses Sonia so much.' He paused and looked at Charlie, who knew instinctively to stop thinking and just listen. Charlie felt at ease with Jésus, sensing the kindness within him.

'When I was nineteen, I had relations with my older cousin,' Jésus went on. 'It was my first time. She became pregnant and I promised her if she kept the child, I would raise it on my own. So Sonia lived with my mother and me in San Vicente. She calls my mother Tía Rosa. When Sonia was fourteen, I went to make a life in America. After I knew I could support us both, I sent for her. She is good at her job. The customers like her. I haven't told her yet.' He paused again. 'Now, when something like this happens, I feel I could lose everything. This is all I have.'

'What are you two yacking about?' said Victoria, who'd been eyeing her son and hairdresser as they whispered in the corner.

'Just stuff,' said Charlie, realizing how worn his mother looked. 'How are you doing?' he asked.

'I'm hot and I'm bored and if this isn't over soon, you're going to have to call the men in the white coats to haul me the hell out of here.'

Charlie pulled a piece of the curtain aside. 'Looks pretty quiet out there,' he said. He parted the curtain even more. 'It's empty.' He opened the front door and walked out. He came back a few seconds later. 'It's all over. I guess we can go now.'

They all blinked and opened their eyes wide the way people do when the lights go on after a movie. And just as in the movies, the world that they'd been living in for the past two hours was finished, gone. No one stirred. There were many ways this afternoon at J. Baldy's could end, and between them they had considered all of them. All except one: that they could just walk out the door and go back to their lives.

CHAPTER 16

Dear Dottie,

When I come on Saturday, I would like to bring a new friend with me. I have told him all about you and the sweethearts and though he didn't say it in so many words, I could tell by the look on his face and the way that his eyes shone that you and he will have a special bond. Don't worry about food, I'll bring it. He has simple and specific tastes. So do I, and you suit them to a 'T.' Wear something loose and informal. My friend can be *very* playful. Yours, Barone

Around the words 'Yours, Barone' he'd drawn pictures of someone who looked like Tessie doing summersaults and headstands. Maybe the circus had come to town and he had befriended one of the performers. 'Señor Swanky is bringing someone for us to meet on Saturday,' Tessie told the girls that night. 'He's being very mysterious and says we should wear clothes that are comfortable and playful.'

'Neat,' said Crystal. 'I have a pair of Charlie's old overalls that would look real cute with my gingham shirt.'

'He better not be bringing one of those nausea boys he works with at Jai Alai,' said Dinah.

The girls fell into one of their giggling fits.

'Hmm, and I was hoping it was someone to help me with chores around the house,' said Tessie.

Dinah thought back to two weeks ago, when she called Barone to tell him that Tessie was trapped inside J. Baldy's.

'Does she sound scared?' Barone had asked.

'Actually, she sounds annoyed. She says Victoria won't shut up and that Jésus has cut Ella's hair within an inch of its life and that sometimes she thinks she made a terrible mistake moving us to this stupid little redneck town. Yeah, I guess she was scared.'

'Your mother is alone too much,' he'd said. 'It makes her sad and anxious.'

'She's got me and Crystal hanging around all the time.'

'I know she does, sweetheart. I'm talking about a different kind of alone that has to do with your father, and with me not always being available.'

Whoever this mystery guest was, Dinah wondered if it would have something to do with that conversation.

On Saturday afternoon, the three of them were

standing at the front door when Barone pulled up in his Impala.

'He looks very by himself to me,' said Crystal.

'Maybe he's got a new imaginary friend,' said Dinah. 'That's so cute.'

Tessie smiled. 'You never know. That man is full of surprises.' He walked toward the house, an 'I've got a secret' smile on his face. He kept his hands over a pouch on his stomach.

'Hello everyone.' The pouch under his shirt started to squirm. Barone feigned a look of surprise as he stared down to his belly. 'Well, what have we here?' A fuzzy ear poked out from where the shirt should have been buttoned. Barone scratched at the fuzz with one finger until the full head of a kitten popped up. Its nose was pink as a pig's, and there were black-, white-, and copper-colored patches on its face. It stared out with unblinking eyes like globes of lapis lazuli.

'Oh my God, a kitten,' cried Crystal, reaching to pick it up.

It dug its claws into Barone's shirt. Gently, he lifted the animal and cupped it in his hands like water. 'He's a scared little fellow. I found him on the beach at Crandon Park. He was hanging around the refreshment stand looking for scraps. I asked the guy behind the counter if he belonged to anyone, and he said no, that it seemed as if someone had left him there the day before. The guy said he was very gentle and sweet, and I said

I knew someone who was also gentle and sweet and that I thought they might become fast friends.' Barone shot Tessie a look. 'Want to hold him?' he asked, offering her the blotchy ball of fur.

Tessie stepped back. 'No, that's all right. He's comfortable with you.' Tessie had never owned a pet before. Cats, in particular, scared her. They weren't to be trusted. There was something stealthy about them; they were too quiet, too fast. Those sharp teeth and razorlike claws, even their whiskers felt wiry and abrasive. If she had to choose, she'd pick a dog, any day. They were dumber, less subtle, not as judgmental. Though Jerry was slim and graceful, in temperament he was much more doglike. Barone had a large chest and short, thick arms, like a bulldog maybe, but he had the sleek wily character of a cat. Even this: making sure the girls were here when he brought the creature to her house, knowing full well that they'd love and cuddle him right away. What a typically conniving, feline thing to do.

'Can I hold him?' asked Dinah. Barone placed him in her arms. The cat twisted and splayed his paws before settling into the crook of her elbow. She noticed that he had four toes on his hind feet and five on his forefeet.

'Would you like to keep him?' asked Barone.

'Yes,' cried out both girls. 'Can we, Mom?' asked Dinah. 'Please, Tessie,' said Crystal.

'I don't know the first thing about raising a cat,' said Tessie firmly.

'I'll take care of him,' said Dinah. 'So will I,' said Crystal.

'Cats are nothing compared to adolescent girls,' said Barone. 'You'll grow to love him, you'll see.'

Crystal grabbed the cat by its front paws and tried to wrench him away from Dinah. The cat arched its back and gave Barone a knowing look: *So this is what it's going to be like.*

'Let's name him Elvis,' said Crystal.

'No,' said Dinah. 'We're going to call him Eddie.'

'Oh. After Eddie Fingers,' said Crystal, and then turned to Barone. 'The boy who died.'

Tessie hadn't thought about that funeral for a long time. It got her thinking about her early days in Gainesville and how frightening everything had seemed: the new house, the job, Dinah's friendship with Crystal and the first time she picked her up from the Landy's house, the time she ran over the cat. She had told Barone about the cat, and he'd never brought it up again. For that matter, Dinah had never brought it up either, even after the barbecue at the Landy's, when Charlie got up and sang 'The Cat Came Back.' Charlie Landy had a curious intuition. He always seemed to know what she was going to say. Maybe that's why she felt so at ease with him. Most of all, thinking back to those days made her ache with how much she missed her Jerry.

The cat. Jerry. Who else? It suddenly made sense. Jerry had sent her the cat.

'Eddie sounds right,' said Tessie. 'We need to make him a sleeping box.' She went to the hall closet where she stored the carton from her Magnavox hi-fi. She took an old sheet and folded it so it filled the box. 'He'll sleep in my room.' Later, when Tessie and Barone were alone, he said to her, 'The cat will be a real companion. You'll feel a lot better having him around.'

'The cat is a cat,' said Tessie. 'It's just another thing I need to take care of.'

Of course, almost immediately, Eddie took over Tessie's heart. At night, he'd jump onto her bed just before she'd go to sleep. He would snuggle up next to her and sleep with his head on her collarbone. During the day, when no one was around, she would carry him on her shoulder and talk to him. Nothing personal, just little asides like, 'Let's open the window and get some fresh air,' or 'I wish Crystal would make her own bed, don't you?' Remarkably, with his purrs and meowing, Eddie always seemed to answer back. Tessie couldn't remember when the nicknames began, but not long after he arrived, she began calling him Mr Paws, and Eddie Bear. After a couple of weeks, she started calling him the Bear, and Pooh Bear, but never in front of the girls. She even gave nicknames to his toys. Tessie felt such love for Eddie that she'd find herself laughing when he would jump onto the kitchen table and lap up whatever food was left on the plates. 'You'd kill us if we jumped on the table and started licking the plates,' Dinah teased.

'No I wouldn't. It's kind of cute,' said Tessie, scratching the top of his head.

Eddie was definitely her cat. He tolerated the girls when they took pictures of him in silly poses, but Tessie was the one he lived for. It was Tessie he'd greet at the door whenever she came home, his tail up, ears forward, as happy to see her as if she'd been away for months instead of hours. He'd sidle up to her and rub her legs with his whiskers and muzzle, *Welcome home. This is the greatest thing that has ever happened.* Sometimes she hugged him so hard, she was afraid she'd crush his little bones.

One morning, after he'd been there a month, Tessie found herself sitting on the kitchen floor, mesmerized by Eddie, sound asleep, a swirl of fur bathed in sunlight. He had a little black marking on his upper lip, like a smudge of charcoal, and she had to stop herself from burrowing her head in the softness of his pink belly. Tessie wondered how she ever lived life without a cat, and what Jerry would think of her infatuation. Before she left for work, she placed a note in the Jerry Box:

I have a new friend. His name is Eddie, and he's black and white and rust colored, and the cutest thing I've ever seen. He

259

makes me laugh and seems to understand things that I say. Have I mentioned he's a kitten? I never understood about people and their pets, but I have a kind of love for him that makes me feel protected, loved, and less alone. He never disappoints me. Who knew?

That night, for the first and only time ever, Eddie peed in her bed.

'She loves that cat more than anything,' Dinah told Charlie a couple of weeks after Eddie arrived. 'I know she loves me, and she probably even loves Crystal. But this is different. No matter what he does, even disgusting things like puking up hairballs on the couch, she thinks it's cute.' They were sitting in Charlie's car at the canoe outpost near High Springs.

The first time they went out at night, he drove her home from the movies right afterward. This time, when the movie ended, he suggested High Springs, a favorite place to go parking. She'd visited him in the store every day for the past two years, and he'd seen her at her house at least once a week when he came to visit Crystal. But being with him alone in his car reminded her of the time she saw her math teacher, Mr Halstead, walking down the street holding his son's hand. Mr Halstead was wearing shorts and sandals. She had never really known he had a kid, much less one whose hand he would hold. The whole thing, the shorts, the bare feet, the little boy, was intimate and embarrassing at the same time, which was exactly how she felt with Charlie now.

'That's what they say about animals, that they give you unconditional love,' Charlie said. 'They don't hold grudges, they don't care how you look. They just live to love you.'

Dinah stared at him and said nothing. He stared back. The Everly Brothers were singing 'Devoted to You.' The music was sweet and the words made you want to believe that love could be forever. He put his arm around her and she softened into it. She was beautiful, Dinah, so full of spirit and life, like her curly fiery hair, which could never be completely tamed. He could see how her father came up with the name Boing Boing Girl. He imagined what his father felt like when he fell in love with his mother. The way he had told it, she was a fractious beauty in her day: wild, eccentric, already divorced at twenty-two. To her, Maynard must have seemed solid and safe and a world apart from the boys she had known. Charlie had never thought of either of his parents that way, but it must have been like this.

He kissed Dinah. She brushed his cheeks with her fingers. He kissed her again and wrapped his arms around her, holding her as tight as it was possible to do. She put her arms around him and tried to pull him closer. They kissed and rocked back and forth through the Everly Brothers and at least three other songs. It was as if they had found this place of refuge after a long journey, and neither was about to let go.

'I love you.' It was the first time he'd ever said those words to a girl.

'I love you, too, Charlie. I've always known it, I guess, I just didn't know what it was.'

Her breath was warm on his face as she stared at him with expectation. He had no words. He said, 'I'm sorry, I never get this tongue-tied.' She said, 'Don't be crazy. Besides, I feel the same way.' He kissed her again and their bodies folded into each other. For so many years they had watched each other and secretly reveled in the familiarity of a voice, a smell. Now it was as if someone finally opened the door and both of them were home. Dinah heard herself groaning, 'Yes,' she said. 'Yes. Please.'

Suddenly, he got still and pulled back.

'We should stop.' His voice was gravelly. 'It isn't right.'

'I don't care,' she whispered.

'I do. I mean I don't right now, but I do in the scheme of things.'

'How can you think about the scheme of things at a time like this?'

He sucked on the tips of her fingers then said, 'I never stop thinking about them. Can you stand that?'

'I can stand everything about you,' she said.

On Saturday nights, Gainesville came alive. The fraternity houses were lit up and the music from their parties filled the streets. Charlie and Dinah drove down Fraternity Row, a beautiful street with giant oak trees, and old Victorian houses grown shabby from neglect. This is what I'm missing, thought Charlie at the same time that Dinah was wondering if Charlie was a little too perfect to be true.

Out of habit, Charlie followed West University onto University Avenue, and went another four blocks past the liquor store. The first thing he noticed was the glass. It picked up the reflection of his headlights and shone like glitter. There was a giant hole where the front window used to be. Someone had shattered it with a rock. Charlie and Dinah got out of the car and walked toward the store. 'This is just the beginning,' he said to Dinah. There had to be a punch line to the Harmon's incident. Charlie knew that. He just didn't think it would happen so fast.

That night, he dreamed that he was standing in front of a room full of people and words were coming out of his mouth that weren't his. He kept saying the words and afterward people came up and told him how much what he had said meant to them. The following night, he had the same dream and after that, the dream became part of the texture of his days and the puzzles of his night. What did it mean and why did it keep coming back?

First thing Monday morning Huddie Harwood showed up. Huddie seemed smaller, more tentative than that day in the street.

'Huddie Harwood, how glad I am to see you,' said Charlie, who was boarding up the window. He clapped him around the shoulder and shook his hand. 'I owe you a big thanks for me and my friends. You really got us out of a jam. For all I know, you saved my life.'

Huddie smiled his jagged smile. 'It was nothing, Mr Landy. Sorry about your window. Stupid hoods.'

'Don't go calling me Mr Landy, buddy,' said Charlie. 'As far as I'm concerned, after what you did, we're friends forever.'

'That's what I came to talk to you about, sir,' said Huddie. 'Well not exactly, but sort of.'

Huddie looked so serious and tight with determination.

'What say we take some of these chairs, have a beer, and sit out back?' said Charlie, trying to put him at ease. 'C'mon, we can watch the loading dock at Florsheims.'

They dragged out the two folding chairs and placed them on a mottled swath of grass. Charlie kept moving his chair to try to escape the sun, but there wasn't a sliver of shade to be found.

Huddie pressed his lips together, trying to figure out how to start. He took a swig from his beer.

'It's about your sister,' he said. 'Crystal.'

'Oh yes, my sister, Crystal. I know her well.'

Huddie didn't crack a smile. 'Seeing as though you're the man in the family – I mean, well your mother, um Mrs Landy, is probably the head of the house, but you're the only man – so anyway, your sister, Crystal. I love her very much and I wanted to tell you that I would like to marry her.'

Huddie continued. 'Well, of course we can't get married right away, us both being in high school and all. But I've been thinking how when I graduate, I want to go into the army and serve my time. If Crystal will wait for me, then we could get married when I get back.'

'Does Crystal know about any of this?' asked Charlie.

'No, sir, at least not about the army part.'

Every day, more soldiers were being shipped to Vietnam. Talk of the draft was hovering around young men like a virus. 'Why do you want to go into the army?' asked Charlie.

'Well, you know, to serve my country. The communists are getting closer and closer. I'll get drafted, and besides, it's my duty as an American.'

Huddie was only five years younger than Charlie, but he seemed to Charlie like such a boy, a boy with an idealized version of what it was to be a man. The way he said those words, Charlie knew they weren't his.

'I'll bet your dad is real gung ho about you going,' said Charlie.

'You know my dad?' Huddie was startled.

'No, but I'm guessing.'

'My dad says that you go into the army a pussy and you come out a man. He says the only people who don't go into the military are communists and Jews and that most of them are faggots anyway.'

Charlie asked, 'How does your dad feel about his son saving two black old ladies from a rowdy group of segregationists?'

'Nothing personal, Mr Landy, but you must think I've got no sense in me at all. There's a lot of stuff I don't tell my father, and what happened that day would be top of the list.'

'Do you think your father ever thinks about you getting killed if you went into the army?'

Huddie leaned forward in his chair and clasped his hands together. They stared in silence as two men got out of a truck across the way and unloaded a half a dozen boxes with the word *Florsheims* in big black type. Underneath it, in a hastily crayoned script, were the words *penny loafers*. Finally Charlie spoke. 'My mother wants me to stay in Gainesville forever and run this liquor store. I don't want to make her unhappy, but I know there's more to life than this.' He pointed to the broken window. 'It's coming time for me to leave. Finally, it's our lives. You know what I mean?'

They watched the deliverymen get back into their truck. Huddie put his empty can of beer under his chair. He pulled a Zippo lighter and a crushed pack of Lucky Strikes from his back pocket and offered Charlie a smoke. Charlie liked everything about smoking: the flicking sound of the lighter as the flint caught fire, the way the tip of the cigarette turned the color of bubbling lava when it was first inhaled, the smell of burnt tobacco. People with cigarettes looked cool and reflective, as if in swallowing the smoke they had ingested some profound secret. He wished it didn't burn his throat and make him choke. Smoking kept your hands busy and required attention. It passed as an activity which would have been perfect at a time like this when there was nothing left to say.

'I don't have to tell Crystal that we ever talked about any of this,' said Charlie. 'And as far as I'm concerned, I can't think of anyone I'd rather have for a brother-in-law.'

For the first time that afternoon, Huddie Harwood smiled broadly. 'I might like to marry her just so I can be related to you,' he said.

'Huddie. What a jerk,' said Dinah later that night, when Charlie told her that he'd seen him that afternoon. They were parked at their favorite spot near High Springs.

'He's not really,' said Charlie. 'He's kind of decent, if a little mixed up.'

'I guess I feel protective about Crystal. I just worry that he'll go off with one of those irritating Little Miss Pep Clubs and break her heart.'

'I think you've got him wrong, Dinah. I think he really likes her.'

'He better,' she said.

Charlie wasn't ready to talk to Dinah about his conversation with Huddie that afternoon and how much it had meant to him. He wasn't even sure he knew why it had, other than it stirred something inside of him, something he couldn't wait to talk about to Ella. But not to Dinah, not now.

'So have you told Crystal about us?' he asked.

'What should I tell her?' she teased.

'That her brother has fallen for her best friend and that she's turned his whole life upside down, though nobody would know it to look at him. You could tell her that for starters.'

Dinah put her hand on his thigh. They kissed. They kissed again, pressing their lips so close together that the next day his lips were swollen and bruised. This time, their bodies knew what to do, where to go. And once again, it was Charlie who stopped them just when he felt he might lose control.

'I'm sorry,' he whispered, his mind drunk with the smell of her. 'I can't. I can't now.'

'Later maybe?' Dinah asked.

'No, I'm serious. You're not some girl to have sex with. To me it would have all these implications, responsibilities, and I just need to figure out a couple of things first. Does that make any sense?'

'Have *you* told her?'

'Have I told who what?' Now Dinah wasn't making any sense.

'Have *you* told Crystal about us?'

'No, but I'll make a deal with you. You tell Crystal tonight and I'll pick you up tomorrow at one and you can tell me everything she said.'

'Deal,' said Dinah. 'Then you have to tell your mother.'

When Dinah came home that night, Tessie was out with Barone, and Crystal was with Huddie. Eddie was only vaguely interested in her arrival. 'Hi, kitten face,' she said, picking him up by the scruff of his neck and placing him on her lap. 'I might as well tell you,' she said, holding his paw in her hand. 'I love Charlie Landy.' Eddie stared into her eyes and slightly cocked his head as if what she was saying were the most interesting thing he'd ever heard. 'Can you believe it? Charlie Landy! And he loves me too. We've made out.' She lowered her voice. 'Here's the weird part. I'd go all the way with him in a minute. He's the one who won't.'

Eddie had heard quite enough. He squirmed off her lap, and made a soft thud as the five toes of his front paws and the four of his hind paws hit the wooden floor.

'Thanks a lot,' she called after him. 'Gee, I'm not having a lot of luck with boys tonight, am I?'

She brushed her teeth and got into her pajamas.

As she lay in her bed, the same bed she'd been sleeping in since she was ten years old, she remembered how big this bed used to seem to her. In her worst days, it was her world: the miles and miles of cotton sheets, and the worn ribbon around the edges of her blue blanket, her flat pillow with the brown sweat stains in the middle indented part. These were the parameters of her safe place, the place she longed for during the day at school and where she retreated gratefully and willingly in the late afternoons. The outside world in those days was distant and scary and her connections to it were as fragile as spider legs. Now this bed was too small – too short for her long legs, too cramped for her oversized dreams. The things she'd done with Charlie, they were womanly things, not girl things. She loved him. She was in love with a boy and yearned to have sex with him, even marry him. Could the little girl who so often hid in this bed ever have imagined she'd have these thoughts? She wondered about her father and what he'd say about all this, though it embarrassed her to think that he would know. Would he even recognize her, so grown up? She supposed that he would. Just because he was dead didn't mean he'd lose sight of her. If she saw him now, would he be fatter, have less hair, be stooped over, or would he look the way he had the last time she saw him?

Jeez, it was past midnight. Where was Crystal?

Dinah wished she'd come home already. She'd force herself to stay awake until she did.

An hour later, Crystal tiptoed into their bedroom and slowly, silently started to undress. Dinah watched her for a while, pretending to be asleep, then said in a hushed voice, 'Don't be quiet on my account.'

'Holy moley!' Crystal jumped. 'You might warn a person before you go spying on them in the dark.'

'I wasn't spying, I was just resting,' laughed Dinah. 'So how was your date?'

'Huddie.' said Crystal, her voice melting. 'I love him so much. If I tell you something, you promise not to tell anyone?'

'Promise.'

'Huddie and me, we're talking about getting married. Not right away, of course, but after I go to college.'

In the gray shadows of the night, Dinah could see Crystal's profile. Her eyes were half closed and she was smiling as if she were listening to beautiful music. 'Have you and Huddie done it?' whispered Dinah. 'You know, gone all the way?'

Crystal didn't change her expression. After a time, Dinah asked her again. 'C'mon, you can tell me. You've done it, haven't you?'

'Huddie and I love each other, and it's the most beautiful thing in the world.'

Crystal devoured mushy romance comics and it

was right out of those comic books, the way she talked about Huddie. Normally, it drove Dinah crazy, but tonight she was so caught up in her own melodrama she didn't even notice. Instead, she shared an intimacy of her own. 'If I stay a virgin any longer, I swear I'll break out all over. Does it hurt the first time?'

'The thing is, you're so passionate that even if it hurts a little, you don't care.'

'Mmm,' said Dinah, curling on her side and placing her hands between her knees. 'It sounds wonderful.'

'It is wonderful,' said Crystal. 'Huddie is wonderful. I am head over heels.'

'That's great, Crystal, it really is. He seems, um, nice.' Dinah was suddenly out of the comic books and back into real life.

'*Phh*. "Nice." I know you think he's just some dumb jock.'

'No, really. Charlie thinks he's terrific. And he was so brave when he rescued him and Ella and her friend.'

'Yeah he was. But how do you know Charlie thinks he's terrific?'

'He told me.'

'Since when do you and Charlie have so much to talk about?' Her voice was chilly. Crystal didn't like the way she'd said Charlie's name; something about the way it lingered on her tongue and came out in three syllables instead of two. 'Cha-ar-lie.'

Now it was Dinah's turn to get comic-book coy. 'There's something I've been wanting to tell you. It's about Charlie and me. We've been seeing each other. You know, privately.'

'Privately? What do you mean you're seeing Charlie privately?'

'We've been out on dates. I've been having lunch at the store with him for about a year. Stuff like that.' Crystal was jolted out of her Huddie haze. Dinah could see she was blinking hard, trying to hold back tears. Charlie was her brother, the one normal, living person in her family whom she liked. Of course she'd want to keep him to herself. How could Dinah have not thought of that before?

'Stuff like that,' repeated Crystal, as if each word were an invasion. 'Exactly how much of him have you seen *privately*?'

So Charlie had betrayed her too. She imagined their conversations: 'Poor dumb Crystal, she doesn't notice what's going on right before her own eyes.' Even in the dark, her anger was palpable.

'For Christ's sake, Crystal, I was going to tell you. I've been in love with him for years. It's only just recently that I found he loves me back.'

'You're in love with Charlie?' she asked incredulously. 'Were you waiting until you were married and had kids before either one of you told me?'

'Oh come on, Crystal, we just wanted to tell you when the time was right.'

'Does everyone know but me?'

'No,' said Dinah. 'Just Ella.'

'What about my mother?'

'We're waiting on that. You know, saving the best for last.'

'No offense, but I don't think you're what my mother has in mind for Charlie.'

Dinah tried to make her voice sound normal. 'What does your mother have in mind for Charlie?'

'I'm not sure,' said Crystal, turning on her side so she was facing Dinah. 'But I'm guessing it's not someone who is practically his sister.'

'I know, it's weird,' said Dinah.

'It's weird all right.'

Lost in their private thoughts, the girls began drifting off into sleep. 'I'll bet your dad would like Huddie very much,' Dinah whispered.

Crystal whispered back, 'Your dad would love Charlie to death, I know he would. Umm, I didn't mean to say it quite that way.'

This Sunday morning, as on the two previous Sundays since the Harmon's incident three weeks earlier, Charlie went with Ella to the Old Stone Baptist Church. Since the rock was thrown through his window, he'd been receiving threatening notes and hang-up phone calls. This church was one of the few places in town where he felt safe. On his first visit, Reverend Potts even talked about him in his sermon.

'We endure our struggles with dignity and pride,'

he had said. 'As humans are, we are limited by fear and trepidation, yet we are also blessed with the will of the ages – to survive and carry on. All of us, God's soldiers, are marching to His command. There are no heroes in His eyes. The only thing He demands is that we do our best and receive grace as it is given to us. Yesterday afternoon, during the unpleasant occurrences downtown with which you are all familiar, grace appeared in the form of a young man who had the courage to transcend his own nature and put his life in peril in order to protect two elders of this congregation. Had it not been for Charlie Landy . . .' Reverent Potts opened his large pink palm in Charlie's direction . . . 'Lord only knows what would have happened to our cherished sisters Ella Sykes and Pauline Brown. We give thanks for their safety and his presence. Please join me in welcoming Mr Landy into our hearts and our prayers.'

Maybe it was his six-foot-three-inch frame that caused the reverend's slight stoop, or maybe he was swayed by all his years and what he had seen with his hard mahogany eyes. Reverend Jeremiah Potts was a leader in the community, one of the few black men whose voice was heard by all. To the white people of Gainesville, he was a man who could be reasoned with, a man whose wisdom and poise demanded respect. To his congregation, he was exemplary: a leader and a sage. He chose his words carefully and never said more than was necessary. After the service, Charlie felt the urge to talk with him. 'Thank you for what you said in there, but there was nothing I did that anyone else wouldn't do in the same circumstance,' he said. The reverend had folded his hands together as if he were washing them, then moved his lips before he spoke. 'There's a light that shines on you, Mr Landy. Time is too precious. Don't waste it.'

'Reverend Potts, I don't want to take too much of your time, but can I ask you something?'

'Of course. Come, let's take a little walk.' There was a stream that ran behind the church, just a trickle of water that shone copper in the sunlight. There was a wooden bench by the stream where Reverend Potts gestured they might sit. The reverend leaned back against the bench, crossed his legs, and took off his shoes. He rubbed his feet, one at a time. 'By God, it's 1962. You'd think by now someone would have invented shoes that molded to your feet, rather than the other way around. There's a fortune to be made in the comfortable shoe business, I am certain of that.'

'I know what you mean,' said Charlie. 'I'm in a standing profession as well. By the end of the day my feet are just sore and burning.'

Charlie would remember this conversation years later when he bought his first pair of Nikes, sorry that the Reverend Potts, now departed, would never have the chance.

'Reverent Potts, did you always know you'd go

into this business, you know, the preaching business?'

By now the reverend had pulled off his socks and was resting his feet in the cool silt. 'I knew that I had a connection to people and that I had something to say,' said Reverend Potts. 'I also felt an easy connection to God. At church I got to know a lot of people and often they would seek me out to talk about their personal issues. It wasn't any one thing that got me here; it was the only thing. It happened so naturally that I can't remember a time when I didn't know I'd be a preacher. What about you, Mr Landy? What direction are you thinking of heading in?'

'I'm trying to figure that out. I expect I'll be drafted. There's part of me that knows I have to get away from here, that it's not my destiny to run a liquor store all my life. But now there's this girl. I'm in love with her. She lives here and I don't want to be away from her.'

Reverent Potts flexed his feet in the water. 'How much does she know about you?'

'Everything and nothing.'

'Mr Landy, I don't know much about you except that it's clear to me you have a gift. That woman you talk about must see that gift. If she loves you, she will understand that you have to use it. She may not like where it takes you but if she loves you, she won't stop you from doing what you have to do.'

They sat quietly on that bench for a while.

Then the reverend looked at his watch. 'Sunday breakfast, I'm afraid I have to go. Good luck with the girl. I hope to see you back here next Sunday.'

'I hope your feet feel better,' Charlie said. 'And yes, I'll see you next week.'

On the following Sunday, Charlie sat through Reverend Potts's sermon lost in thought: Dinah's perfume, the freckles on her shoulders, the way she toyed with her hair when she read, each vision its own blessing. He wondered how people in love ever got any work done. He thought about Huddie and the draft and what he'd read in the library this week about Fort Wadsworth.

After church, he asked Ella to walk with him down to the stream. They sat on the same bench on which he'd sat with the reverend. 'You were right about one thing,' he began. 'I am in love with her. With Dinah. Please don't laugh.'

'These old eyes, they see what's there for them to see. That girl has always been the one for you.'

'Is that all you have to say?' he asked.

'What more is there to say?' she answered.

Charlie squinted so that the space between his eyebrows pleated. 'There's something else I've been thinking. The other day, Huddie Harwood came to see me. He's a good kid, but there are things he hasn't figured out yet. We talked for a long time and he told me things he hadn't told anyone else. Maybe I even helped him. It came natural to me.' He told her he knew he would soon be drafted and about his conversation with Reverend Potts the week before. And then he told her what had only come clear to him earlier that week: that there must be a way he could be in the army and do what he felt he was meant to do. He told her how he'd gone to the library and found that there was this place called Fort Wadsworth in New York City. 'They have a program where you can train to be a chaplain in the army. I'm thinking I might try it. How does that sound?'

To Ella it sounded frightening but final. She heard it in the firmness of his voice and saw it in the way he held his head forward, not to the side as he did when he was asking a question. Charlie had already made up his mind. She knew she was supposed to feel happy, that Charlie was finding his calling. But she couldn't ignore the shadow of fear that followed this knowledge: that he would also leave Gainesville. She would be left in that house with Mrs Landy and Reggie. It was an unbearable thought – one that would only burden Charlie if he knew it. Ella vowed that he would never know it.

When someone you love has been taken from you, it is hard to believe that it won't happen again. Each time she said goodbye to Charlie, Dinah had to fight back the feeling of terror that she might never see him again. And each time she laid eyes on him again, she considered it Nothing short of a miracle. As he promised he would, Charlie came over after church. Dinah was watching from the window, waiting to catch sight of his old Pontiac. And when she did, she ran from the house to greet him. She stuck her head through the open window on the driver's side of the car and kissed him on the cheek. 'You're here!' she cried, her voice fresh with surprise.

'I told you I'd be here,' he said.

'I know you did, but you actually showed up!'

'I'll always show up,' he said, 'C'mon, get in.'

They drove to the Ichetucknee River. As a child, Charlie would come here with his family. The smell of the spring-fed water brought back a memory of his father. He was lying on the grass with his head resting on his arm. His face was worry free and young then. They were eating egg sandwiches and drinking Dr Pepper, which his mother poured from a thermos into paper cups. When they finished, they got up to take a walk down by the river. Charlie noticed that his father's arm was streaked with lines that went this way and that. He was too young to understand that they were just patterns of the grass imprinted on his father's arm, and when he asked him what it was, his father studied his arm carefully before answering. 'Oh, this? It's a map of Ireland.'

Charlie loved telling Dinah that story because it brought back his favorite thoughts about his dad, how funny and tender he could be, and how as a young boy, Charlie had hung on his every word. It never dawned on him until years later that it wasn't a map of Ireland at all. Dinah laughed at his story then confessed to him that Crystal had told her version of it many times before. 'Only the way she tells it, she asked your dad what was on his arm and he said it was a map of Sweden.'

They sat down on the grass, and Charlie lay down on his side, assuming the same pose that his father had all those years ago. Dinah sat down cross-legged beside him.

'So I told Ella,' he began. 'She didn't say much. She just said that she always knew that you were the one for me.' Dinah held his hand and rubbed her thumb back and forth over the knuckle on his thumb. His words and the sureness in his voice made her indescribably happy. When a baby sucks its thumb, it rubs the bridge of its nose back and forth as if to say, 'I've staked out this place and I am safe here.' Dinah's hand took ownership of Charlie's thumb that way.

'And Crystal? How did she react?'

Dinah wondered how much she should tell him about their conversation, how hurtful it had been. 'She was really upset that we hadn't told her. She said that given you were almost my brother, the whole thing was a little weird.' That's as much as she wanted to say.

'And?' he asked.

'And that's pretty much it.'

'So she thinks this is *weird*?'

Charlie was like a dog sometimes. Dinah knew he wasn't going to let go of the subject until he'd picked this bone dry. She supposed it was a compliment, the way he studied her words and held her accountable for them, but it was also an encumbrance. She took a deep breath. 'I think it's more than that. Crystal and I share everything – same classes, same house, same bedroom, my mother. You're her big brother – the one thing she has that I don't. She's not in the mood for sharing you.'

'But she's got Huddie.'

'That's different, don't you see?' Her voice went up a notch. 'She knows I think Huddie's kind of a clod. She idolizes you. You and Huddie are in entirely different leagues. You're not even in the same ballpark.'

He didn't get it. 'Let me understand. Crystal is worried that you and I are like brother and sister, so our relationship is kind of unnatural. Yet she's upset that we're together because, while she already has a boyfriend, I'm the real thing? What's that if not a little weird?'

Were all boys this dense, or was it just Charlie? 'Don't be silly, she's gaga about Huddie.'

Charlie buried his head in his arm, trying to figure out how she could obliterate his logic in one sentence. When he looked up again, there was hope in his eyes. 'So then she doesn't have strange feelings toward me?'

'Forget it,' said Dinah. 'She and Huddie will be married by the time we finish this conversation.'

'She told you that?'

'Told me what?'

'About her and Huddie getting married.'

Dinah nodded.

'He told me that too. Did she also tell you that he wants to enlist in the army?'

'No!'

'I don't think she knows yet,' he said. 'We can't tell her.'

'The army? Why would anyone volunteer to go into the army?' She was grateful to be talking about something other than Crystal and weird relationships.

'He's got all kinds of reasons. The draft, his father, trying to do the right thing.'

'Why doesn't he just go work for the phone company, like everyone else in our class?'

Charlie sat up. 'That's a pretty snotty thing to say, don't you think?'

'No. Most of them are nitwits who only care about football and beer anyway.'

'Do you think only nitwits would join the army?'

'Nitwits with suicidal tendencies.'

'You're in rare form today,' Charlie said. 'Have you been spending time with my mother lately?'

She knew that wasn't a compliment. 'Why, because I have an opinion that might not agree with one you're having?' She had let go of his thumb by now.

'Are we having a fight?' he asked.

'We are having something in which you seem to be judging me for the way I see Huddie and all those other kids at school.'

'Oh that. My mother has a word for it. She calls me "a prig" when she thinks I'm acting self-righteous. It drives her crazy.'

'I can see why,' said Dinah.

A shadow of hurt crossed his face, only for an instant, but long enough for her never to want to see it again.

'I'm sorry,' she said. 'Please, let's not ever fight again.'

'It's okay,' he said. 'Everyone has disagreements from time to time.'

Dinah folded her lips so they looked like a straight line in a stick-figure face. Then she said, 'Not us. We're not like everyone.'

Charlie knew he was at an unfair disadvantage. He tried to convince himself that this was the perfect time to tell her his plans, but deep down inside he knew he'd always regret it if he did.

When Charlie returned home that night, he found his mother and Reggie in the living room, hunched over a Scrabble board. 'What kind of a word is "un"? There's no such word as "un."' His mother was shouting at Reggie.

'Yes, ma'am, there is too,' he argued back. 'I want un blanket,' he enunciated carefully. 'Or, "she baked un apple pie."'

'Look it up,' demanded Victoria. She slammed the dictionary so hard next to him that his letters jumped out of their rack. He jumped too. 'There's no such a thing as "un blanket," or "un apple pie,"' she glared at him. 'Honestly, why do I bother?'

'Hi, Mom, hi, Reggie. Having fun?' he asked.

'Me and Mrs Landy playing Scrabble,' said Reggie. 'We're working on my spelling.'

It amazed Charlie how Reggie was able to keep up his spirits in the face of his mother's outbursts.

'That's good, Reggie,' said Charlie. 'You'll be a spelling bee champ if you keep this up.'

Charlie leaned over his mother. 'Can we talk? I have some news.'

Victoria got a vague look in her eyes, then turned toward Reggie. 'Reggie and I have some news too, don't we Reggie?' she said, her voice going up and down like she was leading a singalong.

'Yes we do,' said Reggie. 'We sure do.'

'Reggie and I saw Dr Simons today.' Up and down, up and down. 'Dr Simons is going to make Reggie some teeth. He says it will take him about six months to finish a mouthful and that no one who ever meets Reggie afterward will ever be able to tell.'

'It's been so long since I've had teeth,' said Reggie. 'Seems like I've been sucking food all my life.'

'It'll be great,' said Charlie, while studying his mother. Her hair had been freshly cut and teased by Jésus. Her nails were perfectly oval and pink as a baby's blanket. She had more clothes in her closet than places to go in them, and however age chose to play itself out on her face she had some product to cover it. The thought struck Charlie that his mother had run out of ways to make herself over. Now she would work on Reggie.

Again, he asked his mother if they could talk. 'Darling, can't it wait until we finish this game? I think he's beginning to get the hang of it.'

'It's pretty important,' said Charlie. 'But sure, finish your Scrabble game.'

'Damn, I hate when you do that, Charlie Landy. Pulling that long face, and that pitiable tone. "But sure, finish your Scrabble game,"' she said in a voice that was petulant and unflattering. 'What is so important that Reggie and I can't even enjoy a little learning and recreation without you having to interrupt us? This better be good.'

This wasn't the time to argue with his mother or raise her temper. So he said what he had to say as neutrally as a TV weatherman. 'I've decided that I'm going to become a chaplain in the army. I'm going to attend a school right outside of New York City. Then I'm going to enlist in the army. There, was that good enough?'

Victoria never took her eyes off of her letters.

'Mom, did you hear anything I said?' Charlie was losing his weatherman composure. 'I'm due to report to Fort Wadsworth by Labor Day.'

'Sure I did,' said Victoria. 'What, do you think

I can't do two things at once? You said some hogwash about wanting to join the army and become a chaplain. I heard every word. Reggie, it's your turn. Don't go taking hours. And here,' she tapped the cover of the dictionary. 'Look it up before you put down gibberish.'

'So what do you think?' asked Charlie.

'What do I think about what?' answered Victoria, leaning over ever so slightly to catch a glimpse of Reggie's letters.

'About the army? About me becoming a chaplain?'

'You've always been a dreamer, sweetheart. Of course you aren't going into the army. And why on earth would you want to go to New York City? Besides, who will run the store?'

'Mom, I really am going into the army. I'm going to become a chaplain. And I've given the store a lot of thought. I think you should run it. You're great with details and organization. I have a hunch you'd be terrific at it.'

Victoria looked at Charlie as if he had just told her she had lipstick on her teeth. 'I don't run stores,' she said, fixing her gaze back on the Scrabble board.

'We're not getting anywhere with this conversation,' said Charlie.

'I've gotten where I want to get,' she said. 'You're not going into the army, and I'm not taking over any liquor store. It seems clear enough to me.'

'Mom . . .' But why bother?

Charlie's shoulders dropped and he started to walk away when Reggie spoke up. 'Mr Landy, If you don't mind my saying so, I think it's a great thing you doing, becoming a man of the cloth like Rex Humbard.'

'Thanks Reggie. I won't be as famous as Rex Humbard and you won't see me on TV, but I do hope to have my own ministry someday.'

Reggie stared at the floor, as if he'd already said too much. Charlie turned to back to his room.

Victoria stared at Reggie because if she looked at Charlie, she knew she would cry. Charlie had a big head, just like Maynard's, and his round face, as smooth and impassive as a slab of marble, was remarkable for its lack of guile. She envied his clarity. When Charlie knew what he needed to know, there was no changing his mind. With all of her petulant fits and refusal to see the truth, Victoria was able to put off reality for a time. But eventually even her own tricks of denial would wear her down. Charlie was different that way. She knew he meant it when he said he was leaving. She didn't know if she could bear another loss.

Victoria still hadn't recovered from the fire. She was still bereft over the things that had been taken all at once. Things of no value, like her music box with the skaters on top and the remains of her tooth inside, were as precious to her as the antique bone china in the dining-room cabinets. Where did Crystal's pink bedroom go? Did all the chocolate syrup from the soda fountain melt into the ground? Their wedding album, with its heavy gilded pages and white leather cover that said 'Victoria and Maynard Landy, September 22, 1936' in gold letters – did that fall as soot into a neighbor's backyard?

It became a ritual. Victoria would be about to fall asleep or be driving into town, and out of nowhere, something small, Maynard's prized model of the Orange Blossom Special locomotive, or big, like the white leather couch in the 'Rocky Graziano' living room, would appear and burst into flame. She'd watch the vinyl melt and twist and curdle into a small mass, or the couch burn to cinders. She'd see Anita Bryant sitting in the living room, and hear the sweetness of her tentative voice as she sang, ''Til There Was You.' Was that just a vapor of memory or did it really happen? The police never discovered the exact cause of the fire. The fact that there was an explosion pointed to faulty electric wiring, but they would never trace its origins. After that, life became divided into 'before the fire,' and 'after.' She still wore the five-carat ring that she'd retrieved that night. It made her feel close to Maynard and was the only gift of his that survived. Somehow, she was able to put aside the fact that the ring was the reason Maynard ran back into the burning house.

Now there was going to be another marker: 'after

Charlie.' This time, she worried that whatever glue and willpower had kept her together after Maynard's death would crumble and turn to dust. Maynard's steadfastness and decency had been the cornerstone of her life. His kindness and reliability had allowed her to be who she was, to live the life she'd always dreamed about. Then Maynard was gone, and Crystal moved in with Dinah, and now Charlie, who gave himself over to her and Ella and Reggie so that their lives could continue as best they could, was deserting her as well. It was time for him to live a life that was his for a change. How could she deny him that?

Nothing was the way it was. The fight with Crystal, the fact that she would be graduating from high school in a few months, being in love with Charlie, the realization that this was but a moment in her life and, like it or not, everything was about to change – these things were like a jitterbug in Dinah's brain. They were loud and constant and always moving. When Señor Swanky called one night, she answered the phone.

'Hi sweetheart, how are you?' he asked. Normally, she would have said, 'Fine, how are you? Here's Mom.' But on this night, his emphasis was on the 'are' and she thought he really wanted to know.

'To tell you the truth, I'm kind of confused.' She told him about Charlie. 'He knows things I don't know, and it scares me sometimes. What if he thinks I'm someone I'm not?' And she told him about Crystal. 'She's so cold to me, we barely speak. How could I tell her about Charlie and me before I was sure myself? We're best friends. We can't suddenly not be best friends because of this.'

Barone listened and never tried to hurry her along. 'I'm talking your ear off, aren't I?' she said, suddenly caught in her own embarrassment.

'This is a funny time in your life, sweetheart,' he said. 'You're not a little girl, but you're not quite grown up either. Being somebody's girl-friend, especially somebody like Charlie Landy, calls for a kind of maturity. It's like Eddie the cat. Suddenly somebody counts on you for things no one's ever wanted from you before. You're still somebody's daughter – you'll always be that. But you're becoming more, how shall I say, womanly. That's different for you and for Crystal. Don't worry, you'll both get used to it.'

It was so queer that he used the word *womanly*, thought Dinah, though it was neat that he listened and treated her like a grown-up. 'You're probably right,' she said, 'it just feels that everyone suddenly has secrets and it didn't used to be that way.'

Dinah remembered one August night when she was six years old. The air was close and sticky, as if it hadn't been changed in days. They'd finished dinner at around seven o'clock. Her mother had cleared the table and stacked the dishes in the sink, getting ready to wash them. 'Those can wait,' her father had said, taking her mother's arm. 'Let's hunt down a Good Humor man before it gets dark.' They'd headed toward the park downtown and sure enough, as the sky turned a dusky shade of purple they heard the familiar chiming of the ice cream bells. Her dad had waved down the truck. He'd ordered her mom a Cherry Twin Popsicle, himself a Fudgsicle, and her a Creamsicle, her favorite. They'd gone into the park and sat on swings, each with the faraway look that people get when they eat ice cream. As Dinah pumped her legs back and forth, a little bit at a time, she'd lost her concentration and dropped the Creamsicle. In moments, an orange and white river was running beneath her feet. 'Don't worry, sweetie,' her dad had said. 'If we run, I'll bet we can catch up with him and buy you another.' The truck was slowly clanking down the street. In no time, they were standing in front of the square freezer door, and the Good Humor man was reaching into what seemed his bottomless supply to find her another Creamsicle. 'We could use a few extra napkins,' her mom had said. By the time they'd gotten back to the park to mop up the mess, it was nearly dark. The river had stopped flowing and a mass of black flies had formed a crust above it.

'How did they all know to come here?' asked Dinah.

'If you see one, you can be sure there are dozens nearby. It's not in the nature of flies to be singular,' her father had said.

She loved to tell Crystal that story. 'No one even got mad at me for spilling my ice cream,' she'd say. 'We just ran after the truck, and he bought me another.'

She never forgot about her father's words: 'It's not in the nature of flies to be singular.' They came back to her now only in a different configuration. It's not in the nature of secrets to be singular, she thought. If there was one secret, there were probably dozens more close by.

CHAPTER 17

It was typical of Charlie to sense when people –
Jésus, Huddie – had a secret they wanted to
reveal to him. That was Charlie's gift, plucking
a filament of a thought out of the air. The paradox
was that when it came to himself he could be just
the opposite. 'I swear, sometimes you're as thick
as a big fat slab of pork,' Victoria had said to him
the day after he told her he was going into the
army.

All morning she had been screaming at him.
'You're leaving me high and dry, trapped in this
house with Reggie and Ella. Do you have any idea
what position that puts me in? I know it's hard to
tell from looking at me, but I AM NOT A
FRIGGIN' SOCIAL WORKER. People say, "Oh,
that Charlie Landy, he's so kind, he's so empathetic."
He is to everyone but his own mother! I know what
you are. You are a selfish, hypocritical egomaniac.
That's what you are!' Then she said the thing about
the slab of pork. 'If your father were alive today, you
wouldn't be doing this to me.'

'If my father were alive today,' he answered sadly,
'I would have been gone long ago.'

She made aggressive staccato sounds as she cracked her gum. Her lips curled and contorted, and she never took her eyes off of Charlie. It was as if all the gum chattering was Victoria duking it out with herself. Finally she stopped and put one hand on her hip. 'Go on, go to New York City, go to the army, just get the hell out of here.'

'I'll always come back,' he said, trying to soften her fury.

'Nah. Once you're gone, you're gone. I know that.'

'No one is ever completely gone,' he said.

Victoria turned and walked out of the room, the sound of her cracking gum diminishing the further away she got.

Charlie thought about that conversation later that day as he drove over to the Glades area. He'd told Dinah he had something important he wanted to discuss with her. 'Oh no, not more about Crystal,' she had said.

'No, it's not that. This is pretty serious.'

Charlie knew he would have to explain things about himself that he never thought would matter to anybody else but Ella. Dinah had always accepted his intuitions. She never questioned how he knew what he knew, or whether or not he was right. Often, she'd made fun of how much he talked – 'enough for both of us,' she'd say – but she never seemed to realize where his words were coming from.

When he got to the Lockhart house, no one was

there but Dinah and the cat. A house takes on a different personality depending upon who's in it. When Tessie was there, the place bustled with her nervousness. She'd run into the kitchen to get a pack of Marlboros from the cabinet where she always kept two cartons at a time. Then she'd skitter around to every other room wondering where she'd left her matches or last put down her ashtray.

Crystal always left droppings of clothes, food, or whatever was occupying her at the time. She still hadn't gotten used to the fact that there was no Ella to pick up behind her. Occasionally Dinah would sweep through the house, gather all of Crystal's detritus into her arms, and dump them onto her bed. 'There's more to you than meets the eye,' she would say, and Crystal would sass her right back: 'At least I have things to leave around. Unlike other people who might as well be living in a *nunnery*.' But all that was before Dinah told her about Charlie, when they were still as taunting and bitchy to each other as only two sisters can be.

Charlie found Dinah sitting alone in the Florida room with Eddie in her lap, and the house felt peaceful. The late afternoon sun was like a benediction. Dinah had a look of expectation on her face and was holding on to Eddie the way a frightened child might cling to a stuffed animal. Charlie sat opposite her on a love seat with a bamboo pattern. The cat glared at Charlie. *What you have to say better be important, Buster. I don't have all day.*

'Where is everybody?' he asked.

'Crystal and Huddie are off *studying*,' she winked. 'If you know what I mean. My mom's at a barbecue at the Bechs'. She was hilarious before she left. She gulped down a glass of white wine and said, 'I'll never make it through the night on Flora's apple lemon punch.' God, those people seem like such morons.'

'Oh, you mean the Baptists?'

'Yeah. They're such creeps, always acting holier than thou then cracking these stupid dirty jokes and double intendras or whatever they're called.'

'Some people make religion look silly,' he said. 'It doesn't have to be that way.'

'Don't you think anyone who blindly believes all that stuff is pretty silly to begin with?' she asked.

'Sure, if they believe it without thinking about it they are. But if they feel it in their hearts, well that's something else.'

Dinah could tell that Charlie was about to set off on one of his jags, but she wasn't in the mood.

'Charlie, didn't you say you had something important to discuss with me?' she asked.

'Oddly enough,' he said, 'what we were just talking about has something to do with what I wanted to say.' He cleared his throat and wiped a stream of sweat from his neck. 'I'm one of those people, you know, who feels God in his heart.

'Ever since I was little, I've known things – things

297

I don't know why I should know. Sometimes I can tell what's going to happen before it happens. It's like finding out you can paint or you have a good voice. You want to test it and use it and do the best you can with it. Lately, it's become clear to me: I want to become a preacher. I want to have my own congregation.'

Dinah held Eddie tighter.

'In order to do that,' Charlie continued, 'I'll have to go away for a while. There's a school for chaplains that the army runs in New York City. I can go there for three months and then go into the army as a chaplain. After that, they can send me anywhere in the world.'

It was so quiet Charlie could hear the refrigerator rumble like a hungry stomach. Even the cat seemed frozen in place.

'That's nice for you,' said Dinah, her words rigid.

'I know this probably comes as a shock,' he said. 'But here's the thing: I want you to wait for me. Whatever I'm going to do, I want you to be a part of it. Do you understand?'

By now, the sun had set and the house was shrouded in darkness. Neither of them budged from their chairs to turn on any lights. It was dark enough so they couldn't read the expression on each other's faces. All they had to go on was the sound of their voices and the articulation of their gestures.

Dinah covered her eyes with her hands. Eddie tried to nuzzle under her knee. Charlie got up from the love seat and sat at the edge of her chair. He tucked his arm around her shoulder. 'Don't you see what I'm saying? I love you and I want you to wait for me. We can do this together, Dinah. We can give each other strength.'

Dinah put her hands down. She spoke with long spaces between her words. 'I love you, Charlie. I respect what you're saying and what you want to do. I'm glad you and God are so chummy. I've been around for nineteen years and He hasn't said a word to me. I don't mean that sarcastically. I just mean that how am I supposed to go on this mission with you when all I know about God is that he took my father when I was ten and now he wants you. It doesn't exactly make me a fan.'

Charlie dropped his chin to his chest and thought hard. 'This doesn't have to be about you and God. It's about you and me. It's about you being who you are, and me being who I am. Who I am happens to involve Him. Who you are, doesn't. That's fine.'

Dinah squirmed as she pulled her legs from under her. Eddie rubbed his head against Charlie's arm. *Just leave things as they are and pay attention to me.* 'Supposing we get married,' said Dinah. 'Not that I'm proposing, but just suppose we do. Then you become a minister and you have a congregation. Every Sunday you go off to church and I do what? I play tennis? I go fishing? How would that look to everyone? And don't preachers' wives have to do stuff like hold bake sales and visit sick people? What if I don't want to do those things? Don't you think you need a wife who will be in the front row each Sunday smiling up at you as you deliver your sermons? And what about the army? Am I supposed to sit around and wait three years while you go to New York City and study to be a chaplain, and then when you get sent off to some godforsaken place?'

Her eyes filled as she comprehended the weight and consequences of his plans.

'I love you, Charlie. I really do. But you have a hell of a nerve making me fall in love with you, then telling me you're leaving, and oh, by the way, you want to become a preacher. Shouldn't you have come with some sort of warning label? "Do not fall in love unless you are prepared to sit around waiting for many years, after which you will get to bake lots of cookies and iron your husband's dresses." That's asking an awful lot, Charlie, it really is.'

'Ministers don't wear dresses,' he said. 'You're thinking about priests.'

'That's not the point. You know what I mean.' Her voice was so charged with anger that Eddie figured he'd done something wrong and scooted under the couch.

'I want to marry you, Dinah. I thought you wanted what I did. I can't imagine my life without you.'

'You've done a pretty good job of imagining your life without me,' she said. 'It works fine for you. There's not one bit of it that works for me.'

Orange Blossom might look like. Every day they'd sit at the dining-room table making lists, jotting down notes of what would go where to make it as authentic as they could. It was the fall of 1962, during the time that Reggie was getting his teeth fixed and Charlie was off to Fort Wadsworth in New York City, so the two of them were happy for the distraction. For Victoria, it was a return to a life she thought she had left behind: fabric swatches, paint chips, decorators, workmen to order around. She'd nearly forgotten how she thrived on all of it, how it got her creative juices flowing in a way that nothing else, not even Reggie's makeover, had.

For Reggie, all those hours in the dentist's chair, watching his reflection in Dr Simon's spectacles as he slowly filled in all the spaces, was a time of rebirth. He would go from having no purpose to becoming a citizen of the world. Reggie, who'd always been on the other side from where he felt normal people were, was now closer than he'd ever been to not being different. He renewed the vows he made to himself after Maynard's death, only this time with more vigor and determination. He would help Victoria. He would help Ella. No, he would take care of Victoria, he would take care of Ella. He would become the man of their odd little household and pick up where Charlie Landy left off. He'd work in the saloon and make it a success. He knew how to do lots of things that no one would guess he knew. All along he had things to say. He was just waiting for teeth so that he could say them in the way they needed to be said.

Victoria hired Frank Bowman, the decorator who was responsible for the successful specialty restaurants like Sundowners and Pelican Point. She told Reggie that Bowman had a rare appreciation for thematic design. 'He gives himself over to it like nobody's business,' she'd said, in what was surely one of the understatements of her life.

Bowman embraced the train theme the way he once had crab and lobsters. He even took to wearing a blue-and-white-striped engineer's hat while he worked. His philosophy was consistent and surefire. 'The moment a customer walks through the doors of one of my establishments, he should be transported to another time and place. If the establishment is properly executed, the customer will be in such a state of psychological disorientation that he will be oblivious to the usual restraints associated with spending money.'

The doors to this particular oblivion would be made from extruded aluminum. They would be double swinging doors, as shimmery as fish scales. Each door would have a round glass window the size of a man's head and at eye level for most people. In the train itself, these windows served a useful function, giving the traveler the opportunity to see if someone was coming through from the opposite direction. On the streets of Gainesville, the daytime sun would bounce off the aluminum like lightning. At night, the reflection of the blinking orange and green neon Orange Blossom Special sign would beckon like the giddy entrance to a funhouse. How could you not come inside?

The walls would be sheathed in crimson satin. Pale yellow Venetian blinds with slats the width of rulers would cover the windows. There would be rattan seats with high backs and broad arms, exactly like the handsome ones they used in the old parlor cars. Bowman had an obsessive eye for detail and faithfully reproduced the ornate counter with all its flutes and flowers, and the marble countertop, the marble veined with green and purple. Even the cash register would be from a time when cash registers were representative of art deco design rather than functional boxes. Overhead, two natural palm-leaf fans would churn the cool air. The light fixtures would be electric replicas of old gas lamps, and the soft light they gave off would bathe everything in sepia. Framed artifacts such as a white linen towel with an embossed orange and a menu featuring caviar, turbot, and crème caramel for five dollars would hang behind the cash register.

The Orange Blossom Special was a perfect jewel, a treasure from another time tucked between Florsheims and the Fremac luncheonette. Even the drinks had train-related names like Full Steam Ahead and First Class Only. A sign above the bar invited patrons to 'Chug Chug.' And just in case they missed the point, Bowman had another brainstorm. The coup de grâce, he called it.

'The two of you will wear what the porters would have worn on that train. Modern, of course, but they'll be reminiscent of the old uniforms. A soft melon-color. An A-line skirt short enough to accentuate your shapely legs.' He winked at Victoria. 'The fabric will be lightweight and wrinkle resistant. A little capped sleeve and Peter Pan collar.' He touched Victoria's shoulder. 'Precious. Maybe a vest instead of the jacket.' He folded his hands together. 'For him, white pants with the melon stripe down the side. A vest with 'Sykes' embroidered above the breast pocket. A hat perhaps.'

It gave Victoria the chills to watch Bowman in action.

'No porter's outfit for me. No, sir, no, thank you.' Reggie broke the spell. 'I've already worn that uniform. I'm a businessman now and that's how I'll dress.'

Victoria flushed. 'I'm certainly not going to be the only one prancing around here like a goddamned cantaloupe,' she said. 'C'mon Reggie. It'll be fun.'

'I've made my decision and that's that,' he said.

'Never you mind,' said Bowman waving his hands as if to clear the air of confrontation. 'I've come up with an alternative plan. Pins. You both, will wear Orange Blossom Special pins. Subtle but authentic.'

*　　*　　*

There was so much buzz around the opening of the saloon that in the days leading up to it, everyone's letters were filled with some news of it. Crystal wrote to Huddie at the Marine Recruit Depot on Parris Island:

> How I wish you could see what's going on here. Everyone's gone nuts over the redesign of Charlie's old liquor store. They've turned it into a saloon. My mother is spending a fortune to make the place look like the replica of some fancy old train that Reggie used to work on. She's hired that phony baloney decorator who does all the stupid fish restaurants with the fake nets and rusty anchors. If you ask me, the place will look more like a dance studio than a bar, but at least it gives her something to do. Reggie's got a bunch of new teeth that are whiter than any Colgate ad you've ever seen. It's amazing what a difference a set of choppers can make.
>
> I hope they are not working you too hard. In your last letter you said you'd lost a little weight. Don't lose any more. I want as much of my Huddie to hold on to as possible. I love you. Your adoring wife to be, Crystal

Ella wrote to Charlie:

Crystal joined a sorority at the University. She seems to be very popular. I saw Dinah a few weeks ago. She asked how you were doing. I told her you were doing the work you set out to do. She said she is working hard at the University. She asked to be remembered to you. Your mother and Reggie seem to have gone hogwild over the saloon. I never thought I'd live to see Reggie Sykes and Mrs Landy fighting over the color of shelf paint. You wouldn't recognize him. He hasn't smiled this much since he was a boy.

It is hard for me to picture the things you are seeing in New York City. I am glad to hear that you feel you are finally fitting into your own skin. I pray for you every day. Your friend, Ella Sykes

Tessie wrote to Jerry:

Dinah's having a hard time going to college and living at home. Crystal's whooping it up in her sorority house and seems to have no time for her. She has made one girl-friend – a mousy little thing named Hedda who is always apologizing for herself. Dinah says she's a genius. There is no sign of a boy on the horizon. Her grades are good but her mood is horrible. Everything I do embarrasses her and we fight a lot. What am I supposed to do?

The man is getting old. He's sixty soon. Now that his wife has died he wants me to move to Miami Beach and be with him. How can I leave Dinah? My job? My life here?

V is spending all her time with Reggie getting the new bar ready. They're having a big grand opening next week. I bought a new shift to wear to the party. I envy how V can get so caught up in stuff like this. She doesn't seem to be bothered with depressions and moodiness like some other people I know.

Sorry to talk your ear off. I don't expect you to have the answers to all my questions, but who else can I ask?

And Barone wrote to Tessie:

Of course I'll be there for the party. It's the biggest thing to happen in Florida since Jai Alai!

The big bed in the big room is empty. The sound of the waves outside is sometimes so loud and hungry. Without you here, maybe I will feed the bed and the room to the sea. Dottie, you are *my* Orange Blossom Special.

(Here, a drawing with Tessie's face, arms, and legs sticking out of an orange that is rolling down a lane about to hit the pins.)

Yours til' the Orange Bowls, Barone (STRIKE!)

On the night before the big opening, Dinah and Tessie had a fight. It started when Tessie asked Dinah what she was going to wear to the party.

'Do you think I've given it a moment's thought?' Dinah snapped.

'Well yes, I thought maybe you had.'

'Has it occurred to you that I don't care at all about the party?'

Tessie knew that tone of voice, filled with nettles. But this time it had something woeful and disappointed in it as well.

'Sweetie, you don't have to go,' she said.

'Oh, yes I do,' said Dinah. 'I have to go, all right. Not only that. I'm bringing a date.'

'Wonderful.' Tessie's eyes lit up.

'I'm bringing Eddie,' she said hugging the cat close to her. She rested her head on his and started to dance around the room singing the pop song 'Eddie My Love.'

Silently, Tessie entreated Jerry. 'Give me a hand here. Help me say the right thing.' Then, with some trepidation, she said to Dinah, 'You're not really thinking of bringing Eddie. That's a joke, right?'

'Hell it isn't.' Dinah whirled around. 'I go, he goes. Why's that a joke?'

'Honey, you know what they say about spinsters? How no one will love them but their cats?'

The moment those words left her mouth, Tessie knew she'd said the worst thing possible. She tried to recover. 'Of course, I'm not implying that you're a spinster.'

'Of course not,' said Dinah. 'But if no one in the world loved me but Eddie, that would be fine too.' Eddie tried to writhe out of her arms.

'That's ridiculous. There are so many people who love you.'

'Yeah. Name three.'

Tessie hated being put in a corner like this. 'Don't be silly, I don't want to play this game.'

'It's not a game,' insisted Dinah. 'Name three. And they have to be living.'

'Well me, naturally. Crystal. And Charlie. Charlie Landy.'

Dinah got that tone in her voice again. 'You're my mother, so that doesn't count. You have to love me. Crystal has barely said a word to me since she became a Tri Delt. And Charlie Landy will never speak to me again after how awful I was to him before he went to New York City. So that makes one.'

Tessie stared at her little girl, all grown up now. Her body was all taut and sharp, at peace only when she was asleep. She still had the same large, searching eyes, but her expression had changed from one of a quizzical child to a wary adult wondering when the next blow would come. When she smiled, which didn't happen often these days, the world was sunny.

'Your dad makes two,' said Tessie. 'Who says we can't count the dead?'

Dinah got a faraway look in her eyes and started singing again as she and Eddie waltzed out of the room.

That night, Tessie went through her drawers looking for a pair of gold hoop earrings to wear with her new shift. Tucked way in the back of everything was a rumpled old red bandanna that she used to wear like a turban over her pin curls. Jerry used to say that she looked like the Maharani of Mars.

The next morning, when Dinah came to breakfast, she found the neatly ironed bandanna folded into a square next to her orange juice. On top of it was a note in her mother's squiggly hand:

> This is for Eddie. Tie it around his neck tonight and he'll look like the coolest cat at the party. I love you, and it does too count. Mom

When Tessie opened her sandwich later that afternoon at her desk at Lithographics, she found this note from her daughter.

> Thanks Mom. I've got you, dad, and Eddie. That's more than enough.

And early that evening, before Barone came to pick her up for the party, Tessie slipped this note into her Jerry Box.

You are one shrewd son of a bitch. Pardon
my French.

To Tessie, Christmas in Gainesville always seemed
like an apology. There were no fireplaces. Those
fake Santas coming down the chimney and silly
snowmen with their carrot stick noses and zigzag
twig smiles seemed to be trying too hard. She
hated the fake fir trees that looked to her like
Fuller Brushes, and the pathetic carpets of white
felt that were supposed to pass for snow.
Christmas was the hardest time without Jerry. She
knew that Barone would shower her with expensive gifts – including the little orange something
that he promised in his note – and that Dinah
would get her something, grudgingly and at the
last minute. But all of it seemed like a record
playing at the wrong speed, a warped reminder of
a past that never stopped playing over and over
in her memory. So Tessie was grateful that Victoria
and Reggie had decided to hold their big opening
bash on Christmas Eve. A lot of people in town
thought it was selfish, even a little high-minded.
But it didn't keep any of them from showing up
at seven p.m. when Victoria, splendid for this night
in her white tight pants with a melon stripe down
each leg and a matching melon-colored vest, threw
open the shiny double doors and shouted to the
waiting crowd 'The Orange Blossom Special is
open for business. Y'all step aboard for the ride
of a lifetime.'

Klieg lights blazed through the night skies beckoning everyone to the party. There was a band that included a kazoo, two fiddles, and a banjo, and it serenaded the crowd all night long. There were pretty girls dressed in short white skirts with melon-colored vests serving platters of crab cakes, thick pink slices of steak, and little black squares of bread with dots of sour cream and caviar. Of course the liquor, all of it free, was everywhere. In the background, the sound of a chugging train played nonstop punctuated occasionally by a tooting whistle. At midnight, everyone was told to step into the street for a special surprise. Fireworks cracked open the sky. The smell of sulfur and champagne filled the air. People clapped and shouted out drunken accolades: 'Holy Toledo!' or 'What in the Sam Hill was that?' It was the kind of party that made people feel as if they were having a good time, even if they weren't. Before they left, all the guests got gifts: cloisonné pins with the Orange Blossom Special diesel and the logo beneath it.

Turned out that Eddie was more of a party cat than anyone imagined. He spent most of the evening calmly snuggled in the pouch that Dinah had fashioned for him with his head buried under her arm. Only once, when the photographer from the *Gainesville Sun* came around and said to Dinah, 'Who's the little guy?' did Eddie poke his head out and look up for a picture.

The next day, under a photo of a smiling Dinah

holding a solemn Eddie staring right into the photographer's lens, there was a caption in large boldface type that said: 'Is There Anyone in Gainesville Who WASN'T at the Orange Blossom Special Last Night? (see story, page 3). Dinah Lockhart on board with pal Eddie.' In the article, Victoria was quoted as saying, 'It's about time that Gainesville entered the Sixties. Keep your eyes on Landy, Bowman, and Sykes. You haven't seen anything yet.' Frank Bowman told the paper that in all modesty, he thought that the Orange Blossom Special was his greatest masterpiece to date. Phil Ryan, owner of Ryan's Bar and Grill, called the whole extravaganza a tasteless farce. 'It was like a circus, for Pete's sake,' he said. 'Whatever happened to plain old elbow grease and hard work?'

Ella clipped the story and the picture from the paper and sent it to Charlie.

Your mother, bless her heart, is very happy. I believe that she and Reggie will be very successful with the saloon. It was a sight to see last night, Reggie talking and smiling at everyone he met. He is the toast of the town. I thought you'd like this article and picture of Dinah and her cat. She is such a pretty girl. Her eyes are sad. I pray for you every day. Your friend, Ella Sykes.

Charlie was walking back to his barracks after a long day of classes. It was snowing. Not the fluffy white stuff he'd imagined as a child. These were meager snowflakes that melted the moment they hit the ground. Nor was it the winter wonderland of storybooks, just lead skies and banks of ice black with soot. How odd to yearn for Christmas in Gainesville, he thought, dreading the upcoming holiday. At least at home he'd be with people he loved, some of them anyway. This was going to be one bleak and lonely Christmas. Thank God he could go home for New Year's. Funny, for all the thought he'd given to getting away, it never once dawned on him that he'd be homesick. Remember how this feels, he said to himself. It will come in handy when you're talking to young recruits who feel the same.

When Charlie got to his bunk, he found Ella's letter. He lay on his bed savoring the thick envelope in his hands. He'd lain on this bed staring at the gray cement walls around him so often, that he'd identified figures in the irregularity of the surface. There was a duck face, a mushroom cap, and a lumpy area that he could swear was the map of Florida. Since he arrived at Fort Wadsworth, he felt the way he had after the fire and his father's death, like who he was and where he belonged had been pulled out from under him. He opened the envelope and pulled out the newspaper clipping. For a long while he studied Eddie's guileless face and Dinah's sweet round eyes. He ran his fingers over Eddie's nose and could feel it, damp and cool. Then he brought the picture to his face and closed his eyes. His fingers remembered being entwined in Dinah's hair and the sudden softness of the back of her neck. When he looked up again, Eddie was staring down at him. He saw the cusp of the moon in the cat's eyes and felt a great tide of loneliness. Eddie's gaze was impatient and insistent: *What are you waiting for?*

Charlie leaped ahead in his thoughts. There he was with Dinah. That was right. There was something else, though he couldn't quite make it out. That night, as he lay staring at the duck face, the mushroom cap, and the map of Florida, he wrote to Dinah.

How can I tell others to listen to their hearts when my own is breaking with how much I love you? I know how you feel about itinerant preachers, but I now know that this one will only be at home when you say you will marry me. Forgive my mushiness. It's been nearly three months since I last saw you and every day that goes by without you is a painful reminder of how quickly life passes. I'll be home for New Year's Eve. Will you ring in '65 with me? I want to start the new year with you. And Eddie of course. He came so alive in the *Gainesville Sun* picture. All my love, Charlie

Tessie was late coming home from work on the day that Dinah received the letter. She'd been at the annual Lithographics Christmas party, much as she hated it. But how would it look if she didn't show up? As head bookkeeper now, the Bechs kept reminding her she was one of the principals of the company. That night, at dinner, as she started to tell Dinah about how the Bechs kept sneaking rum into the punch, she noticed that Dinah had this slippery grin coming and going on her face.

'You look like the cat that swallowed the canary,' she said, then looked down at Eddie. 'Don't you go getting any ideas.'

Dinah put on her highfalutin voice. 'While you were out partying and drinking rum with the Bechs, your daughter received a marriage proposal.'

Tessie looked confused. 'Either you've met somebody awfully fast, or I'm missing something.'

'It's Charlie Landy,' said Dinah. 'It's always been Charlie Landy.'

'You're going to marry Charlie Landy?'

'I can't marry Charlie Landy. He always goes away,' said Dinah.

Tessie pushed her plate away and propped her elbows on the table. 'When you were a little girl, your father and I would play a game called Who Will Dinah Marry? The answer was always different, depending on what phase you were going through. We had you married off to a ventriloquist, an airline pilot, and a dry cleaner.' Tessie laughed at the memory. 'The last time we played that game was just before he died. You got an A on some paper you wrote for school and the teacher wrote, "This has real soul." Your dad said to me, "Jo" – he used to call me that – "Our girl really does have soul. I hope whoever she marries recognizes that and has some of his own.""

'He's sure got plenty of that,' said Dinah, tapping her foot against the chrome kitchen chair.

'You're lucky if once in your life you meet someone like him.'

'He's going to Vietnam,' said Dinah in a tight voice. 'I don't mean to sound harsh, but the thought of being a young widow . . . I just can't stand it.'

Tessie touched her forehead to Dinah's. 'I wish things were different,' she sighed. 'But I can't say you're wrong.'

PART THREE

1966

CHAPTER 19

Jésus wiped his hands on his apron. 'You are too flippant,' he whispered. He was standing with Sonia, who had put Mrs Landy under the dryer after coloring her hair with Miss Clairol's Blondest Beige. Victoria had urged Sonia to add more peroxide. 'I'm a tycoon now,' she said. 'I need something that sizzles.' But Sonia refused. 'Too much blonde, you look more like Twiggy than Mr Rockefeller.' Victoria laughed wildly. 'You are too much Sonia. You crack me up.' It settled things for both of them, this give and take. Sonia loved everything American and was proud whenever she could throw out a cultural reference. Victoria egged her on, admiring her enthusiasm and grateful for her forgiveness. But Jésus worried that Sonia was becoming too disrespectful, too American.

'Ahh, Mrs Landy. Her bark is bigger than her bite,' she answered.

'That's not how we talk about our customers,' he said.

She told him, in Spanish, that he was becoming an old fogey. He told her, in Spanish, that she was getting too big for her britches.

'Does anyone care that I'm frying my brains under here?' shouted Victoria as she extricated herself from the hairdryer. 'Where are y'all?'

Just then, Tessie arrived for her twelve o'clock. She and Victoria listened to Sonia and Jésus in the back, exchanging bursts of Spanish like two people snapping towels at each other. Tessie slipped into her chair and glanced over at Victoria, raising her eyebrows in the direction of the supply room. Victoria shrugged. 'Do I look like U Thant? Why can't they do this on their own time?'

Tessie could smell the ammonia from Victoria's hair dye. It made her remember the ordeal of feeding Dinah a tablespoon of castor oil each morning when she was a little girl. Dinah would scrunch up her face and her body would shudder as the castor oil made its way down to her stomach. After she stopped making gagging sounds, she would say, 'It tastes like liquid eyeballs. I'm not kidding.' Thinking of that now, the pungent ammonia smell caught in the back of her throat, Tessie felt as if she were going to be sick, maybe even pass out. She placed her head in her hands and doubled over.

'You all right?' asked Victoria.

'Uh uh.'

'Can I get you something? Water? A cold towel?'

'Uh uh.'

Victoria put her arm around her friend. Tessie felt the ammonia filling her insides, expanding and pushing everything else out of its way. She began to heave and retch. She heard guttural moaning sounds that seemed to come from a cave within her. Then she threw up: globs of yellow, brown, and white liquid all over the front of Victoria's red plaid miniskirt.

Sonia ran from the closet. 'Mrs Lockhart, are you okay?'

Jésus turned his head away. It would be offensive to Mrs Lockhart if he should stare. And Victoria, eager to clean the vomit from her skirt but wanting to show her compassion, did what she knew best. She told Sonia what to do. 'Have her lie down,' she ordered. 'Bring her a Coca-Cola. Get a cold towel for her face. I'll be right back.' Tessie, meanwhile, remained bent over in her chair, strangely serene and content.

When she first missed her period, she thought it was the beginning of menopause. At forty-six, Tessie no longer worried about slipping up or taking precautions. Besides, Barone was sixty-six. How likely was it that her eggs or his sperm would have the energy to dance together, not to mention do all the dipping and gliding and fancy footwork it takes to make a baby? The impossibility of it dogged her until the reality of it became indisputable: the nausea, the tender breasts, bone-aching fatigue. Pregnant at her age? It was mortifying! Inconceivable! Conceivable? Even the pun of it was a bad joke. Finally, she went to her gynecologist, old Dr Gasque, who seemed as surprised about the whole thing as she was. After probing around inside of her, he shook his head. 'Yup, there's no question about it. You've got one cooking.'

She was still lying on the examining table when he leaned over her and said in a conspiratorial manner, 'I am speaking to you as a friend now, not as a doctor. If you want to do away with it, I can give you the name of a person to see.' His face was so close to hers that she could smell the tuna fish on his breath. 'Excuse me,' she said, 'I don't feel very well.' Before she could get her feet out of the stirrups, she threw up everything she had eaten that morning all over his Cordovan loafers. She never knew if it was the tuna fish or the thought of killing the child within her that made her sick, but after that day she never again visited Dr Gasque.

She waited to tell anyone until she couldn't wait anymore, then tried to predict how they would all react. Dinah was in graduate school, sharing an apartment off campus with Hedda. Eager to be on her own, she rarely visited her mother. When Tessie said to her, 'I have to make an appointment to see you. Can you imagine that?' Dinah had snapped back, 'Mom, I'm grown up now. Things will work better between us if you consider me as a contemporary rather than a daughter.' Tessie wondered, Will the news that she's about to be somebody's older sister bring her closer to home or make her run farther away?

Victoria will have a cow when I tell her, she

thought to herself. For all I know, I'll have a cow too. That was funny. How come Dinah didn't think she was so funny? Maybe this child will think its mother was a riot. Hope has to start somewhere. Maybe Victoria is so caught up in the success of the Orange Blossom Special, she'll barely notice. She and Reggie are even talking about turning it into a franchise. She and Reggie: she and Reggie this, she and Reggie that. They are inseparable. The two of them plus Ella in that house, of course people talk, what would you expect? But Reggie's such a friendly guy, always remembering everyone's name, you can't help but like him. He's so different from Victoria, who can be – you know – such a bitch. 'Bitch.' Tessie said it out loud. She never used language like that. She'd preferred not to call attention to herself in the way that cursing does. But she was about to flaunt her womanliness, her sexuality, in front of the world. She and Barone might as well strip naked and make love right there at the Orange Blossom Special, for everyone to see. That's what they were all going to think about anyway. So big deal if she called Victoria Landy a bitch. What was that compared with having sex at forty-six with a man you're not even married to?

Of course, Barone. How will I break it to him? What in the world will he think? He and Fran were childless and, aside from the friendship he'd formed with Dinah and Crystal, children played no part in his life. She remembered how, years ago, they'd gone to the opening night of the opera at the Dade County Auditorium in Miami. They went because Dania Jai Alai was sponsoring a party afterward. 'Do you like the opera?' she'd asked him. 'I feel about the opera the way I feel about children,' he'd said. 'I can take them or leave them.' Wait until I tell him he's about to have a little diva of his own. Tessie chuckled. That was funny too.

The only person she told was Jerry. She wrote to him,

> I have no idea what a 46-year-old woman does with a new baby or how I will be able to have the patience to be a mother. Somehow I will manage. Do you think I'm totally crazy?

That night, as she lay on the couch, Eddie jumped up and curled up on her stomach. He'd been doing that a lot lately, and she wondered if he could feel the warmth and the life inside her. 'Can you keep a secret?' she whispered to him. 'I'm pregnant. I'm gonna have a baby.' He stared at her, his stern little face never losing its composure. 'I hope everyone else takes the news as well as you,' she said.

A month went by, and there was still no sign from Jerry. By then it was time to start breaking the news. She invited Barone to dinner on a Friday night in late November. They ate outside, the damp humidity finally out of the air. She made steak and rice and a green salad. When he poured her a glass of Bordeaux, she brought it to her lips, then put the glass down without taking a sip. It had a metallic smell. Just a whiff of it made her stomach curdle.

Barone noticed how little she ate.

'Are you feeling a little under the weather?' he asked.

There it was, the perfect opening.

'I am feeling a little under the weather,' she said.

'I'm sorry, maybe you have a touch of something.'

'I do. I have a touch of pregnancy.'

He laughed as if it were a passing joke. 'Have some wine,' he said, 'it will make you feel better.'

'Really,' said Tessie. 'I'm pregnant. Eight weeks.'

She could tell he was figuring backward to eight weeks ago. That would be the end of September. The weekend in Palm Beach to celebrate their tenth anniversary.

'Quit counting.' She smiled. 'It's yours.'

She watched his face as he absorbed the news. After some moments, he threw his head back and laughed. She could see the gold fillings in his molars, and thought that when this child was Dinah's age, he would be eighty-seven. Old.

He stopped laughing, then shook his head. 'A gambler, a hustler, even an artist. All of these were things I could have become. But a father? Never.'

'The doctor asked me if I wanted to get rid of it,' said Tessie.

329

'I will understand if you want nothing to do with it, but I'm keeping it.'

Barone grew serious and took her hands in his. 'Dottie. This is something we made together, something precious. I knew there was a reason I kept the big house. It is for us, for you and me and our family. Of course I want it. Now you have no excuses, you must marry me.'

Tessie placed his hand on her stomach. 'Let's get through one thing at a time,' she said. 'A baby and a wedding. That's one change too many for me.'

CHAPTER 20

With Charlie gone, there wasn't anyone in whom Ella could confide. She kept house for Victoria and Reggie and sometimes helped out in the kitchen of the Orange Blossom Special. She'd also started to teach Sunday School, grateful for the company of the young people. In the evening, she'd stay in her room and read. She wrote to Charlie nearly every day but was careful not to say what was really on her mind. Given where he was and what he was doing, he certainly didn't need the additional burden of Ella Sykes. So she kept to herself the things that she was seeing right before her eyes.

Reggie's hair was now slicked back and shiny. He wore shirts with crazy colored patterns and a white vest. People at the Orange Blossom called him Reg, and the name stuck. When Ella asked him, 'Reggie's been a perfectly fine name for all these years, why are you suddenly calling yourself Reg?' he answered, 'New man, new name,' sounding way too jaunty for her taste. He had no time to do the things he used to do, fix a broken light or take the car in for repairs. 'Reg is a businessman now,' Victoria would say when Ella would ask him to do an errand. Instead of Reggie mowing the lawn and tending to the shrubs and trees as he always had, he hired a gardener.

He still called Mrs Landy Miss Victoria, and she still ordered him around but there was something different about the bickering between them. It had more of a teasing nature and wasn't as mean spirited. When Victoria got a new haircut or bought some new clothes, she would dance around Reggie the way she used to in front of Ella. She'd taken to wearing those miniskirts that left nothing to the imagination. The first time she brought one home, she modeled it for Reggie, smoothing it over her thighs and bending over like a cheerleader. 'Not bad legs for a forty-six-year-old, are they, Reg?' she asked him. He laughed and looked her up and down in what Ella felt was an inappropriate manner. 'Nope, not bad,' he said. 'Not bad at all.' Ella was reading *Valley of the Dolls* and knew she was somewhat under the spell of Jacqueline Susann, but that didn't account for her feeling a stranger in her own house. That was just plain wrong.

Anyway, it didn't take any Jacqueline Susann to see what was going on with Mrs Lockhart. Beginning to burst at the seams, she was, and Ella had overheard Mrs Landy tell Reggie that Mrs Lockhart was going to raise this child herself, she had no intention of marrying that older fellow from Miami. Ella never saw Crystal anymore. She left town right after graduation. All she knew was that she was living in a little house in Atlanta. She had a job at some advertising agency where they thought up snappy little jingles about why people should buy deodorant or wax paper. Ella couldn't understand why people would get paid for work like that. She and Huddie were planning a big wedding for when he got out of the army after the first of the year. The last time Ella talked to her, which had to be nearly six months ago, she had said, 'I miss you, Ella, but I'm never coming back to that nut house. I want to get as far away from her and Reggie and that stupid Orange Blossom circus as I possibly can.'

With Charlie gone, there was no reason for Crystal to stay. Charlie was the only reason Crystal ever saw her mother. He'd call up and say, 'Just come over for a quick bite. We'll watch *I Dream of Jeannie*, and catch up.' At some point in the evening, Victoria would come into where they were watching television and stare down at them. 'Isn't it wonderful to have the whole family together?'

Then she'd leave the room and Crystal would shake her head. 'She can't really mean that, can she?' she'd ask. Charlie would rub her arm and say, 'She knows that she's fooling herself. It's just that if she admits it, everything else will come undone. Let her be.'

With Charlie gone, Crystal and Dinah fell out of touch. His secret relationship with Dinah had ended their friendship, yet as long as Dinah and Charlie were a couple the two girls still had him in common. Without the push and pull of him, there was nothing left. Charlie's absence reinforced what Ella always felt in his presence: he was the glue that held them all together. These days, she felt things were falling away. Things were falling away that she used to believe in. All that was left was trouble. The world was in trouble: the fighting in Vietnam, all those young men getting killed. And people in America protesting in the streets. She'd seen the protestors on television, throwing things and calling the policemen terrible names, and the policemen hitting them with their sticks until there was blood streaming down their faces. She'd heard about how young people were leaving home and living on the streets in California. She couldn't understand that. She heard about the civil rights activist who got shot in Mississippi after all the trouble they'd had up there at the university. Why was it all so violent and scary? Most of all, she was troubled about Charlie, or maybe it was the absence of Charlie. It wasn't what he said in his letters, it was what he didn't say. For all the nights they'd spent sitting on her bed talking about the things they'd never tell anyone else, his letters were distant and impersonal. He wrote about the weather and the men in his company and how much he missed everyone at home. There was nothing she could put a finger on, only the hollow feeling that like her, Charlie was slowly falling away.

What Ella couldn't understand was that for Charlie to endure what he saw, it wasn't possible for him to think – much less write – about what was happening. All he could do was get through one hour at a time, one day, one week. Maybe it would start to add up. Sometimes he just wanted to lie on his bunk and cry, but he always stopped himself, afraid if he let himself start, he would never stop. Later, when it was behind him, the visceral memories were all he had left of Vietnam. The heaviness of his boots as they sucked up the mud on the unmarked trails, each step requiring a mental note. The loneliness, like a parasite, draining him of everything but fear and sadness. The stink of his own body as if it were already beginning to decay. His skin, blotchy and angry. And the jungle: he could see none of it and yet nothing but it, thick and impenetrable, always wanting to reclaim itself no matter how much they hacked at it. Not a place meant for humans. In the end, he reckoned, it would be the jungle that would win the war. He remembered the soldiers; most of them scared, wounded, and too young. He remembered trying to say the right words and hoping they came out as if he meant them. On his worst days, he envied the dead. But even on the bearable days, the truth was that he had lost God and in the darkness, he had lost himself as well.

No matter what she questioned, Ella never stopped going to church. Church was home and one thing had nothing to do with the other. On an afternoon late in October, Reverend Potts stopped her as she was leaving a morning service. 'Ella Sykes,' he called as she was walking down the steps. 'How are you? I've been reading all about your brother. And you? Have you got a little Orange Blossom in your life?' He had a fine broad smile and his gums looked purple against the sunlight. 'Oh sure, I'm doing all right,' said Ella.

The reverend had been in his job long enough to notice things: how people dressed, their demeanor, the passion or lack of it they brought to singing the hymns. Ella Sykes, with her beautiful braid running down to the middle of her back, and her neatly ironed dresses, always looked impeccable. But now she kept to herself and didn't want to mingle with the other parishioners, even her old friend Pauline. That caught his attention.

'Come, sit with me,' he said, leading her to the green wooden bench at the side of the church. Ella took out a handkerchief and wiped off the seat. The reverend took a deep inhale as they settled down. 'This is the best time,' he said. 'The air is clear and the world feels crisp again. Do you find it to be that way?'

'Yes, sir,' said Ella. 'This is certainly the prettiest time of year.'

Reverend Potts unbuttoned his collar. 'I hope you don't mind, it gets a little tight sometimes.'

'Oh no, not at all. Make yourself comfortable.'

'So Ella, I'll get to the point,' he said, pulling a tissue from his pocket and dabbing the sweat from his neck. 'I don't mean to be intrusive, but you seem a little sad lately. I know you must worry about the boy over in Vietnam, and I wonder if there's something you'd like to talk about. Maybe I can help.'

Ella sat with her purse on her lap, rubbing her hands over the white vinyl, wondering how much she ought to say. 'I appreciate your generosity, but I don't think there's much you can do. It's just that, lately, I have a hard time making sense of things. Of everything at home, in the country, where Charlie is. I used to believe there was a reason things happened, and I accepted that, even the bad things like when Mr Landy died in that fire. Now these things are going on and I can't find any reasons. Forgive me for saying this, but sometimes I wonder if God is paying attention.'

Reverend Potts closed his eyes against the sun. 'If you knew how many times I have been down that same road,' he said. 'When I see cruelty and suffering, especially amongst the little children, I often ask myself how this can be. I question God and sometimes I get so angry I curse His name. Then I think what in the tarnation am I doing? Should I really be preaching to people about how they ought to live their lives when I myself am full of doubts and questions?'

Ella looked startled, then tentatively touched his shoulder. 'There couldn't be anybody better at it than you,' she said. 'That's why we believe you. Because you're like us and you don't hold yourself apart as someone high and mighty.'

'That's kind of you, Ella, but I have my moments.'

They each sat with their thoughts for a while until Reverend Potts said, 'Do you believe He was there at the creation?'

'Absolutely, I do,' she said.

'I do too,' he said. 'Now and then I believe that He did the big job, and decided to leave the rest up to us. Sometimes we do all right and sometimes we make a mess of it. I suppose I think it's okay for us to be upset with Him at times, even rage against Him. What doesn't seem okay is to let Him out of our hearts.'

Ella saw the beads of perspiration on the reverend's forehead and understood that these were difficult truths for him to admit. He must trust her and consider her a friend to confide in her like this. Gifts didn't come to Ella Sykes often, but when they did she received them with grace.

'Reverend, you are very kind to share your thoughts with me. You can rest easy that this conversation will stay between us.'

'And Charlie,' said Reverend Potts. 'When you next write to Charlie, tell him I wish to be remembered to him.'

Three weeks later, a telegram arrived at the Landy house. The letters, all capitals and dark purple, blazed against the drab telegraph paper: 'Please be advised: Captain Charles Landy, US army Chaplain, injured in landmine explosion near Danang STOP Flown to a VA hospital in the Philippines and will be returned stateside as soon as possible STOP Nature of his wounds unconfirmed but not life-threatening STOP For his bravery and courage, Captain Landy is eligible for a Purple Heart. STOP'

Over the next couple of days, everyone close to Charlie Landy was left to deal with the news in their own way. Victoria lashed out at whomever she could: at the army, for starters. After phoning the Pentagon for more information and being told there was none available at the time, she told the officer at the other end of the phone, 'How do you expect to win a war when you can't even keep track of your own men?'

When Tessie called to commiserate, she told her, 'I hope you have a girl. The life of a boy isn't worth shit in this country.' Reggie tried soothing her. 'Miss Victoria, we should be grateful that his wounds aren't life threatening,' but she shushed him away: 'Thank you Mr 4-F.' Ella retreated to her room, where she read her Bible and tried to find Charlie in the inky shadows that floated between them.

Because Charlie was well known around town and because of Maynard's tragic death and the popularity of the Orange Blossom Special, the news spread swiftly around Gainesville, especially in the black community, where his actions on the day of the sit-in were now legend. Reverend Potts conducted a special prayer service for Charlie. Even Reggie and Victoria showed up. Victoria held on to Ella's shoulder as Reverend Potts struck a bargain. 'One of Gainesville's finest is in your hands today. Please return him to us with the fullness of his body and soul. If you hear our prayers, we here – his family, his friends, and his community – promise to do everything in our power to sustain him.'

Two days after the telegram, Victoria received a phone call from Charlie's commanding officer. Charlie had suffered severe hearing loss, he said. He would be arriving at Tyndall Airforce Base the following week. Victoria posted a picture of Charlie in uniform above the cash register at the Orange Blossom Special. Underneath, she stenciled the words, 'Welcome our hero home. Wednesday, Tyndall Airforce Base at 4:15.'

A nice-size crowd showed up for Charlie's homecoming. The high school even sent some members of the band to greet him at the airport. As soon as the door of the plane swung open, the band broke into 'Grand Ol' Flag.' Charlie stepped out of the plane looking noticeably thinner in his neatly pressed uniform. He rubbed his eyes, as though he'd just awoken from a nap, and looked out at the crowd with confusion. He assumed they were there for somebody else. Then Victoria rushed up the stairs. She threw her arms around him and planted a kiss on his cheek. Charlie put his arm around her. It wasn't a hug really, more a pat on the back. 'You've drawn quite a crowd sweetheart,' said Victoria.

'Who are all these people? Why are they here?' he asked.

'Darling, they're here for you, to welcome you home.'

'I don't want all this fuss. I just want to go home in peace.'

People clapped as Victoria and Charlie walked down the steps. Only Ella, who saw the anger in his eyes, held her applause.

A reporter from the *Gainesville Sun* greeted Charlie with a handshake but was pushed aside by a crew from the local television station. Victoria and Charlie both spoke though neither knew what the other said until they watched the news with Ella and Reggie that night.

'He grew up in a household where respect and honor were valued above all else,' said Victoria. 'From an early age, he understood sacrifice. It

341

doesn't surprise me that he's a hero. I am just so proud of him.' Victoria was a natural. She smiled and tossed her head and seemed to be flirting with the cameraman.

Then the interviewer turned to Charlie. 'What does it feel like to be home again?' he asked. Charlie read his lips carefully, then took a moment to compose his answer.

'It's as if I was trapped in a hell so dark and grotesque that I'd given up hope of ever getting out. Then all of the sudden someone opens the airplane door and I'm here like it never happened. I can't describe it.'

'Looks like you'll be eligible for a Purple Heart medal. That's some honor, isn't it?'

Again, Charlie took time to prepare his words. 'I don't really care about any medal. That's all it is, some lousy hunk of metal. It has nothing to do with the men I knew and the men who are still there who are a hell of a lot braver than I am. Uh uh, no medals here.'

It broke Ella's heart to hear him sound so bitter. It pissed Victoria off to see him so indifferent. She turned to him. 'Now there's a surprise, Charlie Landy acting holier than thou in the face of one of the greatest honors a man can receive from his country.'

'It's bullshit,' he said. 'Can't you see that?'

'Isn't that a nice howdy-do. You're gone for nearly three years and that's all you have to say?'

'Yes ma'am, it is,' said Charlie, who had discovered that by merely turning his head away he could tune people out.

Across town Dinah was also watching Charlie on TV that night. His eyes were dull. His voice was a little too loud. Even his sentences seemed to be mechanically pieced together. It made her sad. In all the excitement of his homecoming, the one thing everyone seemed to overlook was the nature of Charlie's injury. Talking with Charlie was what always held her – how he could say things that she was thinking but could never articulate or just bring up new subjects out of the blue. And when he listened, he'd cock his head forward as if what she was saying was the most important thing in the world. She wondered if he still planned on being a preacher and hoped that the sound of his voice – deep and rumbling – and the Southern sprawl of his language would survive his hearing loss. Her roommate, Hedda, was watching the news with her.

'That's the guy. The one who left me.' Dinah touched her finger to the glass screen.

Timid Hedda, who usually never dared tell anyone else what to do, studied the television. 'He looks like he's had a hard time,' she said. 'I mean if you don't mind my saying so, it might be nice for you to go see him.'

Hedda and Dinah were going for their master's degrees in business. They were both drawn to

343

the precision and lack of gray areas in business, though for different reasons: Hedda because she lived her life in gray areas, Dinah because a world bound by economic theories and numbers seemed a whole lot safer than the precarious one in which she lived. 'He abandoned me once,' Dinah said. 'I'm really not looking to open that wound again.'

'Of course,' said Hedda. 'Except you're not who you were then, and neither is he.'

Hedda came from a wealthy suburb in Chicago, Lake Forest. The youngest of two, she had an older sister who was a beauty and parents who mistook her tentativeness for vapidity. Her straight brown bangs covered as much of her pale face as possible; the rest, she tried to hide behind her hands. She had an apologetic slouch and a baby whisper voice. When she spoke up in class, which was rarely, she never took her eyes off the floor. But Hedda was smart. She was the kind of un-assuming girl that is wildly successful twenty years after graduation, yet none of her classmates ever remember her. But she was completely devoted to Dinah.

Dinah recognized that in this relationship, she was the brazen and outgoing one and Hedda was the one always following behind. It emboldened her to play Crystal to Hedda's Dinah. She hadn't bothered to tell Hedda that Crystal was another reason she didn't want to contact Charlie. Like her brother, Crystal had gone away. Dinah doubted that Crystal ever gave her a second thought. Many times over the past years, Dinah had written letters to Crystal and to Charlie, and inevitably, after reassuring herself that they sounded friendly and not too lonely, she'd rip them up.

Dinah had trained herself to push away sad memories. When she was younger, she would do it by counting the steps between school and home or the minutes until she could get into bed. Now, alphabetizing her books and arranging her books according to color gave her the same comfort. She thought about what Hedda had said: 'You're not who you were then, and neither is he.' It reminded her of when Barone called, just before she broke up with Charlie, and how she babbled over the phone to him. Good ol' Señor Swanky, he always took her seriously. 'Everything is changing,' he had told her. 'But you'll always be somebody's daughter. That will never change.'

Later that night she called Tessie. 'Do you want a date for dinner tomorrow tonight?' she asked.

'Sure,' said Tessie, trying to keep the gratitude out of her voice.

'I'm available.'

'Great. My place or yours? Oh, I guess they're both the same, aren't they?'

'That's funny, Mom,' Dinah said with a laugh. 'See you tomorrow.'

Probably it was a reach to think that Dinah's laughter was a sign from Jerry, but after a month of not hearing from him, Tessie was hard pressed not to think so.

Tessie fussed over dinner. She bought some creamed spinach and cut up potatoes to make french fries. She made sure to cook the lamb chops the way Dinah liked them: crusty, brown, and flavorless. She even bought syrup for Cherry Cokes. It felt ridiculous to be nervous about having your own daughter to dinner, but Tessie believed that how she heard the news about the baby the first time would color how she felt about it forever after.

The next night, Dinah walked the mile and a half to the other side of town where her mother lived. The sky was black and starless, and by the time she got there the light from her mother's kitchen shone like a yellow rectangle in the darkness. It reminded her of coming home late from school when they still lived in Carbondale. Seeing the lights from the house shining in the cold dark night and knowing that soon she'd be there too, warm and together with her family, gave her a feeling of safety then that she never thought she'd feel again.

Tessie stood waiting for her on the front porch. She wore a forgiving red muu muu over black pants 'Hi sweetheart,' she said. 'I'm so happy to see you.' As they walked through the door together, Dinah could smell the lamb chops and the creamed spinach cooking on the stove.

'Yeah,' said Dinah. 'It's nice to be here.'

As they ate, Dinah told Tessie about school, about Hedda. They talked about what she might do when she graduated and how Gainesville had changed in the years since they'd been here.

'Do you think you'll want to move away from here when you graduate?' asked Tessie.

'It depends on who I end up marrying,' said Dinah.

Tessie did a doubletake. She had treaded so carefully around the subject of boys and dating, not wanting to pry. 'Hmm, do you have anyone in mind?' she asked.

'No. Everyone I go out with turns out to be a jerk in some way. But can I ask you something? You know Charlie Landy's come home, right?'

'Yes. Victoria was just talking about him the other day. Seems he has real hearing problems. She says he barely speaks to anyone, is really down and moody.'

'I was thinking of paying him a visit. You know, just to say hello. Is that crazy?'

'No, it would be a very kind thing to do. I'd say, just what the doctor ordered.'

Buoyed by the intimacy of their conversation, Tessie felt now was as good a time as ever to bring up her little bit of news.

'Speaking of things that are crazy,' said Tessie, already wishing she could rephrase her opening sentence. 'I have something to tell you.'

Dinah took another lamb chop and seemed distracted.

'Are you ready?' asked Tessie, trying to get her attention.

'Yeah, sure. What is it?'

'Well, I might as well just say what it is. I'm pregnant.'

Dinah put down her chop and stared at Tessie. 'That's a joke, right?'

'Nope, I'm two months and then some pregnant.'

'Mom, aren't you the one who's supposed to be telling me not to get knocked up and not the other way around?'

'Do you go around saying things like "knocked up"?'

'I may say it, but at least I don't do it!' said Dinah. 'Are you going to keep it?'

'Why does everyone ask me that?' asked Tessie impatiently. 'Yes, I'm going to keep it.'

'It's Señor Swanky's kid, isn't it?'

'Of course it's his. Do you think I just sleep around?'

'Why not,' shrugged Dinah. 'You're just full of surprises. Are you going to marry him?'

'He wants to, but no, I don't think I will. He's got his life down there and I'm here. You're here. Besides,' she said glancing at her Jerry Box, 'I've already been married once, I don't need to do it again.'

They looked at each other as if each knew what the other was thinking.

'What do you think Daddy would say if he knew?' said Dinah.

'I've given that a lot of thought,' said Tessie. 'I think he would say that we've both lived with the dead for so long that having a new life among us is a blessing. He'd also say that I'd better name it after him.'

'What if it's a girl? And what about Barone's dead wife, Fran? Won't he want to name it after her?'

'We haven't had that conversation yet,' said Tessie.

Dinah reminded her mother about the first time she met Barone. They were in the car on the way back from Eddie Fingers' funeral and he was sitting in the driver's seat muttering to himself, 'A fine pickle, a fine pickle.'

'He always says that,' said Tessie. 'Everything's "a fine pickle" to him.'

Tessie giggled then placed her finger over her mouth. It was the coquettish gesture, the side that was somebody's girlfriend that Dinah had never seen. It occurred to Dinah that she must be scared about this new baby, even though she was determined to go ahead with it by herself.

'You know, Mom, this baby thing could be fun,' she said, suddenly wanting to reassure her. 'I'll help out with little Fran or Jerry or Ferry or whatever you call it.'

'It's nice that our little family is growing, isn't it?' said Tessie, lighting a cigarette. 'Now if I can only figure out how to break the news to the Glenns.'

Dinah smiled at the realization that her mother worried about things the same way she did.

'What do you think I should say to Charlie?'

'About the baby?'

'No, you know, I haven't talked to him in all these years.'

Tessie took a long drag on her Marlboro. 'You know that whatever you plan to say isn't what's going to come out anyhow. Besides, you and Charlie never had problems in the talking department.'

Dinah left her mother's house that night with too many thought fragments bobbing in her head. She grew up having imaginary conversations with people; a lifetime of being an only child necessitated that. Lately she'd been practicing what she'd say if she ever ran into Crystal. Sometimes, she would even conjure up things people said about her when she wasn't there. Dinah could get lost in her thoughts that way. So it was inevitable that by the time she actually went to see Charlie Landy, she'd scripted their conversation dozens of ways.

It was the week before Thanksgiving when she finally got the nerve to call. Ella answered the phone and seemed genuinely happy to hear from her. After some small talk, Dinah said, 'I was wondering how Charlie was doing.'

'To tell the truth, I'm worried sick about him. He stays to himself. He barely talks to anyone, doesn't eat a thing. I've cooked all his favorite foods, and he just says to me, "Ella, let's take it slow. A little at a time." I tell you, it's a hard thing to watch.'

Dinah could feel her heart squeeze. 'I'd like to visit him. Unless you think it's a bad idea.'

'Miss Lockhart, if there is anything that can bring the sunshine back into that boy's eyes, you're it. When would you like to come?'

They arranged that she'd come to the house at three the following afternoon. It happened that Reggie was taking inventory at the store and Victoria was home. When Dinah rang the bell, it was Victoria who answered. She hadn't counted on the lioness at the gate.

'As I live and breathe, it's Dinah Lockhart, daughter of the blessed virgin Tessie Lockhart.' Victoria sure knew how to crack herself up. Dinah suddenly remembered why Crystal chose to live with her and Tessie for all those years. When she finally stopped laughing long enough to invite Dinah inside, she gave her the once-over. 'You have turned into one pretty thing. Mia Farrow. That's who you look like, Mia Farrow with a little fat on her bones. You sure as hell are not here to see me, are you? The warrior is in his room. Have a seat, I'll tell him you're here.'

One of the virtues of Victoria Landy was that you never had to worry about what to say to her: more than likely, she'd have the whole conversation for you. Dinah wondered, as she had so many times in the past, how Crystal and Charlie managed to be pretty normal, despite their mother. She noticed that the living room had been newly decorated in the current mod style, and thought about how the saloon business must be booming. How should she talk to someone with a severe hearing impairment. Should she yell or exaggerate the way she moved her lips? Before she could figure it out, she heard the sound of Charlie's footsteps. They were lighter now. 'Hello Dinah,' he asid, standing before her. 'It's really nice to see you again.'

It made Dinah sad, the way he smiled apologetically.

'Hi Charlie, it's so good to see you, too.'

The conversation might have frozen there had it not been for Victoria, who was bouncing around the living room like a moth off a lamp. 'You two need to get the hell out of here and go off by yourselves. Charlie honey, take the car,' she said shoving the keys into his hand. 'Reg will be back with the other one soon enough.'

They were barely out the front door when Charlie broke into a smile. 'Don't ask me what the "Reg" business is all about, I have no idea. My mother, what a piece of work!'

'Well at least your mother isn't about to start a serious relationship with "Captain Kangaroo"!' said Dinah. 'Can you imagine?'

They stood in front of the car: Victoria's behemoth Oldsmobile 88. Something passed across Charlie's face as he handed the keys to Dinah.

'Will you please drive? That way, I can watch your face and understand what you're saying.' Dinah took the keys and pretended that it was no big deal. 'Sure thing, I'd love to drive this little beauty.' But it broke her heart to think that if Charlie were the old Charlie, he'd hear the catch of sadness in her voice.

It would have been natural for them to go to the lake but neither of them mentioned it. 'If you don't mind, I'd like to just drive around,' said Charlie. 'So much has changed, I'm still getting used to it.'

They drove in silence until Dinah said, 'It's true, everything is different than when you were here last. Does it feel different?' He studied her face, squinting to read her lips.

'You have no idea. I feel as if I left the world altogether.'

'Where did you go?' she asked, wondering if articulating her words so carefully would ever feel normal.

'I don't know,' he said. 'I could never see it. All I saw was mud and vines and the jungle, and I knew if I ever stood still too long, it would grow around me and in me and eventually strangle me.'

'Do I take that to mean you're glad to be back?' asked Dinah, as they drove by the new mall at the edge of town. She could tell he missed that completely. She spoke louder: 'Oh, look in there, there's this gigantic fountain in there shaped like a seahorse. It's what Crystal and I would have called the Nausea Seahorse Fountain, it's so ugly.'

Charlie understood that she was trying to lighten up the mood.

'I'm sorry,' he said. 'I don't mean to be melodramatic. You're the first person I've spoken to about any of it.'

'It's hard, isn't it?'

Charlie shook his head. 'My mother, even Ella, they just stare at me waiting for me to say something. They mean well. Ella's cooking everything I've ever said I liked. Even my mother, in her own imbecilic way, is trying to be nice. The other day she offered to take me shopping now that I have – and these are her words – a new physique.'

'What would you like them, us, to do?'

'Time. I need time. Don't expect me to come home and be me right away. Eight weeks ago, I was there. Then, like in some science fiction comic, there's this great KABOOM! My body flies through the air, and the next thing I know it's three years later and I'm sitting in my mother's car with my old girlfriend. I've got a lot of catching up to do.'

Dinah noticed how the words loosened in Charlie's mouth. Sometimes they stuck to his tongue like toast crumbs; other times they came out in gummy misshapen syllables. Occasionally he'd touch his fingers to his Adam's apple to make sure he wasn't speaking too loud. The conversation was difficult and unnatural. She was driving this tank of a car and trying to make herself be heard. He never took his eyes off her, afraid he'd miss something. There had to be a better way. 'I have an idea,' said Dinah. 'Let's walk around the mall. I promise, after a half an hour, you'll know exactly where you've landed plus what everyone there is wearing. What do you say?'

'Good idea.'

She showed him the seahorse, a dragonlike creature spitting plumes of water into a tiled pool. They looked through the men's clothing stores and had a slice of pizza at Genero's. He'd often dreamed about pizza in Vietnam, he told her. When Dinah thought how this day might go, she'd envisioned them sitting by the lake talking about the war, about his injury, and, of course, about them. Funny how after an hour at the mall, none of it had come up.

Then they went to the bookstore, where the best-selling titles seemed to wink at them from their shelves: *Masters and Johnson Human Sexual Response, The Games People Play, In Cold Blood.* The joke followed them into the record store, where there was a poster for *The Sound of Music*; another for Simon and Garfunkel's 'The Sound of Silence.' Was Barry Sadler really singing 'The Ballad of the Green Beret' in the background? Dinah remembered a skit she had seen somewhere, maybe on the Jackie Gleason show. For some reason, Alice and Ralph were about to meet Sammy Davis Jr 'Now, Ralph,' Alice said in that whinnying voice of hers. 'Remember: Sammy Davis Jr has a glass eye, so don't stare and don't bring it up.' Ralph is visibly nervous when he is finally introduced to the singer. He shakes his hand and says out the side of his mouth, 'Very nice to meet you Mr Davis. How's your eye?' That's what this felt like.

Thinking about it, Dinah couldn't help laughing out loud. Charlie didn't know why she was laughing, but he started to laugh too. Suddenly, they were both breathing the same air again. They sat down on a bench in front of the spitting seahorse. He told her to imagine that someone was talking to her while she was swimming under-water.

'That's how I hear things now,' he said. 'I read lips, I hear sounds, I feel the vibrations of things. It's just hard for me to distinguish words some-times.'

She watched the effort that it took for him to hear her and to speak back. Life had always been full of struggles for Charlie, and this particular one was just beginning. She told him about Hedda and how she missed Crystal and was hurt by her absence.

He pulled out his wallet and showed her the now-frayed and yellow clipping from the *Gainesville Sun*. It was a picture of her and Eddie taken at the opening of the Orange Blossom

Special. He said he'd kept it in an old tin of rolling tobacco. 'All the guys had good luck charms. This was mine, I had it in my rucksack the whole time.'

She studied the photograph. 'God, was I in a bad mood when that was taken. In fact, this is the first time in a long time that I haven't been in a bad mood.'

He said that he'd felt dead for so long and that being here reminded him how much he liked being alive.

'Time,' she said. 'You need time. Remember?'

He was grateful she understood.

They kept talking for nearly an hour. The shopkeepers were beginning to lock their doors, and a nighttime chill crept into the air. 'I only have one more thing to say,' said Charlie.

'What's that?'

'This seahorse is the most hideous creature I've ever seen.'

When Charlie's hearing was intact, he'd barely noticed Reggie's limp. It was just another of his features, like the mole on his neck. But since he'd come home, each of Reggie's steps sounded like thunder. He could feel the vibration of Reggie's steps humming up his legs from the wooden floor. It made him jumpy and was another reason he chose to stay in his room.

But on the night he came back from the seahorse fountain, Charlie didn't go straight to his room.

He went into the kitchen where Ella was grilling pork chops. 'My favorite,' he said. 'I am so hungry I could eat a horse.'

'There's enough here for Miss Dinah,' said Ella.

'Too late, she's gone. But I'm sure she'll be back.'

It was the longest conversation he'd had with Ella since he'd come home.

At dinner, the four of them sipped a musky Cabernet. As his mother and Reggie fussed over the wine, Charlie winked at Ella. Ella rolled her eyes, as if to say, 'Here we go again.' Afterward, Charlie asked if maybe they could have one of their chats.

'It's about time,' she said.

They sat on Ella's bed the way they always did. Charlie ran his fingers over the reassuring lumpiness of her cotton bedspread. When he leaned back against the wall, his legs didn't touch the floor. He dangled them back and forth, and a warm feeling came over him. Was it possible that he was the same person as the little boy who used to sit on this bed and talk about everything under the sun? Not much had changed in here except the books. How many times had he imagined this room and tried to put himself back in it?

'It sure was lonesome around here without you,' said Ella.

'It sure was lonesome where I was, too.'

They didn't talk about everything on this night, but they did become old friends again. Once, she stroked his hair and said he'd gone away a young boy and come back with the face of a man. He moved her chin so that he could look directly at her face.

'Everyone thinks it will be easier for me if they talk louder,' he said. 'It doesn't help. I just need to see their faces and for them to speak clearly.' He told her that the sound of Reggie walking made him realize how painful each step must be for him.

'No need to worry about Reggie, he's doing fine, thank you.'

'The Orange Blossom's been quite a success.'

'To think that people in this town drink enough liquor to make Reggie Sykes a rich man is beyond my comprehension.' That brought to mind Reverend Potts and the conversation they'd had only weeks earlier. Charlie stared at Ella's down-turned mouth as she told him about her troubles. Then he said, 'I know what trouble looks like.'

'Honey, I'm afraid we all do.'

'No, I mean I can really see it.' His voice got louder. 'It has a color and a shape and a certain smell even. I can tell it's coming before it shows up.' He folded his arms across his chest. 'It's not anything I choose to know.'

Ella caught his eye. Was there something of the old Charlie, or was she just hoping?

'How was your visit with Dinah?' she asked, hoping to see a smile on his face.

'You and she are the only people I can bear being around.'

'What about Crystal?'

The smile vanished. 'I need to see her soon. I'm thinking I'll go to Atlanta this weekend.'

'Why don't you take Dinah with you?'

'You read my mind.'

Talking on the phone wasn't possible anymore, so Ella called Dinah to ask if she would meet Charlie tomorrow at four by the seahorse.

'I won't beat around the bush,' said Charlie as they sat beside the fountain. 'I'm driving to Atlanta this weekend to see Crystal. I'd like you to come with me.'

This invitation was fraught for so many reasons, and Charlie and Crystal were just two of them.

'Let me think about it,' she said. 'I'll call Ella tomorrow.'

It was Hedda who convinced Dinah to go to Atlanta. 'You told me about the car rides you and your parents used to take in Carbondale, and how much you enjoyed them,' she said. 'Atlanta is six and a half hours away from here. It could be fun.'

Dinah's father had loved Broadway musicals. Often the three of them would try to sing the entire score of *Pajama Game*, or *Guys and Dolls*, in one car trip. She could still hear his warbling falsetto as he reached for the high notes in 'Younger Than Springtime.' Tessie never stopped listening to musicals, and after dinner some nights, they would trail off into 'Oklahoma' or 'On the

Street Where You Live' as Tessie washed the dishes and Dinah dried. Maybe six and a half hours in the car with Charlie would be fun. And even at the risk of being snubbed by her, Dinah was eager to see Crystal.

'Tell him yes, I'll go,' said Dinah when she called Ella the next night. 'If it's okay with him, I'll borrow my mother's DeSoto.' She secretly hoped that somehow he would know all the words to *Carousel*.

That night, Ella called Crystal. 'Charlie sure would like to see you. We were thinking that maybe, this weekend, he could drive up and visit with you.'

Crystal answered in what Dinah used to call her sorority voice.

'Why, sure I am dying to see Charlie. Just last night I was bragging to my friends about how my uppity older brother turned down the Purple Heart. Tell him I have more than enough room here if he doesn't mind having some of my friends around who just happen to be the cutest girls in Atlanta.'

'Charlie is planning on bringing Dinah Lockhart. He hopes you won't mind.'

Crystal's voice lost its bounce. 'I haven't seen Dinah in years,' she said. 'We haven't even spoken on the phone.'

'Between us, I think Charlie likes her company,' said Ella. 'He's been having a pretty bad time.'

Crystal didn't answer. It was her tough luck, she

thought, to have her brother, now half deaf, come visit with her once best friend who had kept it secret that she was dating him. 'It's them against me again,' she said out loud. 'How can I say no?'

'I know she'll be happy to see you,' said Ella. 'It'll be fine, you'll see.'

'I guess so,' Crystal sighed. 'He can stay in the guest room, she can stay in the fold-out in the living room.'

'That's good,' said Ella. 'They should be there by late Saturday night. Thank you, Miss Crystal.'

Carousel never happened on the car trip. They spent most of the time talking about Crystal and how peculiar it was to pretend they were one big happy family again after so long. 'It'll be awkward at first,' said Charlie. 'She'll remember how betrayed she felt by both of us. Then she'll realize how happy she is to see me, her thinner, deafer brother. And who knows, she might even be glad that he brought along his sneaky little friend as well.'

'That certainly is a comfort,' said Dinah, leaning over to his side of the car and sticking her face into his. 'Thank you for the reassurance.' They spent the six-and-a-half-hour car ride getting to know each other again. Tessie was right: talking was never their problem.

They arrived in Atlanta at about six on Saturday night. The front light was on, but the house was dark inside. 'Maybe she left,' said Dinah. 'No, she's there,' said Charlie. 'She's just doesn't want to be caught watching us.'

Sure enough, the moment they rang the bell, Crystal appeared and opened the door just a crack. All they could see was her face: cute as ever, just a little heavier.

'Hi Charlie, hi Dinah,' she said in her most unsorority voice. 'C'mon in.' She opened the door slowly. Sister and brother smiled shyly before falling into an awkward hug. Then the two girls locked eyes.

'Your hair looks good in a flip,' said Dinah.

'Yeah, it's very "That Girl,"' said Crystal.

'But without the bangs, thank God.'

'I know, I hate the way bangs cut your face in half.'

They were still standing at the door, Charlie with both bags in his hands.

'Whatever you're talking about, could you please do it later?' he asked. 'These are heavy.'

'Oh silly me, come in,' said Crystal grabbing one of Charlie's bags.

Dinah looked around the little house. There was a braided rug with blues and yellows and a touch of orange on the living-room floor. The couch was covered in a green and maroon paisley fabric and the kitchen table and chairs looked to be mix-and-match flea- market furniture. Chianti bottles covered with dried wax sat on windowsills, and there was a Lava lamp on a wooden coffee table that was painted raspberry. Crystal's decorating taste was decidedly different from her mother's. Nothing matched; there was no concept décor. The only things that looked familiar were the dozens of pictures of Huddie all over the house. 'Guess your mom's decorator is busy on another job,' said Dinah.

Crystal had to laugh. She'd hoped the jealousy she'd felt about Dinah and her brother would be gone, but still something tugged at her when she saw them together. Crystal was emphatic about where they were going to sleep. As she hoisted Charlie's suitcase onto the bed in the guest-room, she commented on how much it weighed. 'You planning to stay a couple of months?' she asked.

'We'll stay as long as you'll have us.'

That night, they sat around Crystal's kitchen table eating Chinese food from a nearby restaurant. They talked about what they'd been doing for the last couple of years, each of them realizing how they'd missed the others.

'Why on earth would you go to business school? You're such a good writer?' asked Crystal.

'Mmm, it's hard to explain,' said Dinah.

'And who's Hedda?'

That was another thing Dinah wasn't ready to explain yet.

Crystal told her about her work at the advertising agency, and how she loved all of it: working with the clients, coming up with the concepts, putting together the catchy slogans and phrases.

'I believe I have found my life's work,' she said in typical Crystal hyperbole. 'This is what I was meant to do.'

They gossiped about Tessie and the baby, and Victoria and Reggie.

For the first time since he came home, to Charlie's great relief, he wasn't the center of everyone's attention. For the most part, he sat quietly and watched the girls talk, though he understood half of what they said. Every time they laughed together he visualized colored lights blinking on a Christmas tree.

'How's Huddie doing?' asked Dinah.

'Only two more months, and then: dum, dum, da dum . . .' She hummed the 'Wedding March.' 'We're getting married on Valentine's Day. I know it's sappy and all, but if me and Huddie don't have the all-American love story, who does?'

Dinah felt a tight band around her throat, as if she were going to cry. How could the woman who lived with her like a sister all those years be getting married and she not know it?

'Big wedding?' Dinah managed to ask.

'Yeah, probably,' she said. She reached into her bag. 'Wanna see a picture of the dress?' She unfolded a picture from a wedding magazine and shoved it under her nose. 'How do you like it?'

It was an ivory strapless A-line dress with what looked like a hundred tiny mother-of-pearl ivory buttons running down the back.

'It's beautiful. I hope your maid of honor has thin fingers,' said Dinah, hoping that didn't sound the way she thought it did.

Crystal didn't answer and turned her attention to Charlie.

'So you were on the Vietnam diet, huh?'

Charlie smiled and ran his hand up and down against his stomach to show how flat it had become.

'You look handsome, a little like Burt Reynolds.'

She stared Charlie in the eye when she spoke, and kept her words clear and succinct, as if she'd been dealing with his hearing loss all of her life.

When she asked him, 'How do you like Reggie's new teeth?' and he answered that the blisters on his feet had finally healed, she instinctively knew to rephrase her question.

'Reggie has new teeth,' she said. 'What next?'

Charlie closed his eyes and shook his head as if to say, 'I don't know what's next.'

The three of them laughed, grateful to be able to share something. As each day went by, the conversation quickened and the laughter came with ease. A little over a week after they arrived, they woke up early on a Sunday morning to go hiking in Stone Mountain Park. The sky was a cerulean blue and the late autumn air was crisp and bracing. Crystal was at the sink, slicing tomatoes to put on their tuna salad sandwiches. Dinah was filling their canteens and going on about how the wet canteen covers smelled like the dorms at Florida.

Oddly enough it was Charlie who heard the phone ring. He didn't hear it really; he felt it as a tingling sensation in his stomach. Felt it as the quickening of his heart. Saw it. Smelled it. Recognized the color and shape of it.

Crystal, one hand still on the tomato, picked up the receiver.

'Hello.' Her voice trilled with expectation.

Dinah was trying to force an ice cube into the too-small mouth of a canteen. Charlie stood at the kitchen door watching his sister. He sensed the life go out of her and rushed to catch her as she crumpled to the floor.

It was Mrs Harwood, Huddie's mother. Huddie had been reported missing. The helicopter he'd been in, shot down. At first they thought maybe he'd survived the crash and was hurt somewhere behind enemy lines. Though he was officially MIA, they were certain he was dead. As soon as they could locate his remains they would be sent home.

Dinah took the phone from Crystal and placed it back in its cradle. Charlie kneeled down and put his arm around his sister. Crystal wriggled out of his embrace as if it were a blanket of bees. Charlie was still crouching and Dinah was standing by the phone as Crystal sprang to her feet, ran to her room, and slammed the door.

Charlie and Dinah stared at each other, shocked

and puzzled about what to do next. Pain like this was too intimate to share with the strangers they'd become. Charlie sat down on one of the wooden kitchen chairs. Dinah sat in silence next to him. Please help me to do the right thing, he thought. He wasn't praying as much as he was beseeching whatever or whomever it was that gives a person mercy and strength at a moment like this.

Dinah began to cry. Charlie cried with her.

Intuitively he knew that she was thinking about her father.

'I'm going in to talk to her,' said Dinah. The sharp sound of her chair legs scraping against the kitchen floor sounded like determination to Charlie.

Crystal lay on her bed, her body curled in a vise of misery. Her shoulders heaved and horrible aching sounds came from her throat.

Dinah lay down on the opposite twin bed. She turned on her side, put her hands under her head, and stared at her friend. When they were young girls sharing a room, they'd lie in this position at night and talk for hours. Tonight they stayed like this until the sun cast stalky shadows across the bedroom floor, though they said nothing to each other.

At some point before the sky turned into bands of lurid yellows and oranges, Crystal said to Dinah in a tiny voice, 'Do you suppose Huddie's up there with our dads?'

'I'll bet he is,' said Dinah.

'Do you think they're eating dinner together?'

'Absolutely. Steak and potatoes.'

'And beer, lots of beer, I hope,' said Crystal.

'God, I hope so. Speaking of dinner, you must be starving.'

Crystal sat up, her matted hair sticking to her cheeks. 'I can't believe it, but I am hungry.'

'Come on honey.' Dinah brushed her hair off her friend's cheek then put her hand on her shoulder. 'Let's make Charlie cook for us.'

For the next three weeks, Charlie, Crystal, and Dinah were never out of each other's sight. They talked about Huddie, about their own fathers, even about Eddie Fingers. Victoria called at least once a day, begging Crystal to come home. Each time, Crystal refused. After one of those calls, Crystal put down the phone and said, 'She's probably bought some cute new mourning outfit.'

It was the first time they laughed since that awful day.

They didn't see anyone from home except for Señor Swanky, who took the train to Atlanta so that he could drive Tessie's DeSoto back home. Barone hugged Crystal to him. 'Sweetheart, I am heartsick for you. Please let me know if you need money or anything else,' then kissed her on the cheek. Later Crystal told Dinah that it was reassuring how some things never changed. 'He still wears Old Spice,' she said.

On a Sunday afternoon, two weeks later, Charlie was sitting on the front porch working a crossword puzzle while Dinah and Crystal were preparing dinner.

'I'm worried about how Charlie struggles with his sentences,' said Dinah.

Crystal punched her softly on the arm. 'Sugar, you are hearing things,' she said. 'Charlie's talking as much and as right as he's ever talked.' She shouted to Charlie, 'Isn't that right, Charlie?' When he didn't answer, she nudged Dinah's knee with her own. 'He's fine, don't worry.' Then Crystal asked about Tessie and the baby. 'Is she going to keep it?'

'Yes, she's going to keep it. Maybe this one will be normal! But get this, she is not going to marry Señor Swanky!'

Sometimes whole sentences would go by and Crystal would be like the old Crystal. Then suddenly her eyes would get hooded and she'd stare into the distance and Dinah would know she was lost in her own thoughts.

Crystal came back from her silence. 'Remember Mr Reilly and how he used to ask us rhetorical questions,' she said.

'Is that something I would forget?' asked Dinah.

'You and Charlie, it's been so comforting to have you here. One of the reasons is that there's something between the two of you that is so – I don't know – easy, sympathetic. You know?'

'I kind of do,' said Dinah.

'I see how you watch him, like he's going to disappear any minute.'

'Well he has been known to do that, you know.'

'Yes,' said Crystal, 'but he came back. And he's here, right now, with you.'

'And you,' said Dinah.

'It's nice,' said Crystal wistfully. 'I mean that he came back. Don't let him get away again. If you love him, you need to do something about it.' She paused and turned away from Dinah. 'We would have made a good foursome, don't you think?'

'We really would have.'

Crystal allowed the grief to wash over her but fought being drowned by it. After three weeks, she went back to work. Her friends rallied around like a fleet of tugboats that wouldn't let her sink. They'd bring food and send her notes with inspirational sayings and funny poems. One girl named Polly showed up every night. She had striking blue eyes, and pomegranate pink skin. Crystal called her Polly Wolly, and when she called Crystal Dandy Landy, her lips would pucker as if she were sucking on an ice cube. Dinah studied Polly's slender hands and wondered if she was who Crystal had in mind to be her maid of honor.

More and more Charlie and Dinah would find themselves alone in Crystal's house during the day with nothing to do but wait for her to come home. Sometimes they would get on a bus and go to nearby shopping malls to see if they could find a contender for the Ugly Contest. Anything uglier than the seahorse would have won, but nothing ever came close. Other times, they would walk around the neighborhood and talk about where to go grocery shopping, how Charlie would find a congregation to run, and why Dinah didn't want to finish business school. Later, when they reminisced about this part of their courtship, they would call it their hatching period. Finally, it was Crystal, her face sallow and puffy with sadness, who said to the other two, 'I don't know how I'm going to do it, but I need to start living the rest of my life.'

Their final night in Atlanta, Charlie dreamed his old dream again, for the first time in a long while. Only this time, he could tell by their faces that he was talking too loud. And the words that were coming out of his mouth, they were Dinah's.

Dinah and Charlie took the train home to Gainesville the next morning. Things were settling between them; talking would only shoo them off their course. Dinah walked the length of the train and back again. She bought some donuts and bottles of soda. She went to the bathroom and took her time putting on makeup and combing her hair. When she came back, there were still five hours to go. Charlie didn't mind the quiet and the stillness. Sitting next to Dinah and feeling the steady clacking of the train was a comfort. She filed her nails then reached into the seat pocket in front of her. All she could find was a pamphlet. She read every word of it, about safety procedures, various routes you could link up to from this train, and the history of it. 'Get a load of this!' she said thrusting the passage in front of Charlie's eyes. She pointed to the sentence that read, 'Formerly known as the Orange Blossom Special, this is the first train to run from New York City to Miami, Florida.'

'A sign, don't you think?' he said and smiled.

'Not really,' she said, tucking the pamphlet back in its pocket. 'Just a silly coincidence.'

PART FOUR

1986

CHAPTER 21

Nobody who worked in advertising could afford to miss the annual ASAE conference. The American Society of Advertising Executives never had trouble drawing big names to its meetings. Jesse Jackson came one year, Paul Volker another. Sometimes a famous television newscaster spoke or the hostess of an afternoon talk show. A first lady was always a big draw, and one year Steven Spielberg almost made it. His name was already on the program when his office called and said he had to do some last-minute editing on his new movie. The folks at ASAE had to stay up all night hustling to find a substitute so they could reprint the programs in time. Finally, H. Ross Perot said yes. The meeting was always held at a snazzy location, and it was customary to honor the Advertising Executive of the Year at a luncheon on the first day.

In the spring of 1986, Crystal Landy got a letter from ASAE saying that she had been chosen for the honor. The meeting would be held at the new resort, the Windsurfer, which had just been built in the heart of Gainesville,

Florida: 'So don't forget your golf clubs and tennis racquet!'

When Crystal read the news, she let out a hoot-hoot kind of laugh and shouted to her young assistant, Mark, 'Will you look at this? The big boys in New York City finally looked beyond their own peckers.'

Crystal should have received that award years before. Her company, the Harwood Agency, handled every big account in Atlanta including Coca-Cola, Ted Turner's Superstation TBS, his fledgling cable news station CNN, and his hobbies, the Atlanta Braves and the Atlanta Hawks. Everyone in Atlanta knew Crystal. She'd recently been on the cover of *Atlanta Woman* magazine and was always mentioned in any story about Southern women executives. But her picture had appeared just once in the prestigious national magazine *Advertising Age*. It was a postage-stamp-size photo alongside a four-line mention that she had been chosen to do pro bono work for Habitat for Humanity. Every year, the big award went to someone at one of the major firms in New York or Chicago. Even though at one time or another, the big firms had all tried to hire her, it never crossed their minds to make her one of them.

'How can I pass this up?' Crystal asked Mark. 'Even if it is in Gainesville.'

Crystal didn't visit Gainesville often. When she did, it was mainly to see Dinah, Charlie, and Ella.

They lived in a big old farmhouse outside of town. When she went down for her award, she would stay there instead of at the Windsurfer. It had a fresh-water pond on the property, and the last time she was there, they went fishing at sundown and caught some catfish that they cooked up for dinner. Dinah had thought that buying a house with so many rooms was foolish, but Charlie told her there'd be plenty of room for the children when they came. But the children never came. Charlie didn't care about knowing why or getting help. 'If we can't have them naturally, I'm not interested in manufacturing them,' he told Crystal. Charlie had become an avid gardener – corn, mangoes, squash, beans, grapefruits, hibiscus flowers the size of tambourines. The first time Crystal came to visit and saw the acres of vegetation he had spawned, she declared, 'My word, Charlie Landy's seed is spread over half of central Florida.'

Charlie had his own congregation now. After white families started buying up the grand old homes on the north side of town and renovating them, the area became integrated. For a long time, Charlie preached alongside Reverend Potts. And when Reverend Potts passed away, Charlie became the pastor. Each Sunday Ella, who was nearly ninety now, would sit with Dinah in the front row and listen to Charlie preach. Often his words misfired or he spoke too loud or rested too long on the wrong syllable, but never mind that – Ella still said it gave her goose bumps the size of anthills to hear that boy's sermons. Crystal had been meaning to go hear Charlie, but she never quite got around to it.

She'd visit her mother, though mostly out of obligation. Inevitably, the conversation between them would come down to Crystal's weight and who she was dating, and frankly, she didn't feel like discussing either of those things. Victoria still dressed like a former beauty queen. Behind her back, Dinah and Crystal would joke that old Miss Pearly Whites had become Mrs Crowns and Bridges. It wasn't just that she was aging. As Crystal explained to Charlie, 'Look at Tessie and Barone. They're exactly who they've always been, just more creased and frail. But our mother, she leaves herself wide open for ribbing. The whole thing with her and Reggie – excuse me, Reg – is a scream.'

Victoria and Reggie had moved into a big house near where Victoria and Maynard used to live. As far as Crystal, Dinah, or Charlie could tell, they spent their days shopping and renovating. Reg still drove her wherever she went, and they were seldom apart. 'Let them think whatever they want,' Victoria would say if anyone ever brought up the two of them. But since they sold the saloon five years earlier, people in town had long stopped gossiping about the nature of their relationship. Crystal happened to be in town for the last party they ever gave at the Orange Blossom Special in 1977, the tenth anniversary. It was one of Victoria's usual hyperkinetic affairs, and would have been relegated to the society pages but for one incident. Anita Bryant, who now lived in a thirty-three-room mansion in Miami Beach and had become the spokesperson for Florida Orange Juice, was the guest star of the evening. She still had the dark auburn hair and flashing smile that had dazzled everyone twelve years earlier at Maynard and Victoria's anniversary party. Time had only added richness to her voice, and when she sang, 'Til There Was You,' a hush fell over the room. The clarity of her voice and the innocence of that song brought people back to their own thoughts. It was a lovely reflective moment.

Too bad it didn't last. Outside, a crowd had gathered and was shouting, 'Oh No, OJ' and 'Anita Bryant, Save Yourself.' Bryant, who was now a fundamentalist Christian, had recently launched a national crusade against homosexuality called 'Save Our Children.' Across the street from the Orange Blossom were protestors who were pro-testing the protestors and shouting, 'Thank God for Anita Bryant,' and 'OJ, OK.' Shortly after she finished singing, two fleshy men in bulky suits took Anita Bryant by each arm and escorted her out the back door, across the alley into Florsheims, where she safely ducked out the front door and into a waiting car.

The Bryant story was the one that made the front page of the *Gainesville Sun* the following day.

'Why does everything have to be so damn boring and political?' fumed Victoria when she saw the paper. 'Whatever happened to good old-fashioned fun?' The whole thing was too much of a circus for Crystal, and she never went back to the Orange Blossom Special again.

On the Friday morning of the ASAE convention, Crystal flew into Gainesville. A black limousine picked her up at the airport. They passed through the middle of town on the way to the luncheon. Crystal asked the driver to take a two-block detour so they could pass the old saloon. There it was, smaller than she remembered, and a great deal shabbier. The smoky tinge of the window made it look gray and faded. It was still called the Orange Blossom Special, but underneath the orange and green neon sign, the words *Girls* and *Nudes* were also pulsing in garish reds and purples. The place had become a strip joint. Crystal laughed to think how that probably pleased her mother.

The luncheon was being held at the SkyHigh Club atop the newest – and tallest – building in Gainesville. There was a large plaza around the building and two outside staircases that fed inside. She rode the elevator up to the fifteenth floor and when she stepped out all she could see was sky, that and some gulls who had nested in the building's crevices. She walked around the windowed room and looked down on Gainesville, so tiny and used up from this steel and glass perch.

As her eyes adjusted to the view, she could identify neighborhoods, even houses. She searched for the Harwoods' street, now nearly completely obscured by the loblolly pines. She hadn't seen Mr and Mrs Harwood since the funeral and wondered if they still lived in that house. Maybe if things had turned out differently, she and Huddie would have come back to live here. She imagined Huddie watching her today as she got her award. What would he make of her now, big, bawdy, successful Crystal Landy? She picked out the house where she lived with Dinah and Tessie, and trained her eyes on the back windows. For a moment she could swear she saw two young girls lying in bed, their bodies hunched toward each other as though they were sharing a confidence. So many secrets everywhere I look, she thought. She saw the spot where their old house burned down and where the people who bought their land had built a hideous mansion. 'Nouveau riche trash,' her mother would spit each time they drove by it. And what exactly did her mother think she was? She took a deep breath. This wasn't the time to be thinking thoughts like that.

The more than one hundred people in the SkyHigh Club that afternoon cheered when the president of ASAE introduced Crystal. She looked smart in her royal blue suit. Many women her size might have worried that the skirt was too short or the blouse was too tight, but Crystal was as comfortable in her skin as she'd always been. When they called her name, she offered a spellbinding smile and walked quickly to the microphone.

'It's good to be home,' she said, her voice a little tentative. 'You probably don't know this, but I grew up here. My brother's the pastor of a church not far from here. He and his wife got married at the river out yonder.' She bobbed her head from side to side: 'I was the maid of honor at their wedding, of course. In fact, if you look out that window,' she said as she pointed to the back of the room, 'you can see where I went to school. And down that street,' she pointed to the window on the right, 'was Harmon's Luncheonette, where we had our first civil rights demonstration.

'Don't worry,' she caught herself. 'I am not up here to give you Crystal Landy's tour of Gainesville. It's just odd, seeing your whole past in one sweeping glance. Personally, I prefer small sound bites to big pictures, which is why I chose this profession in the first place.' Then she went on with her prepared speech. After it was over, one of the hotshots from New York asked if she would like to have lunch on Sunday with him and another bigwig in an Armani suit. 'Thanks so much,' she said, thinking it was a little late for that, 'but I'm spending Sunday with my family.'

For the next two days, Dinah drove Crystal back and forth from the conference in their old Jeep. Crystal wondered what Dinah, who dressed mostly in jeans and wore no makeup, thought of her fancy life and designer clothes. Sometimes she wondered if Dinah felt left behind. Life hadn't turned out for either of them as they had bargained. Crystal never married after Huddie died, and Dinah now spent most of her time caring for Charlie and doing work for the church. Dinah worried that Crystal resented her domestic happiness. She wondered if, with all her professional success, Crystal was happy. For her part, Crystal wondered how Dinah could stand living in that old farmhouse back home. If she'd had to bet which one of them would have moved on to the big city and success, it would have been brainy Dinah, not party-girl Crystal.

When they passed by what used to be J. Baldy's – now the Cut Rate Hair Salon – Crystal asked, 'Whatever happened to wonderful Jésus and that beautiful shampooist who turned out to be his daughter?'

'Oh Sonia,' said Dinah. 'They moved to Miami. My mother still gets Christmas cards from them.'

'I hope they're happy,' said Crystal.

'Are you happy?' Dinah asked.

'In my own way,' said Crystal. She talked about her job, and how she'd gotten another offer to move to New York. It was a big agency and, just between them, she said, she was scared to take the plunge. 'Big fish, little pond, Big Apple, little fish,' she said, accustomed to packaging things in tidy phrases. 'And what about you?' She turned to Dinah. 'Is being a preacher's wife what makes your clock tick? Tell me the truth, don't you ever get tired of being Mrs Do Right all the time?'

Dinah wondered if Crystal ever had a thought that she kept to herself. In that way, and so many others, she'd become more like her mother than she'd ever want to admit. 'It's funny,' she said. 'You and Charlie were always centerstage, and I always felt like the curtain. Now I've found a place in my life and in Charlie's, so yes, I would say I am really happy. I can't wait for you to see him preach on Sunday. You'll be so proud.'

The plan was that after the conference, Crystal would go to the Old Stone Church and hear Charlie. Then they would have an early Sunday dinner with Tessie and Barone before she flew back to Atlanta. Maybe they'd get Ella to come, too.

There was a reason Crystal had never heard her brother preach. She was scared he would stumble over his words or garble things. She couldn't stand to see him humiliated. So it was with some anxiety that she sat in the front row with Ella and Dinah on that Sunday morning.

Charlie stood at the podium, all eyes upon him. Clearly he was completely at home here. As he began speaking, he leaned forward and propped his elbows up on the lectern. 'I've chosen as my topic today "Listening." You may think that's an odd subject for a nearly deaf man to talk about, but I didn't say "Hearing." I said "Listening."'

The audience stirred a bit. Crystal started paging through the prayer book.

'When I ask God to watch over one of your

children or to protect our homes from a hurricane, He doesn't say, "Speak up, Bub, I can't understand what you're saying." He doesn't move me to the end of the line and say, "Take a number, I'm too busy planning the next solar eclipse." He doesn't judge me by how well I articulate my words or by how loud I speak. He hears the truth of what I ask, then answers as He sees fit. And no matter how confounding or untenable His answers may seem, it is up to me to accept them.'

Crystal glanced at Dinah as he spoke. Her face was filled with pride. Then Crystal noticed something else. Slowly, almost imperceptibly, she was moving her lips, mirroring every word that Charlie was saying.

'Since my injury,' he continued, 'I hear more than ever. I hear the people who are gone now, my father, Maynard Landy, whose temperate voice would quiet the chaos in our house. I hear my father-in-law, Jerry Lockhart, a man I've never met but whose voice lives within me though he left this earth many years ago. Old friends, like Huddie Harwood and other men I knew in Vietnam, speak often to me. The voices of the living fill my head always: I hear my sister, Crystal, funny and perceptive; the wisdom of my friend Ella; the unvarnished truth that comes out of my mother's mouth. When I step inside this house of worship, the walls resonate with the kind and knowing truths of my friend Reverend Potts. If I never hear another sound again, the words of these people will always be alive in my heart, and I know too that God hears them just as I do.'

Crystal saw Dinah mouth the words 'just as I do.' Next to her, Ella closed her eyes and bowed her head.

No one spoke until they all got back into the Jeep. 'Man, am I starving,' said Crystal. 'I gave up eggs and toast with Mr and Mr Armani. This better be good.'

'My mother's still a terrible cook,' said Dinah. 'Only the silverware has improved.'

TESSIE HAD SINCE moved to a bigger house in the fancier section of town, near where the Landys used to live. She and Barone had never gotten married, though he lived with her now since his crippling arthritis made getting around difficult. She was slim as always and still had her hair pulled back in a Joanne Woodward ponytail. Barone wore his flashy sports shirts and the silver ID bracelet, scratched and nicked but with the initials B.V.A. clearly readable. By now Old Spice flowed in his veins. His hair was white and thinner, but curly as it was when Tessie first met him. Their house was filled with pictures of Fran and Jerry. They talked of them as if they both were running errands and would be back at any moment. Their son, Jann, was twenty now. He had Jerry's will and Fran's salty humor, and could well have been the child of the four of them. While he went to school, Jann worked part-time for Glenn Bech Jr at Lithographics.

'Oh, the Bechs,' said Crystal. 'Did Glenn Jr turn into the same lech his father was?'

'Let's just say that I wasn't there but two weeks when he said to me' – Jann winked and imitated the older man's lascivious voice – '"Your mother was quite a dish in her day. We all thought she was the cat's meow."'

Barone lifted his arm slowly and placed it around Tessie's shoulder. It was obvious what pain that gesture cost him. 'She's still the cat's meow,' he said.

Tessie rolled her eyes and the six of them looked around the room at one another. Once again, it was Crystal who broke the silence.

'So Charlie, Mr "I-Can-See-the-Future." What do you predict is in store for this motley group?'

Charlie had a smile on his face, the same one he'd had as a little boy who said if he met Khrushchev he could achieve world peace. But before he could even open his mouth, Ella gave him a hard glance and spoke in slow, carefully delineated words: 'Charlie Landy, don't you go answering that question.'

ACKNOWLEDGMENTS

My gratitude always to Kathy Robbins, whose friendship and wisdom means the world to me. Elisabeth Scharlatt, new friend, and editor, has made my collaboration with her and Algonquin Books a joyous one. Thank you to Brunson Hoole, Kathy Pories, Tammi Brooks, Anne Winslow, Dove Pedlosky, and everyone else at Algonquin for their care and time.

I am fortunate that my friends are also astute editors: Lisa Grunwald, Kathy Rich, Victoria Skurnick, Jill Bauer, Carl Lehmann-Haupt, and my sister, Miriam Brumer, read early versions and made valuable suggestions.

Lisa Auel, executive director of the Matheson Historical Center in Gainesville, Florida, provided me with history and photographs of the area, and I am grateful for her generosity.

My husband, Gary Hoenig, welcomed the characters of this novel into our home and then nurtured them onto these pages. Like so many things in my life, he has made this book possible.